A Touch of Charm

Miracles on Harley Street, Book 3

Sara Adrien

ARE YOU SIGNED UP FOR DRAGONBLADE'S BLOG?

You'll get the latest news and information on exclusive giveaways, exclusive excerpts, coming releases, sales, free books, cover reveals and more.

Check out our complete list of authors, too!

No spam, no junk. That's a promise!

Sign Up Here

www.dragonbladepublishing.com

Dearest Reader;

Thank you for your support of a small press. At Dragonblade Publishing, we strive to bring you the highest quality Historical Romance from some of the best authors in the business. Without your support, there is no 'us', so we sincerely hope you adore these stories and find some new favorite authors along the way.

Happy Reading!

CEO, Dragonblade Publishing

ADDITIONAL DRAGONBLADE BOOKS BY AUTHOR SARA ADRIEN

Miracles on Harley Street Series
A Sight to Behold (Book 1)
The Scent of Intuition (Book 2)
A Touch of Charm (Book 3)

The Lyon's Den Series
Don't Wake a Sleeping Lyon
The Lyon's First Choice
The Lyon's Golden Touch
The Lyon's Legacy

Dedication

For Andrea,
A princess honoring my career
with her friendship, wisdom, and support.

And

For my little son F.
Everything is a matter of perspective.
May your explanations for the world always ring as true as the
chirping of crickets sound to you, like stars sparkling.

PREFACE

Welcome to Harley Street!

Though Andre and the other doctors and nurses are linked to my *Miracles on Harley Street* series, and very dear to my heart, their brilliant and visionary stories are works of fiction. The medical techniques and tools featured have been meticulously researched to ensure accuracy within a three-to-five-year historical timeframe. For more details on the historical research and where I took artistic license, check out the "Author's Note" at the end of this book. Enjoy your adventure into the past, where historical fiction and romance intertwine! You can find more about my other *Miracles on Harley Street* books at www.SaraAdrien.com.

And if you are new to the doctors on Harley Street and this is your first story, keep the following short overview handy so you already know who is coming back from other books. Think of the doctors on Harley Street as a group of friends, almost like in television shows such as *Grey's Anatomy* or *Friends*, in which the stories bring everyone back even though the focus may only be one person and his or her love interest.

Philippa "Pippa" Mae Pemberton in book 1 is the cousin of the heroine in book 2, Lady Beatrice Wetherby "Bea." In book 1, *A Sight to Behold*, Pippa fell in love with Dr. Nicholas Folsham, "Nick," who is one of the doctors at 87 Harley Street. Bea lived with Pippa at Cloverdale House, a large estate surrounded by parks with an abutting orangery, which belongs to Pippa's family, and which will be converted into a rehabilitation center in the book you are about to read.

Dr. Nicholas "Nick" Folsham is an oculist at 87 Harley Street, and the best eye surgeon in London. He studied in Vienna with Alfie Collins and some of the others, including Felix. Nick's story is book 1, *A Sight to Behold*.

Alfie Collins is the apothecary at 87 Harley Street. His and Bea's romantic story is book 2, *The Scent of Intuition*. He studied in Vienna and completed an apprenticeship in ayurvedic medicine in Delhi, India, before he returned to London and opened the practice with his friends.

Dr. Andre Fernando is the orthopedist at 87 Harley Street, originally from Florence, Italy, and he is quite the heartbreaker. Although his past overlaps with that of his friends Alfie and Felix, his future has very different surprises in store. His story is in the book you are about to read, *A Touch of Charm*.

Wendy Folsham is Nick's younger sister and the nurse who lives and works at 87 Harley Street. Alfie, Andre, and Felix treat Wendy as their little sister, too, watching over her and keeping her safe. In reality, it's Wendy's wisdom and good heart that help the young men. Her story is book 4, *The Sound of Seduction*.

Dr. Felix Leafley is the dentist at 87 Harley Street, a master of his craft. He suffers from a broken heart because he hasn't been able to be reunited with the love of his life. Read his story in book 5, *A Taste of Gold*.

Baron von List is a Prussian villain in this series and some of my other series, too. Suffice it to say that his morals are questionable, his methods brutal, and his intentions violent. For more books with this villain and his story, please visit www.SaraAdrien.com—this is also where you can find out when he will be gloriously defeated by the heroes and heroines in my books.

There are several other doctors and nurses who come in and out of 87 Harley Street and who work at the clinic across the street. Find those stories as part my contributions to the Lyon's Den series. For more information and a complete list of Sara Adrien's stories, please visit www.SaraAdrien.com.

Chapter One

1818. Silvercrest Manor, a country estate two hours from London…

O N THE NIGHT of his friend's wedding, Andre was *en garde,* like a parent watching their child on a swing. Because of his experience in life, his mind wandered to the dangers he wanted to prevent rather than the enjoyment of the festivities at hand.

"Why are you on the sidelines?" Alfie, the groom, asked in a conspiratorial tone—they were among close friends after all—with a polite nod to Prince Stan, but his gaze remained on Andre.

Because I am not supposed to dance with any of the aristocratic ladies; I'm not good enough for them.

"Just keeping the Prince here company," Andre smiled, hoping Alfie didn't catch on. "It's a beautiful celebration." Andre bowed to Bea, the bride who was approaching them. She returned a warm smile and a slight blush, just as the perfect daughter of an earl ought.

"He's looking at us. Baron von List hasn't let me out of his sight all night," Prince Stan remarked, a hint of friendly mischief in his tone when he arched a brow and gestured in the direction of a man watching them from afar. Stan, too, was an anomaly in this crowd; his princely bearing matched with a warmth that belied his station. But for Andre, Stan was a friend.

And Andre cherished his friendship too much to jeopardize telling Stan the truth about his heritage.

"As long as he's just looking," Alfie said with palpable disdain.

"He's probably plotting his next—" But before Andre could finish the sentence, the bride had come within earshot and hooked her arm into Alfie's as if their love celebrated on their wedding day made them invincible.

The most precious kind of love.

And Andre felt deep in the pit of his stomach that he'd do anything in his power to protect his friends.

Andre's gaze sharpened, focusing on the baron. Knowing the man's reputation all too well, a chill settled over him. "I see him," Andre replied, his voice dropping to an indistinct murmur. "We should be wary." Baron von List, a Prussian baron with criminal tendencies and an appetite for brutality, preyed on the weak and subverted money from those who needed it. Andre despised violence above all else. Since Baron von List was often the instigator of violence and pain, Andre despised the man, especially his smug face and cold, calculating eyes.

"He's an entitled Prussian aristocrat who inflicts pain to get rich," Stan said.

Everything I stand against. All Andre wanted was to hide his noble lineage—it had to remain a secret—so that he could continue to heal people. He didn't need riches as long as he had his friends, and he knew he was doing well in life. As an apprentice in India, he'd only slept in a small tent for a week while tending to patients in the rice fields—and their appreciative smiles and a bowl of water were all he'd needed for thanks.

"Baron von List would siphon the blood from the dead if it served him."

Andre nodded in agreement with Stan.

"He's disgusting even when dressed impeccably in all of his finery," Stan said. Andre knew the baron as well as Stan. "There's nothing but blackness that even List's sleek blond hair couldn't hide from his character."

Dr. Andre Fernando was a man of science and facts and believed that hard work paved the way to honor—not titles. He firmly believed that only a select few members of the nobility had genuinely earned the honors passed down through heritage, and the man staring at him was not one of them.

"He came uninvited," Alfie said as he crossed his arms.

Stan nodded, a shadow crossing his features. "His presence sours the evening for me. Shall we make our escape back to London?"

Andre hesitated, glancing once more at his friends. Duty weighed heavy on his shoulders, yet a sense of belonging to his friends tugged at him. "There could be emergencies. One of us ought to be there."

"Oh, Andre, you'll miss the festivities," Alfie protested with a frown, but it was plain to see that the apothecary agreed. Alfie was the groom and should enjoy the celebration. Having a ball after the wedding was unusual, but his match was just as unusual. Particular was the better word.

Romantic, Andre thought with a pang in his heart.

"The patients need one of us to be there at all times," Andre added when Alfie's mien fell. They were more than friends and colleagues; the doctors on Harley Street were a family. "I know you left the apothecary well-stocked, and I will ensure you can enjoy a few more days with your bride."

Andre bowed to Bea and reached for her hand to kiss her knuckles. He was glad to show his respect to the new addition to their family of friends. Of course, she wasn't a doctor nor an apothecary, but she and her cousin Pippa founded the rehabilitation center that Andre helped to start. And where he might be needed.

"But I can't abandon the patients," Alfie protested.

"You can't leave your bride alone on your honeymoon. I will ensure that none of the patients feel abandoned." Andre put a hand on his heart. It was the truth—whether or not he told Alfie—the doctors on Harley Street would prioritize their patients over all else, and Andre was no exception.

No further words were necessary; Andre was the one who could most easily leave and not be missed for the remainder of the celebrations.

"You'll tell me everything when you return to London," Andre said, thinking wistfully that Alfie would return to the practice at 87 Harley Street, but it wouldn't be his home anymore. He'd move into the townhouse prepared for him and his bride, Bea. Although Andre was happy for his friends and glad they found love, he felt a pang of sadness that the practice was emptying like a nest. One by one, the doctors were taking flight.

"Let's go to my carriage," Stan said. "I'd like to return to London before the baron does."

"I think it's time. My patients await, and so does the rehabilitation center." Andre nodded to Alfie and watched him escort Bea into the bustling ballroom.

"And I have to get back to my task at hand," Stan added. "After all, I've come to England to find the reason for the trade problems at home in Transylvania."

"You said that it had been a surprise, even to you, to pinpoint all the trouble to the Prussian baron." But Andre decided not to push his friend further, he knew it was a matter that caused him much distress.

"Yes, I need to heal my country, and you need to heal your patients. Let's hope they don't share the same source of the violence," Stan said with one last glance in Baron von List's direction.

Andre Agreed. What took a moment to inflict could forever occupy a person's life, as was the nature of many of his patients' injuries.

With a final wave to his friends, Andre joined Stan, stepping away from the warmth of the ballroom. The night air was crisp, filled with the scents of blooming flowers and distant rain. His heart felt light despite the weight of responsibilities, his resolve firm as he climbed into the carriage beside Stan. The road to London stretched ahead with uncertainty and promise. Andre settled back, determination mingling with the soft rhythm of hooves against cobblestones, his mind already shifting to those who awaited his care. *Yes*, he thought, his place was at the practice with his patients and not among the nobility.

And it was never going to change.

Upstairs in Silvercest Manor…

EVERYTHING HAD CHANGED since Thea had come to England. Her full name, Princess Josephine Theodora Andrea Hohenzollern-Sigmaringen, seemed as far as her home these days, for she didn't feel very royal. Well, she wasn't letting anyone know that she was—royal that was—and liked the predictability and freedom of life as a governess, except when the mattress's spring poked her in the back. Plus, letting people know where she was would allow the one person she was hiding from to find her.

Never!

But even though she was purposefully hiding, in the spartan room designated as the nursery for her six-year-old ward, Mary White, Thea couldn't sleep. Although Mary should have had her own room, there wasn't enough space, and Thea was glad to be there for the little girl and not at home awaiting her wedding just in time for her twenty-first birthday.

Silvercrest Manor, where Mary's parents stayed for a ball underway downstairs in celebration of a wedding Thea knew little about, was only supposed to be a stop on a longer journey while Mr. White pursued his business. They'd already said their goodbyes before dinner and planned to reunite in London at a later date. In fact, Thea was to take Mary to London and tend to her on the morrow until Mr. And Mrs. White returned from their travels. Thea felt a deep empathy for Mary, understanding her loneliness and promising herself to be present for her own children, just as she and Mary were there for each other now.

Mary put her fingers in her ears. The music from the ball two floors down was altogether too loud, and she was too secluded;

this was the first time in Thea's life that she wasn't the princess with a filled dance card.

"I can't sleep," Mary said, sitting up in her frilly white night-gown. She brushed her hair out of her face. She usually slept like a log, but not tonight. "I can't go to Europe with Mother and Father. It's not fair."

"How can I help?" Thea asked, moving as little as possible lest the bed screech with the shrill sound that made her cringe every time. It had been her fault for running away; from her elegant silk pillow covers and the comforting canopy over her bed, in the same dusty pink as her favorite roses in the gardens outside Bran Castle. Instead of her sizeable four-poster bed, she was in a cot. But she was free, anonymous, and there wasn't a royal in sight forcing her hand in marriage—not her father or her alleged betrothed. She was free.

Alone.

Penniless, lest for the small salary she received from the Whites to look after Mary.

And it wasn't easy for a princess to make do without her lady's maids and all the little luxuries she took for granted before she left Bran Castle.

Thea shifted, and the bed screeched again. She grimaced when the sound assaulted her ears. She didn't mind working as Mary's governess; the little girl was darling. However, life without the comforts of being a princess in a castle proved to be exhausting. She had to wash and dry her clothes, and there were no gowns tied in the back but rather sensible and simple dresses with buttons in the front.

"Are you thirsty?" Thea asked, noting that the water jug on the side table was only half full. "Or cold, perhaps?"

"So many questions," the little girl waved grandly. Her philo-sophical streak often gave Thea reason to suppress a chuckle.

"Tell me." Thea spread her arms, and Mary pulled her white sleeping gown up and climbed onto her lap. Mary's thoughtful expression was a welcome interruption to Thea's musings.

"Well, why do girls pull all the time?" Mary asked.

"Pull what?"

"In the Latin declination you put on the board today. Nominative: *puella*, the girl, genitive: *puellae*, of the girl, dative: *puellae*, to or for the girl."

"*Puell*, not pull," Thea said when she realized the clock on the mantel showed eleven o'clock, which was long past the time of a Latin lesson—or Mary's bedtime. Thea yawned and blinked groggily.

"Do the boys in Rome pull the girls because of their pigtails?" Mary asked again.

"Why would they do that?"

"Because girls are called *puellae*."

"First of all, boys in Rome speak Italian these days. They're not like the stories you learn to translate; they are ancient. Nobody truly speaks Latin anymore."

"You do."

"I speak several languages that came from Latin, and studying it as the basis of proper grammar was part of my education, but I still don't speak it in conversation." Mary didn't need to know exactly how extensive Thea's education had been; she was a princess in hiding. It was unheard of. Rebellious. Dangerous. It was empowering, in moments when she didn't sit so uncomfortably on the cot. Her new sense of freedom had come at the cost of comfort and security. How odd that freedom and security were like two geometric shapes that never overlapped.

"Then why do I have to learn it if I could much better learn Italian to fend off the boys in Rome who pull my hair?"

"You've never been to Rome, dear. And as long as I'm watching out for you, nobody will pull your pigtails." Mary looked unconvinced. "Remember, '*Lingua viva sensus revocat*'—a living language revives the senses. Even if Latin isn't spoken commonly, its essence lives on through the languages we use today."

"The roots are common for all?"

"Perhaps yes. Everything has the same origins. All people are equal; the differences are nuances like shapes on paper, but the essence of what they are made of, ink on paper, is the same for all."

Mary seemed to contemplate that for a while as Thea put her back into bed and draped the covers over her. "So, words are ink on paper, and all share communities?"

"Communication," Thea corrected her. "Yes."

As sweet as Mary was, the life of a governess was not what Thea had had in mind when she'd left her home, Bran Castle, in the Grand Principality of Transylvania, which was under the control of the Habsburgs. They had been in search of her brother, Stan. She'd hoped to escape from the fangs of her parents, eager to organize her arranged marriage to Prince Ralph Maximilian von Habsburg, whom she'd never met; only her brothers had, and her father had promised her to his father under the pretense of a charter to prevent the exploitation of Transylvanian gold from its mines. But, there had to be another way to unite her family with the Habsburgs and give her people more power under the Habsburg rule.

And that's why Thea needed to speak with her brother. She wanted to find out what he'd accomplished, not merely read the occasional letter with a three- or four-month delay. She wanted to be part of the excitement that was her brother's life in resolving their family's conflicts with the Habsburgs and their Prussian followers—*accomplices* was a better word, but that was neither here nor there in the nursery.

Thea drove her fingers through Mary's soft ringlets of curls that fell from her night bonnet, her braided pigtails peeking through. These days, they only had each other.

Mary jolted back, her eyes wide as saucers. "A monster!" she cried, leaping out of bed and clutching Thea with tiny, trembling arms.

Thea, feeling Mary's small body's warmth pressing against her, gently murmured, "A tree branch hit the window." Her voice was calm, a steady anchor in Mary's storm of fear. She stroked the girl's hair, a gesture intended to soothe, as her mother's touch did for Thea when she was little. "Come, I'll show you there's nothing to fear."

With practiced ease, she took up the oil lamp, its light casting a soft glow that danced across the walls. She slipped into her gown, then helped Mary into hers, the fabric rustling like whispers of reassurance.

"Where are we going?" Mary asked, her voice a fragile thread in the quiet room.

"We must meet our fears head-on, little one. We must take the power, or the fear will control our actions." Thea winked, offering a playful smile.

We ladies must always support each other.

Together.

And yet alone.

Together, they descended the servant's stairs, the house around them sighing with the night's sounds.

"Look, it's just dark. Nothing to fear," Thea said when she'd opened the door. "Let's see." That's all she'd intended, a look out through the door. But Mary ducked under Thea's arm and slipped before she could grasp her. "No, Mary! Come back!" When Mary had gone further than the lights from the building reached on the grounds, Thea knew the little girl had gone too far, and had no choice but to follow her. "I didn't mean for you to face your fears outside like this."

Too late.

Thea rubbed her arms and blinked several times until her eyes adjusted to the darkness. Then, she found Mary again and took her hand. Outside, the air was crisp, the remnants of the ball's music still fading to the garden's nightly sounds.

Thea's grip on Mary's hand was firm yet tender, a silent vow to protect her.

Time to face some fears…

The night hummed with life—the distant hoot of an owl, leaves rustling in a breeze—each sound amplifying the unease that prickled at her senses.

As they moved through the hedges, a sudden crack startled Thea, and her heart lurched. The darkness was thick, the moonlight weaving shadows that cloaked the truth. She glanced back, her breath caught as she scanned the gloom. Was it merely a deer moving through the underbrush that had snapped a twig with its hooves? Or a fox? Suddenly, the air erupted with a flurry of wings—bats, their erratic paths cutting through the night. Thea pulled Mary closer, the bonnet slipping over the child's face like a shield. Her eyes darted about for answers, catching a glint—metal, cold and gleaming, momentarily revealed by the moon's light. Once a place of serene beauty by day, the garden now held a chilling mystery, the thrill of the unknown tightening her grip on the nightly dangers.

Navigating the hedges, Thea's thoughts danced between the house's safety and the night's mystery. Had she left her apprehensions behind with the guests who laughed and twirled inside? What shadows lurked in the garden's darkness?

"Do you remember what I told you about nocturnal animals?" Thea asked, gripping Mary's tiny hand with both of hers.

The girl nodded frantically.

"Well, we are diurnal. Humans sleep at night. Thus, we are not easily scared of the animals we are used to encountering, such as rabbits, birds, and butterflies."

"But what about owls? I want to catch a fluffy baby owl!" Mary whispered, her breath hitching as she looked over her shoulder. "Where do we find one? Or a baby wolf, like a puppy, right?"

"I don't think wolves come so close to gardens and roads. I've rarely seen them beyond the Carpathian Mountains."

"Never mind. Mother said there are no wolves in England," Mary whispered again, reminding Thea how different the countryside was from home.

Thea bit her tongue. She'd said too much. Anyone who knew how terribly far those mountains were would question where she was from and who she was.

Note to self: European mountain ranges in Mary's next geography lesson.

But being found out wasn't Thea's problem in this instance.

As they skirted the garden's edge, everything went dark with a suddenness that stole her breath. Her hand grasped the air where Mary's had been, but the connection was severed.

"Mary?" Panic rose within Thea's throat. "Where are you?"

A large, moist hand came from behind and slapped her on the mouth, holding her so tightly that she could barely exhale through her nose. Then the hand disappeared, and Thea's senses flared, every sound and scent magnified, but something rough was shrugged over her head. In the fabric's suffocating embrace, Thea took a deep breath and heard heavy steps. It smelled moldy. The rough fabric poked Thea's skin, probably jute or hemp. A sack enveloped her head, and the world narrowed to the frantic beating of her heart.

Chapter Two

T HE NIGHT SKY covered the countryside like an inky shroud as the landau carriage rumbled back to London along the dirt road. Andre leaned back against the plush seat, a soft smile playing on his lips as he recalled the joyous celebration of Alfie and Bea's wedding mere hours ago.

"What a day." Prince Stan's declaration startled Andre in his reverie. His unlikely but welcome companion sat across from him, staring out the window absentmindedly. "A lovely affair," he murmured, his voice barely audible over the clatter of hooves.

"Indeed," Andre replied, his gaze drifting to the dimly lit countryside. He felt every bump in the road, his overindulgence at the wedding feast making itself known in his queasy stomach. He fidgeted, trying to ignore the sensation. What a marvelous day, he mused, glad for his friend Alfie and his newfound happiness with his lovely bride. Could he also discover a woman who would cherish him with the same intensity as Bea adored Alfie? With such devotion and warmth?

Andre had never thought about getting married, especially after that terrifying night in Florence when he ran for his life.

The marriage of Nick, the oculist, to Pippa brought about changes. Then Alfie, the apothecary, had married Bea. At night, when Nick returned to his townhouse on the same street, the practice at 87 Harley Street would be less crowded, leaving only

Felix, the dentist, and Andre. Even Nurse Wendy had moved out since she was Nick's younger sister and lived with him and Pippa at the townhouse now.

Andre sighed, pondering the day once more.

Stan's demeanor swiftly changed. His eyes sharpened, and he frowned, peering into the darkness. Andre's heart skipped a beat.

"What's happening?" he asked, but Stan didn't answer.

The sound of distant hooves reached Andre's ears, different from the rhythmic trot of their horses. His pulse quickened as he strained to listen. The hairs on his neck stood up when he heard screams in the distance.

Stan hurried, locking the carriage door and balling his fists. The carriage jolted to a halt, the horses neighing and stomping in fright. Shouts filled the air, none of them in English. German, but not the familiar kind from Vienna. Prussian? Andre swallowed hard, fear creeping into his chest. He tried to remain calm, but the tension in the air cut his breath off. His senses sharpened, every rustle and creak amplified in the dark just like that night in Florence…

"Do you have a pistol?" Stan asked.

Andre shook his head vigorously. He never had a pistol. Knowing the wounds those guns inflicted, he hated them. Andre had removed bullets and gunpowder from flesh more often than he could count.

A sudden blow echoed through the night, followed by the sickening crack of bone breaking. Andre flinched; the familiar sound sent a shiver down his spine.

"Get out!" a voice bellowed in Prussian.

Andre's heart raced as he understood the command and the criminals knew they'd understand—they had not been chosen by chance; they'd been expecting them—why else would they speak Prussian in the deep dark woods in England? The door handle rattled, and Stan pushed Andre back but positioned himself, ready for combat. Stan's years of military training and his sense of responsibility as a prince showed. His movements were precise, his posture unyielding, and his gaze steady, as if every step carried the weight of duty and discipline. The way he instinctively shielded others, even in the smallest moments, spoke volumes of a life shaped by command and obligation. But Andre's fear intensified—he despised violence and the lasting damage it could cause.

The door flew open, and chaos ensued. Stan jumped out of the carriage and launched himself at a man whose features Andre couldn't make out. It went too fast, and Andre ducked. As soon as he stepped out of the carriage, he saw the shadows of a fist swinging at him. He saw figures grappling in the dim light, punches landing brutally. A woman pulled away from one of the dark figures, her hands fumbling to tear free the sack that covered her head. Andre blinked, straining to see in the dark. Another figure launched himself at the prince, but Stan fought back, grunting with effort. Amid the confusion, a woman grabbed Andre's arm. She shook wildly.

"Protect her!" Stan shouted urgently.

Andre instinctively wrapped his arms around her, offering the little comfort he could. She burrowed into his chest, her soft hair brushing against his chin. A tiny figure clung to his leg—a little girl. Her brown eyes were wide, and she was sobbing with fear. Tears glistened in the moonlight as they ran down her cheeks, her sobs piercing the night. Around him, shadows morphed and flickered in the frantic dance of the carriage's lantern light, the shouts and clamor spinning his senses into a dizzying whirl. The world felt as though it was teetering between reality and a nightmare, each breath laden with the weight of uncertainty and the urgent need to protect.

"Stan!" the woman shouted when he grunted with pain in response to a blow from one of the men. Something shiny caught the moonlight, and Andre's heart froze when he realized it was a blade.

The woman tried to pull herself away from Andre, but he held her tight just as Stan had told him. Was she trying to help

Stan?

Andre's heart pounded like a drum as he gazed at the woman trembling in his arms. Her delicate frame quivered, and an almost primal need to shield her from the chaos surged through him. The girl clung tighter to his leg, her tiny fingers digging in as if she could anchor herself to him. Instinctively, he gently touched her head, shielding her hair against the dirt kicked up from the road as the men fought.

Time stretched. Each moment was an agonizing test of endurance. The gritty clash of bodies assaulted Andre's ears, the metallic clang of a blunt weapon, perhaps the back end of a pistol, and the desperate, high-pitched whinnies of horses. Dirt from the road grated against boots, a harsh, abrasive sound that made him grimace and pull his shoulders up as if he could shield his ears while bending over the woman and the girl to protect them with his body.

The air was thick with the scent of sweat and fear, a pungent mix that erased the usually comforting earthy scents of the countryside. Andre tasted the dirt kicked up in clouds, its gritty tang invading his nostrils, mingling with the acrid stench of liquor. The girl whimpered softly, a sound so fragile it seemed ready to shatter at any moment, and it pierced Andre's heart like a knife. He could feel her shaking, her breaths coming in quick, shallow gasps, each one a desperate plea for reassurance as she clung to him.

He couldn't bundle them into the carriage for fear that the attackers would take control and whisk them away. Andre considered how long they'd been traveling—they were too far to walk back to the castle.

Finally, the sounds of struggle began to fade. The attackers retreated, their voices growing distant. Andre loosened his hold on the woman, feeling the tension in his muscles slowly ebb away. Stan stood at the open door, panting heavily, his knuckles bruised and bloodied, but he held two pistols and a knife in his hands. He'd removed the highwaymen's weapons and stuffed them in his boots.

"*Eşti rănit?*" Are you hurt? Stan asked the woman in Romanian, his voice gentle yet firm.

Andre understood the question; though he could not speak Romanian, he recognized it quickly. He had heard Romanian many times when he studied in Vienna. It was the closest Romance language to Latin, which he knew, and several students spoke it at the faculty of medicine. That was when he discovered that he could easily understand most Romanian, a combination of his mother tongue, Italian, plus the language of medicine, Latin.

The woman shook her head, her eyes filled with gratitude and fear. She let go of Andre, her body still trembling, and she collapsed into Stan's arms. Andre instantly missed her touch but didn't have time to dwell on the sentiment when the little girl looked up at him and lifted her arms with the plea to be picked up, her tears beginning to run rapidly down her cheeks. Andre lifted her and instinctively hugged her, hoping to ease their fear. He didn't know the girl, but he knew children. And this one needed his help.

Stan's expression softened as he took in the scene before him, clutching the woman against his chest. "You'll be safe now," he assured them, his gaze lingering on Andre. "We must get back to London quickly."

Andre nodded, his mind racing with questions. Who were these attackers? Why had they targeted their carriage? And most importantly, who was this woman who suddenly appeared and seemed to know Stan?

⇢⟫⟨⟨⟨⤛

THEA BLINKED AT her brother barely able to believe that it was him.

"How did you find me?" Stan asked her in Romanian, his voice gentle yet firm once they approached the carriage.

"They did! They pulled a sack over my head and said I'd make a handsome ransom," Thea tried not to cry when she said the words, but she was still shaking with fear. "I didn't know what they'd do to me or where they were taking us. And Mary, I am responsible for her safety. I only told her we'd face our fears because of the branch in the window—" Thea heaved for air. "What have you done that they need to blackmail you with my life?"

"How did they even know—" Stan paused and then kicked the dirt on the road. "List!"

"That's why he was there uninvited!" Andre said. "List's connection to the Prussian attackers is obvious and yet we have nothing against List to report to the authorities."

"Again!" Stan growled.

Thea shook her head, her eyes filled with gratitude and fear, but she wasn't sure she could tell her brother the truth before the stranger—certainly not in front of Mary.

"You can speak, he's trustworthy," Stan addressed her unanswered question. Then he turned to the man and said, "She is my sister."

She had been astonished that Stan had trusted this man so much that he had thrust her into his arms, he was a stranger to her after all. But when she felt his embrace, she knew there was an unspoken truth and wisdom in relying on him. He was a pillar of a man, muscular, warm, and exuding strength beyond muscle—not the strength he'd used to hold her but the feeling of comfort he emitted.

"I lost my bonnet," Mary cried.

"We will find another for you—a new one. With more lace," Thea said, unsure how she'd make good on the promise. What was worse, she'd have to explain to Mary's parents how the last bonnet was lost...

Stan's expression softened as he took in the scene before him. "You'll be safe now," he assured them, his gaze lingering on Andre. "Andre, there's no time to waste. We must get back."

So that was his name, Andre.

"They were expecting us. They spoke like List. Who was that?" Andre asked, but Stan didn't answer. He smacked his lips as if the truth tasted too bitter to say it aloud.

Then Stan ushered them back into the carriage. Thea nodded, her mind racing with questions. Andre handed her the little girl but didn't follow them into the carriage. Looking out of the open cabin door, she saw Andre tending to the coachman.

"Can you move it this way?" He lifted the man's arm, and the coachman nodded.

"He's a doctor," Stan said, eyeing Mary sternly as the little girl settled into the seat. "Who's the child?" Stan asked in Romanian, and Thea was sure Mary didn't understand. She'd been tasked to teach her a little French and a lot of Latin, but her skills did not follow their conversation.

"I'm her governess. It pays for the passage. How would I have a six-year-old daughter in less than a year since you last saw me?"

Stan harumphed and shifted uncomfortably. "So, you did run away?"

"I came to find you."

Stan sighed. "Why?"

Thea had forgotten how well he knew her. Of all their siblings, Stan was the closest in age, and they'd been inseparable as children until he left for university in Vienna.

"Can't a sister miss her big brother?"

"Not if she's supposed to marry the Habsburg prince this year. I'm not your escape, Thea."

I'll be the judge of that.

"Well, what I am supposed to do, and want to do, rarely overlap."

Stan slumped into the seat and rubbed his knuckles. Thea noticed they weren't bleeding this time; he'd been in worse fights.

"He needs a splint, but he can take us to London." Andre climbed into the carriage, then sat next to Stan. "I'll have to take him to the practice first."

Stan nodded.

Andre's demeanor had changed, and he seemed entirely in control now. He was enviable, thinking several steps ahead with a calm mind and the poise of a man with a clear path. Even a commoner had more control over his life than Thea ever had.

"Which practice?" she asked in fluent English, which seemed to take Andre by surprise, judging from his eyes that darted in her direction.

"87 Harley Street. London," he said curtly.

The carriage resumed its journey, the night air cool against Thea's flushed skin. She remained close to Mary, who'd put her head on Thea's lap and soon fell asleep.

It was uncanny how Mary could sleep after the night's excitement, but it was still night, and long past her bedtime. Thea's heart was still pounding from the shock of the attack. Despite the chaos and fear, Thea felt a strange sense of trust. The road ahead remained uncertain, but one thing was clear—this encounter had changed everything.

She glanced up at Andre, his eyes steady and reassuring. She knew she would do whatever it took to protect Mary and stay close to her brother, but she couldn't help but wonder about the man who had shielded them with his body.

"Who is he exactly?" Thea asked Stan in Romanian.

"I can speak for myself," Andre answered in English. There was a sweet lilt to his pronunciation.

"Italian?" she whispered, pressing a hand over Mary's ear; the other was already against Thea's thigh.

"Dr. Andre Fernando is from Florence." Stan said.

Thea shot her brother a glance. "What are you doing colluding with the Florentines?" she reverted to English since there didn't seem to be a language left the handsome stranger couldn't understand.

Stan rolled his eyes. "He's not one of them. He studied in Vienna, and he's a friend."

"A commoner," Thea said and arched a brow and wondered what else there was to the connection between her brother and this doctor. Even in the dim light in the carriage, she could see his intelligent eyes and bright smile, and she'd felt his muscles when Stan thrust her against his chest. Like her brothers, he was strong. Stan, Alex, and the other two had been trained for combat. War. She'd never met a doctor as strong as a warrior.

"What kind of doctor are you?" Thea asked.

"Orthopedist. Bones, and—"

"I know what an orthopedist is. *Orthos* is Greek for straight or correct, and *paideia* means education."

"It's a term coined by the French physician Nicolas Andry. I studied his original treatise."

"In French?" Thea wondered why the muscular doctor was handsome and spoke French *and* German since he studied in Vienna. Most doctors didn't have such a broad education.

"Both. There's a slight inconsistency in the translation from French but the German edition had invaluable citations."

Thea quirked a brow.

As if he'd guessed her skepticism, he explained. "I'm not of noble blood, but I assure you, Your Royal Highness, I'm all but common." Andre arched a brow, and Thea's heart leaped.

He was far too handsome and witty for her to be comfortable near him. As a princess, she'd been taught to keep her distance from rakes—especially the charming ones. He was charming, and this new curiosity about his persona unsettled her.

"All right, let me clear the air here." Stan leaned forward. "Princess Josephine Theodora Andrea von Hohenzollen-Sigmaringen, I'm pleased to present my dear friend, Dr. Andre Fernando, to you." Stan gestured grandly—as if they were not in a tight cabin of a landau in the middle of the night on a dirt path but in the throne room back at Bran Castle. "He knows about the gold mines at home and Baron von List."

Thea dropped her head back against the cabin side. Somehow the Prussian baron had managed to use the political instability in

Transylvania to cover up his exploitation of the gold mines.

"Have you been able to intercept any gold yet? Any evidence?" Thea asked but Stan merely shook his head in resignation. So List was still plundering the country's resources and had so far gotten away unscathed.

"So, why did you run away?" Stan asked.

"I drafted a charter," she mumbled.

"What kind of charter?"

"Charta ad opes extrahendas, per licentias a regia monarchia concessas moderata." Thea reluctantly named the title of her charter draft.

"What?" His eyebrows shot up, carving deep lines across his forehead, while his mouth parted slightly, as if words had been snatched away before they could form. Suddenly, he winced and rubbed his shoulder.

"She drafted a charter for extracting resources, regulated through licenses granted by the royal monarchy?" Andre asked Stan.

"Why ask him? *I* drafted it." Thea pointed at herself.

Andre paused momentarily, and she wished it weren't so dark that she could better make out his expression. Could it be that he was angry because she, just a woman, dared to draft a charter aimed at correcting the political imbalance that drove her father to marry her off for alliances?

"You drafted a whole set of laws in Latin?" Andre asked.

"Yes," Thea said, holding her breath, waiting for his reaction.

"What does it say?"

Oh! He was the first to ask about the content of her charter.

How flattering!

Heat rose to her cheeks, and she was glad the darkness hid her reaction.

"It sets up a licensing system so that the local resources cannot be exploited without reimbursing the local government for the extracted ore by weight." She paused when he leaned forward, and the moonlight shining through the carriage window illuminated his face for just long enough so she could choke on her words. He was handsome.

And she had his attention.

Why was it so hot in the cabin all of a sudden?

"I set up three levels of controls so that nothing can be removed without a signature and ultimately a royal stamp before export papers are granted."

"So that List's smugglers can be caught before they bring him the gold?" Andre said and then turned to Stan. "That's brilliant!"

Thea's breath hitched.

Brilliant. He'd said she was—no, her charter was—brilliant. And he was the first man to give her ideas credit.

Her lungs filled with renewed hope and a sense of pride she thought she'd lost when she ran away from her life at Bran Castle.

"The Habsburgs won't sign it if it means that we'd get the last say about the mining," Stan said.

Andre clapped his hands. "Still, it's a grand idea." Then he leaned forward. "Princess Josephine Theodora Andrea—"

"Just Thea, please," she said, acutely aware of her brother's disapproving snort.

She wasn't sure how to act in this context, so she did as she'd been told, held her hand out for him to kiss it, and was surprised with how he did. Andre bowed from his seated position, took her hand, and kissed solemnly on her knuckle lingering for just a fraction of a second too long.

It felt as though he were bending the etiquette on purpose.

A jolt of prickling shot through her, and she withdrew her hand quickly.

He's dangerous… OH, this is going to be fun.

Chapter Three

MARY WAS STILL fast asleep on Thea's lap.

"So, how did they find you?" Stan asked. The clatter of hooves echoed against the dirt path as the landau carriage rocked gently, the wheels churning up small dust clouds in the dim moonlight Thea could see from the window.

"I'm afraid I don't know," Thea said. "But I know List and his people are dangerous."

"He has associates everywhere," Stan mumbled. "His political nets are cast wider than I can ascertain."

Still, Thea couldn't decide what was more surprising, the well-educated doctor with irritatingly dark eyes that she tried not to stare at in the dimly lit carriage or the fact that Stan spoke near him about the existential threat List posed for their family as if Andre were a long-time confidant.

Andre smiled crookedly and narrowed his eyes to indicate he was up for the challenge. Thea swallowed hard when she realized it was impossible not to stare at his dashing features.

"Who's the girl?" Stan pressed on.

"Miss Mary-Elizabeth White." Thea nodded primly.

Stan pursed his lips and made a roll with his hand in the air, waiting for Thea to continue.

She sighed. "She's my ward. I'm her governess."

Stan coughed. "You are serious?"

Andre sucked his lips in as if he were suppressing a laugh, and Thea shot him a that's-not-funny look.

"Well, I had little with me and met them on the way. They needed a tutor for Latin, French, and mathematics. When I said I could teach it all plus geography—"

"They hired you because you could give their daughter the education due to a princess?" Stan's voice was slow, and he didn't even try to hide his anger from Andre. At this moment, however, Thea wished Stan didn't speak to her in such a patronizing manner. So, what if he was her older brother? He was only one year older than her.

"Indeed." Thea feigned nonchalance and straightened her back.

"Because you are a princess, Thea." Stan's tone grew stern, and Thea's skin tingled with an unsettling warmth. Knowing that the handsome doctor in the cabin overheard their conversation, heat crept up her neck as she shifted uneasily in her seat. She fidgeted, her hands finding no rest, fingers nervously tracing the embroidered pattern on her gown.

"And I had the best education."

"For a specific purpose, yes," Stan nearly growled. It was most unbecoming for a prince.

"And what is that? Being the breeding stock for the Habsburg runt of the litter or merely a trading chip in a political charade?"

Andre watched her intently and ran a hand through his tousled hair, casually drawing attention to the effortless grace surrounding him. Heat crept up Thea's neck, her cheeks again betraying her as she struggled to hold steady under the heat of his smoldering stare.

Perhaps it was better to have this conversation in the dark carriage after all.

"Thea, I've been working on the gold deal. Why didn't you stay at home and wait your turn to fix—"

"Wait? My turn? To do what exactly? Watch the hand of the clock until one day, the Habsburg prince finally decides that his mistresses and adventures bored him enough to claim me as a consolation prize. Or worse…" She held her eyes wide open and leaned toward her brother. "Should I wait for you to solve the problem and make my marriage to him superfluous?"

"What do you mean?" Stan asked.

Thea cradled Mary gently, her gaze drifting through the carriage window to the pinpricks of light twinkling in the distance—a small town, a promise of something other than what she fled. The memories of Bran Castle's imposing walls clung to her like a shadow, a reminder of the life she had left but not its burdens. As the carriage rolled on, she pondered the path ahead, wondering if perhaps she had to reshape her fate rather than run from it.

"Think about it! I won't be a bargaining chip if you solve the political crisis. I'll go from the coveted princess to a shelved spare part."

"Well, if I do solve it—which I haven't—perhaps. But it's not as easy as I thought. And you're not safe."

"I wouldn't know; you didn't address any letters to me, and Alex, nor any of our brothers, ever shared your news with me."

"Because you're a girl!"

"But I'm not stupid, you know! And I missed you. I worried about what you were doing in England."

"So, you came to find me?"

Not exactly.

"It was stupid to run away!" Stan raised his voice, and Thea gave him a stern high-chinned look.

"How dare you?"

"Thea." Stan rubbed his forehead and gave Andre a cursory glance before he addressed her again. As the family's representative in England, her older brother had the demeanor he typically assumed before formulating some verdict that would decide her future. And even though Thea bristled against the thought, she'd have to obey lest he send her back to Bran Castle, where her betrothed might await her. Thea shuddered at the thought.

"Have you considered what might happen if I don't defeat the Prussian baron?"

"No." There was no doubt that her older brother would succeed until this moment. There had always been one of her brothers ready to come to her rescue, whether she'd climbed a cherry tree and didn't know how to get down, rescued a puppy that turned out to be a wolf cub, or accidentally locked herself in the western turret at Bran Castle where a nest of bees had been lodged. "So this Prussian is really that dangerous?"

Andre let out a groan and buried his face in his hands. "Baron Wolfgang von List," he said in a perfect German accent.

"How does he know the baron?" Thea asked Stan, who only gave her a faint nod.

"I can hear you." Andre raised his brows and then dropped them when he dropped his hands loosely over his knees.

"You know our enemy. You speak Italian, English, French, and German?" Thea asked. "Wait, and Latin because you're a doctor?"

"And a little Hindi. I picked it up when I was in India," Andre said. He had a lovely deep voice, resonant and youthful with a typical Italian smoothness, Thea thought.

"As a soldier? Or missionary?" How was that possible, a man that young, having lived so much?

"As an apprentice. After I graduated from Vienna."

"Goodness," Thea managed. His curriculum vitae was impressive indeed. And there was that cocky smirk that made her chest flutter most uncomfortably.

"I came to find you." Thea wrung her hands now and turned back to Stan.

"You came all the way to England and didn't tell our parents? And we are on the way to London and the only reason you're here is because you've been abducted," Stan said sternly.

She cringed. "Yes."

"Where the seat of the English monarch is, the one with a dozen Habsburg cousins, being one of the most influential royal houses in Europe."

"I hadn't considered that." *I just wanted to get away and find you.*

"So have you any plans for how I am supposed to protect you from a nest of bees this time?" The bees being the Habsburgs, Thea didn't want to get stung.

Stan started again. "If I don't stop List in time, and mind you, he's behind all this, perhaps even the highwaymen, then what will become of you? You'd be safer at one of the Habsburg seats than ours. They are connected to the Prussians."

"That doesn't mean they'll protect me. What if they want to use me as a sacrificial lamb?" Thea laid back in the seat. Mary was still nestled with her upper body on her lap, and she smacked her lips in her sleep.

Stan deflated and groaned her name. *Yes, embarrass me further by showing your annoyance with your little sister.*

"What would you have done if I hadn't been there tonight? And Andre? Can you imagine what those men could have done to you and the little girl? You are responsible for her."

Thea grimaced and her hands went cold. He was right. She'd been so proud of making her way to London she hadn't truly considered the dangers.

If she were compromised, or worse, she couldn't even return as a bride for Prince Ralph. She'd be ruined. On second thought… Thea's eyes shot to Andre again.

Mary suddenly turned and flapped her arms in the air. She must have been dreaming. With another swing, she moved her right leg and swung it over Andre, seated across from Thea.

He caught her leg and steadied it, letting the child rest half-sprawled over his already tight space in his seat. Thea tried to lift the girl, but she was so heavy in her relaxed state that she couldn't find the right angle to pull her up. Andre gave a reassuring "Shh" and nodded, indicating that she shouldn't wake the child on his account.

The doctor was surprisingly at ease with the child and didn't seem to mind being discomforted by her.

Shadows danced across Andre's face, cast by the flickering lantern swinging on the hook outside the carriage cabin, highlighting the intensity of his gaze and the tension that crackled between them.

"So what now?" Stan asked Andre as if he had a say in Thea's future.

"I'm staying in London with you," she declared, unwilling to let the men decide for her.

And to her surprise, Andre gave her a pleased look—controlled, as if he didn't want Stan to see, but Thea had noticed it.

"I'll tell Alex you're here. He's in Cornwall and will escort you home," Stan declared with a sense of finality. "I'll call him back sooner. He can help me before he meets Miss Lyndon. He's supposed to meet—"

"It doesn't sound like Alex is very keen on meeting his politically arranged betrothed or else he wouldn't be hiding in Cornwall."

But Stan didn't pay Thea any heed. "I'll send him a note from London."

"I'm not going with him."

"So you want to miss your brother's engagement? He's come to England to meet his betrothed. These alliances could save us."

"Or ruin our lives." Thea deflated. "I'm not going back to meet mine."

Thea's gaze held steady as it met Stan's, her curiosity piqued by the silent clash of wills reflected in his eyes—a familiar scene reminiscent of the stubborn exchanges she often navigated with her kin. A wistful ache whispered through her, yearning for the comforting chaos of familial debates and shared laughter—but this was about her future.

As the carriage journeyed on, the rhythmic creaks formed a haunting symphony, echoing the relentless beat of her heart. Her lashes fluttered subtly, each glance towards Andre a silent entreaty for recognition. With every surreptitious look at the doctor, the air thickened with an unspoken tension, a tantalizing curiosity enveloping her. Thea felt an irresistible pull, a desire to delve deeper into the enigma that was Andre, if only she dared to uncover more.

Chapter Four

London, later that night...

IT WAS NEARLY two o'clock when the carriage finally pulled up before the practice when Andre hopped off, his boots landing softly on the cobblestones. Harley Street was dark, and the lights inside the other white houses in Marylebone were off. He approached the driver, whose arm hung at an awkward angle. Stan gave Andre a nod; he'd escort Thea and Mary inside, so Andre could tend to the driver.

"I'd like to take a better look at you now," Andre said, his tone firm but kind. He offered the man a supportive arm and guided him toward the door of 87 Harley Street, where his practice was located.

The house, usually bustling with activity, stood oddly silent tonight. The others were still at the wedding, leaving Andre as the sole occupant of the practice. He unlocked the door and flicked on the gas lights, the warm glow casting familiar shadows in the hallway.

Leading the injured driver past the door marked *Apothecary*, Andre paused at the second door on the right. He turned on the light and helped the man onto the examination table.

"Stay here. I'll get something to clean your wounds," Andre said, his voice steady despite the unusual quiet around them. The practice was usually bustling with activity.

He stepped into the hallway and froze. Stan stood there,

having already brought in the luggage, and beside him was Thea, cradling the sleeping little girl in her arms. The unexpected sight tugged at something deep within him.

"I need to tend to him." Andre's upbringing required that he'd set the table and be a perfect host but his impulse was to tend to the injured driver.

"I'll take the horses to the back."

"You'll what?" Thea asked Stan with a quirked brow.

"I can do it later," Andre said. It really wasn't a job for a prince.

"No. It's different here, Thea. Everyone's the same and pulls their weight." With these words, Stan went back outside.

"He's good with horses, don't worry. I just never expected him to show it—" Thea said with a smile as she shifted under the girl's weight in her arms. They were an odd sibling pair, not at all haughty or arrogant like many aristocrats of Andre's acquaintance. They were nice.

Well, Thea was more than nice, and Andre had tried not to dwell on that thought for the last two hours in the carriage. He hadn't dwelled on her faint violet scent, the shimmering light of the moon, and the orange glow of the lantern reflected in her curly blonde hair. No, he didn't dwell on any of those aspects, not even the slight bobbing of her chest—*No!* None of it.

She was a princess. Stan's sister.

"Here, let's bring the child to Wendy's old room. She can sleep there. There's a connecting door to Nick's room, where you can sleep." Andre closed the distance to Thea and bent over her to lift the girl out of her arms. "Nick's the oculist here but remained at the wedding ball. Wendy is the nurse. They've moved out but their rooms are still there, safe and warm."

Andre gently carried the little girl upstairs, and Thea followed him. When they arrived in Wendy's room, Thea noticed the furniture was modest, but everything was clean, and the bed looked invitingly soft. Andre set Mary onto the bed and pulled the covers over her. Without needing to say anything, Thea fluffed the pillow and Andre lifted Mary's feet. They understood each other without the need to speak. Thea had removed Mary's shoes before Andre lifted her onto the bed. Just when Andre wanted to unfold the knitted throw and lay it over the child, Thea swept in and gently took it from him, laying it over Mary with the warmth of a mother. But she wasn't a mother; she was a royal of the Hohenzollern-Sigmaringen family. Stan's sister was beyond his reach, and yet she was so close that he could smell the violet in her clean soapy scent.

He wasn't sure how, but they were moving in harmony as if they were of one mind.

"How can I help?" Thea asked when Mary was curled up comfortably.

"Your room is here," Andre pointed to the door that led to Nick's old bed chamber. He couldn't go in there knowing that the beautiful princess would sleep there that night. It wasn't proper.

Thus, once Mary was safely tucked in, Andre walked back downstairs to his treatment room, where the coachman waited, beads of sweat on his forehead betraying his pain.

As Thea moved to follow Andre, he thought he ought to tell her not to. Witnessing the driver's injury was not a matter for princesses.

But he didn't say a word.

And before Andre could make sense of why he wanted to impress the princess, since he shouldn't wish to dwell on any of her qualities, not even her beauty, he heard a groan.

The driver waited, his face pale but resolute on the treatment bed. Andre rolled up his sleeves and prepared to tend to the man's injuries, grateful for the familiar tasks that gave his hands purpose—and kept his mind from wandering too far.

Not that his thoughts needed to go very far—Thea was right behind him.

THE STREETS OUTSIDE were silent save for the occasional clatter of a distant carriage, and Thea felt like a thief in the middle of the night. She couldn't remember the last time she'd had this much excitement in one night.

Despite the late hour, the doctor's treatment room was brightly lit with the gas lamp in the ceiling. A doctor needs light, Thea thought, even though this type of lamp was a rare luxury. His patients must either be very rich and pay him well, or he was that committed to his work that he refused to do it under candlelight. He needed to see well, regardless of the time of day, Thea decided. It was dark outside, and Andre left the curtain closed.

At first, Thea stood in the doorway, watching Andre guide the coachman, wincing in pain, to sit up for his examination. Andre's hands were steady and sure as he supported the man who still cradled his injured arm with a grimace on his weather-beaten face. She watched the doctor's steady hands and composed expression, her heart pounding and hands trembling in stark contrast.

"Can you sit here, please?" Andre instructed, his voice gently commanding. He helped the coachman into a special position on the table so that Andre was supporting his arm at all times. Thea noted the unnatural angle of the man's arm. "They've landed quite a blow."

Thea stepped further into the room, feeling a warmth spread over her in what should be a cold, clinical space. Andre glanced up, their eyes locking briefly before he focused on the task at hand.

"What can I do to help?" Thea asked. Andre hesitated momentarily, but she gave him a soft smile and removed her gloves. She set them on the desk, which she assumed was his. "I'm ready."

"This is not a task for a p—"

Thea put her index finger on her mouth. "I'm just Mary's governess and eager to make myself useful." *I am not just a princess with a trophy title. I can be useful.*

Andre paused and sucked his cheeks in.

Thea gave a reassuring nod.

He sighed. "Could you, please?" He inhaled sharply as if struggling to give a princess order. So she waited, gave a submissive smile that she'd practiced in conversations with Mary's parents, and folded her hands in front of her stomach.

"I'd like to help. He brought us to safety." Thea gave the driver a grateful look, and Andre seemed to notice. The driver, however, winced in pain, and beads of sweat dripped from his forehead.

"Please fetch me the bandages and splint from the cabinet," Andre requested, finally putting the patient before the rank that stood between him and Thea. His tone softened when he addressed her as he glanced over his shoulder at a walnut cabinet the size of a door leaning against the wall.

She nodded, her skirts rustling as she moved across the room. Her fingers traced the rows of neatly arranged medical supplies before she found what he needed and brought them over. Their fingers grazed, the lightest contact, as she passed the tools into his waiting hand. A shiver started at her fingertips and shot up her arm, sending a warm, electric pulse straight to her core.

Her eyes lingered on the veins running along the back of his hand, and she marveled at their strength and precision.

"Thank you," he murmured, setting to work. He gently palpated the coachman's arm, trailing his fingers over the bruise and carefully moving it except where it couldn't move. He felt for the break, narrowing down the exact spot. The coachman grimaced, yet kept his composure, as even more sweat dotted his forehead.

"The radius is broken cleanly," Andre said, his tone clinical as he reached for the bandages. "We'll need to set it and apply a brace to stabilize the radius and the ulna. This will help minimize movement while it heals. It will take time, but you'll recover."

Emotions coursed through her—admiration, longing, and frustration. She yearned to contribute more, to match his expertise with her own. The difference in their abilities pressed heavily on her chest. As she watched him move with seamless proficiency, her eagerness to help felt like a pale shadow. Yet, when their hands brushed, she felt a connection that bridged their skill gap.

"You will be alright," Andre assured him. "But you must avoid using this arm until you are better."

Thea watched as Andre positioned his hands on the coachman's lower arm, his movements confident and precise. The room fell into a tense silence, punctuated only by the coachman's ragged breaths. Andre leaned in close, his ear almost touching the patient's skin as if he could hear the fracture whispering its secrets.

"Would you like to step out for a moment?" Andre asked Thea, his voice calm but charged with an undertone of intensity. "I'm going to set it now."

The driver gasped and seemed to hold his breath.

Thea shook her head, her resolve firm despite the unease twisting in her stomach. She couldn't tear her eyes away from Andre's face, the concentration etched in every line on his forehead.

Andre nodded once, then turned his full attention back to the broken limb. His fingers moved with deliberate care, probing the area around the break. Thea marveled at his focus, noticing how his jaw tightened as he assessed the damage. He took a deep breath, bracing himself, and manipulated the bone.

The sound that followed was a sickening crunch, like the crack of a hard nut underfoot. Thea nearly convulsed, but she was too captivated to even breathe. The coachman let out a cry, his body tensing with the sharp pain, but Andre's grip remained steady. Sweat trickled down the patient's temples, but Andre's eyes never wavered from the task. Thea's heart pounded in her chest, each beat echoing the moment's urgency.

Andre's fingers worked meticulously, nudging the bone fragments into alignment. She saw the exact moment when the pieces slid into place, a subtle shift that seemed monumental. Andre's face showed a flicker of relief. He pressed down a bit more, ensuring the alignment was perfect.

"There," he whispered, his voice barely breaking the tension in the air. "It's set."

It had been no more than a second, perhaps two, but Thea felt as though she'd been through so much more while watching Andre work.

Fascinated, she didn't want to leave his side.

Without pausing, Andre reached for the splints and bandages she'd brought him. His hands moved with practiced efficiency, snugly wrapping the bandages around the arm. The coachman's grimace softened slightly as the support took hold, and the pain eased from his face.

Thea stepped closer, and she admired Andre more with each passing second. She handed him the final strip of cloth, their fingers brushing again. The touch rooted her in the moment, a silent acknowledgment of the skill she was witnessing. And this time, Andre held her gaze. Just for an instant—a meaningful moment in time—Thea felt seen as a valuable person in an important moment, not merely glanced over as a princess who didn't live up to her purpose in life.

There, in the treatment room with the doctor with deep, dark eyes, her existence mattered in a way that she'd never felt before.

And she wanted to matter even more.

I want to matter to him.

Andre tied off the last bandage, his movements precise and sure. He looked up at the coachman, offering a reassuring nod. "You'll need help. Is there anyone waiting for you at home?"

"Yes, I will go home to my wife." The man looked down at the brace. "But I can't work like this."

Thea barely had time to consider how quickly fortunes could turn when a dark cry echoed through the hallway. Thea's eyes widened in alarm, and without a word, they both rushed to the source of the sound.

In the hallway, Stan stood, clutching his shoulder, his face contorted in pain. A heavy piece of luggage lay at his feet, evidence of his ill-advised attempt to carry it despite what seemed to be a grave injury.

"Stan!" Thea exclaimed, rushing to her brother's side. "You shouldn't have!"

Andre was at Stan's other side in an instant, his hands already assessing the damage. "Your shoulder is bleeding," he said grimly. "Come in here." Stan gritted his teeth, nodding his consent.

Andre guided him to Nick's treatment room since the driver was still in his. He lit the lamp on and indicated where Stan should lie. Thea froze for a moment, taking the room in. There were cupboards similar to Andre's room, two desks, one with a stand and a prism on a small velvet cloth.

"This is Nick's room, the eye surgeon and oculist." Andre tended to Stan but must have seen Thea's momentary confusion when she looked at how different this treatment seemed compared to Andre's.

Thea's heart raced as she watched Andre's firm but careful movements, examining Stan's arm with unerring focus.

"Why didn't you tell us you were bleeding?" Andre asked.

"It hurt, but I've been wearing the black evening coat and—" Stan winced. "Ah! I didn't realize how bad it was until I carried the trunks in and saw some blood on my cuff."

Stan shifted on Nick's operating table, and Andre helped him out of his coat.

A large red spot on Stan's white shirt spread from the collar to the elbow, and the ivory waistcoat was also stained.

Thea came to his side. *"Ar fi trebuit să-mi spui!"* You should have told me! Thea's concern was evident in her voice when she spoke Romanian with her brother.

"Nu știam că este atât de rău," I didn't know it was so bad, Stan mumbled. "I've been hurt so much worse than this."

"You didn't pay attention to your bleeding shoulder?" Thea couldn't hide the exasperation in her voice.

"Eu nu am fost atent? Nici măcar nu știam că ești în Anglia și apoi a trebuit să mă lupt cu trei criminali înarmați călare ca

să te salvez!" I wasn't careful? I didn't even know you were in England and then I have to fight off three armed criminals on horses to save you!

Thea opened her mouth to retort, but her words faltered as her gaze dropped to Stan's shoulder. Her fingers brushed against the torn fabric, now soaked through with blood. "You're bleeding," she stated the obvious, her voice softer now, almost trembling.

Stan waved her off, his jaw tightening. "It's nothing."

"It's not nothing," Thea snapped, but her eyes darted to the shadows around them. "We need to get out of here before—"

A sharp crack echoed from the floorboards, freezing them both. Stan spun toward the sound, his hand instinctively reaching for the knife in his boot. Thea's grip on Stan's arm tightened.

"We're safe here," Andre whispered, his voice barely audible.

Stan nodded, his expression grim. "The door's locked. They'll strike again but we don't know when."

Thea's breath hitched, and for a moment, the three of them stood motionless, listening. The forest seemed to hold its breath, the darkness pressing in around them. Then, from somewhere outside on the street, came the unmistakable sound of hooves.

"They'll be back," Thea whispered, hugging herself and rubbing her arms as if she could comfort herself. "But you can't lock me away. Not in England."

Stan straightened and narrowed his gaze with a look so stern that it could have come from their father. "We have to pay attention. You can't ever be out of my sight from now on." Stan winced, seemingly unable to ignore the pain in his shoulder.

Andre glanced at Thea, his voice firm as he nodded to Stan. "I'm here, too. Stay close. No matter what."

As Andre tended to Stan, the sound of hooves grew louder outside. The town on the other side of the walls was alive with the promise of danger. And somewhere in the distance, a low, guttural laugh echoed from a nocturnal animal, sending a chill down Thea's spine.

Chapter Five

A NDRE SIGHED WHEN the prince and princess bickered like he used to with his siblings, except that the stakes were higher now with his high-born guests, one of them injured, and the Prussian baron on their heels.

"The reason I left was so that I could be free here," Thea said in Romanian, cringing when Andre exposed Stan's wound.

"And what has this freedom gotten you? If I hadn't overpowered them, what do you think they would have done with you and the little girl if I hadn't saved you?" Stan growled back in Romanian through his teeth, trying to look at his bleeding shoulder while Andre patted it with a clean cloth.

Observation, diagnosis, treatment. The first step was done exposing the wound; now he had to see how deep Stan's injury was.

"Well, I'll save you now," Andre looked at Stan, "and then I will take care of you," he said to Thea. They both raised their eyebrows simultaneously and gave him the same deadpan look. They looked quite alike, as siblings often did, Andre thought. He sighed at seeing the brother and sister couple and felt that familiar pinch in his heart every time he missed his siblings.

"You understood everything again," Stan remarked, more of a statement than a question.

Andre shrugged. "I had a brother and a sister, too." But before he could say more, he bit his tongue and reached for the knob of Nick's drawer of instruments and picked out the largest of the scissors. "This will hurt," Andre warned, glancing at Thea.

She held her breath.

"No, not the shirt but the wound I mean—" And with a swift motion, Andre cut Stan's bloody shirt open starting at the cuff and exposed the wound on his shoulder. Thea couldn't tear her eyes away from him, filled with concern for her brother and fascination for the doctor.

Stan tsked when he twisted his torso to see the injury at the back of his shoulder.

"It's superficial, and you were lucky they didn't slice any nerves. I'll clean the wound, but you'll need some stitches to keep it closed." With these words, Andre got to work and first rinsed the wound until there was only the red tear visible in Stan's skin. He left for a few moments and returned with a tray of small glass bottles and a scalpel, and he took the needles and thread from Nick's supplies, since he often performed cataract surgeries and had everything at hand.

Andre watched Thea closely, noting the way she seemed to struggle to maintain her composure. He moved with practiced care, soaking a pristine white cloth in the familiar medicinal dilution he'd poured into a metal bowl.

"This is witch hazel; it may sting a bit, but it helps prevent infection." He observed her response, tilting his head slightly, keenly aware of the delicate balance between causing her discomfort and aiding her brother's recovery.

"What does this mean?"

"It's because of the unclean weapon... infections often happen that way." André took a metal probe and gently lifted the sliced skin flap. "It wasn't sharp either. A sharp blade makes a clean cut. This is not one," Andre explained as he picked up the long tweezers and got to work. "I'll have to make it a clean cut, remove some of the tissue, and then suture it—"

"Do it," Stan commanded through clenched teeth, squeezing

his eyes shut.

Andre removed the jagged piece of skin with a swift, practiced motion. Stan gasped, his knuckles white as he gripped the armrests. The pain was evident, but he bore it stoically. It took less than ten minutes for Andre to finish the sutures and place a clean bandage on Stan's shoulder.

"It's done," Andre said, releasing a breath he didn't realize he'd been holding. "You must rest now, Your Royal Highness. Carrying heavy crates is out of the question."

"Don't call her that, you hear?" Stan nodded in Thea's direction.

"Why not? She's—" Andre asked.

"Because the same men who sent the highwaymen might cause her trouble here, too. We're in danger until I fix this problem with List. Until I do, nobody must know who she is." He shifted and sat up, facing Thea. "You have to come with me to the Langleys' and stay inside where it's safe. The Earl of Langley and his countess are close friends. They will shield you from List."

Thea grimaced. "I'm not going to be locked in!"

Stan hissed. "It's not you I'm locking in; I just want you to stay safe until this is resolved."

"Will it be resolved by tonight?" she pressed on.

"No! Do you know how dangerous these people are? If their accent was Prussian, List sent them—"

"It was," Andre mumbled. "I knew it as soon as I heard them."

Stan deflated. "Has there been any doubt? They were List's men. But I don't know how many there are, which means you're not safe here. They could be lurking anywhere!" Stan's words sounded earnest, but Thea seemed unimpressed.

"I can't remember ever not being a target—" she protested. "I'll take Mary to the Whites' townhouse and—"

"No, you can't be in a house full of servants we don't know. Any stranger could be a threat!"

"But Mary is sleeping upstairs. She needs me."

"Then take her with you and just let her parents know she's safe with us. Thea, London is big, and there are so many people; I won't let you out of the house without protection."

"So you'll go with me every time I leave the castle—ahem, house?"

"No, that's my point. You don't leave because I have work and can't take my little sister with me. I can't be your guard."

Thea crossed her arms. "I'm not little and I don't want a guard who locks me in rather than keeps me safe like the ones back at Bran Castle."

Andre pressed his lips into a line. She was most undoubtedly delicate and slim—but not little. He hadn't seen a woman with such perfect curves and—he'd never seen one, truly.

Thea's hand rested on her brother's good shoulder, and her alarm was unspoken but clear in her eyes. *"Stan, nu mă poți proteja mereu de lume."* You can't always protect me from the world.

Andre sighed heavily. He understood Stan's perspective as the older brother. All those years ago, Andre's first impulse was to rush downstairs and fight to protect his family. If Mother had let him, he would have laid down his life to keep his sister safe.

"Then he stays with you at all times," Stan yelled out and pointed at Andre with his good arm.

"What?" Andre blinked rapidly, mouth agape as if trying to process the absurdity of what he'd just heard.

She tilted her head to one side, squinting as if trying to see something far away, her lips twisting into a half-smile that didn't reach her eyes. "Agreed!"

"Wait!" Andre started, barely able to fathom what had just occurred. "I have work to do; I'm the only one here until—"

"Wendy and Felix will be back tomorrow, so you won't be alone at the practice." Stan took on a commanding tone.

"I'm not a royal guard; I'm a doctor." Surely that argument ought to convince Stan that it was absurd to make Andre responsible for the princess.

Stan gave him a stern look and arched a brow.

Andre swallowed hard.

"Thank you," she said softly.

Andre nodded reluctantly. When had he agreed to this?

"This means much to me, Andre. I shall be in your debt," Stan said.

Chapter Six

THEA WAS GLAD they were staying at Andre's practice that night and not only because she knew Stan might need the doctor at night but also because she didn't want to be far from him. Stan was going to sleep in the apothecary's room, right next to Thea. It had been lived in but seemed abandoned now, with no personal items left, except for a shelf full of books about botany, herbs, medicinal plants, and alchemy. They were all upstairs, but she heard Andre moving around downstairs, perhaps cleaning his treatment room or doing something else terribly smart and alluring.

Thea and Stan kept their voices low.

"I have to send Mary's parents a note," she started, looking around the room.

"And explain what exactly? That you are a princess on the run, in hiding, in the aftermath of an attack, a kidnapping, and in London?"

Thea pursed her lips and crossed her arms.

"Please, not at this hour. Let's tell them that Mary's safe tomorrow morning. We should sleep a little," Stan said as he winced and let his arm hang from the freshly sutured shoulder.

"Where?" Thea eyed the bed in the room, a chair behind a desk. It was neat and well-lived in, but most certainly not a large bed.

"Well, we can't stay here at the practice. You won't bring Mary to the Langleys', or will you? It's where I've been staying."

"You can take Nick's tonight if you wish. I'll sleep just upstairs," Andre offered.

"She's not sleeping in his bed, Andre. Thank you, but it's out of the question."

Andre reddened at the implication.

"I need to keep an eye on her; she's bound to run away again," Stan added.

"Oh, am I being kept captive like an animal?" Thea seethed. "Threatened to jeopardize my virtue by sleeping in beds that have been left behind by married men?" True, it wouldn't be proper to sleep in the bed of the oculist, but it probably wasn't as bad as what she was imagining it would be like to sleep in the bed of the dashing orthopedist, whether he was in it or not, but she wouldn't let her brother keep her caged either.

With his good hand, Stan rubbed his eyes and let out a frustrated groan. "Andre, could you leave us, please?"

"Certainly," Andre said with a curt nod. "Let me know if you need anything; I'll be downstairs." With those words, he left.

When the door clicked shut, Thea heard Andre's footsteps, and saw Mary turning in the bed across the hall, but she didn't wake up.

"Do her parents not know who you are?" Stan whispered, giving Thea a frustrated look.

She narrowed her eyes. "It's not your business to pry."

He narrowed his gaze. "As your elder brother and the only one here, I'm responsible for you."

"No, thank you. You delegated the task to the doctor even though I'm quite capable of being responsible for myself."

"By working as a governess to a merchant's family? A princess of your standing?"

"And what standing is that, hmm?"

Stan's eyebrows rose high, but a flash of defiance sparkled in his eyes. Thea knew she almost had him. He was the only brother who could understand her predicament… if he listened.

"Soon, before the altar—"

"Not you, too!" Thea huffed and slipped out of her shoes. She'd sleep a little next door but she wouldn't rest if Stan were going to lock her in an ivory tower again.

"Don't roll your eyes at me!" Stan whispered in the most menacing tone he could muster without waking Mary across the hall. Terribly dangerous indeed, but not too loud to wake a sleeping child.

Thea shook her head. Why was it that men thought she'd submit to their expectations?

"The White family don't know who you are, so they can't tell anyone you stayed with them. As far as they are concerned, you're just an incredibly well-trained governess. If we merely say that you missed me and came to visit before your nuptials, we may be able to save your reputation."

"Stan, I either sleep in the room with Mary or in the one next to her. She's six. Rest assured, my virtue is intact. And I'm not going to lie; there's no shame in working as a governess teaching a wonderful little girl Latin, geography, and arithmetic."

"It's unexpected for a princess."

"Well, it may be. Things happen that are unexpected. Look, I'm here. Surprise!" Thea said with a feigned smile and stretched her arms over her head as if she'd dramatically appeared on stage.

That gave Stan pause. "What has happened at home since I've been gone?"

"Nothing new." She shrugged.

"And yet unexpected enough for you to flee?" Stan cocked his head.

"No, I've been there for the past two months, haven't I? Clearly, I'm still there and trying on veils for the ceremony," Thea retorted and brushed over an imaginary veil that didn't hang behind her back. The idea of trying one on for the Habsburg prince was more akin to a noose than a veil. "I'm the runaway bride now," she added. But then Thea saw Stan's rather sad look, as if he pitied her for the trouble she'd gotten herself into. "Do you know you are the only one who ever understood me? And now you don't!"

"That's not true!" He laughed at that. Their connection was still there. He'd always been the one brother who listened to her before passing judgment on a mere girl.

"It is in matters of power."

"I have no power; I'm the youngest of four brothers. I'm the runt of the litter."

"You're taller and kinder than all the others, so you're not the runt of the litter." She gave her chin a feminine tilt. "And women certainly don't see you as one."

"I don't count."

"Well, what about *me* if you think *you* don't count? The only thing worse than being the fourth son is to have come after him and be a girl. I'm the only daughter, the last one."

"Mother loves you more than any of us boys."

"No, she relates to me more and feels my voiceless pain. For Father, I'm a mere bargaining chip."

"You're a princess."

"A valuable bargaining chip, no more. You should have seen how he looked at me the night I—"

"Thea, please don't tell me..."

"Oh, but I did! And I know what I'm doing." *Some of the time. But he needn't know.*

Stan deflated visibly and sighed deeply as if he'd witnessed the drama of that night himself. "You told Father that you don't want to marry Prince Ralph?"

"Yes. And that was when I presented him with the charter."

Stand grimaced as if he'd seen the disaster unfold. "What happened then?" He rubbed his brow.

She inhaled deeply, but the pain of the heartbreak that night hurt her so much that even the cool air couldn't settle her nerves. "He wailed."

"What?"

"I don't know what else to call it. It's a new sound he made, a cry combined with a deep sort of—"

"Grunt?"

"How do you know?"

"I thought this was his sensational cry of disappointment especially reserved for me," Stan said.

"Well, his look truly broke my heart but solidified my resolve."

"Oh, Thea."

"It did! He looked at me as if I had died in his eyes and as if I had stooped so low that he was the victim of a daughter for whom he'd done everything right to ensure my success, and yet the disappointment of me as a failure was too much to bear."

"Because you gave away the only chance to help our family."

"By marrying Prince Ralph?"

"No. Yes. Well, that charter of yours, it's not a new idea. I've been trying to align our allies and pressure our trading partners to agree to such a charter—well, a treaty actually."

"Good! So you can use some of the text that I've drafted if you like."

"Not if there is no reason to pressure our enemies into signing it. And if word gets out that you've lost your virtue, then only Alex's alliance with the English tradesman Lyndon can help us."

Thea stood and her arms grew cold as realization chilled her to the bone. Her mind raced, as Stan's words crashed over her like a relentless tide. She clenched her fists, nails biting into her palms, grounding herself against the pain of her thoughts.

The dim room felt stifling, the air thick with the consequences of her rashness. Candlelight flickered, throwing her shadow against the wall—a stark silhouette of her turmoil. Each decision replayed in her mind—a cascade of missteps that now threatened the very fabric of her family's alliances. Her brother Alex's happiness hung in the balance, tangled in the web of her making.

"What happened?" Andre suddenly appeared with a flask in hand.

"Ask her," Stan said grumpily.

But Thea didn't want to admit to her selfishness and avoided the handsome doctor's discerning gaze.

"Well, here's something for the night in case the incision pains you." Andre handed Stan the flask and then gave a curt bow. "Please let me know if you need anything tonight. I'll be back to check on Stan."

As Andre turned to leave, Thea retreated into her room without another word to Stan. She left the door ajar to keep an eye on Mary, who slept peacefully. Envy flickered in her heart at the sight of Mary's innocent rest, yet Thea was relieved knowing they were secure at 87 Harley Street. Despite the chaos in her mind, Andre's presence offered a deep, instinctual sense of safety that she couldn't ignore. He was a miracle in a time of need—not only because he'd treated Stan's shoulder, but also because there was something about him that anchored her, so she didn't panic given her troubled situation.

The image of his steady hands and the warmth in his voice had woven themselves into her consciousness, offering a solace she hadn't expected. And somehow, she thought that the handsome doctor could offer even more than that.

⸎

Chapter Seven

A NDRE MOVED PURPOSEFULLY through the dimly lit kitchen, the flickering candlelight casting shadows on the stone walls.

He had royal guests.

Royal.

A prince and a princess.

He selected a plate and began to gather an assortment of foods: a handful of walnuts, almonds, and hazelnuts, each one gleaming in the soft light. He set the kettle on the stove and brewed some peppermint tea, its deep amber hue promising warmth and comfort after the brutal attack and the injuries of the night. The plump and sweet grapes found their place beside the spiced biscuits that Felix had meticulously baked before they'd left for the wedding. He wanted to offer his royal guests some comforting nourishment rather than the stinging scent of witch hazel and the clove oil that hung in the air.

Treating the nobility as long as nobody knew who he was was one thing. But if they stayed with him overnight, they were somehow closer, which felt more dangerous. What if anyone found out that he wasn't merely Dr. Andre Fernando?

He'd never lied about who he was, but why did his omission about his heritage feel like a lie?

As Stan's doctor, he welcomed the opportunity to be close in case Stan became feverish throughout the night or if the stitches didn't hold.

No stitches he'd ever made had done so, but who knew what else could go wrong that night?

And nothing must go wrong because enough had already been done.

First, he was alone at the practice and should be ready for emergency callers. Instead, he arranged a food tray for the beautiful princess down the hall.

Second, he had to hide who he was and live his life, not think about how some brutal highwaymen nearly captured the lovely Transylvanian princess in the other room.

Just down the hall, only a few steps away, her brother guarded the princess with clear vigilance. This brought Andre to the third point: The injured prince was deeply involved in some dangerous diplomatic crisis with Baron von List. And since Prince Stan was injured and Andre was the only other person there, he had involuntarily stepped into List's line of fire. And for the princess in the room down the hall, mere steps away, Andre feared he'd do anything. A woman like her deserved his protection—even at the cost of his conviction that violence was never an adequate response. A pang of something more profound than remorse struck him, for it was the first time in his life that Andre wished he were more. If he had a title, he could confront Baron von List. But as a bastard, he could stand as little more than the princess's guard.

The princess's guard.

Andre plucked a grape from the plate on the tray and squished it in his palm. He had to remind himself that he was no more than a grape that had fallen off the Habsburg vines. He'd never make it into the cream of the crop. He'd never suffice to be the wine that touched Princess Thea's rosy lips.

He sighed.

For Mary, Andre knew fresh milk would be needed come morning, but for now, he placed a jar of golden honey on the tray, its translucent glow catching the light, and neatly arranged spoons, cups, and glasses.

While the tea steeped and cooled, Andre entered the cellar through the kitchen's back door. He needed some ice for Stan's shoulder. As he went down farther into the cellar, the chill seeped through his thin shirt as he approached the cooling cabinet, which he opened with a screech. It was as if the cool realization made his insides scream.

He had to stay away from the princess like he never had to stay away from a woman before.

THEA LEFT HER assigned guest room in search of something to drink. Stan had looked strained after their conversation—or was it because of his shoulder injury? Either way, she knew replenishing his body would aid his healing and perhaps double as a gesture for reconciliation before they went to sleep angry. She went down the stairs and through the corridor toward the back of the building and found an open door that led to a kitchen. A kettle was steaming there, and the fresh scent of peppermint wafted through the air.

"Dr. Fernando?" She saw an abandoned tray loaded with two plates, cups, silverware, grapes, and other food items. It looked unfinished. Where had the handsome doctor gone?

Since Stan thrust her into his arms, Thea had felt a sense of closeness with the doctor, unlike anything she'd ever experienced before. Her stomach fluttered excitedly, and she was curious about the tall, dark-haired man who seemed unlike anyone she'd ever met.

She heard a tapping and then another as if a hammer struck metal.

"Dr. Fernando?" she called louder, venturing toward another door that was narrow and seemed to lead to a storage or cellar.

Thea touched the rough wood of the door and looked into the dark space. It was a staircase leading around a dark cellar corner, and the light flickered from the depths of the darkness.

Carefully, Thea ventured down the steps and found the man she'd been looking for with a big lantern on the floor beside him.

Andre knelt on the floor, the dim light casting long shadows on the damp stone walls. His fingers curled around the chisel and hammer so that Thea could see the veins of his hands and lower arms. He was strong; she'd felt it when he'd held her and Mary mere hours ago in the forest. But now she could admire the muscular arms and envied each tool in his grip. The rhythmic thud of metal on ice filled the quiet space, each strike deliberate and sure.

"Princess, this is not a place for you," he said without looking up from the wooden door. But Thea was curious and didn't want what was for a princess; she tried to decide for herself what was for her. And he most certainly was.

"What is this place, Dr. Fernando?"

"Andre. Just call me Andre. This is our cellar storage. Clutter."

Thea glanced around and saw a few chairs stacked on each other, a broken lamp, metal buckets, and a few old tools that reminded her of the axes the woodcutters used back in Brașov.

However, Andre focused on the cabinet inserted into the wall. Thea stood behind him and bent down to see what the lantern illuminated.

A sizeable sparkling block of ice.

She was accustomed to ice houses, but not tiny cooling cabinets let into cellar walls.

Andre raised his right hand with the hammer and let it fall onto the top of the chisel. Each hit produced a crisp, cracking noise, followed by a satisfying crunch as the ice fractured and broke away.

"This is almost enough," he said, putting down the tools just long enough to hand Thea a piece of ice nestled in a white towel.

The block of ice glistened under the flickering lantern, and Thea felt the cold on her hands. However, a heat built inside her that was so strong that she feared she'd melt Andre's precious ice.

"Did you build this ice chamber?" Thea asked.

"Yes, I need the ice for my patients. It cools wounds and reduces inflammation."

"So, the ice doesn't melt if you keep it here?"

"Not for about ten to twelve days. But I get a new ice block every Tuesday."

"Where does it come from?"

"A patient. I helped him a little while ago, and he has a large subterranean icehouse near Regent Street. He shows his gratitude with a block of ice every week."

"Gratitude for what?"

"I'm not in the habit of revealing information about my patients, Princess Thea."

She could imagine he'd done much for the man if he delivered a precious block of ice weekly. "It's so pure," she observed.

"The finest from the lakes in Norway," he said.

Thea ducked lower again, taking in the egg-shaped chamber that'd been embedded seamlessly into the cool, stone cellar wall. Its smooth, curved interior gleamed faintly in the dim light, a clever design meant to preserve the cool just like a tiny icehouse.

"Why is the chamber oval? Does it involve heat dissipation or the shape's insulation?"

At that, Andre set down his tools and scooted to the side. Thea squatted to look inside the ice chamber, and Andre held the lantern up so she could see.

"Yes," he said, and she thought she had caught a hint of admiration in his tone.

Thea could feel the cellar's chill seeping through her thin gown, yet the contrasting warmth of Andre's presence truly held her focus. The air around them was cool and damp, as if they were sharing a secret in the flickering shadows cast by the lone lantern he held aloft. Its light danced over the walls, illuminating the ice chamber's oval mouth—a hidden alcove of scientific brilliance within the brick wall.

Her gaze lingered on the ice, where each chip caught the lantern's glow, transforming into a cascade of diamonds.

Andre leaned in, his voice a soft murmur that threaded through the stillness. "Notice the curve of the roof," he said, his hand a gentle guide pointing to the chamber's arch. "It traps the warmth, cooling it quickly, much like an igloo."

The rectangular block lay before her, smooth yet faceted. It was a frozen testament to Andre's strength, breaking off the final piece he'd wrapped and setting it on the ground next to her feet. Her warm breath curled like silver tendrils as she breathed, a ghostly ballet in the dim, intimate light.

Her awareness of him was acute; each breath he took matched hers, weaving them together through nothing but the special moment.

She tilted her head slightly, catching the outline of his features—solid and sure in the lantern's glow. Thea felt an unspoken connection, as though the chilled air had conspired to bring them nearer, wrapping them in its embrace.

Her fingers grazed the ice, a cool caress that sent her shivering, mingling with the warmth that blossomed from Andre's proximity. The world outside faded away, leaving just the two of them and the palpable tension, a delicate thread ready to weave them into something wondrous.

"This cabinet is a marvel of practicality," Thea said.

She watched as Andre resumed his work, the rhythmic sound of the chisel against ice resonated in the dim cellar. Each strike seemed to echo the tumultuous thoughts swirling in her mind. She shouldn't be here, alone with him, especially not after the unsettling events of the night. The memory of being kidnapped still lingered, a shadow she couldn't quite shake. Yet here she was, caught between propriety and a curiosity she couldn't ignore. She followed Stan's inclination and couldn't help but trust Andre.

Her gaze lingered on his silhouette, how his muscles tensed with each precise movement. He was more than just a doctor; he was an enigma, and she was inexplicably drawn to him. His presence was a strange comfort amidst the cold and the dark.

Andre paused, lifting his eyes to meet hers, a flicker of something unreadable in his gaze. "You shouldn't have to endure this chill, Thea. It's not proper for you to be here."

His words were like a splash of cold water, a reminder of the boundaries she was teetering on. "Proper," she repeated, almost to herself. The word felt heavy, laden with the expectations she had always known. But something about being with him made her want to defy them.

"I find warmth in different places, it seems," she replied, her voice softer than she intended.

He raised an eyebrow, a small smile playing on his lips. "You find warmth in the strangest places, indeed," he said, returning to his task. There was a teasing edge to his voice, yet a seriousness that told her he understood more than he let on.

Thea's heart fluttered at his words, and fear and excitement swirled within her. With Andre, the darkness felt less oppressive, yet the allure of the forbidden danced around them like a dangerous waltz. She was safe yet on the brink of stepping into unknown territories.

As Andre continued to chip away at the ice, Thea realized that the danger might not solely lie in the dark edges of country gardens or shadowy figures. Sometimes, it lay in the quiet moments, the silent exchanges, and the spaces where propriety and desire collided. And she couldn't deny the thrill of it.

Chapter Eight

WHEN ANDRE CLIMBED back up the stairs with a packet of ice, Thea was in front of him. What an idiot he was allowing a princess to come to his cellar.

"I must apologize, Thea," he said, wrapping the ice tighter in the towel as if the cold seeping through the cotton could also cool his thoughts.

"Why?" She turned over her shoulder while holding the thin metal bar as a railing to the cellar. Andre's heart quickened when he looked up at her. With the light from the kitchen above, her curly blonde flyaways looked like a halo around her face.

He'd been holding up the lantern so she could see where she was going in the narrow staircase connecting the kitchen and the cellar, but the orange glow from the lantern now shone like gold on her perfect features. But her intelligent eyes caught Andre off guard. He swallowed hard and almost forgot how one lifts a foot to climb stairs when his gaze fell involuntarily to her behind. She shuffled and reached the top of the stairs just when Andre thought her backside looked like a fresh pear hanging from a tree in the height of summer. Juicy, delicious, and utterly forbidden.

"This is not a place for a princess."

"I followed you to the cellar, and I'm glad I did. Your icebox is brilliant. I'm glad I had the opportunity to see it." She cast him a smile that nearly made his heart shatter.

Since this was the first time in his life that he couldn't pursue a woman, he wished he'd been born at a different time and titled so he could pursue the princess. She was precious, intelligent, and oh so beautiful. When her eyes met his, his stomach twisted with joy that he got her attention—but he wanted more. But it was the first time in his life that Andre felt inadequate in such a profound, irrevocable way. He was helpless.

The only thing he could help with was keeping the princess safe—from Baron von List, his lackeys, and himself.

Overwhelmed by the desire coursing through him, Andre gathered the food and followed Thea with the tray, the ice nestled beside the fruit meant for Stan.

When they arrived upstairs, Andre pushed the door open with his shoulder, balancing the tray in his hands, expecting to see Stan in the throes of pain. Instead, his eyes landed on Thea, who quickly swept a loose strand behind her ear and blushed furiously upon seeing Stan.

The room held an air of fragile tension. Thea's face, bright pink, showed traces of vulnerability she'd kept hidden before, even in the carriage after the highwaymen kidnapped her. What could have shaken this strong woman terribly in just the past few minutes. What did Stan know and didn't want him to find out?

Andre gently set the tray down on the side table, the clink of porcelain breaking the silence. He straightened, his gaze meeting Thea's, and held it momentarily before dropping it respectfully.

"I gathered some refreshments," he said, his voice steady and calm, though his heart ached at the sight of her distress. "Peppermint tea, for Mary if she wakes up, and other things that might help."

He glanced over his shoulder, confirming again that the child was safe after the earlier attack. The little girl was still sleeping in the room across the hall, cozily wrapped under the blankets he'd provided. *That's good; children need to rest.*

Thea nodded, her eyes glistening but grateful. Stan rose from his bed, giving Andre a slight nod of thanks before coming toward the biscuits and nuts.

Andre busied himself, pouring the tea, the fragrant steam rising as he worked. He placed a cup before Thea and offered her the honey jar. She managed a small smile, a fragile gesture that spoke volumes.

"Thank you, Andre," she whispered, her voice barely audible. Andre inclined his head, carefully placing the piece of ice wrapped in the towel on Stan's shoulder, right where the incision was. Heat was one of the many signs of infections and Andre's suspicion that the cut could have been unclean had been confirmed. He could tell that the wound was infected by the heat emanating from it and how quickly it melted the ice, visible from the wet stain on the towel, and he hoped the cooling would slow the process.

"If you need anything else, just let me know." His words were simple, but they carried sincere depth.

He turned to leave again, but Thea's voice stopped him. "Andre, please stay. For a while."

He paused, studying her face. Something in her eyes was a plea for normalcy, for someone to share the moment's weight. He gave a slight nod and sat on the only chair while Thea and Stan sat on the bed, the room settling into a more comfortable silence.

Andre felt a sense of quiet resolve as Stan chewed the crunchy biscuits, and the scent of tea mingled with the warm spices from the biscuits. He was here for whatever they needed, ready to offer a steady presence amid their turmoil.

"I'm not going to be able to sleep if Thea is still in danger," Stan said.

"Let me stay awake and stand guard," Andre said. "You should cool the incision. Perhaps it will Lessen the effects ofinfection."

"You look like Fräulein Schmidt," Stan said to Thea, but Andre knew it was a joke about him when Stan set the ice down to help himself to a cup of tea.

"Our governess?" Thea tugged at her simple dress.

Stan laughed, then winced and dropped his arm again, pressing the ice onto it with the other hand. "Our governess was a rather stern woman, surely a spinster, with no greater pleasure than conjugating verbs in Latin," he told Andre.

"Mine was called Signorina Bianca. She also made us conjugate and declinate, and I don't remember how many times I had to write the capitals on the map of Europe," Andre said.

"You had a governess?" Thea asked.

Andre was instantly sorry and wondered if he'd said too much.

"Were your parents wealthy?" Stan asked.

Andre pursed his lips. He'd said too much, indeed.

"There were three of us. I had a brother and a sister, and hiring someone to provide our education was worth it." There, that should explain away the expense of a governess for a doctor. Did Stan know that Andre's father was a famous doctor indeed?

Stan arched a brow. "Was that in Florence? During Napoleon's rule?"

Thea inclined her head. "Is that when your family fled to Vienna? It is where you said you studied."

He had undoubtedly overstepped; his royal guests were adept at discerning double entendres and reading between the lines.

"I should let you get some rest." Andre made for the door. "Stan, call me if you need anything. I'll be in my chambers upstairs, the second door on the right."

Andre shut the door and hurried up the stairs, a storm brewing inside him. As he locked his chamber door, he leaned against it, wishing he could lock away his thoughts just as quickly.

The night had been chaotic, but it wasn't the chaos that troubled him the most. It was the sight of Thea and Stan coming together after so long apart. It made him long for his family, who felt like shadows from another life. Would they even recognize him now? He hadn't tried since before he'd gone to India, but what if he'd given up the hope of finding his family too soon? The thought that they might still be alive somewhere tugged at his heart.

But finding them meant giving up the life he had built as Dr. Andre Fernando. It was a life he had carefully crafted, one where his past remained hidden. Yet, with Thea, his heart refused to stay silent. Her presence stirred feelings he shouldn't have. Protecting her was his duty, but it was her heart he wanted to shield, not just her safety.

Andre was no warrior like Stan, skilled in handling danger and diplomacy. He was a healer, grounded in the quiet of his practice. Yet, for Thea, he would brave the unknown. The chill of the night seeped into his bones, but all he could think about was the warmth of her gaze. In the quiet of his chambers, he made a silent promise. For now, he'd keep their secrets safe, all while staying as far away from her as possible.

THE NEXT DAY, Thea blinked at the clock on the desk and realized it was a little after eight in the morning. She needed a moment to realize where she was, that her brother was in the room next door, and she was curled up under a thin white sheet, her back stiff from sleeping without moving. Books about refraction, lenses, and a careful sketch of what seemed like angles of light coming into an eye with various numbers scribbled on the sides lay on the desk. She was quickly reminded that she was in the oculist's room at the practice.

Andre's practice—the handsome and exceptionally kind man who had inexplicably but wholeheartedly earned her and her brother's trust.

What an odd and rare thought. Thea shook her head. Andre must be quite exceptional for the royal family of Transylvania to find someone who earned their trust so quickly.

Thea wanted to know more about him. He had an air of

elegance as if he were bred to be a prince himself, and yet he was strong like a sawyer or woodsman back home, working with large logs of heavy wood.

Warmth spread through her when she considered how hard his chest had been when Stan shoved her against him in the dark of night, when the men had attacked. The unease in her chest built relentlessly.

Before she could think about her brother's imposed rule, that the dashing Italian doctor would accompany her wherever she went, the commotion outside the door caught her attention. She glanced through the open connecting door and saw that Mary had made her bed just as Thea had taught her.

"Thea?" Stan groaned as he turned on the doorknob and grimaced when he tried to move his arm to wave to her in lieu of a "good morning."

"Someone's busy," she said, stepping to the standing looking glass in the corner next to the bed. "I have to find Mary and send a note to her parents. They must be sick with worry by now." Thea tried to iron out the folds of her dress and pulled out the pins from her hair.

A few strokes through her hair tamed her blonde curls just enough so that she could twist them into a knot atop her head and secure them with the pins she'd pulled out.

"In here?" Mary's muffled voice came from outside the door an instant before the knob turned, and she stepped in. "Miss Thea?"

"Yes, dear," Thea rushed to the door and opened it, surprised to find Mary with a bonnet on her head and a little disheveled but cheerful and carrying two cups of coffee.

"Where did you find a new bonnet?" Thea asked bewildered.

"Andre gave me the one from the doll in the children's corner. You know where the watercolors are?" Thea wrinkled her forehead.

"Where?"

"In the waiting area!" Mary slapped her hand on her forehead.

"He gave me this toy cat, too." She held up a wooden cat. "Her name is Lady Felicity Whiskers, she's a figurine." Then she pointed to the cups. "This is for you and your brother."

Yes, brother. Good, Mary didn't know who they were.

They were lukewarm, and Thea's heart melted at the thought that Andre must have ensured Mary wouldn't carry hot liquid.

Andre appeared with a small parcel tied with string. "Good morning." He bowed to Thea and cast a look at Stan. "How do you feel?"

"Hot," Stan grimaced, and his neck cracked when he moved it. His hand came to the opposite shoulder. "Burning," he added.

Andre's face darkened. "I need to look at the incision." He handed Thea the parcel. "Before you woke, I took the liberty of gathering some essentials to ensure your comfort. I realize the highwaymen caught you, and you could pack nothing for a journey to London."

"That's why I said we should go to the Langleys and avoid strangers. Anyone could be a traitor and pose a danger," Stan growled, but Thea ignored him.

"How very considerate," Thea said, accepting the parcel with open arms. "How did you find all this?"

"The coachman's wife is a seamstress on Regent Street." Andre smiled when Thea gasped at the contents of the parcel. There was rose water, a silver comb, ribbons, and a few other things in lovely matching packaging.

"You may go to Wendy's chambers if you wish. You will also find a stack of towels, and I can run a hot bath for you—"

"No, Andre. My sister mustn't take a bath here. I'll bring her with me to Violet's house so that she can be properly chaperoned," Stan interjected, still his hand on the shoulder with the injury. "I am certain that the Earl and Countess of Langley will not mind if I bring some guests," Stan said.

Andre inclined his head, showing his obedience, but Thea could see the disappointment in his eyes. Was it possible that he wished to be with her more, just as she hoped to spend more time with him?

AFTER THEA AND Mary left to freshen up in Wendy's chamber and the shared bathroom, Andre tended to Stan who'd come downstairs to his treatment room looking even worse than after the battle in the woods. The prince was proud and didn't admit it, but Andre could see he was in pain.

"I am afraid that you're showing the four cardinal signs of inflammation," Andre said upon inspecting the incision. It must have bled a little more at night after he'd placed the sutures, so he prepared a small muslin square and a dilution of calendula and chamomile to rinse the wound.

"No inflammation, Andre, don't say the word. I don't have time for that," Stan said, but he winced when Andre touched the wound with the wet muslin.

Andre touched Stan's forehead and pursed his lips. "You have a low-grade fever."

"I'm just a little hot," Stan shrugged, and he cringed because his shoulder seemed to cause pain. It wasn't too swollen yet, so proper wound care could still control the infection, Andre thought.

"You speak Latin, don't you? And Romanian is so close to it, you'll understand. There are four signs of infection: *rubor, tumor, calor,* and *dolor,*" Andre said. "The ancient Romans already described it in this manner."

"Redness, swelling, heat, and pain," Stan translated.

"Very good, so you don't deny that there's an infection indeed." Andre continued to clean the wound.

"I acknowledged that I understood the words, not that I agree to the infection," Stan mumbled.

"Unfortunately, an infection is not something you can agree to; it happens. But you can fight it off and look after yourself."

"I don't have time, Andre. I have to take Thea to the Langleys, I trust them. And then I will confront List. You know he sent the men to abduct my sister. He's dangerous."

"This is dangerous, Stan. With all due respect for your sense of duty and honor, if this infection spreads and your fever gets worse, you could die. And then you neither resolve the issue with List nor keep your sister safe."

"Then who will keep her safe? Who can I trust for so long to look after her and this little girl she has brought?"

At first, Andre remained silent. Sometimes the best defense was retreat. "I'm going to Alfie's apothecary to bring some pine honey and a new wound dressing," Andre said, but Stan grabbed his arm and squeezed.

"You have to do it! Not just tonight but for a while. At least until I sort the mess with List out." Stan spoke with such urgency, and his eyes showed how important this was to him. "Do you understand how precious she is to me?" Stan's brows furrowed deeply.

Andre slumped his shoulders, the weight of the situation pressing heavily down on him. "I do know. I had a sister, too. And I would have given my life to protect her."

I left my family to keep them safe from the misfortune that is me. But those weren't words he could speak, lest the prince before him lose respect for Andre, the bastard, instead of trusting him as Andre, the doctor. It had always been his policy to separate his two personas, even though it was tearing him apart on the inside. If only he hadn't been born at the wrong time.

"Then you know. Can you look after my sister and help me until our brother Alex arrives? Please?" Stan asked, his voice raw. This wasn't the request of a prince but merely of a big brother.

Andre noticed the sheen of sweat on Stan's brow, a subtle tremor in his step as he cradled his shoulder, the protective slump betraying the fever burning beneath. Even as Stan's words charged ahead, Andre's mind weighed the balance between confrontation and the silent peril beneath Stan's bandage.

Andre scratched his head. "Under one condition!"

Stan blinked a few times as if he weren't used to receiving conditions. "What?"

"You take care of yourself until the infection heals. You're under my care until I dismiss you as healed, and you may resume your vendetta against List."

"It's not a vendetta, Andre; he's threatening my country. He's dangerous for our friends. Your friends. For Felix and—"

"I know. But if you die of an infection, you'll make him stronger. Right now, you are his highest-ranking opponent, and you have a chance to defeat him. Take the time to heal and then return stronger on the battlefield."

"It's not a battlefield; it's my life."

"All of life is a battlefield, isn't it?"

"Per aspera ad astra," Stan quoted a Latin proverb.

"True. Through hardships to the stars." Andre nodded and left to retrieve the wound dressing from his treatment room. But he feared that the trial ahead would not be a battle with the enemy but one with himself: How could he protect Princess Thea and be so close to her without losing his heart? She'd captivated him in a way that he felt in his bones—this battle he would surely lose. In promising Stan to look after his sister in his stead, Andre had implicitly agreed to have his heart broken by the fierce and beautiful princess whom he could never have.

Chapter Nine

AFTER THEA AND Mary freshened up in the morning, Thea took Mary back downstairs to the oculist's treatment room, where Andre said they could find paper and quill to pen a note for Mary's parents. Stan looked feverish and tired even though he'd slept all night.

Mary found a large flat case with an arrangement of lenses. Next to each was a small piece of paper glued onto the velvet lining with numbers written on it.

"Oh, this is fun," Mary declared as she switched them with each other in the case. "Can you put them back in order?"

"Mary, don't do that!" Thea rushed to the girl's side. "What is this even?"

"It says on the side of the tray," Mary pointed at the edge. "Re-...reef—"

"Refractive Lenses," Thea read aloud. "Oh, don't mix them up! This is for eyeglasses."

"I want to make some!" Mary cheerfully said, but Thea tried to keep track of which lenses Mary had already switched, but it was too late. "Let's make spectacles!" Mary held two lenses over her eyes and looked like a big fish.

"Do you know where I can find a piece of paper to leave the oculist a note?" Thea asked Stan. "We need to leave him a note to warn him that they are out of order."

"I promised Andre that we'd stay at the rehabilitation center for a while," Stan said with a solemn look when he buttoned his coat. "It's the best for all of us."

"I have to let Mary's parents know where she is and that she's safe," Thea said, scanning the room for said paper and a quill.

"We can send them a messenger. Should I arrange for Mary to return to—"

"No, I am staying with Miss Thea!" Mary hopped off the stool and seemed to forget about the lenses. "I'm not leaving for Europe, so I can be a nurse here!" She put her hands on her hips and tapped her foot on the floor. "I already slept in the nurse's bed last night."

Stan arched a brow and looked at Thea as if she'd said it, but all she could do was shake her head.

"Miss Mary," Stan cleared his throat.

"I'm her governess," Thea interrupted as sternly as she could muster, even though she rather wanted to burst out laughing at Stan's fake look. "I can only return her to the care of her parents, nobody else. And since they are due to travel to Europe, Mary stays with me," Thea said.

"She's my princess!" Mary said, crossing her arms.

All eyes shot to the little girl.

"You heard us last night?" Thea asked with a stern look that hardly hid her astonishment.

Mary beamed at her. "I have my own princess!"

Stan's mien sobered as if Mary didn't understand what a princess was. No matter how much Thea loved her brothers, as the only girl, she felt on an island alone at sea when it came to feminine things—like the universal fascination with being a princess.

Thea tucked a thought into her mind about telling Mary that a princess had many more responsibilities than fairy tales suggested, such as strolling in gardens, dancing at balls, or holding audiences. Judging my Mary's twinkling eyes, twirling in imaginary gowns was her priority in all things princess. But there was time to explain a real princess's life another day.

"For now, I'm your governess." Thea flattened her lips into a line.

"I know! That's even better! I'm the only girl in the world with a princess governess!" Mary twirled and danced through the room until she seemed to grow dizzy and bumped into Andre, who'd just entered.

Even though she didn't mean to, Thea burst out laughing.

"Ouff!" Andre exclaimed when Mary crashed into him, seemingly dizzy from twirling in her pretend ballgown, but the impact seemed somewhat overstated. He bent down and picked Mary up.

"What was that all about?" His face brightened immediately when his eyes met Thea's, but she still shook in mirth.

"I'm the only girl in the world with her own governess princess!" Mary declared, and Andre smiled.

"She's rather extraordinary, Miss Mary. I agree that you are the luckiest girl in the world."

And even though Andre avoided Thea's gaze, she gasped and forgot to laugh.

"I'll be a doctor today," Mary declared when Andre held her back. "Where's my first patient?"

Andre chuckled. "You need to study medicine before you can be a doctor."

"Oh, they won't let me. I'm a girl," Mary said. "Let's pretend today!"

Thea didn't like that. "You will make them let you because you will know so much, and be so smart that they won't deny you a place at university."

With a skeptical glance, Stan surveyed the scene while moving his injured shoulder ever so slightly, his eyes narrowing slightly as he silently communicated his discontent and pain.

"Where did you study?" Mary asked as she cupped Andre's face.

"In Vienna," Andre answered.

"Then I must learn German in addition to Latin, Miss Thea… ahem, Princess—"

"Yes, dear. And I shall help you to learn everything that I can. But until then, why don't you begin as Dr. Fernando's assistant?"

Stan let out a groan of disapproval but didn't say anything else.

"I could be a nurse!" Mary clapped her hands together, and Andre shot Thea a look.

"Nurses know almost as much as doctors, sometimes even more," Andre said, which only earned him a frown.

"I want to be your nurse today!" Mary said, pursing her lips when Andre set her down.

He smiled and extended a hand to her as if asking the little girl to dance. "It would be my honor, Miss Mary, if you agreed to be my nurse until the real nurse, Wendy Folsham, returns."

Mary put her hand in Andre's, and he escorted her out of the room and down the hall. Thea followed them and felt the smile melt away. She'd never been jealous, but there was a tinge of envy that she couldn't deny, for she wished it was her hand in that of the dashing doctor.

Again. Thea thought she had to banish this infatuation from her mind. She couldn't possibly fall for the doctor, could she?

A few minutes later, still pondering Andre's most pleasing physique, she couldn't recall why it was that she didn't merely throw herself into his arms. Ideally naked.

No, she mustn't.

She was a princess on the run, trying to escape a loveless union with a Habsburg prince from Austria.

She wasn't free to let love fall where it may.

But could one stop it from falling, then? Didn't the Romans already say, "Alea iacta est?" The die is cast. It was a phrase attributed to Julius Caesar as he crossed the Rubicon River, signifying a point of no return. She wasn't going back either, so forward and onward was the only way.

Could she follow her heart?

Thea felt heat creep to her face as she stood quietly in the doorway of Andre's treatment room, watching him work with an intent focus that captivated and comforted her.

Mary unfolded and refolded a muslin. Andre said he'd need it as a bandage soon.

While Andre tended to his patient, he also gave Mary a barrage of useless instructions for the "important help" he needed from his would-be nurse, which made her feel vital and proud. Thea could see it in her expression and demeanor. Somehow, Andre had inspired Mary to learn in a way that Thea hadn't. He was brilliant.

Truly amazing.

And oh so handsome and kind.

Thea shut her eyes and exhaled deeply. The die was cast.

She'd escaped to England, but now there was truly no return.

She was falling for Andre.

Chapter Ten

S CARCELY HAD THE clock ticked away a handful of moments, when the air of Andre's treatment room seemed transformed. And Thea's state of mind was also altered.

She admired Andre from her vantage point, keeping an eye on Mary, who was dutifully assisting him. The room was bathed in the soft glow of the afternoon sun, and the air carried the soothing blend of dried herbs and beeswax.

Mr. Hollingsworth, an elderly tailor with a neat white mustache, sat across from Andre, his face a mix of hope and worry. Thea observed how Andre's demeanor shifted seamlessly from the light-hearted charm he often displayed to a gentle seriousness. "Let's have a look, then," he said, his voice steady and reassuring. He reached for the tailor's wrist with a gentleness that spoke of his practiced care.

"Push against my hand," Andre said, holding up his muscular hand, which looked youthful and strong compared to his patient's. The man seemed strained as he pushed, but Andre didn't wince.

"How long have you suffered from the loss of strength?"

"Since the accident, Dr. Fernando. But it's gotten worse. Especially in the evenings."

"After a long day's work?"

"Yes."

Andre nodded and examined how far the man's fingers could bend. Not very far, Thea thought.

"Limited range of motion and loss of strength, Mr. Hollingsworth," Andre said.

"I agree," Mary nodded as if she had all the expertise in the world.

"Thank you, Miss Mary. It's good to have a second opinion that finds approval of my diagnosis," Andre said. Thea suppressed a chuckle.

"I have nine grandchildren, Dr. Fernando," the older man said, his warm gaze pointing toward Thea. "Congratulations on your young family."

Thea gasped. He thought she was… oh but…

"Thank you so much, but she's merely a dear friend's sister, and this is Miss Mary White. She's our guest until her parents pick her up when they return from Dr. Folsham's wedding." A white lie to ward off further questions and keep Thea's identity secret.

Keep her safe.

"Oh," the patient's eyes darted from Andre to Thea and then to Mary. "I assumed wrong. My sincere apologies."

Thea noticed that Andre blushed a furious red color. He seemed like a man who wasn't accustomed to lying to his patients and it tugged at her hear that he had done so for her, but she appreciated it nonetheless.

Suddenly Andre furrowed his brow with concern. "Mary, we really must ask you to step out for a moment," Andre said, his tone both firm and kind. "I have a patient to attend to."

Mary, her curls bouncing with every nod, crossed her arms defiantly. "But I can help! I want to be your nurse."

Thea couldn't help but smile at the girl's determination. "Mary, it is very kind of you to offer, but—"

Before Thea could finish, Mr. Hollingsworth paused, taking in the scene with a knowing smile. "Ah, but how could one possibly refuse such an offer?" the patient declared, a playful glint in his eye. "Surely any old man would be most fortunate to have not one, but two lovely nurses to fuss over him."

Thea felt a warm blush creep up her cheeks, a mixture of amusement and mild embarrassment. Mr. Hollingsworth's charm was somehow endearing. She glanced at Andre, whose mouth twitched in a reluctant smile.

"Very well," Andre conceded with a sigh, though his eyes twinkled with good humor. "But Mary, you must promise to do exactly as you're told."

Mary clapped her hands in delight, her enthusiasm infectious. "I promise!"

As Mr. Hollingsworth settled in the chair, Thea caught his eye, and he winked conspiratorially. Despite the seriousness of the situation, Thea felt her spirits lift. This unexpected task may benefit her and Mary, not just the patient. Or was it the doctor who had this effect?

⇒⟫⟪⇐

ANDRE RATHER WISHED he hadn't said anything. He couldn't introduce Thea as the princess, he'd promised Stan to keep her safe, and the best way to accomplish that was not to show off who she was. He could barely hide a ravishing beauty like her, but a princess? If anyone found out, the news would spread through London like wildfire, and List would know where to find her.

It was too dangerous.

Yet, he'd done her a great disrespect by introducing her as a friend's sister. But it wasn't a lie. She was his friend's sister. Some of his friends were in high places, and it wasn't very much his fault that their sisters—this one in particular—were extraordinarily beautiful.

And smart.

And kind.

And she was staring at him so intensely that the hairs on his neck pricked up.

"If your diagnosis is bad, Dr. Fernando, don't tell me! It's my livelihood. I can't sew with the left hand, much less use the scissors. I work with wonderful fabrics—"

"I understand," Andre said and rose from his stool. "There isn't a cure, but we can treat the symptoms to alleviate your discomfort."

Andre noted the slight wince on Mr. Hollingsworth's face as he examined his elbow and shoulder next, the subtle tremor Andre seemed to detect without a word. He could see the worry in the tailor's eyes, the way his fingers struggled to obey his will. Andre's hand rested on the back side of the patient's shoulder.

"Does it pain you in the morning when it's cold?"

Mr. Hollingsworth quietly confirmed the question, seeming both relieved and resigned.

Andre's attentiveness was unwavering as he explained the nature of the ailment.

"It seems you're suffering from what we might call a craftsman's ailment," Andre said, pointing to the affected area precisely. "You have rheumatism, which causes inflammation of the joints. Combined with the severe wear of the joints, we need to watch it very closely."

A flicker of hope danced in Mr. Hollingsworth's eyes at Andre's words, but he didn't want to mislead the tailor into thinking there was a remedy.

"Rest the hand as much as your trade allows," he advised. "A menthol bath can increase the blood supply and ease your discomfort on days when cooling helps. I will also ask the apothecary, Mr. Collins, for an ointment with arnica if you experience days of swelling. Choose whichever feels good because it may alternate at times. And don't hesitate to come to see me if the pain increases."

"Thank you," the old man said as he stood with renewed determination, gratitude evident in his posture.

As Mr. Hollingsworth departed, after thanking Mary profusely for her outstanding care as a nurse, Mary's satisfaction was palpable, a quiet pride that filled the space between them. Thea remained in the doorway, her arms crossed and her gaze warm with a seeming appreciation for the treatment.

"Once I clean up, I shall take you to the Cloverdale House," Andre declared. "It's not quite ready yet, but it will be an adequate accommodation for you and Stan. We're turning it into a rehabilitation center. I mean, the other doctors and I. I can look after Stan there, too."

Thea nodded. "You have transformed a moment of pain into one of promise," Thea said, admiration coloring her voice.

"He was very grateful for your assistance," Andre told Mary, unsure if he'd found the right words.

Andre sighed. "I cannot help him much. His muscles atrophy, lessening his strength. If he continues to make the same motions for hours every day, he will further wear the joints down, and once the nerve is pinched, he won't be able to work with the pain."

"How can it be stopped?"

"It can't. Every profession has its own pattern of wear. The body shows it after years of hard labor. All I can do is ease the symptoms and perhaps slow the progression. But time takes its toll on people."

And he had a sinking feeling that the more time he'd spent with Thea, the harder it would be when she left his life again.

As Mr. Hollingsworth left, Mary tugged gently at Andre's sleeve, her eyes wide with excitement about her recent role. "Andre," she chirped, "will I be your nurse for real when I grow up?"

Andre chuckled, patting her head affectionately. "Perhaps, Mary. You did a splendid job today."

Mary beamed, then glanced shyly at Thea, her curiosity seemingly piqued. "Miss Thea," she asked innocently, "will you be Dr. Andre's nurse, too? You look at him like my mama looks at my papa."

Thea's cheeks turned a soft shade of pink, and the child's candid question momentarily swept away her composure. She exchanged glances with Andre, whose eyes danced with amusement and something deeper.

"Well, Mary," Thea replied with a gentle smile, "I think I will leave the nursing to you, the expert."

Mary giggled, satisfied with the answer, and twirled around the room, her energy infectious. The air between Thea and Andre shifted in the silence left by Mary's innocent words. Andre shifted awkwardly, a warm flush creeping up his neck at Mary's audacious suggestion. His gaze darted to Thea, who seemed to be battling her own rising color. He told himself it was merely the absurdity of the notion that painted her cheeks with such a rosy hue. Yet, as he fumbled for words, a glance at Thea's eyes, wide with surprise, reassured him that decorum would soon restore their composure.

However, as Andre watched Thea wring her hands, Mary's simple question lingered, weaving their unspoken feelings into something tender and hopeful.

It may be doomed, but that didn't mean it didn't exist.

Chapter Eleven

A FEW HOURS later, there was nothing for Thea to do but wander through the practice at 87 Harley Street. Stan had gone to retrieve his belongings from the Langleys'—the earl and his countess with whom he'd stayed since he'd arrived in London—while Mary took her midmorning nap on the armchair in the oculist's treatment room.

Thea returned to Andre's room diagonally across the hall, leaving the doors open to hear Mary if she woke up. Or worse, if she snuck up on her, curious as she was.

Thea had a strong desire to be near Andre, ideally alone.

Andre was gathering Mary's folded muslin bandages and putting them in a neat pile on a metal tray. Since no patient was in sight, Thea ventured into the room to speak with him.

She eyed the skeleton that hung from a nail on the wall.

"Is this real?"

"Yes," Andre answered.

"Who is it?" She rubbed her hands uncomfortably.

"I beg your pardon?"

"If this is a real person, then who is it?"

"I don't know." Andre leaned back and eyed her curiously, as if there were a stain on her collar. "Every group of students is assigned a skeleton at the university. We had to study every detail of human anatomy, and when Alfie and I finished the anatomy course, we purchased the skeleton for a small fee."

"So you know what all the parts of this are called?" Thea stepped closer to the bones and noticed they were connected with metal pins and wires. She lifted the skeleton's hand, which didn't feel real. There was little left of a person, and the hand felt like a thing, a model of what may be inside a human or what may have been a human long ago. "What's this called?"

"The fossa or the attachment?" Andre asked with a swift glance at the second bone of the index finger.

"All of it. Everything has a name, right?"

"This is the tuberosity of the distal phalanges."

Thea blinked at his explanation. "All of these protrusions have names?"

"Of course. The grooves, too."

"Why?"

"Well, think about how you'd localize an injury or a fracture."

Thea let go of the skeleton's hand and opened her left palm, inspecting it closely and trailing her right index finger along the lines on her palm. "What about these folds? Do they have names, too?"

"This is the anterior palmar view, with many names." Andre put his hand under hers as if she were a precious treasure he barely dared to touch.

She looked at him, unsure what to say.

"But there's a big difference between the mere skeleton and a living person."

"Blood and flesh, as they say in English?"

"It's not that simple." He gently turned her hand over, and she instinctively held it at the ready to receive a kiss on the knuckles. It was an impulse she'd learned and honed over the years, almost like the habit that betrayed her mannerisms as a high-born lady.

Andre seemed unperturbed by her gesture and didn't seem to give it as much thought as she did. He aptly guided her hand and articulated her wrist. Thea gasped at the depth of his knowledge. He ought to know every bone, muscle, vein, and fiber—and yet Thea wished he'd discover her anew as she was discovering him with a new awareness.

"Innervation is the main difference between the living and everything else. See, here?"

He trailed the index finger of his other hand over a line that started very thin and then disappeared over the back of Thea's hand. A shiver followed the light trail of his touch, and Thea's insides quivered with something he couldn't quite name. He turned her hand over and bent her wrist to expose the lines. Under his expert gaze, a jolt of excitement made her break into goosebumps. He must have noticed, for he first inspected her cheek, then his gaze moved to her neck, and finally he looked ather face as a whole. Of course, a doctor would know everything about the body.

And this doctor affected every fiber of her being with only a chaste touch and scorching look.

"You can't always see them, but the veins and arteries constantly pump blood through your body." He showed her the branched veins of her wrist and then turned her hand back over.

Thea felt the air drain from her lungs as if her pulse had quickened under his gaze. She felt breathless in a way she had never felt before when she was near him.

A long pause followed, and she grew restless under his intent gaze. He knew everything about the human body, and she didn't know why her response to him was so strong and how to handle the fervor building in her stomach. Her body seemed to react to Andre in a completely unfamiliar way.

"Thank you for explaining this to me," Thea marveled.

Then he bent down and placed a kiss on her knuckle, lingering for an instant longer than she'd expected.

"I'm always at your service, Your Royal Highness," Andre said. He didn't quite say it the way most people, who knew who she was, would. An undercurrent of mischief made the tiny hairs on Thea's neck prick up.

ANDRE THOUGHT SHE was exquisite. He'd seen his fair share of nice girls and pretty women, and he'd had enough unchaste encounters to allow him to deepen his knowledge of female anatomy to the level of ultimate mastery. But none of them had prepared him for how Thea's intelligent eyes met his. No, they didn't just meet; they connected. They were linking his soul to hers so profoundly that it almost ached not to stare at her. It wasn't nice, of course, staring… and yet, she sparkled with a curiosity about the human body that awakened his most basic urges, for he knew all too well he could show her just what her body was capable of—over and over again he wished to hold her and let her reach the peak—*Stop!*

Andre shook his head, hoping these ideas would leave his mind.

He was not worthy of a princess, and she'd been set aside for a Habsburg prince—not a Habsburg bastard.

He sighed and took heart, but he already knew his would break.

She was beautiful, but not because of her dark-rimmed eyes, lush curly hair, or perfect smile—Andre was fascinated by her thoughts about the world and her questions.

"How long did it take for you to learn everything about his body?" Thea asked, trying to direct his attention back to the skeleton.

"It is a she. Well, it was. This woman has been dead for more than fifty years. I don't know where she came from, but she had a short life."

The crinkled her forehead. "How do you know that?"

"I don't know, but she probably never had a baby."

"Why not?"

"Her hips are wide and open, so she was of child-bearing age, but they are still connected at the pubic symphysis, so no baby has passed through her birth canal yet. It's not a certainty but a likelihood."

Thea cocked her head and made a grimace that spoke volumes of her innocence.

"Her spine was very straight, and there was much cartilage to protect the vertebrae, so she was healthy and strong until her death." Now Thea looked sad and flattened her lips into a frown, so Andre continued with what he knew: bones. "If you ask Felix, he can narrow her age further based on her teeth."

"Because they were healthy?"

"No, because she didn't have all of them yet."

Thea's eyes flew to the skeleton's mouth, and she noticed the largest back teeth were lower than they should be. They hadn't grown yet.

"That's so sad," she said, eyeing the skeleton as if it were a recently deceased friend.

"Yes, it is unfortunate. She didn't die of a sudden injury, so perhaps she had an infection. The traces are long gone."

"And yet, she's continuing to serve people."

"What do you mean?" Andre asked the question even though he knew the answer. But if she did and had concluded what he'd learned no sooner than in his second year of studies, she was much more intelligent than him.

"You're performing miracles; I'm in awe of you," Thea said. Her dark eyes sparkled in the very shimmery gold of the lightest parts of her blonde curls. She had such a sense of perfection that Andre almost felt she wasn't real. She was too good to be true.

And certainly out of his reach no matter how close she stood to him.

"You can't stay here," Andre stepped back, tasting the words he wished he hadn't uttered.

Thea let her hands drop to her sides and blushed.

"I mean, this is not adequate for a princess. Not even for

Mary."

She swallowed visibly and lifted her chin in defiance.

"I already arranged for a room at Cloverdale House," Andre added. "On Abbotsberry Road."

"What is that, a hotel? I'm afraid I can't pay for it."

"No, Cloverdale House is going to be the rehabilitation center I spoke of earlier. It's a grand estate in London, near Pall Mall."

Why was speaking so difficult when Thea looked at him so intently?

Andre raked his hand through his hair only to realize she followed his every motion.

"So the oculist's room you slept in last night, Nick's room, remember?" An unexpected compulsion seized Andre to present Thea to the others, the physicians who were both his confidants and companions—much akin to a gentleman's desire to acquaint a lady with his family. Yet, he mused inwardly, with a touch of humility, there was naught of significance or grandeur to parade before them. He had no claim on the princess.

"Of course I do." She narrowed her brows.

Stop rambling and get on with it.

"Well, he recently married a duke's daughter, an heiress. She wishes to convert Cloverdale House into a rehabilitation center, but a few patients have arrived early, since Nick and Pippa's wedding. It's still in the transitional phase, but the building and the grounds are much more suitable for you. There's a staff and gardens—abutting a park—and Pall Mall is only a short walk away." *It's so much better for a princess than this.*

Andre waved at his treatment room, set up to be practical, easily cleaned, and bright. It was not the elegant ballroom with sparkling chandelier he'd imagine for the princess. And yet, even in his modest practice, her eyes sparkled brighter than even the crystal chandeliers at the Hofburg Palace in Vienna.

"It's a nicer prison to keep me safe for as long as Stan wishes, isn't it?"

"It's big but safe. And elegant. Plus Stan could have a nurse when I'm not there."

No, it's a way for me to see you every day.

Thea quirked a brow that was so un-princess-like that Andre nearly laughed out loud.

"I arranged for a room for Stan so that I can look after him every day. There's a nurse and at least one of the doctors there at all times."

"Who's there now? If you are here and the others are still at the wedding,"

"Dr. Rosen, the surgeon, and his wife, Nurse Shira. They remained there with two wounded soldiers. Those are the first two patients. I am going to see them later this afternoon, too."

"So this would be the best for Stan? A hospital?"

"A rehabilitation center," Andre corrected her.

"Why don't you call it a hospital? It seems like one to me," Thea said.

Andre cocked his head. "Because there are certain patients in need of higher levels of care." Privacy. Diplomatic neutrality while they recover, too.

Thea sucked her cheeks in. "Because they don't wish to be found?"

Andre pressed his lips into a line. "I assure you of my utmost discretion regarding patients."

"I see. I'll be hidden among other aristocrats. Wounded war officers?"

Andre bent down and took the bag he'd packed with a new ledger and a few other things he thought he'd need when he started seeing the patients at Cloverdale House.

"There's room for Mary, too. And her parents could pick her up there when they return." Andre saw that Thea looked a little unconvinced. "It's lovely. Let's go, I'll show you."

There's more to me than this treatment room.

Chapter Twelve

Later that day...

AS THE HIRED hackney turned off the busier Abbotsberry Road onto a deserted gravel road, Thea felt anticipation mingling with trepidation. Cloverdale House loomed ahead, its grand silhouette outlined against the afternoon sky. Surrounded by a relatively flat patch of manicured land and a private park open to the public, the mansion was like a castle with small turrets and exuded an air of both invitation and majesty. An ivory tower to lock her away from the freedom that had already been within her grasp.

Andre's presence beside her was a steady comfort. His calm demeanor and reassuring smile made the journey feel less daunting. Mary, perched between them, could scarcely contain her excitement. Her blue eyes sparkled, and her small hands clutched her toy cat tightly.

Thea leaned slightly out of the window, taking in the sight of the sprawling grounds. Despite its grandeur, the place had a welcoming charm—perhaps it was the clusters of wildflowers dotting the grass, or the gentle curve of the pathways beckoning visitors to explore—a glimpse of freedom Thea decided to hold on to. In fact, the sense of openness of Cloverdale's design starkly contrasted with the enclosed, rigid confines she often associated with stately manors.

"Is this like Bran Castle, where you grew up?" Andre asked.

"No, Bran is on a mountain. It's not as easy to get there."

"Ah, a secluded fortress?"

Yes, he saw straight into her heart. She grew up secluded. Alone.

Of course, her family had been there, but Thea had never been allowed to mingle with other children in the village of Bran. "It's situated between the localities of *Măgura* and *Dealul Cetății*, offering a strategic view of the surrounding hills and valleys."

"But no access to people?" Andre asked.

"Exactly."

"You sound as though you felt rather alone."

Thea shrugged. "It's the price of being safe and sheltered." Thea reached for Mary's hand and rubbed it as she continued, "But there's much to discover here in London, and we shall do it together."

"And I'll keep you safe," Andre said reassuringly.

Mary chuckled with glee.

They'd arrived.

As the carriage drew to a halt in front of the grand entrance, Thea took a deep breath, trying to still the fluttering in her chest to return to the realm of aristocrats. She already missed the more unburdened life of a governess.

Andre descended first, then turned to offer his hand to Thea. She accepted it gratefully, feeling the warmth of his touch steady her nerves. Mary scrambled out next, her energy boundless as always.

The coachman tipped his hat respectfully in Andre's direction, clearly expecting his response. "Will you be needing anything else, sir?" he inquired.

Before Andre could utter a word, Thea interjected with a grateful smile, "That will be all for now. Thank you." She cast a quick glance at Andre, seeking his approval for her decisive interruption, a habit born from her upbringing as a princess, where she was accustomed to issuing commands.

Andre's eyes widened momentarily, caught off guard by her forwardness, which did not go unnoticed by the coachman, who frowned slightly. "Quite forward, this wife of yours," he remarked, his voice tinged with mild surprise.

"She's used to having the world at her feet," Andre said, quickly disseminating the coachman's suspicions. Thea sucked her lips in, sorry she'd misspoken. If she was hiding that she was a princess, she had to remember all the lessons she'd learned as a governess.

She had to, but it seemed impossible. She'd run away from her life and duties as a princess, but she was still a princess at heart, whether in her elegant gown at Bran Castle or not.

"You have a nice family," the coachman said, turned, and climbed back onto the driver's seat.

The second man who'd thought Andre and Thea were a family with Mary as their child.

"You look perfect together," he added.

With a final nod, the coachman guided the carriage away, leaving Thea, Andre, and Mary standing slack-jawed before the imposing front doors of Cloverdale House. Before Thea could say anything, the doors swung open with a creak, revealing a grand hall that seemed to pulse with history and elegance.

Andre offered his arm and escorted her inside.

"I need to tell you that we didn't think the rehabilitation center would be open for a while, but since we had three new patients who needed to be admitted, we made do," Andre explained as they walked down the giant white marble steps to the double-winged front door.

"Did you operate on them?" Mary asked.

Andre chuckled. "I can't tell you, I keep my patients' confidentiality." He winked at her.

"So there's another surgeon?" Thea asked.

"You mean, Dr. Philip Rosen? He works across the street from us, at 91 Harley Street but comes here, too. That's all I can say."

With these words, the door clicked shut behind them, and a young woman with a full head of curly black hair and a white apron appeared.

"Andre, there you are!" Her smile was infectious as she greeted Thea kindly and immediately told Mary the cook had just taken fresh honey buns out of the oven.

"That way, the fourth door is on the left. Tell her that Shira sent you."

Mary darted off without another look at Thea.

"Mary!" Thea called, but Andre chuckled merrily.

"This is Nurse Shira Rosen, Dr. Philip Rosen's wife." Andre turned to Thea, but she hesitated. "You can tell her, if Mary knows, the secret's out, and yet it will be safe among us."

"I already heard, Your Royal Highness. It's an honor to meet you and your secret is as safe with me as a diagnosis." Shira took a deep bow.

"See? Confidentiality," Andre said with a satisfied smile.

After Shira assured them that the house staff had prepared the rooms for Thea and Mary and another for Stan, she left to look after Mary in the kitchen.

Again, Thea and Andre were alone, this time at the elegant entrance of a lavish London estate. The grand hall was lovely, even for someone like Thea. Its walls were adorned with intricate moldings and paintings depicting pastoral scenes and noble ancestors. A grand staircase with a carved oak balustrade swept upward to the upper floors, promising more rooms filled with riches.

Andre's touch on her arm brought her back to the present. He was looking at her with a mixture of concern and encouragement.

"Are you quite well?" Andre asked softly.

Thea nodded, though her emotions swirled within her. "Yes, I think so."

"Would you like a tour?"

"I'd love one."

"I won't leave you alone."

His words were a balm to her soul. Thea took another deep breath, this one steadier, and allowed herself to take in the beauty of Cloverdale House.

As the golden light of the setting sun filtered through the grand hall, casting a warm glow over the polished marble floors and ornate furnishings, a sudden disturbance shattered the tranquil atmosphere. The sound of clanking porcelain preceded the raised voices, growing louder with each passing second.

Thea and Andre exchanged concerned glances. The tension in the air was palpable.

There was a thud in the adjacent room.

Thea felt a knot of anxiety tightening in her chest. She could discern the harsh, clipped tones of German and the flowing cadence of French, both voices rising in anger.

Stan had warned her of the person he suspected ordered her abduction.

"Baron von List," Andre mumbled as if the name tasted bad.

"Is he here?" Thea fought the impulse to hook her arm into Andre's and hold him tight.

"I don't think so, but I might not know all the patients who arrived while I was at the wedding." Andre moved closer to her, his presence a steadying force. "Stay here," he murmured, his tone protective yet calm. "I'll go look what's happening."

"Don't! He's dangerous!" Thea pulled Andre back.

"Yes, you're right. He's a threat. Let me see if it's him at all," Andre said.

But before he could step, the door swung open again, and two men stumbled into the hall, locked in a furious argument. Though different in style, their uniforms bore the marks of nobility and military distinction. Judging by his attire, the taller of the two, a Bavarian soldier with a proud, aristocratic bearing, had eyes that blazed with anger. His opponent, obviously a French imperial guard in a blue coat with golden epaulets, was of equal stature and spat his words with venom, his accent thick and unmistakable.

"How dare you, Heinrich!" the Frenchman shouted, echoing off the high ceilings. "Your kingdom benefitted from Napoleon's brutality! Do not pretend to be above reproach!"

Heinrich, his jaw clenched in righteous anger, fired back. "And what of your own country's sins, Jacques? France tore Europe apart for the sake of one man's ambition. You have no right to lecture me on honor!"

Thea's heart pounded as she watched the confrontation unfold. She observed the two men and the subtle indicators of their noble status, the quality of their uniform materials, the intricacy of their embellishments, and their demeanor. The German-speaking man wore a *Rittmeister's* cavalry uniform that was so finely tailored that Thea had no doubt he was of highest ranks. And the Frenchman wore reinforced breeches like the Hussar's of Napoleon's Grande Armée. These were not just soldiers; they were men of noble descent, their titles and lands intertwined with the turbulent history of post-Napoleonic Europe. And they were at odds, seemingly trying to provoke one another by wearing formal uniforms even when they were patients at the same rehabilitation center.

Andre cleared his throat. "Dr. Andre Fernando, an orthopedist. And this is—"

"Princess Josephine Theodora Andrea Hohenzollern-Sigmaringen." Thea knew her rank was higher, and she didn't hesitate to use it in this instant. "I was assured of diplomatic neutrality at this establishment." *And I will not submit to either of you, lest you threaten the independence of Transylvania.*

Both men straightened their postures, their expressions shifting from anger to something more controlled and respectful. As the tension in the room dissipated, Heinrich and Jacques seemed to recognize the need for civility.

Heinrich was the first to step forward. He removed his hat, inclining his head in a gesture of deference. "Please allow me to introduce myself properly. I am Heinrich von Thurn und Taxis,

Count of Bavaria." Though still tinged with the remnants of anger, his voice held a note of genuine respect. "It is an honor to make your acquaintance, Your Royal Highness."

Thea nodded graciously. "Count Heinrich, thank you. I appreciate your introduction."

Jacques followed suit, his expression softening as he approached. He offered a formal bow, his French accent smooth and refined. "Your Highness, I am Jacques Devereux, Marquis of Lyon. I apologize for the disturbance we caused. It is an honor to make your acquaintance."

Thea returned his bow with a slight curtsy. "Lord Jacques, thank you for your introduction. Let us hope that from this moment on, we can find common ground and peace within these walls."

"May I ask, Your Highness, whether you are the same Princess Josephine betrothed to Prince Ralph of Habsburg?"

Thea swallowed hard, and her breath shook. "Yes, I am."

When Thea answered, the marquis gave her a knowing look, almost like the once-over of a matron at the balls. Although she'd accepted a dance with their sons, her reputation as the runaway princess seemed to have caught up with her. The marquis didn't offer any congratulations on the betrothal. *So, news had spread indeed.*

Andre truly must have heard what had been said. The words, careless and cutting, still lingered in the air. She was the runaway princess, the stupid and selfish one who didn't want to marry a Habsburg prince. And yet, there was so much more to her she wished to show Andre. She longed to explain herself. Thea's gaze darted to Andre's again, searching for a sign, a reassuring glance that might dispel her fears that he wouldn't care for a chance to know her better. The air around her felt charged with uncertainty. Thea's fingers clenched into a fist at her side, desperate to hold onto something tangible, preferably Andre.

But Thea remained steadfast as her upbringing commanded.

Both men nodded politely, their initial hostility giving way to mutual understanding.

Thea's outwardly calm demeanor and grace had set the tone for a more amicable interaction, and for a moment, it seemed as though peace might indeed be possible—if not in her life, then at least between the nations of the nobles present. Amazingly, neutrality at Cloverdale House seemed to work.

"Dr. Rosen said you'd come to see me," the count said. "*Sie sind aus Wien?*" Are you from Vienna? The question was directed to Andre.

"*Ich habe dort studiert, jawohl.*" I studied there, yes.

Andre bowed and turned to Thea stiffly, his expression un-readable as he barely held her gaze. "Perhaps we should have tea," he suggested, his voice measured, lacking the warmth she had come to cherish.

Thea nodded, her heart fluttering with a mix of apprehension and hope. "Yes, tea would be lovely," she replied, though her voice wavered despite her efforts to keep it steady. Her mind swirled with the fear that his formality signaled a shift, a retreat into the safe confines of decorum, which would ruin her hope that he felt as she did.

The room's ambient noises seemed to swell in her ears as they proceeded to a room off the main hall, the muted conversa-tion in German between the men weaving a tapestry of distraction as she tried to decipher Andre's intentions. Her palms felt clammy against the fabric of her gown, a tangible reminder of her unease. Would tea merely be a polite obligation, a preamble to distance?

As they moved toward the tearoom, Thea was acutely aware of the space between them. She longed for reassurance in his gaze, a flicker of the connection they had shared, yet his face remained impassive, a mask she could not penetrate.

The plush carpet in the drawing room muffled their footsteps, the rich scent of black tea with bergamot wafting through the air as they neared the table set for four. Thea settled into her seat, her fingers tracing the delicate rim of the teacup before her, seeking comfort in its familiar texture. She watched a footman pour the tea, each movement precise and controlled, and wondered if the ritual would be the last thread tying them together.

After tea, Andre rose and made to leave. "Please excuse me, Your Royal Highness. *Monsieur le Marquis. Herr Graf,*" Andre bowed to all of them, addressing each in a nearly impeccable accent in French and German. "I must attend to my work."

Thea forced herself to meet Andre's eyes, determined to bridge the gap with sincerity. She hoped for a thaw in his demeanor, a sign that their bond could weather this storm but all she could make out was his fear. Could it all be traced back to Baron von List or was there something else? She wanted to know more.

Everything about the handsome doctor.

Andre withdrew to a separate room, first with one and then with the other of the two men, to examine their injuries. Nurse Shira returned, informing Thea that Mary would be an adorable assistant nurse.

"My husband operated on them, but it is Andre who will see to their recovery from now on," Shira explained when she joined Thea and oversaw a footman clearing the tea set once Andre had left with the count and the marquis. "He's very talented, and it certainly helps that he can speak with both of them in their native tongues."

"Indeed." Thea marveled at the broad education Andre had for a doctor. It still didn't make sense to her that he had had a governess and spoke so many languages. Something about him made him fit in with the lords more than the working class.

"Yes, he speaks so many languages fluently. Isn't he amazing?" Shira smiled, but then another woman in a white apron called her. "Would you pardon me, please? Andre needs my assistance."

"Certainly," Thea said.

"Please feel free to explore the castle. I will send someone to show you your chambers shortly." With these words, Shira disappeared into a corridor.

Thea continued to walk down the other direction of the hall. She was surrounded by the elegance of England's craftsmanship and artistry. Lavish draperies, gilded mirrors, and finely upholstered furniture whispered tales of a time when beauty and elegance were life's priorities. Although distinct from Bran Castle and other European palaces, each space exuded a warm sense of welcome. Everything felt quintessentially English—from the floral tea service to the embroidered settee cushions—and Thea was enchanted by it all.

Her gaze swept over the lavish room, and each intricate detail sparked dreams of a life with Andre. She envisioned them moving gracefully through these elegant spaces, their fingers gently touching, and their laughter floating in the air. She pictured intimate dinners, where every word exchanged over candlelight promised a deeper connection, filling her heart with a delightful mix of joy and longing. If this castle was nice on the inside, then there would be even more to explore outside, wouldn't there? Perhaps, while Stan was healing, Andre could show her more of London? More than she'd seen in the short time with Mary's family. More time with Andre—yes, that was what she longed for even though she couldn't quite explain the urge.

But reality always found its way in, a stark reminder of the barriers between them. The class divide was undeniable, with Andre's status as a commoner casting a shadow over her dreams. Her engagement to Prince Ralph felt like an unyielding burden, now amplified by her notoriety as the runaway princess. The whispers of scandal swirling around her urged caution. Still, even as her imagined world began to dissolve, its beauty lingered, urging Thea to hold on to every stolen moment with Andre.

She wasn't ready to let this newfound tingling sensation go when she was near him—not yet. No matter how much Stan wanted to lock her up at Cloverdale House while he was a patient—she wasn't in need of treatment. But she did want more time with the doctor.

This is not over.

Chapter Thirteen

T HEA WANDERED THROUGH the house alone after Andre went to tend to his patients, and Mary decided to follow the nurse again. It was early in the afternoon, and the light coming through the large windows at Cloverdale House cast a golden-orange hue onto the damask wallpaper. Thea's fingers brushed lightly against the shimmering fabric wallpaper. Rich, intricate patterns danced beneath her touch, each thread reminding her of the opulence she'd left behind at home when she ran away. It hadn't been hasty, nor had it been avoidable to run away; she was still convinced, but it was a big step though one that should help her to achieve her freedom. She was perhaps known as the runaway princess, but that didn't mean she was free to follow her heart.

Yet, despite the familiarity of luxuries, there was something different in England. She took a deep breath, letting the cool air under the vaulted ceiling of the staircase fill her lungs as she continued her exploration. The air was fresh, as if the wind whispered promises of new beginnings. It invigorated her, filling her with a newfound confidence that she rarely felt at home.

When Thea approached an open door, a light-flooded room made her stop. Blinking, she stepped cautiously through the open door. Her eyes adjusted, revealing a cozy sitting area bathed in the afternoon's sunlight, and the silhouette of a woman caught her attention. She seemed relaxed yet poised in an armchair with one leg stretched onto a cushioned stool. She hadn't seemed to notice Thea come in, for she appeared caught in her thoughts—gazing out the window onto the lovely park surrounding the castle that Thea had noticed earlier from the carriage.

She appeared not much older than Thea, perhaps only two or three years her senior. Her dark brown hair was swept up in a simple yet elegant coiffure, revealing a delicate neck and refined posture.

Thea cleared her throat, and the woman turned toward her with a practiced smile of the sort Thea knew all too well from a refined upbringing.

"Come in!" the woman called out, her voice clear and inviting. "Is it time for my tea already?"

Thea hesitated for a moment, then stepped fully into the room. The woman's warm eyes were framed by long lashes that cast gentle shadows on her cheeks. Her kindness and openness drew Thea in.

"I'm afraid I'm not here with tea," Thea said, offering a small smile. "I was just exploring the castle and found myself drawn to this room."

The woman's mouth curved into a genuine smile as she gave Thea the once-over. "Well, you are most welcome. I'm Isabella Victoria von Habsburg, Lady Ashford. And you are?"

"Thea," she replied, inclining her head slightly in greeting.

"Just Thea?"

"Princess Josephine Theodora Andrea von Hohenzollern-Sigmaringen," she said with a curtsy.

"Your Royal Highness." Anna gripped the chair's armrests tightly and tried to push herself up. She must have tried to rise and bow to Thea, but Thea rushed and lay her hand over hers, for it was evident that the woman who'd introduced herself as Anna was hurt.

"Don't get up on my behalf. I see you're injured." The woman sank back into the chair. "It's a pleasure to meet you, Lady Ashford," Thea assured her, hoping the need for etiquette wouldn't take over the newfound freedom she'd enjoyed since she arrived in London.

"Please, call me Anna," she said, waving away the formality. "What brings a princess here? Have you also been injured?" Anna gave her the once-over and then nodded toward a chair opposite hers, also turning toward the lovely window bathed in the afternoon sun.

"I'm here with my brother; he's the patient," Thea said, careful not to give away too much to a stranger. But there was something familiar about this woman.

"Nothing too serious, I hope?" Anna asked.

"No, he just needs some time to heal." Thea couldn't help but warm at her dark eyes. She felt as though she'd seen their questioning look before.

Thea moved toward the indicated chair. The overwhelming light streaming in from the window cast an inviting glow on the plush upholstery. She sat, smoothing her skirts and taking in the details of the room—the richly colored Persian rug, the fine china displayed on a nearby cabinet, and the faint scent of jasmine that she attributed to Anna.

"It's quite lovely here," Thea remarked, her eyes meeting Anna's again. "Very different from home, but beautiful in its way."

"Where did you grow up?"

"Bran Castle in the Carpathian Mountains."

Anna dropped her hands on her lap and smiled softly. "I've seen drawings, and they must be rather stunning. This castle has changed to convert it into a rehabilitation center. It's a very hush-hush affair and reserved only for nobility. Think of this place as Almack's for the invalid. I'm lucky to have obtained a spot even before it opened officially."

"How did you? I heard it wasn't supposed to open for quite a while."

"Oh, my husband can be rather generous in ensuring his privacy. When I caught him, he realized he needed to lock me away." Anna hesitated, momentarily interrupting the bubbly nature Thea had just begun to appreciate. "He probably didn't expect ever to be caught with his mistress."

Thea blinked incredulously, but she knew she'd heard right. Then Anna pulled at her gown, and a tightly bandaged ankle gave Thea a pretty good idea of her injury.

"It's all of my own doing," Anna sighed. "I fell off my horse because I rode too fast. Thus, I broke my foot."

"How did this happen?"

Anna's eyes twinkled with tears, and she leaned toward Thea, holding the armrests on either side of the chair. "I was on an outing in Somerset. We have a country estate there, and I had planned to surprise my husband there after he returned from a business trip. I had some important news to share with him." Anna patted her stomach, and Thea instantly understood. "That's when I saw him with a woman. Under our apple tree!" She threw her hand in the air. "It was unmistakable." Thea swallowed hard, her eyes flickering with shock and empathy as she listened to Anna's tale. "It's the same tree under which he proposed to me. He promised lifelong love and fidelity, and now look at me. With child and injured, locked away for his convenience." Thea clutched her chest with both hands. What a terrible fate for such a young woman. "I rode so fast and aimlessly in my rage when I caught him." Anna wiped the tear from her cheek that rolled down.

"Did you speak to him?"

"He wouldn't speak to me! He said we'd discuss it later."

Just like Father used to say when I tried to address the topic of my unwelcome match.

"But then you fell and got injured," Thea whispered, her voice trembling with the sorrow of newfound understanding.

"And now I'm here until my leg heals," Anna said and then pursed her lips.

"And the baby?" Thea asked, but she was afraid of the response. Pregnancy was a precious state, and she wasn't too naive to underestimate the dangers a horse's fall could cause under such circumstances.

"I have only been seen by the nurse, and she said she didn't suspect any injuries to the baby. But I have yet to see the doctor."

From the following of Anna's brow with a tension Thea recognized from a woman who'd exhausted her last resort, Thea realized that Anna's heart hurt more than her broken bones.

Thea took Anna's hand, and their eyes met. It was a moment when two women sat in the simple understanding that even their titles were insufficient to protect them from society's patriarchal structure. And just like that, Anna wasn't a stranger anymore. Even as far away as Thea had fled to England, she recognized a commiserating soul, and a new friend in Anna.

"I ran away from my betrothal."

"Did he…?" Anna's falling tone implied the worst.

"Oh no, no! I've not seen him since I was three years old. I don't remember him at all." Thea pursed her lips. "But I just wanted more from life than being his wife."

Anna deflated. "I understand. You are very wise for your young age to realize it in time."

"Nobody else sees it that way."

"Perhaps not, but it's your life. At least until you marry, and your husband dictates what you may do." She sighed.

"What is it that yours won't let you do?"

Anna looked out the window and blinked profusely. Was she trying not to cry in front of a princess, or was there another reason for the emotions she seemed to try to hide?

"I was rather hoping to search for someone," Anna murmured, each word heavy with melancholy.

"Who is it?" The thought of being trapped in a loveless marriage had been terrifying enough, but now, considering losing one's flame and then being trapped was unbearably cruel. "A flame from your past?" Thea pressed on as the feeling of commonalities with Anna grew into warm friendship in Thea's heart.

"No, my brother. We lost him, but perhaps he's not dead. How could I ever stop trying to find him?"

"Of course you cannot." Thea couldn't fathom the thought of losing one of her brothers, she'd undoubtedly try anything in her power to find them.

"My husband won't entertain the thought. He said it's not his responsibility to search, and I… I loathe him for this, Thea." Anna covered her mouth with one hand. "I've never spoken the words aloud, but it's true." A tear rolled down her cheek, and she wiped it with the hand already on her face.

A comfortable silence settled between them, punctuated only by the distant chirping of birds outside and the rustling of leaves in the gentle breeze that made the light flicker in the room.

Thea wished she could help Anna and suggest ways to put out the word about a missing person.

"I will speak to my brother and ask if he can aid your search," Thea said.

"No, if he's injured, let him heal. This is something I can't share with… Hohenzollern, you said?" Anna cast Thea a questioning look, and Thea nodded.

"You are connected to Prince Ralph?"

Thea tasted acid. "He's the one I'm running away from."

Anna tilted her head back and her chin up.

Surely, Thea had misspoken now, and she already regretted trusting Anna. It was just that her eyes were so warm, and a certain familiar *je ne sais quoi* prevented Thea from putting her guard up.

After a few moments, Anna spoke again, her tone more serious. "I shall help you hide."

Thea inhaled deeply, her chest filling with renewed hope that she'd found a new friend indeed.

"I know him, and he would make a worse husband than even mine. He's his distant cousin, I'm afraid.

"You know, I must admit, I wasn't expecting company today," Anna said warmly. "The best connections often start in the most unexpected ways."

The simple conversation and shared understanding brought a sense of belonging that Thea hadn't realized she was missing.

As they continued to chat, the afternoon light shifted, casting long shadows across the room. Thea felt a contentment she hadn't felt in a long time—a sense of being exactly where she was meant to be.

"Would you like to stay for tea, after all?" Anna asked, a mischievous glint in her eye. "I promise it will be much more enjoyable with company."

Thea smiled, her heart light. "I would love that, Anna. Thank you."

As the sun dipped lower in the sky, Thea and Anna sat together, sharing stories and companionship, forging a bond that Thea knew would carry them through the challenges ahead.

Chapter Fourteen

T HE NEXT DAY, it seemed nothing was unfolding as Andre had anticipated. Sleep had evaded him the previous night, leaving him restless and awake before dawn. By seven o'clock, he had already visited the Patisserie de La Loire, a charming bakery nestled near his practice. He had collected a parcel of delicate madeleines, their sweet vanilla aroma a small comfort as he held the parcel in his lap during the carriage ride to Cloverdale House.

Upon arriving at his treatment room at the rehabilitation center, Mary's delighted smile greeted him.

"This smells so good!" She beamed. "Did you hear that my parents sent word that I can stay as long as I like?"

"Until they return?" Andre asked and Mary nodded. To a child, a few days or weeks meant as much as an adventure of unascertainable duration. He smiled. "Fresh madeleines from the patisserie near the practice on Harley Street," Andre said and instinctively passed the pastries to her.

"Can I take them to the study? Miss Thea is waiting for me with a bilo-logy lesson."

"Biology?" Andre chuckled.

He handed the parcel over, and Mary immediately took it.

"We have scissors there to cut the cord," she called as she skipped down the hallway, tugging at the cord that tied the parcel, and Andre hoped she'd share them with Thea. The gesture felt right in the moment, yet he knew deep down that he had acquired them for Thea, not just as a mere treat. There was a longing in his chest, an unvoiced wish to present her with something more fitting—flowers, chocolates, tokens of affection he could not openly bestow.

In fact, Andre had not seen Thea again after tending to the patients at Cloverdale House.

He had only caught sight of Stan arriving to confirm their dinner plans with Thea once nurse Shira had attended to the task of cleaning his wound and refreshing his bandage. Earlier that morning, Andre had inspected Stan's shoulder, noting with a twinge of disappointment that it wasn't healing as swiftly as he'd hoped either. The other doctors would return shortly, marking the official opening of Cloverdale House as a rehabilitation center. Likewise, his friends would soon arrive, and a steady flow of patients would provide a welcome distraction from the princess who had occupied his every thought.

Andre's heart ached for the unlikelihood of a formal courtship. He could have sent a calling card, requested a proper visit, and perhaps invited her on a chaperoned stroll along Pall Mall. But he was no aristocrat, and she, a princess, stood on a pedestal he felt forbidden to reach. His mind lingered on possibilities that dared not take form, constrained by the chasm society placed between them. Mainly because of the secret of his birth, the jeopardy he'd put his family in, and the shame he'd bring upon Thea's lineage. He could tackle impossible love, but what he'd realized he harbored for Thea was beyond words. All he could call it was hopeless—a fatal diagnosis of heartbreak was the only possible outcome.

Thus, he hoped Mary would share the madeleines with Thea so that she could at least taste some of his favorite pastries. He could offer his protection and friendship without admitting to the ardor of his feelings, couldn't he? Thea had sounded as though she felt rather alone, and perhaps the spongy cakes could offer her some comfort—that's what Andre's mother had always said:

"There's comfort to be found in food."

With several patients in residence, although the other doctors hadn't returned, Cloverdale House buzzed with activity. But Andre needed solitude to think. He slipped through the side door, emerging into the secluded area at the back of the estate, where a long medieval wall still stood. The wall seemed pointless, not enclosing anything of significance. "Hedges along a pointless wall," Andre muttered to himself. The blackthorn, meticulously pruned and perfectly aligned, stood staunchly in its place. Pruned, trimmed, and unwavering. Andre felt like that hedge—close to a piece of history laden with royal legacy, yet unable to expand or grow. His lineage was too diluted to claim any throne, although it allowed his family to brush shoulders with the elite of Europe. But not him. He was merely the hedge, vibrant and robust, deeply rooted yet not truly part of the grand scene. Plus, he wasn't going anywhere, just like the hedge.

Frustrated, Andre kicked a pebble across the gravel path. He'd never felt so trapped by his station—angry, yes, especially when his siblings had been invited to the Hofburg Palace in Vienna, the epicenter of imperial social life. As the eldest son, he should have escorted his sister, but his younger brother, Lorenzo, donned the evening attire and took his place. At their mother's behest, Andre had stepped aside.

He was the outsider, pruned by tradition to stand firm in his place. When the Napoleonic army invaded Florence, his survival hinged on discretion. That fateful night had severed him from his family, and he missed them now more than ever.

"Andre, listen to me," his mother had whispered, her voice steady despite the chaos unfolding outside. "You must go to Vienna. Study at the university. They won't acknowledge you, and it's all my fault. Your future depends on your education. Do you understand?"

Downstairs, heavy boots thudding against the wooden floors grew louder. Napoleon's soldiers were raiding homes, searching for any sign of resistance. Andre's heart pounded, his instincts urging him to rush downstairs and defend his family. But his mother's grip on his arm was firm, her eyes pleading with him.

"Papa already reserved a spot at the Faculty of Medicine for you. Go early; they will let you work until the semester begins." She handed him more money than he could count and stuffed it in his waist pocket. "This is all we have in the house." Why did she assume she wouldn't have any use for it?

Dread settled in Andre's chest, and his heart pounded with an unfailing yet new sense of panic.

"I can't leave you and the others," he protested, the weight of responsibility as the eldest son pressing down on his shoulders. "I need to protect you." But he didn't want to leave his family's side. What would life be without his family?

Mother jerked back.

A loud crash echoed from below, followed by the unmistakable sound of a struggle. His father, Dr. Johann von Dürer, was trying to fend off the invaders. Andre heard a grunt, a shriek from his little sister, then silence. His breath caught in his throat.

His mother, Isabella di Lorenzo, quickly moved, gathering a small bundle of essentials. Her usually composed face was etched with worry lines, her lips pressed tightly together. The faint glow of a single candle illuminated her features, giving her an almost ghostly appearance.

Mother's eyes were so wide open that he saw the white around her dark brown irises, the same color as his own.

"Go!" her voice cracked, and she avoided eye contact. It would have shattered her resolve; he understood that much. She kissed his forehead, pushing him towards the window. She hurriedly opened it, the cold wind biting at their faces. "If I can, I will find you. But it would be best if you survived despite my mistakes. Nothing else matters, my love, except your life and survival. Remember that! I wish you only happiness in life."

"But Mama!"

"Please go, my love!"

Andre hesitated, torn between his duty to his family and the urgency of his mother's command. He glanced back at her, but she turned away, moving towards the stairs. A faint cry escaped her lips, and she disappeared. Andre didn't know it then, but it would be the last time he'd see his mother.

The night air carried a chill that seemed to seep through the stone walls of their villa in Florence. Andre, eighteen and brimming with youthful idealism that was doomed that night, stood by the window of his dimly lit room. Florence's terracotta roofs stretched before him, their familiar reddish-brown hues muted under the cloak of darkness. The undulating pattern of the tiles formed a mosaic, each piece fitting seamlessly into the next, creating a familiar and treacherous landscape.

Half-hidden by storm clouds, the moon cast intermittent patches of silver light across the rooftops, making the wet tiles glisten like polished stone. The rain had turned the usually warm, dry surfaces slick and dangerous. Andre could see the rivulets of water streaming down the curves of the roofs, pooling in the dips, and cascading down to the cobblestone streets below.

Propelled by panic, Andre climbed onto the roof, the shingles slick with rain. The metallic scent of iron filled his nostrils, a gruesome reminder of the bloodshed below, dull hits, and the stench of brutality emanating from the streets. He moved cautiously, heart racing, as he navigated the treacherous surface. With every step, the image of his family's villa, not as he knew it during his happy childhood, rather that night, fraught with violence, burned into his memory.

The streets were scenes of horror; lifeless bodies lay sprawled in the mud, victims of the violent raid. The mingling scents of blood and rainwater created a horrendous odor. Andre's stomach churned, but he pushed forward, driven by desperation. He found a hidden corner on a faraway roof and crouched, his body trembling with cold and fear.

Andre's memories flooded his thoughts, destroying his unrealistic imagination to woo Thea. Again, he looked at the small green blackthorn along the old wall. His parents had repeatedly advised to remain inconspicuous until they found him. He waited semester after semester at the university but they never came for him. And when he went to pursue his apprenticeship in India with Felix, he knew the traces of his old life would be erased. The one thing he'd promised his parents was that he'd do well as a doctor—his only link to his family. And yet, Andre was like a hedge in the wall's shadow, forbidden to blossom like other plants. But he felt a change around Thea, as if his feelings might finally unfurl and bloom.

"I want to find one first!" came a cheerful voice, starkly contrasting his stormy emotions. Little Mary bounced out the side door and held a small glass jar. "Oh, Andre!" she called, holding her straw bonnet with the other hand.

"Good morning, Miss Mary. How do you do?" Andre initially feigned politeness, unable to forget his gloom, but when the little girl came to stand before him and looked at him, donning her baby teeth in a bright smile, his mood lightened instantly.

He squatted to face her. "What have you here?"

He inspected the jar, which seemed empty but for a few wrinkled leaves she'd stuffed in.

"We're looking for Lyc-… ahem… Lyca—"

"Lycaenidae," Thea said from behind Mary.

Andre hadn't seen her coming—in the literal sense because he'd been squatting and focusing on Mary, but also in the figurative sense because his heart lurched when she smiled at him. She wore a straw bonnet, too, tied under her chin with a pink ribbon.

Do not look at her lips.

Speak.

Say hello, at least.

"Thank you for the madeleines. They were delicious," Thea said.

"You're welcome." What Andre meant to say was something entirely different. *I'd bring you fresh pastries every morning and lay the world at your feet if allowed.*

But he was frozen, mesmerized by Thea's dark eyes sparkling in the shadow. She'd bring light even to the simple pruned hedges behind the castle that wasn't hers; that's how brightly she shone. And suddenly, all the gloom was lifted from Andre's chest, and he took heart. He was there now. And he'd cherish any moments he was allowed to share with her.

It would suffice for someone like him.

"Do you have many patients waiting today?" Thea asked politely.

"One here at Cloverdale House. And then nobody else on Harley Street until tomorrow."

Thea smiled and blinked as if it were as difficult for her to break their eye contact as it was for him. "We are looking for butterfly eggs. Today's lesson is the metamorphosis of insects," Thea explained.

"With all this blackthorn, Miss Thea said we might find some *Polyommatus*. They have shiny blue-and-purple wings," Mary declared cheerfully and walked along the hedge, inspecting the undersides of the tiny leaves.

"These hedges are a treasure trove," Thea said when she and Andre strolled leisurely behind Mary, who was mumbling to herself.

"They're just green to me, nothing special," Andre lied, still convinced he was no more than one of those unmovable hedges.

"On the contrary," Thea started. "They seem inconspicuous, but they are the cradle for life. The butterfly eggs blend in seamlessly, but the blackthorn provides the ideal protection to keep them safe. Sadly, mother butterflies never see their hatchlings, thus the blackthorn protect them instead."

Andre thought she was adorable in her philosophical diatribe of insect nurseries, and he felt meager next to her, just the cradle for something that would hatch and leave—just as he feared that Thea would leave. She had more important things to do in her life, princes to wed, diplomatic relations to foster, as Stan had explained. She'd leave him behind like the butterflies in the hedges when they emerged from their chrysalis.

"Without the perfect blackthorn leaves, the caterpillars would starve when they hatch. And the entire agricultural system could collapse."

"The entire agricultural system? Because of some butterflies?" Andre stopped on the gravel path.

"If the caterpillars cannot pupefy and remain protected under the leaves, they won't become butterflies. And without butterfly pollination, there'd be no fruit trees. Many plants we eat depend on pollination—"

"Butterflies are beautiful, but the fruit trees also require bees and the support of the wind for pollination."

Thea inclined her head. "Wind is strong but moody. A little gust makes them fly higher, but a storm can kill them. And perhaps some trees would rather have butterflies than bees?" Thea gave a playful smile over her shoulder.

She was flirting.

Don't engage.

A storm like her father's wrath if Andre laid a hand on the princess.

Just then, the wind blew stronger, and the rim of Thea's bonnet flapped backward. The ribbon holding it to her chin slipped off, and the bonnet nearly flew away, but Andre caught it.

Instinctively, he put one hand on the back of Thea's head and the other under her chin, ensuring that the bonnet stayed put to protect her from the sun but, more importantly, that the ribbon didn't strangle her. Not that it was strong enough, but he wouldn't let any discomfort come to her under his watch.

"Thank you," she beamed.

He held her gaze, for it was too beautiful to look away. Under the brightness of her gaze, Andre felt he might be growing the courage of the stray leaves pricking up from the hedges no matter how carefully they were pruned. He wanted to rebel against everything he'd chastised himself for and kiss her.

"How long have you lived in London?" Thea asked as they walked on, following Mary, who'd carefully stuffed more leaves into her jar.

"About two years now. I was born in Florence but attended school in Vienna. My father had a post at the faculty of medicine there."

"Is that why you became a doctor?"

"In a way, I always thought I was. Even when I was little,

about the same age as Mary, he took me to the lectures and even the laboratory. He gave me grapes to practice sutures when he was occupied with his colleagues. I helped him grade exams by the time I was fourteen."

"You must have learned very much. I am certain he's proud of you," Thea said.

"I wish I knew." Andre felt that familiar clipping sensation in his lungs whenever he spoke of his family. "When I completed my studies, I traveled to India with Alfie Collins and Felix Leafley."

"I saw their names on the sign at 87 Harley Street," Thea smiled.

"Yes. When we came to England and learned of the opportunity to open the practice together, I lost track of my family along the way."

They were forced to lose track of me under Napoleon's rule.

But he didn't want to burden the princess with too much sadness. He hated the pity and much preferred to be judged not for his heritage or the terrible timing of his birth but for the accomplishments that were of his own doing.

"You must miss them very much. I am certain they are looking for you."

"I had to run away to save their lives; it's a long story," Andre said, but then he noticed that Thea grew sadder.

"I only ran away for my own selfishness."

HE WAS BREATHTAKING, and Thea wished she could brush the curl off his forehead and draw him in for a kiss to distract him from the pain and loss he'd suffered. If only she were allowed to act on her feelings, to be free like the butterflies, and land where she wanted, for she would surely choose him.

"It's not my place to say anything," Andre mumbled, trying

to control the anger bubbling up within him.

"Speak freely. I don't need the royal etiquette here," Thea said.

"I know you well enough not to wish to speak freely. You deserve all the respect of a princess, whether you are at court or not."

Thea eyed him curiously for a moment, then smirked and let her mischievous side shine through beneath the facade of the mere princess.

"Then consider this an audience. Now, speak freely," she started again.

"It's not selfishness that made you run away, I think. Self-preservation and pursuing a happy life are more basic than that."

"Basic, such as instincts?"

"Some instincts for self-preservation are fundamental, yes."

"Such as…"

"The search for companionship, for instance. Humans usually don't want to be completely alone. Some wish to have large families or simply a dog to walk for company, but complete solitude is rarely welcome. And one can be lonely in a loveless marriage."

"Do you want a large family?"

That made him laugh. "I am from a very large family. We have members scattered throughout Europe."

"And you miss them."

"Every single day."

"I'm from a large family, too. Two branches, even. It's exhausting to keep the names in mind sometimes."

Andre chuckled. "I don't think I even met most of my extended cousins."

"Parents never forget their children. My mother always followed our lessons and holiday schedules and attended our music recitals."

"And your father?" Andre asked.

Thea sighed. "He didn't forget either, but it was different. He always had expectations that we feared to fall short of. None of us wanted to disappoint him."

"I doubt you could ever disappoint anyone."

Thea's smile faltered. "If I don't marry whom Father chose for me, I'm afraid I'd disappoint him so gravely that he'd never recover."

"Doesn't he merely want what's best for you?" Andre seemed ignorant of the dynastic responsibilities of a princess.

"He wants to use me for what is best for the kingdom. That's not the same."

"Isn't that the same as what Stan is working to achieve?"

"And if he achieves it after I marry—and I am not saying I will marry Prince Ralph—then I sacrificed my happiness for naught." She balled her fists. "I always do what's expected. I am satisfied with every element of what the only princess of Transylvania ought to do, and then I do some more. But every time my father looks at me, he grimaces with pain because I fall short in the one way that counts for him—marriage."

"That's so difficult," Andre said with a frown.

"It's inevitable. That's why I'm hiding.

"And yet you can't wait indefinitely or prolong the engagement?"

"No engagement happened. I am promised to him, but I've never agreed to any of it. I've never even met him since I was three."

"Don't you wish to—"

"No! I… there's someone else I—" She stopped mid-sentence and blinked profusely, even though they were walking along a shadowy path.

"Someone else caught your affection?"

If only you knew…

"Yes, I think he's caught my heart." Her eyes locked with his, and he swallowed hard.

"That man is incredibly lucky."

Chapter Fifteen

WHEN MARY CAME between Thea and Andre, he wandered away in thought. He seemed consumed by something that held him back, needing to cool his mind for some reason Thea couldn't guess.

"Let's not go back to conjugating verbs, Thea," Mary pleaded when their break had ended longer than Thea had planned. "I want to do something exciting!"

"Isn't it exciting to learn to converse like a lady?" Thea gave a superciliary glance, suspecting Mary felt about the answer just as she had as a child. Few things were more boring to a little girl than Latin grammar.

But Mary's long and heartfelt groan response made her laugh. It was true, even if Thea would have expressed it differently than Mary. A lady in England was expected to converse about topics ranging from the dull to the mundane when in polite society.

The life of a princess wasn't like fairy tales made it out; the pomp and luxury had felt more constricting for Thea than a privilege. Her most important duty was to obey her father.

No more!

Thea shook her head and hoped that Mary didn't notice. She'd escaped, yes. But it wasn't a permanent solution by any means.

"Can we stay out here, please?" Mary pleaded.

"All right, a little longer then." Thea feigned reluctance to draw out their break but strolled through the park's lush expanse surrounding Cloverdale House, the morning sun casting a gentle glow over the dew-kissed grass. The air was crisp, carrying the sweet scent of blooming flowers, and the distant chatter of London seemed to fade into the background. Beside her, Mary skipped with the boundless energy of a child, her laughter ringing like a bell.

Suddenly, Mary's eyes widened with delight. "Look, Thea! A rabbit" she exclaimed, pointing to a small, fluffy creature with a white cotton tail—just as in children's books—nibbling on clover. Without a second thought, Mary dashed after it. Her curls bounced in ringlets with each step, peeking out from her bonnet.

"Mary, not too fast!" Thea called with a mix of amusement and concern. She quickened her pace, her skirts rustling against the grass. Thea's gaze drifted over her shoulder, and her heart skipped a beat.

Andre was there, running effortlessly up the hill toward Mary with long and graceful strides. Thea's breath caught in her throat. His presence was magnetic, drawing her in with an intensity she couldn't quite understand. She hadn't moved with such freedom since her childhood even though her breath came in ragged bursts as she sprinted up the hill to ward off Andre, her feet pounding the earth with a rhythmic urgency. But the closer she came to Andre, the stronger the exhilarating sense of boundlessness swept over her, unshackling her spirit—as if he'd set her heart free. When she reached his side, the sunlight danced on his dark hair, and his eyes, focused and determined, seemed to hold a secret just for her. He cast her a boyish look from the corner of his eyes.

"Again!" Mary cried out joyfully, reaching her hands up to Andre. He picked her up and twirled her in the air, and the little girl screamed with joy—as if Mary's voice made the exact sounds Thea felt in her heart when she saw Andre.

"Hello, Thea," Andre said, "I have my hands full." He

laughed heartily, and Thea saw his perfect white smile. Everything about him was packed, handsome, muscular perfection. He held her gaze and set Mary down.

It was such a hot day—or was it just Thea's chest and face heating when Andre looked at her as he did.

She swallowed and blinked to regain her composure. She tried to, at least.

"I can see you are busy," Thea jested when Mary's sudden squeal pulled Thea back to the moment. The little girl had flung herself onto the grass with a delighted "wheeeeee," rolling down the gentle slope with abandon.

"I always did this with my brother and sister." Andre's rich and warm laughter echoed, and Thea found herself momentarily stunned by the thought that he must have had a family he missed even though he never spoke of who was exactly part of his family.

He was tall and seemed careless in a cultivated way, as if he made an effort to push aside his woes and consciously revel in the pleasures of life.

Then Thea realized he was one of them for her—he was a pleasure to look at, with his deep mahogany eyes, ebony waves of hair, and broad shoulders.

But Mary's laugh woke Thea from her reverie. The girl's joyful squeal was louder than any other noise around Cloverdale House. It was a laugh that spoke of joy and freedom, a stark contrast to the reserved world she'd fled.

And it had to do with Andre, didn't it?

Suddenly, Mary plopped into the grass and chuckled with playful glee as she rolled herself into a ball. It had been years since she'd done that, but not too long since she'd watched the peasant children playing outside Bran Castle just like that, rolling down a grassy hill. It had grown typical for Thea to look out her window from her ivory tower and smile at the people outside the castle walls, enjoying the sunny weather while she sat there with a pile of books and her hair pinned up to prepare her for a marriage she didn't want.

Whoosh!

Mary's rolling form collided gently with Thea's legs, and before she could steady herself, she tumbled backward. Strong arms caught her, pulling her into a firm embrace. Thea's heart raced as she pressed against Andre, their fall cushioned by the soft earth. They rolled together, tangled limbs and laughter until they stopped.

Thea lay still for a moment, the world spinning slightly. Andre's grip was secure. His touch sent a thrill through her. She let out a small scream, half surprise, half exhilaration. It had been years since she felt this alive, unburdened by society's expectations.

Andre's eyes met hers, a playful glint in their depths. "Are you alright, Thea?" he asked, his voice teasing yet gentle.

Alright? *That isn't the word to describe how I feel with you wrapped around me.* Delicious? Magical? All the most wonderful tingling feelings mixed together and even better!

She nodded, breathless and smiling, catching sight of Mary, who'd started to pick some flowers. "I haven't done that since I was a child," she admitted, a hint of wonder in her voice. The grass tickled her skin, and the sky above seemed impossibly blue.

Considering that she'd already disgraced herself—because it was unseemly for a princess to frolic in a meadow—she let all the rules go and plopped on her back, allowing the sunshine to tickle her nose.

Andre's presence was intoxicating. In his company, the world felt brighter and more vibrant. Thea realized quickly that she was falling for him, this man who brought laughter and light into her life.

For an instant, she thought Stan called her name but if it were just her conscience preventing her from enjoying Andre's presence, she'd better ignore caution. She didn't want to care about the trouble of escaping Prince Ralph or her dynastic responsibilities. As they lay there, the sounds of the park around them and Mary talking to herself as she collected the bouquet of dandelions, Thea knew she was on the brink of something extraordinary. And for the first time in a long while, she was ready to embrace it.

⟫⟫⟪⟪

ANDRE HAD NEVER been more challenged to hide his arousal and hoped it wasn't obvious when Thea all but toppled into his arms. He tried to stop her fall, but he lost his balance on the slant of the hill and the uneven ground. Instinctively, he caught her.

There hadn't been time to consider the consequences of feeling her body pressed against his; he'd merely wanted to prevent her from succumbing to an injury.

Yes, in the soft meadow, on a little hill, rolling around like a lovesick farmer's boy on the meadows in south Tirol. But this was London; he wasn't just a boy but a physician, and in his arms was a princess.

Not just any princess, but the princess.

The one whose heartbeat he felt against his chest.

The one whose sweet breath made him want to kiss her.

The one who was laughing out loud, ignorant of the forbidden thoughts he had.

He mustn't betray her trust, nor Stan's. His task was to look out for her.

Basta! Enough!

Basta, Basta, Basta! That was all.

It had to be enough. He'd help her up, feign utmost regret for the mishap, and let her run off, leaving him disgraced for not stopping her fall, for harboring the most unchaste thoughts for a princess whose virtue he ought to protect.

Yes, he was going down, especially if Stan saw him like this.

She'd probably scream and run away.

How could he possibly explain himself if Stan confronted him about the situation?

Thea rolled off him and onto her back in the meadow just then. She closed her eyes and just lay there.

This was the moment, Andre knew, he ought to seize. It all unfurled so perfectly in his mind's eye. He'd climb over her, put one hand on either side of her shoulders, she'd blink at him when he blocked the sun from her, and then she'd smile that perfect smile of hers. So he'd lower his mouth onto hers, and they'd topple in the meadow, under the bright sky and surrounded by fragrant flowers, for that's what he felt like near Thea—wild and free.

But he couldn't do it.

She was a princess, and he was just a bastard of the distant Habsburg branch. They weren't even alone since Mary was there. Again!

Thus, he propped himself on his elbow and looked at the lovely princess crinkling her nose under the sunshine.

"It tickles, doesn't it?" she asked, her eyes still closed.

"What does?"

"The grass on our necks."

She thought he'd been lying beside her. She couldn't know that he had been admiring her. He knew he'd hardly have another chance to commit such perfection to his memory. Perhaps, if he were lucky, he could remember this moment forever and draw from it when he was alone at night. He was sure he would be because something had changed in his heart, and he never wanted to look at another woman again—only Thea, the princess of his heart, since she couldn't ever be the princess in his life.

"You are so beautiful, I have no words," Andre said, half hoping she hadn't heard him.

"No words?" she asked.

"None."

"Not in any of the languages?"

She's flirting.

He took heart. "Perhaps in a combination."

"Which ones?" Thea blinked into the sun, but he felt her gaze on his skin like a wave of something he didn't dare describe either.

"Let me think about it." Andre lay beside Thea, the world around them a blur of soft sounds and gentle warmth. The sunlight poured over them like thick honey, slowing down time as Andre tried to stifle his impulse. A halo of flyaway hairs and the lace rim of her bonnet made her too inviting as she lay with her eyes closed, her expression one of pure tranquility. Every detail of her seemed etched into his mind—the way her breath created a gentle rhythm in the air, the slight upturn of her lips that hinted at an unspoken joy.

"Thea," he began, "the superlative of *bella* is *bellissima*, and it's not enough for you in Italian alone." She looked at him as his words lingered between them, delicate as the sunlight that seemed to wrap around her blonde curls. "Painters couldn't capture your golden glow. But even that pales, for *éclatante*, as the French say, gleaming with a radiance as if the heavens shaped you, blending the skies with their most precious hues, still isn't enough."

"Andre…" she whispered, her voice almost trembling, "I don't know if I am worthy of such words." Her hand fluttered to her chest, resting lightly as though to steady the rapid beat of her heart. "No one… no one has ever spoken to me this way before."

"Should I stop trying to find the right words?"

I have overstepped.

"No! Tell me."

"I know I shouldn't, Thea. I'm greedy to even want to find the right words to capture your beauty because nothing about you can be captured. There's a spirit and freedom of liveliness around you that I've never found anywhere else." Andre paused as if to steady himself, his breath trembling, his voice now a whisper of fervor and longing. "You are not just a passing vision, not the sight of a dream. You are a constellation of stars that transcend the humble ideas I am capable of, *stella mia*, my star, the light that guides me through every shadow and every silence since I've met you."

Definitely overstepped. Stan would kill him for how he spoke to the princess.

She glanced down for a moment, shyly, before looking back into his eyes, her cheeks flushed with a hue that rivaled the poppies in the meadow.

His heart pounded with a fervor that matched the vibrant colors of the meadow. The scent of crushed grass mingled with the sweet aroma of nearby honeysuckle and primroses, creating a heady mixture that danced around them. Every fiber of his being urged him closer to Thea, the princess of his heart, the woman who had unwittingly woven herself into the very fabric of his soul.

But he mustn't.

As he shifted, the earth beneath him seemed to whisper encouragement, and he edged nearer, the proximity to her a sweet, torturous bliss. The gentle murmur of her breath, the soft rustle of her gown, created a symphony that played solely for them. He reached out, his hand hovering, before daring to smooth a wayward strand of hair from her face, his touch as light as the breeze that played across her skin.

"You make me feel," she faltered slightly, her voice soft but laden with emotion, "as if I am not just Thea, a mere princess... but something more with you than when I am alone. Something beautiful, luminous, as you say. But it is you who paints me such with your words. Do you not see?" She tilted her head slightly, her voice dropping to a tender whisper. "It is your gaze that gives me light, Andre."

Despite his attempts to remain still, Andre felt his body lean toward her, an unconscious movement that defied his better judgment. Thea's cheeks colored the softest shade of pink, a delicate hue that spoke of innocence. Her lips parted slightly, drawing his attention like a beacon, and his pulse quickened, each beat a drum echoing in the silence that enveloped them.

His fingers brushed against hers, a light touch that sent a thrill through him, sparking a sensation that traveled up his arm, to settle warmly in his chest. Thea's hand trembled slightly, yet she didn't withdraw. Her fingers rested against his with a tentative trust that meant more than he dared hope. Her gaze held his, and they had a silent conversation that needed no words, each glance a question, an answer, a promise:

I won't betray your trust.

Yet, he leaned in, their breaths mingling, the space between them electrified with a thrilling and terrifying tension. The subtle rustling of grass beneath them became the background music to their shared moment, a soft symphony that accompanied the beating of his heart.

He leaned in, the air between them charged with electricity, making his heart race. Her breath mingled with his, and he could almost taste the sweetness of anticipation. Her closeness was intoxicating, a promise of something beautiful and profound.

Just as their lips brushed the edge of possibility, a whisper of a breeze stirred, cooling the warmth between them. Thea blinked, and the spell wavered; the moment held in a delicate balance. Andre paused, the space between them widening, yet the connection remained, silent sparks hanging in the air.

Thea's eyes flickered with a return to awareness, and Andre paused, the tantalizing moment stretching like gossamer between them. Though the kiss remained beyond reach, the bond forged in that instant was undeniable, a shimmering connection that promised more. As he leaned back slightly, the meadow resumed its gentle song, but Andre knew this moment would linger.

He lay back, the ache of the almost-kiss a bittersweet memory already etched into his heart.

"Look!" Mary called, interrupting Andre and Thea's leisurely moment in the meadow.

Andre rose and squatted beside Mary, secretly grateful for the child's interruption because he couldn't possibly apologize enough to Thea for what he'd almost done.

Mary's bright curiosity momentarily captured Thea's attention. The child's fingers danced over the jar, her eyes wide with wonder at the discovery.

"I have enough," she announced, her voice bubbling with triumph as she held up her jar, its interior a miniature world of green leaves and promise.

"Are there butterfly eggs in there?" Andre asked, his voice gentle, indulging Mary's fascination with nature. His interest in medicine started when his father brought home a stack of sketches of the skeleton. Father had indulged him and nourished his curiosity. But as Andre looked up, he caught Thea glancing over her shoulder, her brow furrowed. The wind whispered through the trees, carrying a sense of unease.

"Have you seen anything odd?" Thea inquired, rubbing her arms as though warding off a chill that had nothing to do with the low sun of the afternoon.

"Look! A tiny white dot on the bottom of this leaf," Mary interjected, pointing to her jar with a mix of pride and wonder.

Andre's attention flickered back to the girl, but the prickling sensation at the nape of his neck refused to fade. Thea had been standing a few paces away, her silhouette framed by the dappled sunlight filtering through the canopy while Mary showed him her jar with butterfly eggs and was adorably excited about her finding. But something was amiss. Andre felt an inexplicable tug in his chest, an urgency that settled like a stone in his stomach.

A rustle in the underbrush snapped his focus back to reality. "Thea?" he called softly, the name barely more than a breath, apprehension threading through his veins.

She was gone.

Chapter Sixteen

WHERE WAS HIS princess?

Andre's heart lurched. The space she'd occupied mere moments ago was now a void that screamed louder than words. Panic surged through him with a force that left him breathless. The world tilted, and his vision narrowed to a tunnel of urgency and fear.

The orangery doors swung open with a sharp click, the sound echoing through the quiet space as Stan stumbled out. His face, customarily composed, was drawn and pale, the absence of his coat revealing a hastily wrapped bandage stained with fresh crimson.

Andre's heart lurched at the sight. A dash replaced Stan's usually assured stride, his eyes wide with urgency. The sunlight streaming through the glass illuminated the stark contrast of blood against his white sleeve, each droplet a vivid reminder of the danger that lurked unseen.

"Where's Thea?" Andre's voice cut through the air, a mixture of fear and determination woven into each syllable. "She was just here."

How could she be so close one moment and gone the next?

Stan grimaced, his expression a tapestry of pain and frustration. "Someone was inside and hit me. He ran away, and I came to find you. Where is she?"

The words hung heavy, pulling Andre into a harsh reality. The familiar warmth of the surrounding greenery, usually a sanctuary filled with the soft rustle of leaves and the gentle hum of bees, felt suddenly oppressive—the danger was anywhere. The distant chatter of birds seemed muted, the tranquil atmosphere disrupted by the moment's urgency.

Standing beside Andre, Mary gasped softly, her hand instinctively reaching for support.

Andre's mind raced the peaceful serenity of moments before, shattered by the intrusion of danger. The vibrant colors of the garden seemed to dull, the vivid greens and bright floral hues paling in comparison to the stark red of Stan's injury. Fear coursed through him, sharpening his senses and urging him to action.

Andre's resolve hardened, and the need to protect Thea overrode everything. His gaze met Stan's, a silent promise exchanged—a vow to find her, to ensure her safety amidst the chaos that had descended upon their world.

"Stan," Andre barked, urgency sharpening his voice.

Stan's eyes widened, darting between Andre and the space where Thea had been. Understanding dawned, stark and cold. "I'm going to find her."

He winced and Andre saw Stan's tension originated from his shoulder.

"I'm going."

"No, she is my sister."

She is my Thea. Andre gave Stan a hard look. "We're wasting time. And you're hurt, it'll slow you down."

Stan nodded, scooping Mary up with his healthy arm, her jar clinking as she clutched it tightly. "Take Mary. Get inside. Lock the doors. Don't open them for anyone." Andre watched them retreat toward Cloverdale House's orangery, the child's questions trailing behind them like specters.

"Where's Miss Thea?"

But Andre had already turned his back to Cloverdale House,

his gaze sweeping the park, taking in every shadow and whispering leaf.

"I'll find her," Andre called, but he was already running along the hedge, past the giant oak tree, and onto the open grassy part of the park.

He moved, each step purposeful, the ground firm beneath his feet yet somehow distant. The park stretched wide and empty, a labyrinth of paths and hedgerows. He ran, his breathing harsh and ragged, but he dared not call her name. He couldn't risk drawing attention, couldn't risk his capture because there wouldn't be anyone else to save Thea.

In the distance were a few men on horseback. Near the fountains, he could make out the silhouettes of women and parasols. But they couldn't have gotten that far with Thea.

The air was alive with the scent of damp earth, the faint, sweet perfume of wildflowers, and the bitterness that Thea was missing. The sun dipped lower, casting elongated shadows that danced across the grass. He pressed on, his senses honed, listening for any sign, any hint of movement that could lead him to her.

Ahead, a cluster of trees loomed like a dark giant with mysterious shadows, their branches whispering secrets he wasn't privy to. Like so much in his life, he was excluded from something that mattered. Andre slowed, his heart pounding a relentless rhythm in his chest. He paused, straining to hear beyond the quiet rustle of leaves.

A muffled sound, barely audible, reached his ears. He pivoted, the motion fluid and intuitive. His gaze locked onto a figure moving swiftly through the trees, and his heart clenched with recognition. He followed. Shielding his face from the branches, he stepped out of the park's sunlight into a corridor of darkness between the dense trees, his steps cushioned by the fallen leaves on the ground.

He hadn't seen much of the highwaymen when they traveled back to London, but he smelled liquor and sweat just as he had that night. It was the same man, at least one of them.

In the dim glow of the tree shadows, Andre strained his eyes to discern the figures standing too close to Thea. The air was thick with anticipation, and each breath was laced with the scent of damp stone and tree needles. His mind raced with calculations—how many was he up against? The shadows seemed to multiply, an indistinct mass that shifted between the trees in the distance.

He approached cautiously. Cold sweat slid down the back of his neck, the clammy dampness clinging to his skin like a second, suffocating layer.

It was then that he heard it—a slight gasp that sliced through the oppressive silence. The sound sent a tremor down his spine, unmistakable in its familiarity. It was Thea. He would know her voice anywhere, her breath's gentle rise and fall like a melody etched into his very soul.

Andre's heart hammered in his chest, a mixture of relief and dread colliding within him. His vision wavered, narrowing to a pinprick focus on the point of dread before him while the rest of the world dissolved into a distorted blur. There she was, emerging from the shadows, her movements a blend of grace and urgency that he had come to admire. The sunlight caught in her hair, casting a glow around her determined features, beads of sweat forming along her hairline. She looked terrified but held her gaze stern and her back ramrod. Andre had never admired her more, and for a moment, time seemed to hold its breath.

Flanking her were men whose intentions were as clear as the sharp glint of steel at their sides. The sight of these shadowy figures, their menacing and purposeful postures, ignited a fire in Andre's chest. The air seemed to hum with tension, and each second stretched taut with the threat of violence.

"I'm taking a turn," one of the men said.

"*Ich zuerst!*" Me first! The other pushed him.

That was the moment to strike.

Thea's wide and unyielding eyes met his, and Andre found the courage he needed in that silent exchange. The fear that had gripped him melted away, replaced by the need to protect her, for she became more important to him than his own life. The subtle rustle of fabric and the muffled footfalls of the approaching figures spurred him into action.

His foremost strength was that the men hadn't seen him yet.

Surprise was the best attack.

Every muscle in his body coiled with readiness, and his resolve settled over him like armor. The space between the trees seemed too narrow, focusing his attention solely on Thea and the danger surrounding her. The world beyond faded, leaving only the urgent rhythm of his heartbeat and his fierce drive to reach her and pull her away from the encroaching threat.

As he moved forward, the chill of the stone floor seeped through his boots, grounding him even as his spirit soared with the fierce need to protect. Andre's spot between the trees became a battlefield of wills—his resolve clashing against the shadowy figures that dared threaten Thea, the one he cherished most. Despite his aversion to violence, he knew it was the only means to save her.

He moved silently, using every ounce of stealth honed from countless days spent in Delhi's crowded bazaars. The ground softened beneath his feet, damp and yielding. His pulse thrummed wildly, propelling him onward.

As he closed the distance, he could see her struggle, the defiant tilt of her chin, the fire in her eyes. She fought against her captors, her spirit unyielding even in adversity.

"*Ihr Bruder wird schon nachgeben, wenn wir sie ein wenig abnutzen.*" Her brother will give in all right if we use her a little.

Andre understood every bit of the slurred German, nearly convulsed at the idea of those do-no-gooders laying a hand on Thea.

Still, he couldn't tell precisely how many there were, but there were at least two.

"*Ich will zuerst 'ran!*" Me first! A different voice called out, a slight Prussian accent clashing with the other.

"*Nöh! Zusmamen macht's mehr Spass!*" No, together is more fun! The first voice again.

Three drunkards, Andre thought. His stomach churned.

Then a squeal.

It was Thea. He'd seen and heard her distress.

Andre's breath caught a fierce pride swelling within him. There was no angle to surprise them, so he stepped into view, his presence a sudden, defiant interruption in the unfolding drama. One held Thea's arms behind her back, the other bent toward her far too close for Andre's taste.

Then, a twig broke with a loud crunch under his boot.

Fear flickered across the captors' faces, a hesitation that Andre seized.

Andre moved with precision, each strike intentional yet reluctant. He ducked under a wildly swung fist, delivering an elbow to the man's ribs before him. Even as his body responded with the speed and certainty of combat, his thoughts wavered, hoping that his blows were not causing irreparable harm. Though ruthless, these men were still human, and the nature of his heart was to heal, not hurt.

His eyes darted to Thea, standing at a distance, fear etched across her delicate features. That look drove him further, each punch and kick a vow to keep her safe. His instincts honed not for battle but for mending, now fueled his determination to protect the woman who had become so important to him.

The chaos of the fight seemed to stretch time, each moment heavy with consequences. Around him, the clash unfolded, but his focus remained unwavering—Thea was the only thing that mattered as he dodged another kick from his opponent's boot. In the heat of the fray, every heartbeat echoed with the urgency of his mission, his oath to shield her from harm.

Andre ducked beneath a swinging arm, his counterattack swift and decisive, yet his mind was plagued with the hope that his actions wouldn't leave lasting scars. The woods vibrated with the sounds of struggle, but Thea's presence grounded him, her safety his guiding star.

As he subdued each attacker, a path to Thea cleared, and with it, a realization. Protecting her was not only about defending her body but also about safeguarding the tender connection that had grown between them. And amid the violence he hated, Andre realized he never thought he would feel this deep need to protect someone other than his family.

And then, it was over. The captors fled through the thick foliage. Andre stood, chest heaving, his gaze locked on Thea. Relief crashed over him, leaving him momentarily weak. The dim glow of the low afternoon sun lingered between the trees, casting long shadows across the secluded clearing where Thea lay crumpled on the earth floor, her gown torn. Her sobs were muffled as though afraid to disturb the heavy silence that had settled after the chaos. Andre knelt beside her, his fingers brushing tenderly against the damp streaks on her cheek. His heart pounded not with the exertion of the battle but with the fury that still roared through his veins, demanding justice for the affront committed against her.

He didn't deserve her; he mustn't love her, but even he knew that he was the one to console and protect her because of how he felt.

"Are you hurt?" he asked.

Thea's eyes, wide and filled with panic and relief, met his. She furrowed her brow and then winced when she tried to stand up. She tried to speak, but words failed her, choked by the tremor of unspent fear. Her fingers clutched at his sleeve, seeking assurance that this nightmare was truly over. Andre's gaze softened, though the storm within him did not abate. He wrapped his arms around her, drawing her into the fortress of his embrace, where he vowed no harm would dare trespass again.

"May I carry you?"

She nodded. And then she burst into tears.

As Andre lifted Thea into his arms, the weight of her vulnerability pressed heavily upon him. Her slender frame trembled, and as she buried her face into the crook of his shoulder, he felt the warmth of her tears seep through his shirt. Each sob was a dagger of doubt, piercing his heart with the fear that perhaps he had not reached her in time, that her injuries were more grievous than they appeared.

The sun shone as if nothing had happened, as if it were normal to illuminate the brutality of the moments just passed, as he made his way toward Cloverdale House. He hated the violence that had brought them to this moment, the brutality that shattered peace and inflicted pain. Violence was a beast he despised, a force that left injuries both seen and unseen. Yet, he knew in his soul that sometimes, it must be confronted to protect what one holds dear. And from the violent encounter, he'd emerged with single-minded clarity: he, Dr. Andre Fernando von Dürer, was better for Thea than any man who'd hurt her—he'd lay his life down to ensure her safety. And even if he wasn't the one who deserved her, there wouldn't ever be another who'd cherish her as he did.

"Thank you!" Thea whispered.

"I vowed to protect you at all costs," Andre said, but he wasn't pleased with himself. He wondered if he could have done less damage in the heat of the moment. But that was the problem with violence. In the quiet, his voice emerged, a gentle murmur against the afternoon's chaos. "You're safe now." Each word was a promise, a vow as unwavering as the princess in his arms. He tightened his grip, feeling her heartbeat against his chest, a rhythm that reminded him of her fragility and his duty to safeguard her.

As they neared the house, its silhouette a looming sanctuary, he hoped that Thea's injuries were not severe. He could not bear the thought of her enduring further pain, regardless of whether it was physical or emotional. His mind clung to the singular truth that mattered: he would lay down his life to ensure her safety, to see her smile again, unburdened by the shadows of that day.

Chapter Seventeen

T HEA INSTANTLY REGRETTED it when Andre set her down after he locked the door behind them. It was absurd to think it at the moment, but when he'd cradled her in his arms and carried her to safety, she'd never felt more—it was challenging to think it—at home. Yes, that was the right way to think of it. She wasn't merely safe in Andre's arms, but felt like she'd arrived precisely where her path had led her. It may have seemed odd in theory, but practically—she felt it deep in her heart—she was meant to be close to him. And when he'd carried her, she became his.

Not because he touched her or because she'd risked—and perhaps succeeded in—getting compromised. That wasn't it at all. She became his as soon as he scooped her up in a moment of vulnerability and weakness, and she felt she'd never be alone with him. She'd never feel bare or insignificant because she was a girl—she was a princess and no fairy tale damsel in distress. With him, even in a moment of need, she was more. He hadn't patronized or removed her from danger because she couldn't defend herself—even though that was precisely what happened, it wasn't how Andre made her feel—instead, he'd asked if he could assist her. He left her in control and merely offered his support. All of that tact and humility after he saved her—there wasn't an aristocrat, her brothers included, who would have wanted to support her more than save her. It was a fine line, an insignificant

131

nuance to most, but it meant the world to Thea.

The handsome, tall doctor with a chest and shoulders as hard as wood, Thea thought when she wrapped her arm around Andre's neck. In the woods a few moments ago, she'd reeled in his closeness. This was different. He hadn't merely saved her; he was her protector in a way that it seemed he was doing it for himself more than her safety. She meant something to him, didn't she?

And he'd felt so good.

Wise.

Brilliant.

And oh, so close.

Thea realized she was still clutching Andre's arm and looked up at him. He was nearly one head taller but just the right height for their eyes to meet again.

And Thea's breath hitched when he blinked at her with those dark lashes as if he'd heard her thoughts.

"What happened?" Stan called out when Thea limped and held on to Andre's arm as they stepped into the orangery at Cloverdale House.

"Thea!" Mary cried as she threw herself against Thea's legs and hugged her tightly, nearly making her topple again. But Andre's arm was already on her back.

He offered his support.

Again.

And hopefully forever.

"Thea!" Stan called out in horror as he eyed her intensely.

"Andre came out of nowhere, and then he lunged at them. The taller one hit him, but Andre ducked." Thea heaved for air, but suddenly, tears came in a torrent of emotion when she realized what could have happened.

Oh, it was embarrassing to be so overcome with emotion, but now that she thought about the danger she'd been in, she hoped she may have just gotten away with her virtue and her life.

"I recognized one of them; it was the same man as in the

woods," Andre said. "A Prussian."

Stan froze and looked at Andre and Thea with resignation at first, but then it turned into fury. "They're attacking my family," Stan mumbled.

"They already did. Twice!" Thea winced when she tried to put weight on her leg.

"Come, I'll take a look," Andre said as he put one hand again on her back and the other under her bottom. Before she could say anything, Andre had lifted her into his arms.

He was carrying her. She liked it more than she cared to admit.

While Stan and Mary were momentarily ahead in the brief moment that they walked through the halls of Cloverdale House, Thea closed her eyes. Still in Andre's arms, she let the tension go. After one last deep breath, she managed to stop crying.

"If you hadn't come in time—" she started but choked on the horror that he saved her from.

His grip tightened, and he looked deeply into her eyes. "I wouldn't have stopped trying to find you."

"Until what?" Thea asked.

"Ever." Andre's voice grew serious, and there was a certain heaviness to it that spoke of deep sorrow. Just a few more doors down the hall, and they'd be in his treatment room. Thea had never been inside, but it was close and soon, he'd have to set her down. Too soon.

Of course, she loathed the circumstances of her injury, but being in this man's arms was like reaching for the stars and grabbing one. In touching him, she committed a transgression she could not ignore—she knew it all too well. Yet, as he carried her through the solemn halls of Cloverdale House toward his treatment room, the moment felt charged, as if she were stealing a forbidden chance to connect with Andre, one she could not bear to lose.

"Did they hit you?" Andre asked in a low voice as they followed Stan with Mary in tow.

"The taller one shoved me against the wall. I think that's when the sutures burst," Stan mumbled. He seemed in quite some pain.

As soon as they arrived in the treatment room, Andre gingerly set Thea down on the elongated treatment table and lifted her leg with one swift motion under her knee onto the edge. "Can you straighten it?"

She nodded.

"Good. Then it's probably not broken." Then he turned to Stan. "Can you open your shirt so we can clean the wound, please?"

"Where's Nurse Shira?" Mary asked.

Thea followed Andre's gaze to the small clock on the wall. "I think she left for the day. There's no time to send for her. Can you be my nurse?"

Mary inhaled with an air of encouragement and enterprise. "I'll ask a servant for water to rinse his shoulder."

Stan arched a brow at the little girl, but Thea was rather proud. Mary felt visibly useful and had learned so much since she'd come to London with Thea. Even though she was so tiny, she'd become her own person.

When Mary left, Stan spoke to Andre. "This is getting out of hand. I've notified my brother, and he's coming here." Then he turned to Thea. "Alex will arrive any day now. Together, we will confront List."

"May I?" Andre asked and touched her boot. "I need to examine your leg."

Thea cast a look at Stan, but he seemed unperturbed. Andre had his trust, and he was there, so Thea lifted her skirt and let Andre bare her leg.

SHE'S JUST LIKE *any other patient*, Andre tried to tell himself as Thea exposed her bare leg.

Just a woman like any other.

His insides churned as if every fiber of his being resisted what he tried to convince himself of.

She was a patient now, and he mustn't think of her as the most precious and beautiful woman on Earth—perhaps the whole universe.

The confines of the treatment room felt intimate, almost conspiratorial as if the walls were listening to their every breath. Andre stood before Thea, his gaze unwavering as he gently lifted the hem of her gown, uncovering the delicate curve of her leg. The sight of her skin, usually flawless ivory, now marred by a fresh bruise, sent a fiery rage coursing through his veins.

He'd imagined it at night, unveiling her beautiful legs. And they were perfect, long, feminine, smooth—precisely as he'd pictured and better—but the moment was overshadowed by her injury, forever stolen from the magic his gentle touch would have revealed. And that made him even angrier.

His fingers trembled slightly as they hovered above the discolored mark marring her knee. "Thea," he murmured when he palpated the bruise, his voice a deep rumble laced with barely contained fury, "does this hurt?"

She nodded.

He lay his hand on her knee, trying to soothe the pain that the criminals had inflicted.

"Can you bend your leg?" he asked, gently gripping the ankle and pushing it up.

She winced, but her range of motion did not diminish. "It's not broken."

"How long till it heals?" Stan asked from behind Andre, seemingly watching them together.

But Andre didn't want to hide his raw emotions anymore. "It will look terrible for a few days and then fade from blue to green to yellow."

"It's not worse than when I fell off the cherry tree at Bran," she said wistfully, but Stan shot her a piercing look, one reflecting the concern of a brother for his sister.

"It's very different. That was an accident back then, and you were nine. This was a crime against a member of the royal family." He swallowed. "And what's worse, it was another attack on my family. And for that, List shall pay. I need Alex here while my shoulder is healing."

Andre wondered what Stan planned that he needed his older brother Alex with him, but he knew it wasn't his place to ask.

Mary arrived, a metal bowl of water in her hands and a muslin towel over her shoulder. "I'm ready to tend to the princess," she declared solemnly, setting the bowl down.

"Mary, this is too small," Andre said but Stan had already come to Mary's side.

"There must be something else we can use. Take some of these muslins, please, Nurse Mary." The little girl beamed at Stan. "And then, could you help me to find my valet?" Stan asked and left before Andre could tend to him more, but he was grateful that his little nurse distracted Stan so that he could speak to Thea.

"I shouldn't have let this happen," he whispered.

She hesitated, her lashes fluttering as she sought the courage to speak. Her vulnerability sharply contrasted with the usual vivacity that danced in her eyes, a reminder of the violation she had endured. "They… they kicked me," she whispered, the words tumbling out, each one a dagger to Andre's heart. "When I bent over, they shoved me against a tree."

Andre's jaw tightened, and his neck muscles corded with tension as he fought to contain his emotions. The thought that those no-do-gooders touched her was insufferable, the reality spreading with bitterness in his throat so that he could hardly swallow, as if he couldn't allow the atrocities of the crime to sink in.

Her vulnerability drew him in and wrapped him in a protective haze that was both tender and fierce.

"I should have been there," Andre said, his voice a low growl of self-recrimination. "I promised to protect you, and I failed."

Thea reached out, her fingers cool against the warmth of his cheek. She tilted his head until his eyes met hers, luminous and steady despite the turmoil reflected within them. "You saved me, Andre. You found me when I was nearly lost to them."

"This will take a while to heal, and you're in pain." He shook his head as if he couldn't believe the horror of his words.

"It will heal, and it will be forgotten."

"I won't forget this, and neither will Stan."

"If this Prussian baron is so dangerous, I'd prefer that you both stay away from him instead of avenging a bruise by risking your lives."

Her words were a balm, soothing the raw edges of his guilt, yet the fire within him only burned hotter. He could not let this transgression go unanswered. The stakes had never been higher; the very core of his being demanded justice—demanded that he ensure such a threat could never reach her again.

Swallowing hard, Andre took a deliberate breath, his resolve hardening like steel. "They will pay for what they've done," he vowed, his voice barely more than a whisper, yet it resonated with the weight of an unbreakable promise.

Thea's fingers combed through his hair, a gesture meant to comfort but which only fueled the desire simmering beneath his skin. The proximity of her body, the scent of her mingling with the vial of arnica oil he uncorked, and the lingering adrenaline of their earlier ordeal were intoxicating. He longed to draw her closer and assure her of safety with more than words.

Her gaze softened, and she leaned forward, pressing her forehead against his. The contact was electric, a spark that ignited the air between them. "Andre," she breathed, her voice a soft caress. "I trust you."

The admission was a heady rush, more potent than the finest brandy, and it took every ounce of his self-control not to close the scant distance between their lips. He cupped her face in his hands, his thumbs brushing softly over her cheeks as if to memorize the texture of her skin, the shape of her resolve.

"I will never let anyone harm you," he declared, fiery and fierce. The promise hung between them, heavy with the weight of all it implied.

And that's why he had to stand back as he did.

"We've got water," Mary called from the door, but it was Stan who carried the heavy bowl.

And that distracted Andre from the heady feelings about the princess coursing through him. Mary got to work and started to rinse Stan's wound, but he guided her since her arms were too short to even reach up to his shoulder.

"You're an excellent nurse," Stan said and winked in Andre's direction with a patient-to-doctor look saying, "I can manage it, don't worry."

Stan appeared busy with the cold water Mary drizzled on his wound. Giving Andre a minute or two before tending to him. For the moment, he had to steady himself, for he almost grew weak and let his emotions get the better of him.

Thea's eyes shimmered with unshed tears, but there was a new light in them, a spark of hope that banished the embarrassment of her ordeal. She leaned into him, her breath mingling with his, and whispered, "I know."

At that moment, Andre and Thea were bound by a shared setback, and a passion that crackled like lightning around them. He lifted her hand to his mouth and pressed a tender kiss to her knuckle, a silent vow of protection and devotion.

And Andre reminded himself that he mustn't cross the line that would soil her with the touch of a bastard.

He couldn't do that to her; he loved her too much.

Chapter Eighteen

A NDRE'S ATTENTION LOCKED onto Thea's injuries, each wound a problem to be solved, and he forced him to suppress the anger toward the attackers. How dare they touch the princess, much less push her against a tree in the park. As much as he despised violence, there was no other response he had for blackguards like that.

The rhythm of his work—cleaning, assessing, bandaging— was a balm against the storm of conflicting emotions that churned beneath the surface. While he emptied and refilled the small wash basin with clean water and picked some gauze and clean towels from the cabinet, he found clarity, a reprieve from the questions that loomed unanswered in his life. Yet, beneath the calm exterior, a muted truth lingered: no matter how proficiently he navigated this world of healing, there would always be parts of his life that eluded his control—his heart among them. He resolved to confront those truths again as he worked, but only after ensuring Thea was safe and whole. For now, this was all he could focus on.

By the time Andre had applied the arnica tincture on Thea's leg and covered it with a wet cloth to cool it while she rested, Mary was sitting on Stan's lap, the bleeding wound forgotten, and Stan told her a story.

"She climbed every tree, I'm telling you; Mother said Thea

was more akin to a monkey than a princess."

Andre saw what Stan was doing and gave him a reassuring nod; the distraction of the patients was always a good idea to calm them and made the work for the doctor much easier, given that Andre had to close some of Stan's stitches again—even if it was the patient, Stan, distracting the little nurse.

Mary's eyes were wide with joyful admiration. "My Thea can climb trees?"

"I'm rather quick, too," Thea called from behind Andre, who'd retrieved a few small white muslin squares to tap Stan's wound clean. The stitches were still intact, and the wound closed. The strain of defending himself had made it bleed again. What concerned Andre was the redness around it and the small white pustule in the corner of the suture.

Infections of flesh wounds were common. The low-life criminals who didn't have anything better to do than to injure innocent and good people used such dull and dirty blades that he had seen patients die from the infections more often than the wounds themselves.

He wouldn't let this happen to his friend.

Andre touched Stan's forehead.

The prince was still feverish.

That explained why he didn't see the intruders sharply and why his reaction had been slowed.

"Stan, you need to rest so the infection can heal." Andre tried his sternest doctor voice, but getting the ton patients to do what he said was difficult, much less a prince.

"I'm fine," Stan said.

Andre cleared his throat. He didn't want to worry Thea, but he had to explain to Stan that this was more serious than he seemed to think.

"Miss Mary," Andre said, "I would be most obliged if you could ensure that our patient, the princess, keeps a healthy fluid balance so her knee can heal." Mary's eyes widened, her gaze focused and alert as she folded her hands in front of her.

"Yes, certainly."

"Can I entrust her to you?"

"Yes," Mary said as seriously as an adult on a mission.

"Thank you." Andre turned back to Stan.

But then he noticed that Mary stood primly and didn't say anything.

"Is something the matter?" Andre asked.

"To what do you entrust her to me?"

"To give her fluids."

"How?" Mary's mien darkened, and she frowned.

"Tea."

"Oh!"

"There's usually tea being served in the sunroom."

"Let's go," Thea told Mary, carefully sliding off the treatment cot and leaning on Mary with more ado than was necessary. "I feel so weakened; you may need to stir the milk in for me."

"Certainly, Miss Thea," Mary said dutifully. "I can do that for you. That's quite a scare you gave me when you up and disappeared."

Mary sounded so precocious; Andre would have laughed if the situation hadn't been so terrible.

"When you disappeared. There's no need for the preposition up."

"Yes, Miss Thea."

Thea nodded gravely and winked at Andre, who stifled a chuckle.

Adult patients created jobs for the little would-be nurse to feel good about herself. It should have been the other way around, but it would never have been; a child was always the priority.

Andre closed the door behind Thea and Mary when they left.

Now to the stubborn prince.

"Stan, this is serious and not a joking matter," Andre started.

"I know, I'm resting."

"The infection could worsen. It would be best to rely on your body's defenses to heal. Rest alone is not enough."

"I need my own nurse." Stan's eyes shot up at Andre. "Is Miss Folsham back?"

"Not yet. Nick and Pippa will probably arrive with Wendy any day now." Even though it was Stan who deflated, Andre could feel the weight lifting at the thought of his friends returning. "But you have to take this seriously. An infection could potentially become life-threatening."

"So can a broken heart." Stan quirked his brow.

And for a moment, Andre didn't know whether it was meant for him or Stan.

But it was true.

"I'm not in the business of breaking hearts," Andre said, resisting the sinking feeling that Stan could see into his heart and find the forbidden affection for Thea.

"You mend bones, I know. But some injuries in life ought to be prevented at all cost." Stan cast a look in the direction of the door that Thea had left through a few minutes earlier. "Look after her, please. I must face List and can't keep her safe when I am like this." Stan tried to move his shoulder but winced. "Please do this for me, Andre. Not as my doctor but as my friend."

Andre nodded. He'd look after Thea regardless of Stan's request.

"She's my only sister, and..."

"Understood."

Agreed. No other words were needed.

Andre thought about how Thea faced the men just minutes ago in the park. She held her head high and didn't show any fear.

Only when she was in Andre's arms did she cry a little.

Andre attempted not to show it but inwardly winced because he was charged with protecting Thea and her heart. Yet the two were at odds with protecting himself, and he knew his heart would shatter if he couldn't be with her—which he mustn't allow to happen—to protect her.

What a dilemma!

THEA STOOD BY the window at the far end of the hallway, the cool pane beneath her fingers grounding her as she stared into the darkened gardens. Somewhere beyond the glass, in the faint silver light of the moon, the world carried on as it always did, distant and indifferent. Inside, however, her thoughts whirled like an unruly storm. She had left Stan to rest, confident in Andre's care, but the uneasy weight of the day still pressed against her chest. Had she attracted those dangerous attackers and led them to Stan?

With a sinking heart, she thought so. Worse even, she'd been so selfish as to run from the groom her father had chosen, thereby fueling the conflict that seemed to target her brother and her own life.

It's all my fault.

Suddenly, the soft sound of approaching footsteps stirred the quiet. She didn't turn, though she knew who it was without question. Andre's presence was unmistakable, an awareness she couldn't explain but couldn't deny. Her breath caught, and her grip on the window tightened as the sound stopped short behind her.

"Thea." His voice was low, carefully measured, as it always was, yet something in its quiet timbre tugged at her.

She turned slowly, heart jolting at the sight of him. He stood just a few paces away, stiff with the sort of control that made her chest ache. She searched his face, taking in the faint shadows under his dark eyes, the set of his jaw, the tension in his shoulders. He held himself carefully, as though even the act of breathing might betray something he dared not reveal. Yet his eyes—they gave him away every time. There, in the fleeting moment before he schooled himself, she saw the look that tore at her. That unspoken softness seemingly reserved for her, restrained and yet achingly clear.

"You've spoken to Stan?" she asked quietly to match the stillness of the hall.

"Yes. He's resting now," he replied. "I hope so at least." His words seemed curt, his eyes now fixed just beside her—not meeting hers directly. She noticed the way his hands had clasped behind his back, and she bit back an odd sense of frustration.

"Well, thank you for looking after him," she said. "He needs to recover."

"I merely fulfilled my duty," Andre said quietly, his gaze fixed somewhere beyond her shoulder. "Nothing more." His stance remained rigid, unnatural. Didn't he know how much it hurt her to see him so formal, so impenetrable? Or perhaps he had to. Perhaps he didn't allow himself to think beyond the rules and expectations that seemed to govern his every action.

When he didn't speak, Thea hesitated before softly asking, "And me, then? Have you come to watch over me, as Stan requests?" She tried for a touch of levity, but her voice faltered slightly.

"You shouldn't be wandering the halls alone until we put some guards in place," Andre said after a pause, his gaze shifting briefly to hers before darting away again. Even that single moment brought a heat to her cheeks she couldn't suppress.

"I'm hardly wandering," she replied, unable to keep the note of defense from her tone. She hated how small her voice sounded just then. "Is there so much danger lurking everywhere I go?"

His lips parted, but no answer came straightaway. Instead, his brow furrowed, and his expression became unreadable—a mask, yet one that seemed to pull tighter with every second. The longer he remained silent, the worse it felt, her stomach tying itself into cold, uneasy knots.

When he finally spoke, there was a stiffness in his voice that stung. "This day has been taxing. You ought to rest."

Thea's breath caught at the gentleness underneath his firm words. But it wasn't enough—not when the strain in his body and voice said so much more. "I don't want to be alone," she admitted quietly. "Could you stay with me?"

His gaze snapped back to hers then, and for a painful, fleeting moment, she thought she saw the true weight of it all—his turmoil, his restraint, his deep, unspoken affection. She stepped closer without meaning to, her skirts brushing the polished floor, her pulse quickening.

"It wouldn't be proper." His voice came low and heavy, as though the very words bore the weight of the impossibility that lay between them.

"Why do you do this?" she asked, her voice no louder than a whisper. "Why do you insist on placing walls where they are not needed?"

Andre stiffened, clearly unnerved at her approach. He dropped his gaze—a flicker downward that lingered for an instant too long before he caught himself again. Thea felt both exposed and dismissed in that single moment. She stopped, her cheeks burning, her heart wavering. Why wouldn't he speak? Why couldn't he simply look at her and acknowledge what simmered between them, what had grown in the silence of these moments where his restraint had failed to hide him completely?

"You are a princess," Andre said evenly, though the words felt brittle. "Your safety… your station… these things are not subjects of—"

"Of what?" she interrupted, her voice faltering but insistent. "Of choice? Of my own decision?"

His expression shifted again—tighter, colder. "Your station demands… Much. Forgive me for intruding upon it. I would not dare—should not dare to drag you down to my level."

"Down?" Her voice came shriller than she'd intended. "Or do you mean up to the man who saved me today. Who's standing with my brother and me against this impossible Baron von List who's sabotaging everything nobility stands for?"

But Andre didn't meet her gaze. So she continued even though her heart dropped further than she thought possible, the carefully erected hope she'd clung to crumbling beneath the weight of his formal reply. "You have seen only the part of the threatened princess in my life, Andre. But there's more than—"

"None of it is for me to see." It seemed as though he couldn't even give her his true feelings masked in those words—only half-measures meant to protect her, or perhaps himself.

"I see," she said softly, swallowing back the sting of tears as she stepped back. "Thank you for reminding me where I stand, Andre."

"It would not be proper," he said, his voice low and heavy, as though the very words bore the weight of the impossibility that lay between them. "We mustn't…" Andre faced the wall, hung his head, and she didn't hear the rest of what he mumbled.

Thea turned quickly, her skirts brushing the floor with a soft whisper, intent on escaping before her composure fractured entirely. Yet as she reached the shadowed corner of the hall, she hesitated, glancing back despite herself. The light from the wall sconce flickered faintly, illuminating Andre where he stood—or rather, where he leaned now, his back pressed against the cold stone. His head tipped forward, his hand gripping the wall beside him as though bracing against the burden he carried. His broad shoulders, always so resolute, sagged under the weight of some unseen anguish. His jaw tightened, but his eyes betrayed him, dark with a tempest of emotions he seemed unable—or unwilling—to release.

From the shadows, Thea watched, her breath caught in her throat, her heart splintering as she tried to make sense of the sight before her. He was not merely composed or withdrawn, as he often made himself in her presence. No, he appeared unraveled, broken in a way that made her chest ache. She had done this. She was certain of it. Her presence, her foolishness, her very existence seemed to bring danger to him and cause pain.

The memories pounced on her like wolves—twice now, the danger that had burst into her life had caught him too. Andre, steady and loyal, had been pulled into the fray not out of duty but because of her. The attackers had seen her weakness, and in their threats, Andre had stood by her side, his life entangled with hers in ways it never should have been. She was a princess, born to a world of privilege but also peril, and he—he was a healer who sought to mend, not to bear the brunt of her troubles. Yet here he was, suffering in silence, crushed by emotions he would never allow himself to voice.

Because of her.

Her fingers trembled where they gripped the edge of the hallway's frame. She wanted to go to him, to speak, to say something—anything—that might ease his torment. But the weight of what she'd seen rooted her in place, guilt pressing down until the idea became impossible. How could she apologize for what could not be undone? Could she unlove the man who'd captured her heart?

No, she realized, her stomach twisting as tears pricked her eyes. She was not good for him. She brought him nothing but danger—and, worse still, despair.

Unseen in the darkness, she lingered a moment longer, her heart unable to look away even as her mind screamed that she must. Then, turning once more, Thea slipped into the stairwell, the soft fall of her footsteps swallowed by the stillness of the night.

ANDRE STOOD IN the quiet hallway, unmoving except for the rise and fall of his chest. He could no longer hear Thea's footsteps and the rustling of her dress. He pressed his hand flat against the cold stone of the wall for even the elegant wallpaper barely hid the hard bricks underneath. His fist was still trembling from both the force of his earlier blow and the raging turmoil within him. Although his knuckles burned in fiery protest, he barely felt it compared to the hollow ache deep in his chest.

The faint echo of Thea's retreating steps still haunted his ears, though she was gone now, vanished into the shadowed halls. He could picture her even now—her slender shoulders stiff with unspoken emotions, her skirts gliding against polished wood, each step purposefully quiet yet heavy with meaning. She had turned from him not just physically but emotionally, and he could feel that distance as surely as a blade had come between them. And it was his fault. He had driven her away.

Andre turned to lean his forehead against the wall, the cool surface grounding in a way the air could not. He squeezed his eyes shut, willing the relentless pounding of his thoughts to still themselves. Stan was just two doors down, close enough to catch any noise—close enough to make all of this unbearably real. Thea had only just walked out of sight, and he could not risk her hearing him break apart in the hallway like a man undone. He owed a princess, at the very least, his restraint.

But his heart did not listen, and neither did his body. The dull throb in his knuckles wasn't enough to release the tension coiled in his stomach, nor was bracing himself against the solid wall. He wanted to hit it again, to feel something sharper, something clearer. He wanted to shatter the thoughts spiraling through his head, dragging him down into a futile, aching place where his longing for her rose undeniably against every shred of logic.

He couldn't move forward—she had left. He wouldn't follow her.

His promise to Stan was a cord wrapped tight around him, binding him not to his emotions but to his word as a man. Protect Thea. Look after her. Ensure she was safe at all costs—that had been Stan's request, given to him in trust. Andre had taken them to heart, perhaps too much so. But what choice did he have now? To fail at that charge, even for a second, was unthinkable. And to compromise her in any way—even just to tell her what simmered inside him—would be the worst betrayal of all.

Thea was a princess. Her title was not a mere formality; it was her entire identity, built on the expectations of a world far above his own. And he—he was no prince. Medicine was his calling, but it was also his boundary, defining him more concretely than any title could. He was not a lord or even a gentleman of means. He had no estate, no legacy aside from the patients he patched back together one broken limb or feeble cough at a time.

What could he offer her? The answer came as quickly as it always did—nothing. Worse than nothing. A life with him would reduce her to obscurity, to whispers from the court and wagging tongues that would follow their union ruthlessly. A doctor's wife. A princess who had abandoned all she was born to for a man who could boast little beyond his skill with stitches. It wasn't just scandalous; it was impossible.

He pressed his aching fist lightly to his forehead, his pulse thrumming in his ears. And yet, even knowing all that, even with the clarity of every reason why he must not—he could not—his mind betrayed him. It betrayed him with the memory of her warmth, her frame pressed to his side as she had sought him for comfort only days ago. He could remember it too clearly, the way her breath had brushed against his neck, the feel of her head resting so lightly against his shoulder. It had been an accident of necessity, a fleeting moment that should have passed like mist. But instead, it lingered, as vivid now as if it were happening again. The weight of her had steadied him and set him aflame all at once.

She sought his closeness and protection. *Him.*

What if she likes me back?

Andre swallowed hard, fighting against the swell of emotion that threatened to choke him. Thus, he drew back from the wall and rubbed at the dull ache spreading through his hand. He had not meant to strike it as he had, just as he had not meant to ache for Thea as he did. But his control slipped further every day. The promises he made to himself—to keep his distance, to do only what was necessary—they were eroding faster than he could rebuild them.

His shadow stretched long against the wall as he turned to gaze down the hall once more, toward the silent stairwell where

Thea had disappeared. The thought struck him then, painfully clear, like stepping into frigid water—what did it matter if he burned for her, if his chest ached and his stomach twisted with longing? It changed nothing.

Only *she* could change *everything*—if she liked him back.

With shaking breath, he clenched his hands into fists again, forcing himself to feel the ache, to bind his emotions within those raw, bruised knuckles. Thea deserved far better. She deserved the life waiting for her, the suitors who could offer her gowns and jewels and castles. She deserved stability, honor, ease—even if Andre himself hated thinking that no other man might fulfill that role. It did not matter what he wanted. He could never earn the privilege of standing beside her, not in this life. All that mattered to him was what she wanted.

Chapter Nineteen

Cloverdale House, later that evening...

THEA FOUND THE upholstered chairs too hard as she sat beside the flickering light of the hearth, her posture straight, her hands folded neatly in her lap. The ticking of the clock on the mantel marked the hour with a steady rhythm, each tick a reminder that it was now past eight and soon Mary's bedtime, but Thea still didn't want to be alone. She glanced at Mary, sprawled on the thickly patterned rug, diligently brushing her toy cat's painted-on fur with a tiny brush. The girl's soft hum of concentration filled the otherwise quiet parlor at Cloverdale House.

"Do you think she misses me?" Mary asked without lifting her eyes from her self-imposed campaign. Her dark curls, like her mother's, tumbled over her face.

Thea hesitated. Mary's tiny fingers paused, hovering over her toy cat, Lady Felicity Whiskers. The fire cracked, sending a sharp pop like an inconvenient truth Thea couldn't ignore.

"I think your mother has been very busy supporting your father's growing business," Thea replied carefully, smoothing her skirt over her knee to avoid Mary's gaze. It was the same answer she'd given before.

Mary sighed, her shoulders slumping. "She said the traveling was exhausting, so she didn't take me along. If she dislikes it so much, why must she go?"

A thorn of frustration pricked Thea's chest. Of course, a child of six could not yet untangle the delicate, relentless strands of social obligation. For Mary, all that mattered was the mother she rarely seemed to see—a mother who avoided goodnight kisses for the promise of brief exchanges in candlelit ballrooms.

"Sometimes," Thea said slowly, "ladies must do things they'd rather not because it's expected of them. You'd do well to remember that when you're older."

Mary snorted—an utterly unladylike sound that made Thea fight the urge to chuckle. "When I'm older, I'll remember not to marry a man I don't know. I want to be exactly like you!"

Surprise unfurled in Thea's chest, warm and disarming. Oh dear! What she'd tried to teach Mary didn't seem half as important as the example she set.

"Like me?" Thea asked, her voice softer than she intended. She leaned forward as if moving closer; she might better understand Mary's bright, earnest expression.

Mary didn't hesitate, her head bobbing with unwavering confidence. "Of course. You don't have to do what anyone else says. You read all those books, and you know so many things. You're brave, too. I can tell even when you're in danger. And you use everything you know to follow your heart."

Thea's throat tightened, and she glanced down at the toy cat in Mary's hands, the cluster of patterns on the rug underneath.

"Oh, Mary," she murmured, searching for the right words. How could she explain that her bravery wasn't a choice but a necessity? That her independence bore a cost that no child could—or should—envision? That she hadn't followed her heart as much as run away from her fears?

If I followed my heart, I'd go to Andre.

"You know, Mary, it's what you know and what your parents give you that you will take on any adventure in life."

Mary blinked as if she didn't understand. "My parents never take me with them on adventures. They left me with you."

"Yes, and it could be much worse, you know."

"I do. But they don't know that I have my very own princess." Mary rose and climbed onto Thea's lap. "And I want to be a secret princess just like you."

I wouldn't wish that it upon anyone.

When Mary put her little hand on Thea's cheek in such an honest gesture of affection and admiration, Thea nearly burst into tears. Stan had been right; she'd missed a chance to help her family secure their geopolitical standing. The girl's usual bubbly enthusiasm was fleeting, though, and soon enough, her head rested heavily on Thea's shoulder. "I can't even remember the last time Mama stayed to hear about my lessons." Her whisper was quiet, yet it carried across the room as if the walls bore witness.

Thea felt a familiar ache open in her chest whenever she made excuses for Mrs. White. She could not say what Mary wanted to hear, no matter how much she longed to put the girl's mind at ease. And yet, Mary deserved honesty, or as much as Thea dared offer. She picked a blue coverlet that hung over the back of her chair and wrapped it around Mary.

"It's not because you've done anything wrong," Thea said when her voice felt steady enough. She reached out, brushing a stray curl from Mary's temple. "Your lessons are perfectly fine. You're clever, and your mother knows it. I keep a record, and she can read about your achievements when she returns."

Mary nodded, sucking in her upper lip. "But you did something wrong. You scared me today."

"Me?" Thea feigned ignorance, but it was plain to see that Mary was worried when Andre brought her back to Cloverdale House. Mary nestled against Thea, and even though it was more than her role as governess allowed, Thea hugged her little ward.

"Were you and my brother very worried about me?"

Mary nodded.

"Don't tell anyone, but he worries too much. Our father always says that. He sent him to learn from the greatest military strategists, and when Stan came back, he came back with a deeper understanding of his worries than what Father had expected."

"What did he expect?"

"Bravery, probably. A warrior spirit and courage." Where to begin with a list of Father's expectations that she and her siblings rarely lived up to.

"I think he's wrong." Mary straightened but remained on Thea's lap.

"Prince Ferdinand is wrong?" *How refreshing!* Thea couldn't stop the smile now. She would like to see her father's face when Mary gave him one of her common-sense lessons. "Tell me."

"For one, one should understand the dangers before going on an adventure. That's what Mother said to me. She didn't know where the business trips could take her and Father, so she didn't want to take me along."

That gave Thea pause, for it was uncanny, and yet she'd not even considered the consequences of running away herself. "What else do you think is wrong with it?"

"Something is missing." Mary had her precocious tone again. "The room for love."

"Room. For love." Thea felt her eyebrows shoot up, but she couldn't hide her surprise.

"Yes, it takes up so much of the heart. I saw the book with the human heart in Andre's office, and the ribcage is made of hard bones that keep all the love inside safe."

If Thea had an answer, she would have given it. She smoothed her hand down Mary's cheek instead.

"An excellent plan," Thea said, unable to hide her smile. "How does one make room then?"

Mary looked at her, her blue eyes glinting in the firelight. Thea snugly tucked the pale-blue coverlet around Mary's shoulders, smoothing it with deliberate precision.

"That's enough stalling, Mary. It's time for bed," she said, her tone gentle but firm.

Mary wrinkled her nose. "I'm not stalling, Miss Thea," she said with an innocence only a child could muster. Yet her hands clung to the edge of the coverlet, her fingers curling into the soft fabric.

Before Thea could press her further, the door opened quietly. She turned quickly, her hand still resting on the blanket. Andre stepped inside, his gaze sweeping the room, sharp and alert as always. "Pardon my intrusion, but is there anything else you need before I go to sleep?" he asked, his voice steady, though softer than usual.

Thea blinked, caught off guard. "You're not leaving tonight?" she asked, straightening instinctively.

"No," Andre replied calmly, stepping further into the room. "I'll sleep in my office here in case you or Stan need me. There are servants at every door standing guard, too."

Though she masked it, a flicker of relief passed through Thea, nodding once. "That's… reassuring," she said, though she wasn't entirely sure whom she was trying to reassure—Mary or herself.

"Can you tuck me in?" Mary asked suddenly, her tiny voice breaking the stillness. She looked up at Andre, her wide blue eyes filled with hope.

Andre hesitated for only a moment before nodding. "Of course," he said, stepping closer to Mary and picking her up.

Apparently, Thea wasn't the only female who enjoyed it when Andre carried her.

Thea shifted slightly to give him space, watching as he crouched beside Mary and took her in his arms. Within minutes, he'd carried her upstairs, and Thea led the way.

Once Mary was in bed, he adjusted the blanket where it had slipped near her feet, tucking it securely along her sides. His hands, always so purposeful, now moved with care Thea hadn't expected.

"There," said Andre, sitting back slightly on the edge of Mary's bed as he met Mary's gaze. "All set. Goodnight, little princess."

"Goodnight," Mary murmured, a sleepy smile tugging at her lips.

Thea reached out, brushing a curl from Mary's temple, her

fingers light and brief. "Sleep well," she said softly, her eyes lingering on the child as her breathing began to even out.

"Now you have two princesses to protect," Mary mumbled, her eyes closed already.

⟫✦⟪

ANDRE STRAIGHTENED; HIS heart did that unsettling leaping again, and his gaze met Thea's.

Two princesses to protect.

For a moment, neither spoke. Then Thea stepped back quietly, letting the warmth of the chamber settle around them.

"Thank you," she said at last, her voice low enough not to wake Mary.

Andre inclined his head. "If you need anything, you know where to find me."

She nodded, watching as he turned to leave the room as quietly as he'd entered. Thea lingered for a moment longer, her eyes falling on Mary's peaceful face. Then, with a final glance at the sleeping child, she carefully closed the door behind her.

Don't even think about staying in the dark hall with her.

Go away.

Andre halted because his upbringing required the lady—the princess—to walk before he did. And yet, he knew he shouldn't linger near her because it was so hard not to look at her. He shuffled uncomfortably and then nodded again. To her, he was just a doctor. Surely, missteps in etiquette could be excused.

"Andre, wait!"

He deflated.

But, of course, he stayed.

Anything for my princess.

"I just don't want to be alone." Thea wrung her hands and came to Andre's side, eyeing him with the innocence of a woman who surely didn't know how alluring she was, especially not in the dim light under the flickering wall sconces in the halls.

Note to self: Tell Nick and Pippa that brighter hallway lighting will be needed at Cloverdale House.

Before Andre could suggest something prudent, bright perhaps, such as enlisting Stan for a nightcap to help Thea sleep, she closed the distance and whispered in his ear. "Mary said the funniest thing, that my father is wrong." Thea chuckled. "If it weren't the words from a child or if I said such a thing, it would be bordering on treason."

Andre got goosebumps from the butterfly touch of Thea's breath close to his neck, and he tilted his head to face her.

Bad move.

Her eyes were aglow, and she licked her lips.

Andre was instantly hard.

"Let's walk a little." He gestured toward the staircase. *Take her to your office. Sit at opposite sides of the desk, putting three feet between you and her.*

"Could you show me the orangery?" Thea asked as she descended the stairs and was only two steps ahead.

"Surely, you've seen it, haven't you?"

"But I'd like to know more about the plants. Perhaps I can teach Mary there tomorrow. I'd rather not venture to the park again."

Andre's chest tightened again when he recalled the danger in which he had found Thea only hours before.

"The orangery has a lock inside the door that leads out. Let's make sure it's closed."

And so they walked downstairs and through the quiet halls of Cloverdale House. Her proximity sent an unrelenting awareness through him, his body taut with a tension he couldn't name. Every fiber of him seemed drawn to her—her warmth, her subtle lavender scent, the unintentional softness of her presence that lingered like a touch.

When they arrived in the glass-encased building of the orangery, beads of water ran down the large windows. A servant rose from a stool next to the only door leading to the park.

"Dr. Fernando, how can I assist you?"

Don't leave us alone.

His hands itched with the memory of holding her, of feeling the fragile strength beneath the silk of her gown, the way her lithe figure had molded so briefly against him. She wasn't just alluring—though even in the simplest attire, she could command his full attention. No, she was something far more impossible to resist. There was a vulnerability in how her hand trembled just slightly when she brushed back a loose strand of hair from her cheek, leaving him inexplicably undone.

"I need to speak with Dr. Fernando alone, please," Thea said.

The princess wishes it, and I will oblige.

With anything.

The servant bowed, and Andre took a step back.

Every time he touched her, a jolt shot through his veins that nearly magnetized him, forcing him to get closer to her even though he mustn't.

When the servant had left, Thea walked through the rows of raised beds and brushed her fingers over the foliage of the many plants. "What are these potted ones? Their leaves look like citrus."

"Oranges and lemons," Andre remained a raised bed away at a safe distance. Thea nodded as if she knew the answer.

Is she testing me?

"And these?" she asked, pointing at a tall, prickly plant that looked like an octopus extending its tentacles into the air.

"Aloe Vera. It's not a cactus," Andre said. "It's used for its soothing properties on skin irritations and burns. The juice is gelatinous and can be applied directly."

He was ready for the next question from Thea, the governess. He could protect Thea, the princess. But he knew he couldn't withstand Thea, the woman.

She seemed most interested in being alone with him and had dragged him to where there were only the plants as their witnesses, confusing Andre's interpretation of her intentions.

Unless she liked him back…. The thought lingered in his mind. *She didn't have any intentions. Stay away from her. Basta!*

"Are any of these useful for my brother?"

Ah, she was being the concerned sister. Andre exhaled deeply. Speaking to her as Stan's doctor was indeed the easiest path forward.

"Neem is helpful." He pointed at a little tree with the elongated, jagged leaves.

"I've never heard of neem," Thea said as Andre came to her side and picked a leaf.

"It tastes bitter, but the powdered leaves promote healing, cleansing of the blood, and speed up the healing of wounds."

Thea took the leaf from him and held it to her mouth.

"No, don't eat it," he murmured, his voice low and laced with concern. Gently, his hand encircled hers, the warmth of his touch slowing her impulsive gesture. "The leaves need to be dried first. As they are, they could upset your stomach."

She stilled under the firm yet tender hold of his fingers. Her gaze slowly lifted to meet his, questioning but unguarded.

"And you care if my stomach turns?" she whispered with a hint of a teasing smile, though her voice trembled faintly.

He smiled—a small, earnest thing, like a secret between them. "I care about more than that."

Her breath caught, the air between them charged yet unspoken. She allowed her hand to rest loosely in his grasp, her lips curving into a delicate smile of surrender. "Then I suppose I'll trust you… about the leaves."

Their eyes lingered, the moment unexpected yet filling the space with more than words could hold.

Don't engage. Look away.

Pick a flower for her.

No!

"I overheard a part of your conversation with Mary," Andre said.

Thea curled her lips downward, and Andre wanted nothing

more in this instant than to kiss the sadness away.

"She's a deep thinker but still a child. I can't tell her how I failed my family."

He studied her as if her words carried the weight of a secret she had yet to share. "Thea, you didn't fail," he said softly, his fingers lingering near hers as though afraid to break their fragile connection.

She looked away. "You don't understand how we were raised," she murmured, her voice barely above a whisper.

I do—more than you know.

But he couldn't tell her that he was a Habsburg bastard. She didn't want a Habsburg prince, so how could he ever measure up?

"Stan was… everything good that came from our family. He bore all their expectations so easily, so gracefully. I… I stumbled with the most important of all steps." Thea flattened her lips.

Silence stretched between them for a moment, heavy but not uncomfortable, like a shared breath before confession.

Andre leaned closer, his tone gentler now. "Thea, strength isn't always measured by how easily you carry the weight. Sometimes, it's about continuing, even when it feels impossible. And that… that is where I see you."

Her eyes flicked back to his, surprise mingling with something unspoken. "You're kind to say that," she said, her lips curving into a bittersweet smile. "But you saw how he endured—how he fought, even when he feared for my life. He's defending our family here in London. Stan is… perfect. Even in his weakness, he is perfect."

Andre shook his head slowly, his gaze unwavering. "Perfection doesn't make a man loved, Thea. You think your parents placed value only on what he could endure, but true love—it's what remains when all the expectations fall away. And I would wager they saw that in you, too, even if you couldn't feel it."

She startled slightly as though his words had brushed against a truth she'd tried to hide. Her voice softened. "I don't know if I'll believe that. Perhaps not for a long time."

He gave her a faint smile, his thumb brushing her wrist—a deliberate, grounding touch. "Then I'll believe it for you until you can."

"What makes you so sure?" she asked.

"My family. They loved me so much, and that love risked their lives. So I had to leave."

"You left out of love?" She narrowed her eyes. "It's as absurd as it is painful, I imagine." Her eyes glistened, but instead of tears, something lighter was in her expression. "You have a most peculiar way of making me feel as if I'm not utterly hopeless," she admitted, a delicate laugh escaping her lips.

He straightened slightly but did not release her hand. "Maybe that's because you aren't." Then, after a pause, his voice shifted, a hint of teasing returning to lighten the moment's weight.

"Now, tell me—did Stan grimace as much as you think he did when he swallowed that neem?"

Thea laughed more freely this time, her fingers tightening slightly around his. "Oh, he grimaced all right. You could tell from the twitch of his nose. But still, he swallowed all of it."

"I'm sure I'd disappoint again if I had to," she said, her smile faltering again.

"But you never did anything to disappoint him!"

"I did! In disappointing Father, I let them all down. After all these years of training to dance, to study French etiquette, to write to ladies in waiting at every notable royal court in Europe, and the countless lessons in pianoforte, mathematics, Latin, French, German, English, and the many, many fittings for dresses so that I always look presentable—after everything, I didn't want to do the one thing my family expected from me."

"Marry Prince Ralph?"

"It was all Father needed me for."

"Thea, you make it sound like your father doesn't love you."

"Not for who I am, no. He loved presenting me as a pretty and well-cultivated bargaining chip. He was proud of all the promise I embodied, my ability to perform my role as the dutiful daughter, and especially the fact that I succeeded."

"Because you're smart."

"But that's not what he sees. Never did! And it's not enough to make him smile at me anymore. Do you know that he avoided eye contact after I refused to dance with Prince Ralph at the ball?"

Andre shook his head.

"It was the result he wanted and the steps leading there," she continued. "When I said I'd refuse Ralph when he came to the ball, Father looked at me as if he'd lost me. But in reality, I lost my father that night."

Her voice wavered, the bitterness seeping through each word. "He never saw me as Thea, just the sum of what I could achieve for him, his ambitions, his plans. When I chose for myself something that didn't align with his vision, it wasn't just disappointment in his eyes—I saw disdain. That night, I realized he never truly knew me, and maybe he never wanted to. He just wanted his perfect bargaining chip, and I could never be that, not if it meant losing who I am."

If only you knew how badly I'd like to catch you.

TEARS WELLED UP in Thea's eyes as the memories flooded back. "Every time I tried to talk to Father after that, it was like speaking to a wall. He wouldn't listen, wouldn't see me. I thought our love was conditional, based on his dreams, not mine. It broke me, knowing I'd never be enough for him."

"Why didn't you tell him how you felt?" Andre asked gently.

"I did. He didn't accept it. He said he couldn't hear it anymore; he couldn't suffer the pain."

"The pain to hear how *you* felt?"

"Yes, he didn't acknowledge my feelings at all. The effect my failure had on him, not how I fared, was too much for him to bear. And every time he laid eyes on me, I saw the sorrow and the disgust. My presence weighed on him. So I left."

"That's not possible, Thea. It's just not—"

"Oh, but he said so! I trapped him at Bran Castle without hope of establishing the rights for the monarchy."

"What?" Andre grimaced.

"Well, think about it. Since I didn't make the liaison with the Habsburg family possible, he will continue to fight the rivalry among everyone who wants a hold of the region."

"Or you fueled it further," Andre mumbled.

"Exactly. I could have prevented it, but I made it worse. And Stan knows it, too. That's why he called Alex for help."

Andre crossed his arms and looked at the gas lamp hanging from the center of the orangery as if the solution to the dilemma could float down from the light source and brighten the future ahead.

"But he's your father, he loves you. There ought to be more understanding."

"Love and hate are close, and the pain I caused him was too great. I tipped the scale and used up the love he had. What's left is something else that runs deep, but it's not love."

"How do you know that's true? Perhaps you need time to heal the wounds. Surely, he won't put the connection with the Habsburg family over his daughter."

His words sank into her, slow and steady, like the warmth of the fire in his eyes reaching her heart. How could he see the fractures in her practiced composure so clearly? Even those she'd worked so hard to smooth over? And why was it so easy to talk to him?

"He already has. How he looks at me—you weren't there, but it was with such disgust." Thea's voice cracked, her eyes burning with tears.

Andre reached out and took her hand, squeezing it gently. "Maybe there's still hope, Thea. Maybe with time, he'll come to understand."

She shook her head, the pain evident in her expression. "I

don't think so. It's like everything I ever did right vanished in that single moment of defiance. He can't see past his disappointment to recognize my pain. I'm a living disappointment, not a daughter with valid sentiments." Thea's voice dropped to a whisper, her emotions pressing down upon her.

"Shouldn't you go home and resolve this misunderstanding?" he asked as if her answer could decide his fate along with hers.

"Don't you think I tried?"

Thea sighed. "All winter, I tried. Every attempt to reconcile was met with resistance, like I'm wounding him anew every time I speak. Mother shields him, protects his broken heart from the truth I carry. She's become this barrier, constantly reminding me to keep my emotions in check, not to upset him further."

"He's under a lot of pressure. That's why Stan came to England and is trying to resolve the problem with the gold mines. And Baron von List is blocking every bit of progress, isn't he?" Andre asked.

"And threatening us now. He even endangered Mary when he sent his—"

"I agree that the Prussian attackers probably came from him, but can we be certain?"

"Alex will help us to find out."

"And if your brothers resolve the problem with the gold mines, it would set you free?"

"Nothing would set me free, Andre. I've lost value as a bargaining chip. I'm a promissory note for a broken promise."

"Where do they think you are? How are they covering for your loss of…"

"Reputation? You can say it, Andre. I suppose they told a lie. Perhaps I'm shopping for dresses in Vienna or taking voice lessons at the opera in Budapest." Thea gestured as if the lies her parents would tell to explain her failures away could be as vast as the ocean.

I don't care anymore.

Andre narrowed his eyes. She realized he believed her despite trying to downplay the rift between her and their father. Yet, he listened to her feelings and stayed loyal to Stan. Andre was an upstanding man in every sense. And she trusted him wholeheartedly.

"Those last few months at home were like walking on shattered glass, trying to navigate a familiarity where my very essence was too painful for them to bear. The conversations that could mend our broken bonds are the ones they refuse to have. And every time they push me away, it breaks my heart again."

Thea's breath hitched as she continued, "I see their avoidance, the way they divert the subject or leave the room when I try to open up. It's as if my feelings are a poison they can't tolerate, and they are the victims of my bad choices."

"But this was the first choice you ever made. You've always been the exemplary daughter, haven't you?"

For the first time, she felt a flicker of hope. Maybe she wasn't entirely alone in this world. Even though she wasn't sure how to continue, the excitement and possibilities were much more encouraging than a life shackled to a Habsburg Prince she didn't like.

And then someone came to mind she thought she might like quite a lot.

Chapter Twenty

ANDRE DIDN'T WANT to be the next bad choice in Thea's life. The weight of her past, the quiet pain that lingered in her words, was enough to make him tread carefully. Yet care wasn't something he could give sparingly, not to Thea—or her family.

After their conversation in the orangery the previous night, Andre couldn't sleep and stayed with Stan, who'd been shivering beneath the thin covering, his skin pale and clammy. Andre knew hesitation had no place there. The fever had worsened, and the wound—raw and angry looking—had deepened its hold. Any delay was a risk he could not allow.

Thea came to look after her brother in the morning when Andre stepped out to get the post, and more ice for Stan's wound. Returning to Cloverdale, he went to call on Stan.

"I sent a message to the others. Soon, we will have a backup at Cloverdale House and the practice. I'm not going to let Thea out of sight," Andre told his friend when he woke up.

"Did Alex send word? Is he coming?" Stan asked. Beads of sweat from the fever ran down his forehead, but he shivered through the cold chills.

"Indeed, there's a letter for you." Andre handed him the note and watched Stan scan the words.

"He'll be here soon," Stan said with palpable relief and plopped his head back on the pillow.

There was a commotion outside and within a few seconds, Thea and Mary appeared with solemn faces.

"How is he?" Thea had been so strong, so composed, but the strain in her eyes had betrayed her fear. She bore it well, as though she'd carried far heavier burdens before. But Andre could see now—this, Stan's suffering, her family's shadow—it wasn't a weight she should carry alone.

"I'm here for whatever you both need," Andre said when he watched Stan hand Thea their brother's note.

For Thea's sake, for her peace more than her gratitude, Andre resolved to look after Stan with all his might. Whatever it took, he'd give her one less thing to fear, even if it meant risking being too close, being another piece of her life she might one day regret. Sometimes, doing the right thing wasn't about avoiding mistakes but about showing up when needed most.

And today, Thea needed him, whether she realized it or not.

"Nurse Shira will be here momentarily," Andre said when he glanced at the clock.

"We are going shopping," Thea declared when Andre eyed the notes for the Bavarian and French lords who would need his care, too.

"I beg your pardon?"

"She's right. There'll be a ball for Alex's engagement. We need to be a united front," Stan said, his teeth clattering under the cold chills.

Andre cleared his throat. "You are planning for a ball while he has a dangerous fever, and Baron von List is out there threatening your—"

But Thea didn't let Andre finish. "I can't spend another day in the same dress. It's time for a change. Let's go!" Thea didn't let go of the doorknob and stood in Andre's way. For a moment, she was so close that... no, he wouldn't.

"She's right. Balls, dances, all of our finery—it's no different from the armor we need in a battle." Stan waved as if Thea had to go sharpen her swords indeed, even if they were made of lace and silk. "We all need to be ready!" Stan's gaze met Thea's, and Andre knew that all he could do was to follow her and ensure her safety. There was no changing her mind.

"Will you be alright?" Thea asked one more time.

Stan nodded and pulled the blanket up to his chin.

On their way out, Nurse Shira already had clean towels ready and gave the servants instructions for an ice bath for Stan's feet. He was in good hands.

"I'll go wherever you go," he said and saw Mary slip through the door that Thea had blocked but kept ajar. The little girl was giddy with excitement about the outing.

"I hired a hackney carriage."

"We call it a hired hack in London," Andre chuckled and flicked the rim of his hat that he'd just put on and buttoned his coat. "After you." He opened the door and helped Thea in. Mary followed, and he lifted her into the carriage.

A few minutes later, Andre stepped out of Bond Street's bustling flow into the cool, inviting interior of Madame Duchon's, the best dressmaker and millinery shop with an attached haberdashery. The shop's bell tinkled softly above his head, a delicate chime that announced his entrance without disrupting the serene atmosphere inside. He pushed the door open so that Thea and Mary could enter ahead of him. Once inside, the rich scent of polished wood and lavender sachets enveloped him, a welcome contrast to the sooty London air outside.

"Oh my!" Mary clapped her hands together and swayed toward a shimmering pink fabric hanging over the back of a chair.

Thea, in contrast, nodded appreciatively.

Gleaming mahogany shelves lined the walls, each meticulously organized with bolts of the finest silks, satins, and velvets. Their vibrant hues—emerald green, royal blue, and deep crimson—seemed to beckon them closer. Glass-fronted cabinets displayed an array of ribbons, lace trims, and buttons, all arranged with an eye for aesthetic perfection. He hoped this would do for the princess, whether she admitted to her title or not, because she had an air of refinement that Andre was confident not even the finest silks could do justice to.

The floorboards beneath his polished boots creaked softly as he moved deeper into the store, their sound muffled by an exquisite Aubusson carpet stretching the room's length. Near the rear of the shop, a window seat bathed in afternoon sunlight offered a tranquil spot for customers to peruse sample books. The light filtered through the lace curtains, casting intricate patterns on the hardwood floor, and it struck Andre that all of this was rather too feminine for his comfort.

"You have to tell me how pretty I am!" Mary called from behind Thea, already wearing a wide-brimmed straw hat with fabric flowers and some beads on a wire as fake berries. She threw a beige lace shawl over her shoulder and took Andre's hand when she was close enough. "Would you like to dance with me, my prince?" Mary's tiny hand clasped his. Her innocent eyes sparkled with uncontainable joy, starkly contrasting his chest's sudden tightness.

He swallowed hard, feeling the dryness in his throat as he looked at her earnest face. She pulled him forward with surprising strength, and his feet almost instinctively fell into step with hers. Every muscle in his body tensed, yet a tender smile began to form beneath the surface tension.

He knew Thea was watching him.

It was all rather silly but in good fun.

"You are an excellent dancer, just like my princess," Mary said, seemingly pleased with herself. Andre had done better, he thought. Before he had to leave his family in Florence, he'd taken lessons with his younger sister. There had been small society balls that his parents attended, and he'd joined them after he turned seventeen.

"Eh-ahem." A woman in a dark brown dress with a strict bun and spectacles pursed her lips. "I am Madame Duchon," she declared, positioning herself behind the polished counter. Her posture was as impeccable as her attire. She acknowledged Andre with a warm yet composed smile, her eyes sparkling with professional curiosity. "How may I assist you today?" Her voice was smooth and cultured, and every syllable was pronounced with care.

Thea stepped forward, but Mary let go of Andre before speaking and approached the lady behind the counter. "My governess needs a dress for a princess! Look how pretty she is!"

THEA STOOD IN the dressing room of the elegant shop, the sound of her heartbeat loud in her ears because she didn't know if she'd be safe. What if one of List's people found them? Surely Andre would be close but if they hurt him, too?

Thea's unease clashed with the décor of the lovely room. Plush velvet chairs, their legs carved with intricate designs, were positioned around the room, offering comfort to patrons as they tried on the latest fashions. Richly embroidered drapes framed the tall windows, which provided a view of the bustling street below. The scent of chocolate and rosewater lingered in the air, adding to the familiar sense of luxury and refinement—but not safety.

The room was obviously designed to cater to the fashionable elite of London. Although she felt mousey in her governess dress, Thea feared being discovered if she gave away how much she knew about the differences between mulberry silk thread counts and the damask designs on the left shelf. She could tell the tiara on the velvet display stand had glass stones set in brass rather than diamonds in gold like hers at home, but she'd left it behind and tried not to be her true self.

No, that wasn't true.

She wanted to be her true self, not merely the girl carrying the princess title, but the person who'd earned the honor associated with it.

Despite the beauty surrounding her, Thea couldn't breathe.

For once in her life, she had the chance to remain unrecognized however slight. It wasn't a privilege she ever had when shopping in Vienna, where the anonymity of the Hohenzollerns was impossible.

The walls were framed by mahogany paneling, adorned with delicate floral wallpaper in soft pinks and greens. A large, gilded mirror stood against one wall, reflecting the light from a crystal chandelier, which cast a warm, inviting glow over the room. But Thea shivered inside.

The seamstress pulled a stool over and wore a pincushion, readying the gown Thea had agreed to try on. She felt a pang of loss as she looked down at her sensible woolen dress and thick white stockings. They had been her armor, her disguise, allowing her to blend in and live a life of relative freedom.

"I'm Margaret," the seamstress said quietly, carrying a magnificent ball gown of deep-emerald silk. Her skilled hands moved with practiced ease as she laid the dress out on a chaise longue, the fabric shimmering in the light. She turned to Thea with a warm smile, and her eyes were kind and understanding.

"Let's get you ready, Miss—" Margaret said gently, her voice soothing.

"Just Miss Thea, please." Thea couldn't allow her surname to be used, von Hohenzollern-Sigmaringen. Her throat tightened as she unbuttoned her woolen dress. She slipped it off her shoulders and let it fall to the floor, revealing the simple undergarments she wore beneath. The thick white stockings followed, leaving her bare legged and vulnerable. Each piece she shed felt like a piece of her freedom slipping away.

Margaret handed her a petticoat, its layers of soft cotton and lace rustling as she held it out for Thea to step into. As Thea climbed into the layers of tulle, she felt the cushioning surround her, creating a barrier between her and the world outside. It was as if a cleft were forming, separating her from the control she had fought so hard to seize over her own life. The fabric felt familiar but confining, a paradox she couldn't quite reconcile.

Next came the short stays, a beautifully crafted piece with delicate embroidery. Margaret stretched it out so Thea could slip in. "Take a deep breath, Miss Thea," she instructed.

Thea complied, inhaling deeply as Margaret pulled the laces of the petticoat tight in the back. A yelp escaped her when she felt the tightness of the stays combined with the bulky petticoat. She'd breathed in to assume her regal stature but felt the pang of losing her freedom as soon as she saw herself in the gilded mirror. Thea held her hair up as it would be pinned into an elaborate upswept coiffure for a ball. And the person she saw was someone she'd wished to outgrow.

And yet, Princess Thea had followed her to London. She wasn't just Thea. How long could she remain hidden, where even a walk in the park around Cloverdale House had proven dangerous.

The many layers constricted her, forcing her to stand tall and straight. On the outside, she appeared poised and regal, every inch the princess she truly was. But inside, she felt herself crumbling. Each tug of the laces seemed to tighten the grip of her past, the gilded cage of her station closing in around her.

Memories flooded back, unbidden and unwelcome. She remembered standing in front of similar mirrors, dressed in opulent gowns, presented like a polished gem to foreign dignitaries and potential dance partners who would please her father in his business ventures. She had been no more than a political bargaining chip, her desires and dreams secondary to her father's ambitions and the demands of her title.

Not even secondary, they'd been outright irrelevant.

Margaret finished tying the stays and stepped back, her eyes meeting Thea's in the mirror. "You look beautiful, Miss Thea," she said softly, her voice filled with genuine admiration.

Thea managed a small smile, though it didn't reach her eyes. "Thank you, Margaret," she replied, her voice barely above a whisper.

Margaret helped her into the ball gown, its rich-emerald silk sliding over the petticoat in a whisper of elegance. Snug across the bust, the fit tapered gracefully before falling into a sweeping silhouette over her hips and legs, ending in a small train that trailed behind. Delicate lace and tiny pearls adorned the bodice, adding a touch of refined artistry to the design. Each movement sent the skirt billowing, a cascade of luxurious fabric rippling like water with every graceful step she took.

As Thea gazed at her reflection, she saw someone who looked like a princess—a vision of grace and beauty staring back at her. The transformation was complete; she embodied the role she had once embraced so effortlessly, a role she thought she'd left far behind. And yet, beneath the layers of silk and lace, she felt like a stranger to herself.

The last time she had worn a gown like this had been at Bran Castle, as the promised bride to Prince Ralph. Those memories stirred something restless inside her—the girl who had been a princess, but also the woman who had run away from that life. They were both still there, shadowing her reflection.

Her hands clenched into fists at her sides, nails pressing into her palms as if pain might ground her. She forced slow, steady breaths, attempting to calm the storm of emotions raging within.

"There, all done," Margaret said, stepping back with a satisfied smile after adjusting the gown's hem. "You're ready for a ball."

Thea swallowed hard, giving a tight nod. "Yes, I suppose I am," she replied, though the words felt as empty as the smile on her lips.

She stuck her tongue out for a fleeting second—the smallest act of rebellion against the suffocating perfection of her appearance, a brief reminder of the girl she still hoped to be.

Margaret patted Thea on the shoulder, reassuring her before leaving the room, leaving Thea alone with her thoughts. For a moment, she allowed herself to close her eyes and breathe. The weight of the gown, the tightness of the stays, the elegance of the dressing room—all of it pressed down on her, a reminder of the life she had left behind.

She opened her eyes and stepped toward the mirror, examining her reflection. The gown was undeniably beautiful, a masterpiece of craftsmanship and design. But it also represented everything she had fled from: the expectations, constraints, and lack of agency over her destiny. Yet, once her brother Alex arrived, she couldn't escape her duties. Somehow, she had to find a way to be as brave as Mary had seen her, following her heart and taking her destiny into her own hands. She had to be the princess Mary saw in her and the woman Andre found worth saving.

Thea took another deep breath, her chest constrained by the stays, but her resolve was hardening. She had come to England seeking freedom and a chance to live on her terms. The ball gown might be a temporary necessity along with a few day dresses, but none of it would define her. She would find a way to balance her past with her future, to forge her identity on her own terms.

But how?

As the shop's door swung open, letting in fresh air, Thea felt a rush of anticipation. The world outside was waiting, and so was she.

Except that the world melted away when Thea caught Andre's eyes.

Her heart skipped a beat as her gaze met Andre's.

The way he looked at her—his eyes softening with admiration and something deeper—made her feel seen in a way she hadn't been for so long. His gaze traveled over her, taking in the transformation, and yet it was clear that he saw beyond the gown and the trappings of her station. He saw something, it seemed, that he'd lost a long time ago and just rediscovered.

He wasn't intimidated by her.

Thea dwelled on this observation for a moment longer than she ought, because he'd also not hesitated to speak freely with her that night in the carriage when Stan introduced her as a princess. Most men reacted differently to her, but not Andre.

Andre took a step closer, his movements measured and deliberate, as if drawn to her by an invisible thread. The warmth in his eyes matched his tender smile, making her heart flutter. In that look, she found reassurance, encouragement, and something that resembled deep vulnerability.

And with that, Thea stepped into the light toward him, ready to show more of herself to him.

Two minutes earlier…

ANDRE TOOK A moment to absorb the scene at the shop. Behind Mary, a young assistant arranged a new shipment of French ribbons, their delicate patterns catching the light—the assistant's quick, efficient movements spoke of experience and familiarity with the inventory. A large, gilt-framed mirror hung on the wall behind them, its reflection adding depth to the already elegant space.

While Thea had disappeared into the dressing rooms with a seamstress, Andre continued to look after Mary. The dressmaker had given her a little wicker basket with several cut-off ribbons. Indeed, they were leftovers from tailoring dresses and all the womanly trimmings of the gowns, but for the little girl, they were a treasure trove.

Andre remained near the counter, occasionally drifting to the dressing room, where Thea had disappeared with the two seamstresses.

Mary was happily occupied with the wicker basket filled with ribbons. She carefully deliberated about pulling out each piece, her face lighting up with every discovery. Andre watched her, a tender smile tugging at the corners of his mouth. Her innocent delight was infectious.

"Isn't this lovely, Felicity?" Mary mumbled to herself, but Andre didn't think much of it. She seemed content.

Andre's mind drifted to Thea, the beautiful princess only a few feet away.

"Mother said that Miss Thea moves as if she always wore a petticoat and a ball gown," Mary said.

"Your mother said that?" Andre tried not to betray the suspicion in his voice. If a lady thought that, she might ask why, and perhaps Thea's cover as governess would be pierced. But Thea did indeed have a graceful manner of walking and moving. When she turned around, her hands stretched forward and down as if she were indeed ready to push a bustling dress down. And when she climbed stairs, she always lifted the front of her dress as if it were a much larger gown than the simple day dresses she wore.

Yes, she was a princess in every way—and indeed used to wearing elegant gowns every day at Bran Castle, where she and Stan grew up.

Hard to hide.

Impossible to resist.

Andre's woolgathering was abruptly interrupted by Mary's sudden gasp. "Oh no! I've lost my kitty!" Panic tinged her voice as she spun around, scanning the floor.

Andre crouched down to her level, confusion furrowing his brow. "Kitty? What kitty, Mary?"

"*My* little kitty!" She twisted her hands together, her lower lip trembling. "It was right here…"

One of the seamstresses who'd been sorting fans on the counter overheard and immediately paled. "A cat in the shop?" Her eyes widened in horror. "It could climb onto the dresses and destroy the fabrics!"

Andre straightened up, trying to diffuse the situation. "I assure you, it's not a real cat. Just a toy."

But Miss Whitmore was already calling for backup. "Madame Duchon! Madame Duchon! We need help! There's a cat loose in the shop!"

Another seamstress hurried over, her hands fluttering nervously. "A cat? Where?"

Andre could see the humor in the unfolding chaos though he composed his expression. "Really, it's just a toy," he repeated, trying to calm the flustered women. "It's made of carved wood."

Mary, looking guilty and worried, held up her empty hands. "I'm sorry. I didn't mean to make everyone upset."

The scene drew a chuckle from Andre, despite himself. He glanced around the elegant store, filled with the mild pandemonium caused by a little girl's imagination. He instantly understood why children didn't usually come to such places. Yet, something was endearing about Mary's disruption, a reminder of life's simple joys even amid luxury.

Suddenly, a rustle of fabric caught his attention. He turned toward the dressing rooms, and his breath stilled. Thea emerged wearing a stunning ball gown. The dress was a deep, rich blue, the front adorned with intricate embroidery of large blossoms in red and gold thread. Her hair was half pinned up, the rest cascading over her bare back in soft curls. Andre knew from his own sister that there hadn't been time to fuss over Thea's hair. This was a haphazard upswept style and her natural, breathtaking beauty.

Andre's senses sharpened, and every detail of the moment imprinted itself on his mind. The gown hugged her upper body perfectly, flowing gracefully with each step. The embroidery caught the light, shimmering subtly and drawing his eye to the masterful craftsmanship. The scent of the faint perfume she wore, created an intoxicating blend that seemed tailored to enchant him.

His gaze traveled from her delicate neckline, framed by her elegant updo, to the gentle curve of her waist and down to the gown's hem, which just brushed the floor. The room seemed to fade around her, leaving only Thea in sharp focus. A warm flush crept up his neck, and his heartbeat was loud in his ears.

Thea met his eyes, a shy smile playing on her lips. "What do you think?"

"A cat is loose! Oh, the gowns, oh, the fabrics!" Madame

Duchon wailed as she combed her hands through her hair and joined the panicked seamstresses. Mary squealed joyfully, probably thinking it was a game since she knew the cat was a toy.

Thea glanced at the chaos in the store and narrowed her eyes. But then Mary climbed on a chair and called out, "There!" All the wailing women darted in a direction. "No, there!" She pointed in another direction.

Thea sucked her upper lip in and suppressed a chuckle.

Andre began to shake in mirth.

"No, over there now! Quick!"

Thea covered her mouth with her hand and took a few steps back when a seamstress appeared from a back room with a tall ladder. "Over there?" she asked, setting the ladder against a tall shelf with neatly folded fabrics.

Mary nodded, her little mischievous eyebrows raised high on her forehead.

"I told them the cat is a toy," Andre shrugged, and Thea giggled. He followed Thea to the secluded corridor leading to the fitting room. It looked like a lavishly outfitted ladies' parlor room with various accessories on display that he didn't know half the names of. There were gloves and fans and a velvet-upholstered board with sparkling pins.

But he only had eyes for the sparkling beauty beside him.

"What do you think of my dress?"

For a moment, words failed him. His mouth went dry, and he had to swallow before responding.

⇒⟫⟪⇐

"YOU LOOK… BREATHTAKING." The sincerity in his voice mirrored the awe in his gaze.

Thea's cheeks flushed a delicate pink. She glanced down, smoothing an invisible wrinkle in her gown. "Thank you, Andre."

Mary, sensing the shift in atmosphere, clapped her hands and whispered, "See, you are a prince! And Thea is a princess!"

Well, he wasn't, that was the problem. But Andre laughed softly, the sound easing the lingering tension in his chest. He extended his hand to Thea, his fingers barely brushing hers.

Thea placed her hand in his, her touch sending a pleasant tingle through him. They stood there, surrounded by luxurious fabrics and the remnants of a child's playful chaos. The moment was simple, a testament to life's unexpected beauty.

In that instant, amid the laughter and elegance, Andre realized this was true happiness: unplanned, unrestrained, and utterly natural.

"Aaaahhhh!"

A crash.

Chapter Twenty-Two

ANDRE TENSED.

Thea looked in the direction of the shop's front.

They rushed back, and Mary clutched her wooden cat amidst the chaos.

Shelves lay overturned, glass shards sparkling like dangerous stars on the tiled floor. Rolls of fabric lay strewn across the counter, their vibrant colors spilling from the shelves to the counter and the floor in a messy heap. Ribbons of every shade and width spilled from their spools, forming a mismatched rainbow that snaked through the shop.

"What happened?" Thea asked when she nearly stepped on some buttons that glittered from unexpected places, having spilled from their containers and scattered.

"I found Lady Whiskers," Mary approached her and raised her arms.

Despite the elegant gown that made Thea look like the princess she was, she bent down and picked Mary up as if nothing mattered as much as her care for the little girl.

At the center of the chaos, a woman lay on the floor, his face contorted in agony, her leg twisted at an unnatural angle. The ladder she'd been using lay beside her, its wood splintered.

Andre's mind sharpened into focus. He needed to act fast. Dropping to the woman's side, he assessed the situation with quick, practiced movements.

"Madame, can you hear me?" Andre asked, his tone calm and authoritative.

She moaned in response, her eyes squeezed shut against the pain. She pulled her leg inward, unwilling to allow a man to touch her.

"I'm a doctor. Dr. Andre Fernando, let me help you."

She relaxed instantly, opened her eyes, and let him look at her leg. It wasn't hard to see that it was her ankle sprain. She'd landed on her foot when she fell from the ladder. Considering how the ladder's rungs had broken off, it hadn't taken much to break. The swelling on her lower leg started showing, and a slight bruise was staining her skin blue. "This is going to look much worse before it'll heal. But it's not as bad as it looks," Andre concluded when he saw that she grimaced. "Is there any sturdy fabric that you can spare?" Andre asked Madame Duchon. "I need long strips, like bandages." He showed the length and width with his hands. The woman nodded. Andre directed, not taking his eyes off his patient. "What's your name?"

"Margaret Brown, Doctor." She leaned backward when Andre straightened her leg.

"Well, Margaret, you were lucky because this will heal independently. But you should not put much weight on the ankle for two or three weeks. I'll wrap it in a splint for you, alright?"

She nodded.

With deliberate swiftness, Andre broke off a piece of the ladder splintered on the tiled floor beside him. The crash had reduced it to fragments, yet Andre saw utility in the wreckage even amid the chaos. He rubbed the jagged edge of the wood against the broken remnants of the ladder, smoothing out any sharp protrusions. Then, he wrapped the splintered end in fabric torn from a nearby roll. This would prevent any loose splinters from causing further injury.

He pushed back a damp strand of hair clinging to his brow, his hands smudged with the evidence of effort. For a moment, his gaze shifted toward Thea, hesitant yet filled with a quiet yearning—not just for her recognition, but for her to see his strength, his skill, the way his hands could heal, and understand him as someone capable of more than protecting her. He wanted to be so much more for her.

Everything.

Just then, Madame Duchon arrived, her arms full of a neat stack of mismatched fabrics. Though their colors clashed, they were all the right size for bandages. Andre glanced up and nodded quickly. "Thank you, Madame," he said, his voice steady despite the situation's urgency.

He secured the proffered fabrics around Margaret's ankle, creating a makeshift but effective bandage. His hands moved with the precision of someone who had done this countless times before, each motion purposeful and efficient. Margaret winced slightly but held still. He felt her trust, and it was precious. A patient who put their injury into his hands always received his utmost attention and care.

Once satisfied with the immobilized ankle, Andre turned his attention to the longer part of the ladder. He got up and examined it briefly, judging its strength and length, then snapped it over his knee with a decisive motion. He again wrapped the top end in fabric, ensuring it would be comfortable to grip.

"Use this as a crutch," Andre instructed, handing Margaret the newly fashioned aid and helping her up. Margaret seemed to take the makeshift crutch with gratitude and hesitation.

He paused for the briefest moment, straightening his posture as if to make himself more noticeable, before glancing toward Thea with a look that lingered just a second too long. Andre reached into his inner waistcoat pocket and produced a card elegantly engraved with his name and the address of his practice. He handed it to Madame Duchon, who accepted it with a nod of understanding.

"I trust that you will give Margaret seated work and not cut her wages?" he asked sternly when Madame Duchon grimaced in the poor seamstress's direction. "Since her injury occurred in your shop," Andre pressed on until the owner nodded.

But the shop owner tsked just when Andre wanted to turn to Thea and Mary, ready to leave.

"Not so fast!"

THEA SHOULD HAVE seen it coming.

She cradled Mary gently in her arms, the little girl clutching her wooden toy cat as if it were a lifeline. The elaborate folds of the ballgown Thea still wore rustled softly as she moved through the shop, starkly contrasting the chaos left in the wake of the accident. She could feel Mary's small body trembling against her, the child's wide eyes darting around the room, still filled with fright.

Madame Duchon, the shop owner, surveyed the mess with a cold, calculating gaze. Her lips pressed into a thin line as she took in the overturned fabric rolls, the scattered ribbons, and the broken ladder. They knew that look; it was the look of someone assessing damage, not just to property but also to pride and order.

"Who will be held responsible for this mess?" Madame Duchon's voice cut through the quiet, sharp and unforgiving.

Before Thea could respond, Mary's small voice piped up, trembling yet earnest. "It was my toy cat," she stammered, holding the wooden feline out to offer it up for judgment.

Thea's heart ached for the girl, who had only been playing moments before the disaster struck. She tightened her hold on Mary, feeling the weight of responsibility settle heavily on her shoulders. Looking at Madame Duchon, she saw the woman's frown deepen, her eyes narrowing not at the child but at her.

The accusation hung in the air, unspoken but unmistakable. This was not about a toy cat; Madame Duchon was looking for someone to blame, and her gaze had landed squarely on Thea.

"A mother usually pays for her daughter's expenses. This is going to cost you, Miss... eh..."

Thea squared her shoulders and stepped closer to Andre, shifting Mary into his arms. He took her instantly, and the girl nestled against his strong body.

"She's not my mother!" Mary said, burying her face in Andre's shoulder. "Thea's my governess."

Madame Duchon raised her chin. "And is he your father?"

Andre's eyes shot to Thea, and she felt his piercing gaze.

"I'm so sorry about the mess, Madame," Thea said, calm and measured despite the unease tightening in her chest. "I shall ensure that this will all be paid."

"No, wait! The ladder didn't give way unexpectedly. It was already too rotten and shouldn't have been used, which is why Margaret was injured," Andre added.

"I can pay for it," Thea whispered.

"But you shouldn't have to if you didn't break it," Andre said, taking a wide stance.

"So you're giving me the fault for all this?" Madame Duchon's frown remained, her tone clipped but losing some of its harsh edge. "This shop is my livelihood. Such chaos cannot be tolerated."

She walked to the counter, retrieved a piece of paper and a pencil, and started to write something down. *"Un, deux, trois...* oh!" She scribbled something, then put the end of the pencil in her mouth and assessed Thea from head to toe. "Five rolls of fabric, the gown you're wearing, at least ten yards of silk ribbon, and the ladder—"

"The ladder was already broken!" Andre seemed annoyed, but his tone was measured. They realized that he was a man who knew all too well how the wealthy were treated, and it was plain to see that Madame Duchon considered Thea and him easy prey. Thea had often been to fine shops in Vienna with her mother, and these in London seemed no different. Once they got a whiff of good-natured people who could pay, they'd multiply the bills several times over.

"Send me the bill at Cloverdale House on Abbottsberry Road," Thea said. "For the dress, too." She picked up the front and turned to the door.

"Not the dress, no." Madame Duchon crossed her arms, creasing the paper she'd written on.

"I beg your pardon?" Thea pursed her lips.

"You're the doctor's mistress and have the nerve to come and let him outfit you while the mother likely thinks that you are taking her on a stroll."

The air felt sharp, cutting into Thea's chest like the edge of a blade. Her grip tightened on the dress, the fine fabric scrunched beneath her trembling fingers. She saw Andre from the corner of her eye. His jaw twitched, his gaze darkening like a storm brewing on the horizon. Yet she didn't look to him for rescue.

"How dare you accuse me of that?" she said, her voice low but with a dangerous edge that even she didn't recognize at first.

Madame Duchon sucked her cheeks in. "So you lied? The girl is yours, and you truly live at Cloverdale House? Then it's him with the illegitimate child?" She snuffed in Andre's direction, dismissively.

Thea's heart pounded like war drums in her chest, the heat of anger crawling up her neck. She'd endured accusations before, endured the whispers behind her back, the runaway princess— but this was different. Thea's breath shuddered out, the weight of who she was pressing against her ribs. All her life, she had hidden, run, swallowed her pride for safety. The old Thea would have turned and fled. But no more.

Her heels clicked sharply against the floor as she strode to Madame Duchon. Composure reigned over her like armor as she straightened, her chin lifting so high it was as though the invisible crown she once wore had materialized again. Her hands uncurled, steady at her sides now, and her voice came out clear and unyielding, cutting through the tension like steel through air.

"I am Princess Josephine Theodora Andrea Hohenzollern-

Sigmaringen." The words fell into the room with the weight of thunder. She allowed a beat to linger, her eyes locked on the seamstress with a resolute flame. "And you have just insulted a member of the royal family on absolutely no basis."

Her pulse thrummed as she met Madame Duchon's stunned expression, but she felt lighter, stronger—like standing tall for once against the torrent of whispers and shadows had given her wings. She would no longer hide.

Thea stood in the middle of the disheveled shop, her heart pounding. Madame Duchon's eyes bore into her with an intensity that made her feel cornered, but it was Madame Duchon who took a step back, only to find the counter blocking her retreat. "How do I know it's not a lie?" she demanded, her voice trembling with anger and fear. "Imposters!"

Thea felt her pulse quicken, her palms turning clammy. This was the moment she'd dreaded ever since she left her homeland. She had hoped to avoid it, but circumstances had conspired against her. She stepped forward, her spine straightening with determination.

"Madame Duchon, I assure you, you will be paid for the items I ordered," Thea began, her voice steady despite the turmoil inside her. "And as for me, I have nothing to hide. I am exactly who I said."

The silence that followed felt like a heavy weight pressing down on the room. Madame Duchon's eyes widened, her mouth opening and closing as if searching for words that wouldn't come. Still clutching her toy cat, Mary looked up at Thea with wide, innocent eyes, clearly confused but trusting.

Andre, who had been standing quietly beside Thea, stepped forward, his presence commanding attention. "Madame Duchon, allow me to explain the severity of Margaret's injury," he said, calm yet authoritative. "The sprain is located at the ankle joint, where the ligaments are most vulnerable. If left untreated or improperly immobilized, it could lead to complications such as chronic instability or further damage. It was essential to immobilize the ankle to ensure proper healing."

Madame Duchon's gaze flickered between Thea and Andre, her skepticism slowly giving way to reluctant acceptance. Andre's explanation left no room for doubt; his knowledge was evident in every word he spoke.

"Why does the little one say you're her governess?" Madame Duchon asked as if the question were a sword she'd wield.

"To protect me. My identity," Thea said. "As did Dr. Fernando until Margaret was hurt."

Thea watched Madame Duchon's reaction closely, her emotions swirling with relief and apprehension.

The shop owner took a deep breath, her composure slowly returning. "A princess," she murmured, still grappling with the revelation. "And a doctor. This day has been full of surprises."

Thea nodded, her expression softening. "I understand this is difficult to believe, Madame Duchon. But I assure you, we only wish to help. Margaret needed immediate care, and Dr. Fernando did what was necessary. We will take full responsibility for the damages and assist in any way we can to restore order. Let me see that." With these words, Thea took the paper on which Madame Duchon had written.

"Ah! The fabrics, ten yards, hm?" She scanned the room. "It's no more than two."

If they thought she wouldn't know because she was a princess, she underestimated how hands-on her education had been in Transylvania. She held out her hand with the aplomb of a princess, and after a moment's hesitation, Madame Duchon put the pencil in her palm. Thea crossed out the ten and replaced it with a two.

"The ribbons came off the spools but are intact, so I'd say two or three hours of clean-up work at a shilling an hour?" That was what the Whites paid her as a governess, and it seemed fair.

Thea glanced at Margaret, who dropped her head.

"No? Half a shilling?"

Margaret shook her head.

Andre cleared his throat and Thea understood. She knew people like Madame Duchon all too well, increasing their business at the cost of fair labor.

"From now on, Madame Duchon, Margaret will receive a fair wage and will not be coerced into climbing rotten ladders. Understood?"

Madame Duchon curtsied and nodded.

"I didn't hear you."

"Yes, Your Royal Highness."

Andre stepped forward. "I need to examine Margaret again in a few days. If her posterior tibial tendon is ruptured, she will need more rest." He turned to Madame Duchon. "It's the tendon that attaches one of the smaller muscles of the calf to the underside of the foot. It helps support the arch and allows us to turn the foot inward."

Thea suppressed a grin. "So Margaret might need about four weeks of seated work."

She crossed out the ribbons.

"And Dr. Fernando's service offsets the rest of the inconvenience you've put a price on here, Madame. Or should I request that he send you a bill?"

"No, Your Royal Highness."

"Very well. Then I will pay for this dress and ensure that my friends and family never find out that you refused to hear the doctor out and threw a tantrum because a little girl lost a toy cat in your shop. It wouldn't sit well with the higher classes of customers, I'm sure, to know that your nerves are so easily frayed, would it?"

"No, Your Royal Highness."

"Then I'm glad it's been settled. As much as I regret that the fabrics have been unrolled, it seems as though nothing has been damaged, and a little clean-up work is all that's needed. Poor Margaret will be able to keep track—on paper"—Thea gave her a grave look, and the girl blushed—"to ensure it's all been done." Then she turned to Margaret. "Do you earn a commission for pieces you sow?"

"Yes," Margaret tried to curtsy, but she winced.

Thea reached out and helped to steady her. "I need a whole new outfit. Now that Margaret has my measurements, can you send me three new dresses to Cloverdale House by the end of the week?"

"Oh yes, yes, of course!" Madame Duchon answered hastily.

Thea held her hand up in the air to stop her. "I'd like to clarify that I'm purchasing Margaret's handiwork. She's exceptionally talented, and her good work should be rewarded." Her gaze drifted to Madame Duchon.

"Yes, Your Royal High—"

"Let's go." Thea turned to Andre. "I'm finished here."

Mary's eyes were so wide, with her mouth agape, that Thea nearly laughed.

The little bell over the door chimed when Andre held it open, and Thea escaped the tension in the shop.

Thea felt a wave of relief wash over her. The confrontation had been intense, but they had managed to navigate it. She glanced at Andre who offered her a reassuring smile. Then, Thea reached for Mary's hand and gently squeezed her.

"That was..." he said softly, his eyes reflecting pride and admiration. Then his face brightened into a broad smile, donning perfect rows of white teeth.

Thea smiled back, feeling a warmth spread through her chest. "I couldn't have done it without your support," she admitted, her voice tinged with gratitude.

Andre waved for a hackney.

A black carriage stopped, and he called to the driver, "Abbotsberry Road. The eastern park gate." Then he held the door open for Thea. "If you don't want to be recognized, perhaps it's best not to stand on the street in a ballgown."

They quickly lifted Mary into the carriage.

But he winked at her just before she accepted Andre's hand to climb in herself. "Not that I mind, Your Royal Highness."

"Will this cost Margaret her position?" Thea asked when they were safely in the carriage.

"Probably after she's healed, yes. I don't suspect Madame Duchon will want to risk her reputation as a shop owner until after I declare Margaret healed."

"For less than a shilling an hour—" Thea shook her head.

"You mean a shilling a day?" Andre said gravely. "But I can ask someone for a new position for Margaret."

"Oh yes! The old man with the trembling hands?" Mary asked clasping her hands together.

"Yes."

Thea knew she had forced Madame Duchon into softening the bill, but it was Andre who had truly left a lasting mark amid the chaos. While she floundered with her title and strained diplomacy, his actions had spoken volumes. He'd cared for Margaret with steady hands after the fall, exposed Madame Duchon's lie about the ladder, and ensured Margaret's wages until she recovered. And when she did, Andre would see to it personally, making sure Margaret was strong enough to stand again before using his connections to secure her a new job with the old tailor.

His ability to weave kindness and pragmatism together left Thea breathless. Andre wasn't just calm under pressure—he was magnetic, a figure who commanded attention and respect without asking for it. He had a touch of charm that softened even the harshest moments. It was everything she admired— everything she desired—and yet, Thea forced herself to tear her gaze away before her heart could betray her. Would being near someone like him undo everything she'd built to protect herself, as easily as she'd used her title today?

Chapter Twenty-Three

ANOTHER WEEK HAD passed, and Stan felt better, to Thea's relief. Yet her heart grew heavier as she noticed that Andre spent less time at Cloverdale House.

Thus, one afternoon, Thea found Anna for tea as Mary pretended she was a nurse for Andre and unfolded his muslin towels. It was later in the afternoon and Thea had changed in one of her old day dresses. The others would be delivered in a few days.

Thea noticed a wistfulness in Anna that made her chest tight. "Does your leg hurt very much?"

Anna looked at her as if she'd been woken from a stupor. "Not at all." She winced when she adjusted in the chair, and Thea knew it hurt, but something else bothered her even more.

"Is this about your husband?" Thea ventured when she poured herself a tea and topped Anna's off. "Milk?"

"Yes, please." Anna's gaze was fixed on Thea's movements, but she seemed to see another horror altogether. "I sent for my mother."

"Is she very far away?"

"Vienna. It's where my father worked before—" Anna's voice faltered, her lips pressing together as though the words were something fragile she feared to break. She looked down at her hands, pale against the coverlet, fingers faintly trembling. "You know I had a brother," she said, almost too softly to hear.

"I have four. They can be rather irritating at times." Thea smiled, hoping to coax even the slightest lightness into the room, but Anna didn't seem to notice.

"My older brother was born before my parents married," Anna continued, her voice quiet, distant. She swallowed, her throat bobbing as though she were trying to force back the ache threatening to rise.

"Oh?" Thea prompted gently, leaning forward as if bracing to catch whatever fragile thread Anna was holding onto.

"When Napoleon's army came..." Anna hesitated. Her breathing grew shallow, and her gaze shifted to the window as if she might find solace in the morning light trembling through the glass. "My mother sent him away. She thought he'd..." Her words wavered, breaking on a sharp inhale. "She thought he'd be safer far from home."

Thea watched her closely, seeing the battle raging beneath Anna's calm exterior. Her hands gripped the blanket now as if anchoring herself.

"You've never found him," Thea said softly, not as a question but a truth that lay between them, heavy and undeniable.

"No. I don't even know if he... if he's—" Anna bit her lip, shaking her head in quick, determined refusal as though even speaking certain words might make them real. Her chin trembled before she forced it still. "Sometimes, I think I've searched all these years not because I thought I'd find him, but because...I couldn't bear the thought of not trying."

Thea reached out, her fingers brushing Anna's wrist lightly. "Anna, you've carried this alone for so long. Maybe telling someone, letting it out—" She hesitated, searching for the right words, "Maybe it could be one way to... to at least see what happens next."

Anna blinked down at Thea's hand as though trying to find sense in the contact. "You don't understand," she said, her tone barely a whisper. "What if I open my mouth and all that comes out is my worst fear? What if... he's truly gone?"

"But what if he's not?" Thea pressed, her voice warm yet weighty. "You said it yourself, Anna—you've been here at Cloverdale with time to think. Maybe you've been preparing for this all along—for the moment when you stop running from the question."

Anna's lips parted, but no sound came. There was a new tension in her expression—a mix of longing and fear, of wanting to believe but questioning if she even deserved to. Her gaze flickered back to the window. She closed her eyes briefly, as if searching for courage in the faint rays of light.

Then she exhaled, slow and shaky, her next words clinging to the space between them like a lifeline. "Mother has been looking for him ever since but to no avail. I think it's slowly killing her, but she's holding on to life because she can't die without knowing for certain."

"It must be tough for a mother to suffer the uncertainty of how or if her child may live," Thea said, sure she couldn't fathom the fear in a mother's heart under such circumstances. And that made her think of her mother.

"Now that I'm with child," Anna suddenly burst out, "it's different."

"I know. Isn't that wonderful?" Thea asked, but already knew the answer. Anna's marriage didn't seem like a loving family. Again, Thea thought of her parents. They were in love and loved her undoubtedly, even if she was just a girl, a mere bargaining chip in the vast net of diplomacy.

"I don't mean the family. There's a settlement clause in my marriage contract. I've never told anyone about it, Thea. I want to use it now. My husband... I wish he'd live somewhere else."

"And this clause can make it happen? A divorce agreement?"

"No, nothing that formal. Just a large amount of autonomy and money in case he cheats on me." Anna looked out the window again as if she could find a better time among the green leaves outside. "Since he brought me to London, I've entertained more guests than I can count, and I've learned more new names than I ever thought I could, but not one of them became a friend. I don't trust any of them." Anna's eyes bore into hers. "And yet something about you makes me trust you."

Thea rubbed her hands together. "I ran away from my family, and I don't know how trustworthy I am."

"You ran from a fate like mine, Thea. It was wise."

Thea blew the air out through her lips. "My brother certainly disagrees."

"About what this time?" Stan suddenly stood in the door. His arm was tangled—one couldn't consider this wrapped—in a knotted mess of white bandages. He bowed and kept the position a little too long. Then Thea realized what this was all about.

"Thea!" Mary appeared from behind Stan. "Look at him! He's all better!"

Stan's gaze caught Thea's. He was stifling a laugh.

"Lady Anna Ashford, this is my brother, Prince Stan."

Mary chuckled and curtsied out of turn. Thea had to explain this to her again later when they were alone. "And this is Miss Mary White, my ward."

"I've bandaged the prince. The prince!" Mary twirled. "And he's all better now!" She danced and sang to herself until she disappeared out the door, and her little voice was audible in the hall.

"She fancies herself a nurse," Stan said as he bowed and took a seat.

"Wasn't it the other arm that was injured?" Thea squinted.

"Yes."

And just like that, Stan's visit lightened the mood.

After introductory platitudes had been exchanged—and Thea was most impressed with her brother's newly perfected skills in British small talk—Stan produced a letter from his waist pocket. "Our parents sent an urgent note." He handed it to Thea.

Her heart dropped, and she was glad she was seated because her knees would have surely given way. This was it—the missive calling her back.

"We don't have much time till he comes to Town, so you need to brace yourself," Stan said before Thea could unfold the letter.

Oh no, Prince Ralph wasn't coming to call her as his bride, was he?

She forgot to breathe.

My Dearest Daughter,

It is with the utmost regard for our family's precarious standing that we write to you. Your brother, Alexander, will soon arrive in London to make the acquaintance of his betrothed. It is now incumbent upon you, dear children, to embrace the duties that accompany your noble stations. Upon your return, we expect you to have secured an engagement befitting our lineage with a Habsburg as you have been destined.

In our absence, we have entrusted your brothers with the authority to bless your union. May this endeavor be successful and honorable, reflecting the dignity of our family.

With all our love and expectations of a bright future for each of our children,

Your Devoted Parents

"What did it say?" Anna asked.

"As soon our brother, Alex, arrives in London, we need to take care of some unpleasant business. And then Thea's engagement can be announced."

"No, it cannot," Thea set her cup down and crossed her arms.

"Wait!" Stan held his hand up. "I have an idea."

"Hopefully a good one," Thea said. Anna, however, seemed much more interested.

"We use it to introduce you to Society. I'm sure my friends, the Langleys, will be happy to throw you a ball. And then you can stay for the whole Season." Stan smiled as if he'd had the best idea yet.

"I'm supposed to remain hidden," Thea protested.

"You didn't manage it too well to date, so perhaps you make a grand entrance when Alex is here. We'll be ready to confront Baron von List then," Stan said.

"Not with Prince Ralph. I'm not agreeing to marry him. So I need no ball."

"I'll throw this ball for you, Thea," Anna said. Color returned to her face. "For once, I'd like to make one of these expensive affairs useful."

"But it wouldn't be an engagement ball, and you can't throw a ball from the rehabilitation center. There're patients here," Thea protested, unsure whether Anne or Stan even heard her. Once aristocrats wished to have a ball, there was no return. So if it had to happen, perhaps it could be the kind that would make Andre feel a little more at home? Could he and the other doctors be invited?

"How about a Viennese ball?" Thea suggested. She saw a smile creeping up Stan's face, but Anna gave a skeptic glance.

"Continue." Anna signaled with her hand in swirling motions.

"Well, the Viennese balls are highly formal, often requiring white ties, evening attire with tailcoats for men and full-length gowns for women, that's different from the London balls, which are more like social events?"

"It sounds more different than it is, my dear," Anna protested.

But Stan smirked. He must have known what Thea was hinting at.

"I'd be making my debut in London's society, so this would require an opening ceremony and a midnight quadrille," Thea continued.

"And a *Damenspende*," Stan said with mischief. Viennese balls included unique customs such as the *damenspende*, a gift given by men to their dance partners.

"Who do you want to present with a token of your affection?" Thea asked, quirking a brow.

Stan shrugged. "It's just the occasion that calls for a gesture, isn't it?"

"There are fewer chaperones and rules of etiquette at a Viennese ball," Anna said as if she were thinking about the potential scandal of throwing such a themed ball in London. Then she smiled. "We will end with Ludwig van Beethoven's contredanse."

Stan clapped his hands together. "You are both rather deviously scheming an overthrow of Almack's it seems."

Anna laughed at that and Thea bit her lip.

"Viennese balls could be themed, like a masquerade."

"I'm not throwing a masquerade ball," Anna shook her head vehemently.

"No, no. I'm merely suggesting that it's not exclusive to the nobility. We can invite more people, perhaps?" Thea blinked in Stan's direction.

He rose and reached for Anna's hand. "It was a pleasure to make your acquaintance, Lady Ashford." Then he turned to Thea. "I think you won't need my assistance to invite the doctors from 87 Harley Street, isn't that so, dear sister?"

With these words, he gave a warning look, and Thea felt the heat creep up to her face.

Was it that easy to see that she wanted to invite Andre?

Chapter Twenty-Four

I N THE LATE afternoon at 87 Harley Street, once the last patient had left, and Andre was heading to the kitchen for an early dinner. He didn't have time to visit Stan yet but would make his way to Cloverdale House soon. Where Thea would be. He sighed, his heart heavy with the unspoken truth about his feelings.

Then there was a knock.

"Stan said it's open during business hours," a female voice said.

Thea?

She stepped in with Mary in tow. "Andre, hello!"

"Good evening. What brings you here? Is Stan's fever higher? Who ensured your safety on the way here?" He went to the window and didn't see the carriage. "Did you walk here? With List threatening… I would have come tonight… I was going to—" A million reasons darted through Andre's mind, but he would have never guessed the correct one.

"This is for you!" Mary held out a folded card with gold-embossed letters. He didn't recognize the initials.

"Stan is all right. He brought us here in his carriage on the way to the Langleys' for a brief visit and he will be back soon. We wanted to deliver this personally." Thea beamed as she shut the door behind herself.

Andre opened the card and read it.

You are cordially invited to grace the Viennese Ball hosted by Lord and Lady Ashford, which will be held at their esteemed residence on Saturday, the eleventh of November.

"A ball?" he asked.

Mary nodded vigorously.

"You risked your lives to invite me to a ball?" Andre crossed his arms.

"It's Viennese. You ought to know about it." Thea blushed and avoided his gaze as she spoke. "Stan kept us safe, and it's hosted by a dear friend."

Mary tapped her foot on the floor.

After a short pause, Andre smiled crookedly. "It'll be an honor to attend. How could I refuse such a charming invitation by the most beautiful young woman," he said to Mary, who was reaching for his hand and climbing on his feet. "Will you be there to dance a waltz with me?" But as Mary wrapped herself around him and wanted to be twirled around, Andre's eyes met Thea's.

"I hope you will grace me with the honor," Andre said.

Thea turned a brighter shade of pink and nodded. "It would be my pleasure," Thea said.

"Just like at your castle, Miss Thea. It will be a Viennese ball with a quadrille, beautiful gowns, and—" But Mary didn't finish.

"That's not what distinguishes the Viennese and London balls," Thea tried to correct her.

But Mary was not letting reality interrupt her reverie. "Just like at your castle," she said dreamily.

"I didn't grow up in Vienna, Mary," Thea said with a chuckle when Mary hopped off Andre's feet, and they followed him to the kitchen. "Would you like some tea?"

"Where's your castle?" Mary asked when they returned to the practice. Andre opened the kitchen door for his guests, not that he usually had guests at the practice. It was strange not inviting them to his treatment room and leading the way to the relatively modest kitchen in the back of the first floor.

"In the Carpathian mountains," Thea smiled, but she seemed absent-minded.

"I don't know where that is. Is it a very magical place?" Mary pressed on.

They'd arrived in the kitchen, and Andre pinched his lips shut. This was usually a place filled with laughter, heated conversations, or intense discussions about how to pay the next month's rent. Still, without Nick, Alfie, Felix, and Wendy, it was a modest kitchen with a relatively old-fashioned stove.

"I need to see the map," Mary declared.

"I don't have your books with me," Thea said helplessly. "And I can hardly draw it for you, with valleys, mountains, the Bârsa and Turcu Rivers." She looked a little at a loss.

"I have an atlas," Andre said.

Mary flashed him a bright smile, showing her baby teeth in two tiny rows.

"One moment, please," he said, rushing out the door, up the stairs, and to his chambers as fast as he could so he could be back and look out for Thea and Mary's safety. If he had known they would leave Cloverdale House, he wouldn't have…

Ah, there was the old atlas on his small and overstuffed bookshelf near his armoire. He grabbed it and, on his way back out of the room, stopped by the small mirror on the wall over the wash basin and picked up his comb. For the lovely princess, he didn't want his wavy hair to look too unkempt.

Andre stilled instantly and then splashed some cold water on his face.

This was not how he ought to think about Stan's sister. His task was to keep her safe.

She'll always be safe in my arms.

And wasn't his job to ensure her safety when Stan wasn't nearby? He wasn't a bow street runner; he was a doctor. He'd certainly ensure her physical well-being, but he worried about her emotional well-being.

She'd run away from her home in Transylvania and hadn't confided in him whether she planned to return.

I don't want to lose her.

But he didn't even have her…

Clutching the atlas in the brown leather binding under his arm, Andre walked down at a more adult pace than he'd sprinted upstairs like a green boy in heat.

"This was my atlas," he said as he handed it to Thea.

"Why did you need maps when you studied humans?" Mary asked.

Andre chuckled, his heavy heart instantly forgotten when she asked her pointed questions. This little girl was astute, direct, and intelligent, reminding him of his sister.

"I didn't always study bones, veins, and muscles. There was a time when I had to memorize borders, capitals, mountains, and rivers, just like you."

Thea seemed to avoid his gaze, surveying the room without as much as the tiniest expression of disappointment. A princess would and should expect to be invited to the finest dining rooms in London, and… that was the idea!

"Are you hungry?" Andre asked Thea, but Mary jumped up and beamed at him.

"Oh yes! Do you have any milk?" Mary asked excitedly.

"Not here, but I'll get something even better for you," Andre said. "Whipped cream and custard."

Mary clapped her little hands and jumped while tugging at Thea's sash. "Can we go? Please?"

"Is it very far?" Thea asked but Andre could tell that he'd already won them over. "Only a five-minute walk from here."

"Do they have the same madeleines you gave us earlier this week?" Thea asked, smiling.

Andre winked. "Even more!"

Said and done.

Within a few minutes, they entered the Patisserie de la Loire, a French bakery on the corner of Harley Street. As usual, the little bell over the door chimed as they entered, and the owner, as soon as he spotted Andre, smiled and called over the two customers ahead of him, "Madeleines are coming fresh from the oven, Monsieur le Doctoeur."

He was a man with a kind smile, chubby cheeks, and an infectious smile, especially because he loved that he had the same name for him and Nick, Monsieur le Docteur.

"Are these the same madeleines you brought me as a gift?" Thea asked when Mary didn't pay attention.

"Would it be alright if I said yes?" Andre asked. *I could forever look into her beautiful eyes and never get enough.*

THEA ADJUSTED HER shawl, the light November chill beginning to seep past the fabric as she took Andre's offered arm. His warmth close to her side was a comfort, though she would never admit how much she relied on it. They walked slowly through Marylebone, the stones of the pavement clicking softly beneath their boots. The street was quiet except for the occasional creak of coach wheels. Rows of identical white houses lined the road, each one neat and proper, without a single crooked window or chipped paint to disturb their symmetry.

Each house had an air of order she couldn't match. Perfectly symmetrical windows framed the entrances, black-painted doors standing steadfast in the center. Some had potted boxwood plants on either side of the doorstep, pruned into clean, round shapes as though their owners had measured every last leaf. The uniformity unsettled her. Marylebone was lovely, but it made her feel like an ink blot on a pristine sheet of paper. She was a stranger here, someone who didn't belong and whose steps could be erased as easily as the morning mist on the glass panes.

Her own situation only deepened the contrast. She wasn't just new to the city; she was in danger, and it was her own fault.

Now, she found herself stumbling through an unfamiliar world, the ground seeming more uneven beneath her every hour, and the future uncertain for her entire family. The only thing she knew was that she wanted Andre close by, and that's why she'd ventured to see him.

For, even when Marylebone's order left her unsettled, Andre made her feel steady. His strong arm beneath her gloved hand kept her from drifting too far into thought. He seemed acutely aware of their surroundings—ever the protector.

Thea's hand rested lightly on Andre's arm, her stride falling in step with his as they walked along the cobbled street. Ahead of them, Mary skipped and twirled, her laughter curling through the air like a ribbon, unbothered by the adults' subdued conversation.

"You never answered my question," Thea said softly, glancing up at him.

Andre's gaze remained ahead, his expression composed, save for the slight tightening of his jaw.

"Which one?"

"The languages," she replied. "You speak so many, but why? And why choose this? A doctor in Marylebone, instead of the larger life you seem capable of."

He paused a moment before responding, guiding them around a cart laden with vegetables. "Circumstance chooses for us far more often than we choose for ourselves."

"Circumstance," she repeated, her tone skeptical but not unkind. "Convenient, but unconvincing."

A slow exhale escaped him. He looked down briefly at her, then back at the uneven stones beneath their feet. "When the world is at war, no one's path is straightforward. I did what I could to ensure survival. For myself, and for the family I lost along the way."

Thea's arm stiffened slightly against his, but she didn't loosen her hold. "You lost them?" she asked, her voice quiet but pressing.

"I did," he said simply. "When I fled... Vienna was no longer safe. For a while, I thought we'd scattered as far as we could. I searched for them after the war, but there was only silence." He kept his tone measured, though the words carried an undertone of resignation she couldn't fail to catch. "So I did as I had promised and cultivated my craft."

"You wanted to make them proud?" Thea asked.

"Yes, my father was a doctor, and my mother was very devoted him."

"Military records must exist if Napoleon's army took them," Thea ventured, her voice suddenly steadier. "You made inquiries, didn't you?"

He nodded once, sharply. "Many. None returned."

Her brow furrowed, her voice dipping lower. "But why wouldn't you use genealogic resources? I mean, wouldn't you—"

"I couldn't examine the parish records in all of Europe. They could be anywhere," he interrupted, though his tone contained no trace of impatience. "Too many dangers remained for those of my blood. Napoleon's hatred did not vanish with his empire, and his old soldiers needed little reason to act."

They walked on a few paces in silence, the smattering of a horse's hooves filling the space. Finally, Thea tilted her head, her gaze searching his profile.

"Do you still hope they will find you?" she asked.

Andre's lips pressed tightly together. "Hope," he murmured, as if testing the taste of the word. "I carried it once, but after a time..." His voice lowered. "After a time, hope becomes another weight to bear."

Her hand tightened on his arm, though he wouldn't—or couldn't—meet her eyes. "That doesn't mean they're lost," she said after a moment, her voice so quiet it barely reached above the breeze.

"They'll never be lost if I carry them in my heart, Thea. I'd give anything to be with my family again."

I ran away from mine.

Ahead of them, Mary's laughter rang out again as she hopped

from one stone to the next. Thea looked up at him again, forcing a faint smile despite the ache in her chest. "Perhaps, hope isn't as heavy as you imagine. If only you would share it."

His expression softened, but before he could speak, Mary called out, skipping back toward them. The spell of the moment broke, and Andre only smiled faintly as he turned his attention forward once more.

"One day, I'll have a family of my own perhaps. For now, Nick, Wendy, Alfie, and Felix are the family I have."

Thea gave his arm a squeeze but could do no more.

Mary, of course, had noticed. Mary always noticed. Just the night before, a maid had commented on how little she had slept and dared to speak of Andre. But how could Thea explain it? Even she couldn't untangle why every stray thought eventually circled back to him. Somehow, Andre had become the pivot on which her world turned, his steadiness the thing that kept her upright when it felt like her knees might give way. She wasn't sure when it had happened, this lived-in certainty of his presence in her life, but it was there now, settled into her like roots twining into soil.

They paused at a corner, and Thea looked down the next street. Another row of identical houses stretched into the evening haze, lit only by the glow of a streetlamp. She tightened her hold on Andre's arm, grounding herself in his solidity. The streets might all look the same to her, but with Andre near, she told herself she might just learn where she was going.

Chapter Twenty-Five

ONCE THEY RETURNED with a parcel of treats, Andre invited Mary and Thea back to his treatment room in the practice at 87 Harley Street.

"Oh, bones!" Mary shouted with glee and ran to the skeleton hanging from the wall. "How spooky!"

Andre suppressed a chuckle when Mary lifted the skeleton's arms and cried "Boooooh…" in a foreboding voice as if she were a ghost haunting a castle.

Thea rushed to her side. "Come now, let's treat her with respect."

"Her?" Mary asked. "Did you know her before she died?" She clasped her little hands together, awaiting an exciting tale.

"We don't know who she was, but she's a real human," Thea jumped in, gingerly removing the skeleton's hands from Mary.

"She's not a toy, I'm afraid," Andre added.

Mary stepped back, pursed her lips, and eyed Andre curiously. "Neither is Thea, you know?"

Andre couldn't help it; his eyebrows rose and betrayed his surprise.

"I do." His voice came out like a slow, dark growl, not at all as he'd intended.

Mary turned back to the skeleton and stuck her hand between the ribs. "Where's the heart?"

Andre received an apologetic glance from Thea, but he was happy to comply and explain basic human anatomy. "It sits here, protected by the ribcage."

"Does bone heal if it cracks, or is it like stone?" Mary asked.

"It can, yes. Often, a fracture in the bone will—"

But Mary interrupted him. "And where are the seams of the heart?" the girl asked.

"Seams? You mean muscles?"

"No, when a heart breaks, I know it shatters. That's why in the skeleton, it isn't there, I suppose. But when it's filled with love and bursts at the seams, where can those seams be reinforced?"

Andre narrowed his eyes. This wasn't anatomy as much as a little girl's interpretation of matters of the heart. He knew he had to tread carefully. "Where did you get these ideas?"

Mary turned to Thea, who was standing behind her, beet red. When Andre's gaze found Thea's, she deflated and put both hands on Mary's shoulders. "We should go now."

"No! I want to know." Mary peeled Thea's hands off her shoulders and looked up at Andre. "You're a doctor, so you're an expert in matters of the heart, whether it breaks or bursts."

"Are these conditions you speak of ailments that require healing?" Andre pursed his lips, steadying himself for a response that would surely make him laugh, but he would not.

"Well, all I know is that Miss Thea said her heart would break if you didn't return her feelings. But if you did, it would be so full that it would burst at the seams." Then, the little girl put her hands on her hips. "Return now what's hers so she stays healthy." Then she reached out to Andre and held her palm up, ready to take those feelings into custody for her dear governess.

Meanwhile, Thea had turned a dark, almost violet shade of red, like spring tulips.

Andre had not seen this coming. His heart plummeted to his knees, and he forgot to breathe.

But Mary's gaze was unwavering.

Thus, he did the only thing he could think of: He bent down

into a squat and took Mary's hand between his own. "You like Thea very much, don't you?"

The girl nodded.

"And she told you all this about her heart?"

She nodded again.

Andre took a steadying breath and found Thea's gaze. A frown line on her forehead betrayed that Mary had babbled. It was a secret conversation that hadn't been meant for Andre's ears. And yet, now he'd heard it, he had to respond. "Well, tell Thea I want nothing more than to keep her heart safe before it bursts."

"What if it breaks and shatters? She's rather afraid of it, and I know what that feels like. It's why I sleep with Lady Felicity Whiskers now." She fumbled for something in the pocket of her dress and produced the small carved cat figurine. It was painted white with a yellow ribbon tied around its neck. "Thea said I don't need to be afraid when my kitty is with me because you gave it to me. That's why I can't give my kitty to Miss Thea. So it's upon you."

"For what exactly?"

"To protect Miss Thea from being afraid that her heart will break. You'll have to keep her safe when she's scared at night."

Andre choked and coughed, unable to meet Thea's gaze now. He would certainly like nothing more than to keep her safe at night, comply with ensuring her heart would soar with love, and be there for her whenever she worried.

That was the pivotal moment when Andre rose to stand before Thea. Her chest rose, and she looked at him with the vulnerability of a girl and the expectations of a grown woman to be loved.

Yes, that was the moment.

Andre knew that they didn't come often in life, but every once in a while, something small occurred that turned life around forever.

"It would be my honor to do as you said, Mary. All of it."

Andre no longer spoke to Mary; he suspected that Thea knew that. His gaze locked with Thea's for a moment, and her pupils grew, the color drained from her face, and her mouth fell slightly open. She'd understood.

I need a moment alone with her.

Somehow.

Now.

Chapter Twenty-Six

T HEA STOOD STIFFLY in Andre's treatment room, her hands
folded neatly as though that might calm their trembling.
Andre's treatment room was neat as an operating room—
polished wood shelves lined with jars of tinctures, a single vase
graced with lavender perched on the windowsill, and the faint
aroma of herbs lingering in the air. It felt too ordered, too clinical
for the storm that swirled inside her. She leaned forward slightly
as Andre moved behind the desk toward the window, when there
was a commotion outside.

How had it all unraveled this fast? She had made a mistake—a
terrible one—baring her feelings to Mary in a moment of rare
weakness. And Mary, well-meaning but utterly tactless, had seen
fit to lay them bare to Andre. Thea's heart clenched, her thoughts
a dull roar of panic. What must he think of her now? The
runaway princess, flitting through England like a moth lost and
without direction—and worse, a wanton woman who had
foolishly lost her heart.

But none of that was true and he ought to know.

If he didn't, she'd tell him.

Nobody had ever looked at her as he had when they'd rolled
down the hill in the park abutting the gardens at Cloverdale
House. Nobody had ever truly seen Thea—beyond the princess—
quite as he had.

No, she wouldn't hide. She'd decided that when she'd stood in front of the modiste's looking glass on Regent Street, her back straight even as her hands shook. The silk gown they tailored that day had served as more than adornment. It was a stand—a vow to herself. Hiding had never saved her, not from her past, and most certainly not from her own emotions. But that didn't make this any easier. Thea wanted, needed, a moment alone. Just the two of them. The weight of her unspoken words pressed against her ribcage, but she couldn't seem to find a way to begin. Would he listen? Could she explain herself? Her gaze flickered to Andre, who still hadn't looked at her, and her stomach tightened. She felt as though she were teetering on the edge of a precipice, the silence hanging between them a thread just waiting to snap.

More noise came from outside and Mary joined Andre at his office window to see what was happening.

"Two carriages have arrived!" she announced.

Andre nodded. "Everyone is back."

"You mean, the nurse is here now?" Mary shouted excitedly. "Miss Folsham?"

Andre gave a friendly nod, and Mary clasped her little hands together in glee. "Can I go speak to her?"

"Of course, if Miss Thea allows it." Andre's eyes met hers, and she saw his Adam's apple bobbing.

Could he feel the same as she did about their time alone coming to an end? The quiet practice has been a refuge, especially with Stan's watchful eye back at Cloverdale House.

"All the doctors? Everyone is back?" Thea asked, but she could see that Andre understood her question; more people meant no chance to be alone.

A door clicked, and footsteps became audible. There were murmurs of voices and a thump. They were probably carrying their trunks inside.

"Go and introduce yourself to the nurse," Thea said, eyes glued to Andre's.

"Her name is Wendy," Andre added.

Thea opened the door to Andre's office for Mary, and she eagerly escaped, calling to the people in the hall.

On the other side of the door.

A solid oak structure and walls shielded them but there was just no time.

I'll make time.

Thea locked the door and left the knob in the keyhole.

"I-I… ahem… I'm sorry about Mary," Thea started.

"I'm not."

"She shouldn't have told you—"

"I'm glad she did. I feel the same."

Thea's heart raced as if it tried to jump out and she felt light-headed—as if she were in a dream and Andre was the only one there with her.

Finally alone.

Andre closed the distance to her but remained silent. His eyes were so dark and hungry that Thea's heart pounded, she forgot to breathe, her words dissolving into nothing as her gaze locked on Andre's. He stood just a step away, too close and yet not nearly close enough. The flickering lamplight cast shadows across his face, sharpening the intensity in his dark eyes. His admission echoed in her ears—he felt the same. She wasn't imagining this incredible, terrifying connection pulling her toward him.

The silence between them hung heavy, charged, her racing heart the only sound she could hear besides the soft crackle of the hearth. Thea's gloved fingers twisted at her waist as she fought to keep steady, though every nerve in her body thrummed with awareness. Andre moved, bridging the short distance between them in an instant, and her stomach twisted with anticipation. When his hand lifted, his thumb brushing over the curve of her cheek, her whole body stilled at the contact.

"You feel… the way Mary said?" he murmured, but it wasn't a question, it was permission. His voice low and stirring something deep within her, as though he knew exactly what caused her trembling.

"I do," she admitted, her voice barely above a whisper, shaky but unhidden.

She didn't realize she had backed against the door until she felt its hard support on her back, their breaths mingling in the scant space between them. His hand drifted lower, curling lightly around her jaw, tilting her face up, and she closed her eyes for just a moment, overwhelmed by the sheer intimacy of the gesture. When she opened them again, his gaze softened, but the glint of something far more primal lingered, just beneath the surface.

Then, without another word, Andre's lips touched hers. Gentle at first, as though testing her resolve. Thea couldn't suppress the sharp inhale, the shock of it shivering down her spine and settling like a spark of fire low in her belly. His mouth was warm, soft yet insistent, coaxing her to respond. She did, her fingers lifting unbidden to clutch at the crisp fabric of his shirt, holding him as though he might disappear if she didn't.

The kiss deepened, his lips moving against hers with a slow, deliberate passion that stole the air from her lungs. Thea's sensation narrowed to the contact—the faint taste of tea on his mouth, the faint scratch of his clean-shave jaw, the unrelenting strength in the firm pressure of his touch as it settled at her waist. Heat blossomed in her chest, spreading outward, until there wasn't a part of her unaffected by his nearness.

Her knees felt weak, and she leaned into him, into the solidness of his frame, the anchor he provided to her dizzy frenzy of emotion. One of his hands slid upward to cradle the back of her head, his fingers tangling softly in her hair. Thea tilted her head instinctively to deepen the kiss, a quiet sound escaping her throat that she barely recognized as her own. The treatment room, the jars of tinctures, and even Mary's meddling all faded into a distant haze.

There was only Andre—his lips, his heat, his strength—and for that singular moment, she allowed herself to be entirely his.

His initial hesitation gave way to a fervent response. His arms encircled her waist, pulling her against him as if anchoring himself to the moment—to her.

He opened his mouth and moved his lips, gently sucking her in, and she gasped into him. He brushed her lower lip with his tongue, and all the questions in her mind were erased. Just like that, he'd answered all of her questions. For all that mattered was that he indeed felt the same.

Oh and how he felt!

The intensity of the kiss deepened, and a rush of emotions surged through her—desire, fear, joy—all blending into a dizzying whirlpool that left her breathless.

This was new for her, and she didn't expect it, but perhaps the surprise made it much more special.

FOR ANDRE, THE kiss was both a revelation and a surrender.

At that moment, Andre knew he was lost to her. Thea was not just a fleeting passion, a moment of desire to be forgotten. She was everything, the center of his world; the one person who could make him forget all else. He wanted to stay and be with her and lose himself in her completely.

Thea's hands cupped his face, her thumbs brushing over his cheeks in a gesture of tender affection. Andre leaned into her touch, his heart swelling with emotions he could not name. He kissed her again, this time with a slow, deliberate passion that spoke of all he felt, all he could not say.

When they finally pulled apart, their foreheads rested against each other, breaths mingling, eyes locked in a gaze that spoke volumes.

In that fleeting instant, they were no longer two individuals bound by society's constraints. They were simply two souls finding solace and strength in each other. The future was uncertain, but for now, in this singular, breathtaking moment, they belonged to each other entirely.

And then there was a thud.

Followed by a knock. "Andre?" Wendy called.

"Thea!" Mary added. "I know they are in there," she mumbled.

"What is going on in there?" Wendy called.

Andre stepped back and let out a heavy exhale.

Thea gave him a humored look, pressing her lips together as if to taste him again.

And he couldn't stop himself from kissing her again. To feel her tender mouth, the heat building for him, and she opened up immediately.

Another knock came from low on the door, near the doorknob. Mary.

Andre put one hand against the door as if the sheer pressure from his arm could keep the world outside at bay, especially the curious girl—and he didn't mean Mary. Wendy mumbled something behind the door, and then he recognized Alfie's voice.

He knew he had to go. If he was supposed to keep her safe, hidden, unseen, scandal was not the right way to accomplish that. But he felt an almost magnetic pull to Thea. Her touch was intoxicating. Her soft, blue gown clung to her in a way that caught the light just right, highlighting the perfectly flaring curve of her waist and the delicate slope of her shoulders when he glanced down. But the rosy blush on her face and the pinkness of her swelling lips was more than a declaration of the word he didn't dare name. Her eyes, a deep shade of blue, seemed to pierce through his resolve, making him question everything he thought he knew. Her movements were graceful and deliberate; it was undoubtedly her first kiss and a silent invitation stirred something primal within him he didn't want to suppress.

Their breaths mingled as she cradled his cheeks. There was a riveting tension in the air, a palpable anticipation that made his pulse quicken. Thea's hands moved with gentle certainty, her fingers trailing a line of fire down to his collar. Andre's heart thundered in his chest as she slid her hands lower, resting on his heart, her tender and commanding touch. He could feel the warmth of her palms, the slight tremor that gave away her rising desire.

Without a word, Thea pressed her back against the door, her body arching slightly as if to meld with his. She pulled him closer, her eyes never leaving his. Andre's breath hitched; he knew this moment was a precipice, a point of no return. But the look in her eyes, the way she silently asked him to stay, made it impossible to turn away.

"Andre? Are you in there?" Alfie called, but Andre didn't hear anything else. A murmur of voices in the hall faded as Thea pressed her chest against his, her hands now on his shoulders.

She kept him there. His audience with the princess was in full swing, and she didn't want anyone to disturb them.

"You have perfumes at the apothecary?" Mary's voice came muffled from the other side of the door.

"I'm not opening," Andre whispered into her mouth.

Thea chuckled but didn't break the kiss.

This was scandalous.

And brilliant.

Then the footsteps grew fainter and withdrew.

For a fleeting moment, Andre smiled, his lips quirking up in a rare expression of pure, unguarded joy. But then Thea's tongue darted into his mouth, and the world around him vanished. His insides clenched a visceral reaction to the soft, insistent pressure of her kiss. He was lost, utterly consumed by her.

Her taste was a heady mix of sweetness and longing. He responded with an urgency that matched her own. Their kiss deepened even further as his hands roamed her back, feeling the smooth silk of her gown beneath his fingers. He could feel every shift in her body, the way she pressed closer, her fingers tangling in his hair. A faint smell of vanilla and custard from their meal only minutes ago lingered, but there was no room for anything between them. The space around them melted away, leaving only the two in a cocoon of shared desire.

Thea's back arched further, pressing her hips against his, and Andre's hands slid down to her waist, pulling her even closer. The feel of her against him was exquisite torture, a blend of pleasure and anticipation that set every nerve alight. He could hear the soft gasps of her breath and feel the rapid beat of her heart against his chest.

Thea's fingers traced the line of his jaw, her touch feather-light and teasing. Andre responded with a groan, his hands gripping her tighter. The need to feel her completely overwhelmed him. Her body molded to his, fitting together as if they were made for this moment—for each other.

Thea's lips left his, trailing a path of fire down his neck. Andre's head fell back, a low moan escaping him as she kissed and nipped at his skin. Every touch was a promise, a declaration of desire that left him breathless.

Andre's hands moved of their own accord, sliding up her sides to cup her breasts. Thea's sharp intake of breath spurred him on, his thumbs brushing over the peaks through the thin fabric of her gown. Her reaction was immediate, her body arching into his touch, a soft moan escaping her lips.

Thea's hands were everywhere, exploring, teasing, driving him to madness. She was a siren, calling him to abandon all reason, to lose himself in the depths of her passion. Andre's control slipped further with each passing second, the need to possess her, to make her his, growing unbearable.

"Thea," he rasped, barely managing a coherent thought.

Their kisses grew fevered. Thea's nails raked down his back, leaving trails of sensation that made him shudder. He responded by gripping her hips, lifting her slightly to press her more firmly against the door. The feel of her heat, the way her body moved against his, was almost too much to bear.

Andre's mind was a haze of desire; his world narrowed to the feel of Thea in his arms and the taste of her on his lips. He wanted to devour her, to claim every inch of her, to make her his in every way possible. The room seemed to pulse with their shared heat, the air thick with the scent of longing and arousal.

Thea's hands slid down to his waist, tugging at the waistband of his trousers, but then she hesitated again. Andre sucked in a breath, his entire body tensing with anticipation. Her touch was both a torment and a blessing, each movement driving him closer to the edge. She looked up at him, her eyes dark with desire, a silent plea for him to continue, to take her completely.

But this wasn't the time nor the place.

"Thea?" Stan's voice came from the other side of the door.

They both froze.

Andre took a significant step back, combing both hands through his hair.

"Are you in there?" Stan's voice was commanding.

Regal. Dangerous.

She cleared her throat, clutching both hands on her cheeks, but she never stopped looking at Andre. "I'm coming out in a moment."

"Is Andre with you?"

Andre shook his head. There was nowhere to go. He considered the window. This would have never happened if he had climbed out and walked around the block to return with pastries from the other side.

But it had.

And the thought of denying it made his heart sink.

"Yes!" Thea called back, straightening her back. An expression of certainty washed over her face.

She was all of the princess he knew her to be and the only one there who matched Stan's rank.

She stood tall, ironed out the folds of her dress, pushed a pin in her hair back up, and suddenly she had the authority to match Stan's.

"Come out!" His voice thundered.

She put her hand on the key and gave Andre a glance over her shoulder.

He tucked his shirt back into his breeches, walked to his desk, and sat down, hoping the flush of the moment wasn't visible and that the authority he'd have behind his desk would hide the evidence of his arousal.

They nodded to each other. Thea turned the key.

And Stan stormed in. "What's going on here?"

Chapter Twenty-Seven

THEA DIDN'T LIKE Stan's authoritative stance when he stood in the doorway.

Andre was firmly seated behind his desk, scribbling something in a ledger.

The room was in perfect order.

Of course, he could put one and one together—better, Thea and Andre, but that didn't mean he could pretend to be her father. And if there was one thing Thea had learned for as long as she could remember, it was how to handle an older brother.

Andre looked ruffled. He sat at his desk, papers neatly stacked, his posture as straight as if carved from marble. Too straight. And Thea felt the thrill of it all because she'd done that to the handsome doctor, her Andre. When he spoke, his voice was calm—polite, even. "Hello Stan," he said, his tone measured, "what's the problem?"

Thea's heart jumped at the sharpness of Stan's reply. "You know exactly what the problem is," he snapped, his words cracking through the air. "You were alone with my sister!"

Heat crawled up Thea's neck, her cheeks burning as if all the sins of the moment were branded there for judgment. She wanted to speak—to defend Andre, to explain that nothing untoward had occurred—but the words stuck in her throat, a lump of fear and shame she couldn't dislodge. And she didn't want to lie about something so wonderful.

Andre, however, remained stiff. He gestured faintly to the desk in front of him, his fingers barely moving as he replied, "As you can see, I am seated at my desk, a respectable distance from your sister. Hardly the scandalous scenario you imply."

Thea's pulse thrummed like a drum as her gaze flicked between the two men. Andre's expression didn't shift, his dark eyes steady on Stan's face, cool and undeniably correct. Stan, by contrast, seemed to falter. His frown deepened, his jaw clenched, a vein in his temple pulsing with frustration. He glanced her way, his brow furrowing further as though searching for evidence to back his accusation.

But there was nothing. Thea stood exactly where she had been moments before, her back near the window, feet planted firmly in place. Five solid paces separated her from Andre's desk—a gulf that no amount of Stan's bluster could overcome. She saw his anger waver in his eyes, his certainty unraveling like a loose thread.

The silence that followed was excruciating, pressing on Thea's chest like a weight. She felt light-headed as if she were caught in the eye of a storm, waiting for it to spin her out. Stan's mouth opened, but no words came, his shoulders sagging imperceptibly before he finally looked away.

"I needed to speak with him about something." Thea gave Stan a piercing look, but he seemed calm, taking in the condition of the room.

"What?" Stan's tone was grumpy, and Thea bristled at that.

"A patient."

"You don't treat any patients," Stan said matter-of-factly.

"I still see them; one in particular caught my eye."

Andre looked up for an instant, and Thea saw his mien falling when his eyes met Stan's. Andre instantly looked down, dipped his quill in the ink pot, and scribbled more.

What was he writing, a novel?

When Stan pursed his lips in the same manner that Father did when Thea didn't want to obey, she bristled, and indignation surged within her. She'd run away to find autonomy and surely didn't come this far to exchange one authority figure for another. She'd decide who she'd fall for... oh, and she'd fallen, that was certain.

For Andre.

Oh dear.

She sighed.

She glanced at Andre again, and he looked at her for a moment, a black hunger flaring up in his eyes, and then he cleared his throat and blinked back down at the ledger on his desk.

Good.

"Thea, explain yourself," Stan thundered.

"Why should I?" She folded her hands before her and stood in the simple dress as if she were in Bran Castle in a ball gown on the top of the stairs, about to descend for a grand ball. Yet beneath the surface, her heart hammered wildly. Heat bloomed under her skin, and she could feel the flush combined with the tingling awareness still lingering on her lips where Andre's had been. She ached with a disorienting mixture of want and mortification, her body betraying the fierce restraint she maintained. The room felt too small, the air too thick, and though she held herself steady, as if carved from marble, inside, she was molten, trembling on the edge of unraveling completely.

My big brother interrupted my first kiss!

Thea was seething on the inside.

"Because I demand it," Stan said, standing ramrod as if he were in military uniform again like he was all those years ago when his father forced him to undergo training and achieve a rank he could be proud of. Father had different demands from each of them and remained unhappy regardless of how much honor they brought back home.

Mary came in, her usual bubbly self, but around her waist was an apron. "I'm the assistant nurse."

Behind her emerged a young woman who looked at Andre as

if demanding to know what was happening. This must be the nurse he'd mentioned.

"Your Royal Highness," the nurse took a bow. It was all wrong, but Thea appreciated the gesture and gave a friendly nod. More and more people knew that she was a princess. Even though Andre's friends were probably not dangerous, Thea worried that there was danger still lurking somewhere.

ANDRE WASN'T PLEASED by the interruption either. A kiss like that—a kiss that left a man's mind and body in utter chaos—deserved far more than the bubbly intrusion of Mary's cheerful chatter. Still, he couldn't deny a flicker of relief as her arrival dissolved Stan's makeshift interrogation. Any reprieve from Stan's suspicious glare was welcome, though Andre was sharply aware of why he had been so quick to corner him—he'd do the same in his place if his sister had been caught with... but one glance at Thea's lingering flush, the soft bloom on her cheeks, and any fool could guess what had transpired. And as for himself—he shifted uncomfortably in his chair, his body insistent on betraying him in a manner most unbefitting of a gentleman. Stiff didn't begin to describe it; bracing himself was perhaps closer to the truth. But even now, despite the interruption and his predicament, he couldn't bring himself to regret a single moment of what had just passed between Thea and him.

"Who needs my help?" Mary asked, ready to take a patient.

"Euhm..." Stan grimaced and shot Andre a look for help. "Miss Folsham is back. Nurse Wendy."

Was Stan stammering her name as Wendy entered the room?

Andre narrowed his gaze.

Interesting, a moment ago, he could have threatened Andre.

"We should look at the stitches," Andre said as he rose from behind his desk. "It's good to have you back, Wendy," he added, and she came to the treatment bed near the wall. "Stan?"

Andre seemed to purposefully not look at Thea lest he betray something.

"I need to see, I'm the assistant nurse!" Mary declared, twirling in her white apron.

Andre suppressed a chuckle and searched Thea's face for help, but she had none to offer.

Wendy retrieved a bowl, a bottle of witch hazel, a few bandages, and a tray with other supplies from a cabinet. Then she paused and gave Andre a look.

He nodded in Stan's direction. "Would you like me to clear the room for you?"

Chapter Twenty-Eight

EVERYONE WAS BACK and the practice had filled with bustling energy. But then Thea noticed that Stan's eyes had wandered to the nurse.

Interesting.

This was mainly because the nurse diligently focused on folding and refolding a towel that Andre then reached for to spread on the treatment bed.

Thea narrowed her eyes and waited for Stan's reaction.

When he met her gaze, he indicated "no" with his eyes, and she inhaled as understanding dawned on him.

"Dacă îmi păstrezi secretul, îl voi păstra și eu pe al tău, frate." If you keep my secret, I will keep yours, brother. Thea subtly gestured in the direction of Nurse Wendy.

Stan inhaled, nodded, and then looked at the nurse again. She was pretty, young, and seemed to blush furiously under Stan's intense gaze. But what struck Thea the most was how well she worked with Andre.

Once Stan had taken off his shirt, it was Nurse Wendy who took the tweezers and held the wound down as Andre removed the stitches. Mary grimaced a little when she first saw the dark scab wash away with the witch hazel solution and the bowl tinged with the dissolved red blood.

"I'll remove the stitches because there's an infection, but I will bandage the wound so that it won't open," Andre explained for Stan's benefit as much as Mary's. "This is called a roof tile bandage," he said when he placed one piece of muslin in a crisscross over the other. "The pressure comes from both sides to draw the skin together."

"How long until the wound closes?" Stan asked, wincing when Mary joined Wendy and patted his shoulder.

"You don't just need it to close; you need the infection to heal. This could otherwise take a dramatic turn," Andre said firmly. Wendy handed him another bandage while gently nudging Mary's so she wouldn't rub.

"Just pat, pat, see?" Wendy showed Mary and Stan shot Wendy a grateful look.

And Thea now knew why Stan inhaled and flexed his muscles for them—well, he didn't want to show the pain of the deep infection to the little nurse, but he wanted to show off his muscles to the adult one. Thea knew her brothers better than herself sometimes.

"We must repeat this at least twice daily until the wound is closed. Only then can we immobilize the arm, so the scar remains narrow and smooth." Andre turned to Thea. "It seems we will keep him as a patient to Cloverdale House after all."

"Wendy, could you—" But Andre didn't need to finish.

She nodded eagerly, and it was a little too obvious that she averted her gaze from Stan, who was pulling his shirt back over his exposed torso.

"I'll look after your wound at Cloverdale House," Nurse Wendy said.

It was a promise that hinged upon a practicality Thea knew should soothe her, but instead, it sent an ache spiraling through her chest. Cloverdale House. The place where he would be— where she could see him again.

The thought took root, unbidden yet undeniable, sparking a restless hope in Thea's chest. She could still see the faint curve of his lips before their kiss, feel the pull that defied reason. Her cheeks warmed at the memory, her pulse quickening with a longing she could neither quell nor justify. She shouldn't feel this way, shouldn't crave that spark again, but the idea of seeing him at Cloverdale House was enough to set her heart racing. It would be her chance—her excuse—to be near him once more.

Except that the next day at Cloverdale House, Andre didn't come. One of doctors said that there was a large carriage accident, and he had a great number of patients, but Thea hadn't heard everything. Instead, some of the other doctors had arrived, introduced themselves to Anna when Thea had been sharing tea with her, and then withdrew into the various rooms Thea didn't keep track of. Thus, Thea distracted her mind from the intense kiss with Andre with a little homework for Mary.

"Why are you making me learn French and Latin?" Mary asked, holding the pencil and writing simple words.

"Because you are so young now, you can learn three or four or even five languages at the same time easily."

"It's not easy," the little girl pouted.

"I know."

"But you said it is."

"It's easier now than learning the languages when you grow up. I never said it's easy altogether."

"How many did you learn when you were five?"

"Five."

"Yes, when you were five."

"No, I mean, I learned five."

"Which ones? French, Latin, and English?"

"And Romanian and Hungarian."

"Say something in Hungarian!"

"Bármit elérhetsz, amit kitűzöl magad elé."

Mary beamed. "What does it mean?"

"You can do anything you set your mind to."

"Even though I am a girl?"

"Especially because you are a girl."

"You're a girl, too! You have to marry and have children

soon."

"That's what my father wanted, Mary. But it's why I ran away."

"Did I run away to learn languages and be free like you without a husband and children?"

Thea choked. If this was how Mary saw her acts of defiance, she had many amends to make. "Mary, darling, you didn't run away. We were kidnapped, then saved, and I sent a message to your parents to let them know that you are safe until they return to London. It's a bit like an excursion with me."

"My princess." Mary hugged Thea.

Now, she couldn't stop the tears from coming anymore.

"Why are you crying?"

"Oh, it doesn't matter." Thea forced a smile and wiped another tear with her free hand while she held Mary on her lap.

"But it's your feelings! Of course, they matter!"

"To you, perhaps, not to my father."

"He is probably too busy and will have more time when the deals are all in order."

"Is that what your mother tells you?"

Mary nodded.

"It's also what my mother told me. But then I grew up, and I realized that when my father had time for me, it was to ensure that I learned well, practiced the dances, that my posture was straight, and my teeth white."

"He loves you and wanted to see you growing up."

"He loves what I can do for him and what I can manage as a grown-up. That's why I had to learn all these languages."

Mary squinted as if she tried to sense what Thea was saying. Thea knew she shouldn't tell a child about all this, but even just thinking it, she felt ungrateful. Who had ever heard of a princess who didn't appreciate her station?

"Let me try to explain this." Thea took Mary's hand in hers and looked at her. "It is indeed important to invest in your education. Languages are important, but so are arithmetic, geography, and water coloring."

"Why?"

"So you build a foundation for what you will learn later."

"Is that what you're doing now?"

That stumped Thea for an instant.

It was indeed a lesson she was learning. She had no guidance or set assignment, but figuring out where she belonged did require all the training, knowledge, and heart.

And it had taken a little girl a few minutes to put it together. *Could it be that simple when one prioritized love?*

"Languages, for instance, show people you are interested in their country, culture, and etiquette."

"So you learned Hungarian before you liked the culture?"

"No."

"The country?"

Thea pursed her lips.

"It's just not very far away from where I lived, so while I like the language, the country and the culture are very close to mine."

"So you picked England instead?"

Thea leaned back in the chair and scratched her nose. "No."

"When are you going to Saxony, Bavaria, or Prussia?"

"Why?"

"Because you learned German. You're learning languages to make friends with the people, right?"

"No." Thea deflated. It wasn't brilliant considering it this way. "Mary, I was raised to fit into any of those cultures with great ease because the man my father wanted me to—wants me to marry," she swallowed bile, "is connected to all these countries."

"So perhaps he will love you and take you there to explore?"

"No, he won't. And I ran away because I didn't want to be with him."

Mary considered that for a moment. "I'll make up my own language."

"What?"

"*Rasinu kalatin plomp.*" Mary gave a self-assuring smile. "*Prumblim.*"

"What does that mean?"

"Whatever you want it to mean so it makes you happy."

"That's not a language then, Mary."

"But it should be. What's the point in learning languages to speak with people who don't make you happy? In my language, anything I say is something that will make others happy when they hear it."

She clapped her little hands and hugged Thea.

"Thank you so much for creating *Quinovinum* with me."

"What's Quino—"

"*Quinovinum* is my language now.

"*Halikanu Peraton,*" Mary added. "I'm hungry."

So Thea took Mary downstairs in the hope to find a small meal for Mary to tide her over until dinner.

"Oh, Andre! *Rasinu kalatin plomp.*" Mary ran toward him, lifted her arms, and he instantly set down his cup on the saucer and picked her up. She took his face in both hands and smiled. "*Prumblim.*"

"PRUMBLIM?" ANDRE'S EYEBROWS rose so high they betrayed his questioning whether he should question what she said. But he thought it better not to ask, considering that Thea stood rather stiff in the doorway. It had been such a long day, one emergency after the other, and he was glad to finally see Thea again. Of course he rather wished to be alone with her but he smiled brightly and hugged Mary. "Thank you, Mary."

"See, he understood!" Mary turned to Thea and slid back down Andre's arms. Thea had come closer, and Mary now tugged at her sleeve. "He knew exactly what I said, and it made him happy. He smiled!" Mary pointed at Andre's mouth and Thea gave him a bright smile.

Yes, rather lovely indeed.

But now Thea burst into laughter. There was no chance Andre knew what Mary had said. They weren't words!

"She made up those words." Thea shook in mirth when Andre gave her a surprised you-can't-be-serious look. Then he laughed, too.

"Would you care to translate the language… ahem, what is it called?"

"*Quinovinum.*" Mary emulated Thea's best governess tone.

"*Quinovinum.*" Andre nodded with an air of grave understanding. "And if you translate what you said to English, it means…?"

"Whatever would make you happy to hear." Mary nodded and gave a tight-lipped smile.

"Which is what?" Andre pressed on.

Thea pressed her hand over her mouth, seemingly trying not to laugh.

Then Mary drove her hands over her face to wipe the frustration away. "You truly don't know?"

Andre and Thea both shook their heads.

"But it's the same thing for both of you! If you say *Prumblim,* you'll both finally be happy!" She threw her hand into the air. "Just say it!"

"Say what?" Thea asked.

"I love you!" Mary groaned, pivoted, and walked away. "*Prumblim. Prumblim. Prumblim.* Is it so hard to say love?" And with this word, she'd left through the door.

Finally, alone again.

And that was a word, indeed.

He knew he hadn't blinked in a while but was frozen. Andre felt his pulse in his knees, but he couldn't locate his legs or feet.

Prumblim.

Love.

Saying it to one another.

He tried to swallow, but his throat was dry.

Thea stood only a foot away, blushing like… like… Andre cocked his head.

Like it was true.

"*Prumblim?*" Andre asked with a half-smile that seemed to return when Thea inhaled and held his gaze.

"She just invented a language that would make people happy."

"It's a brilliant idea." Andre shifted but didn't close the distance to Thea. "She's right. *Prumblim.* Especially when the person they love the most shares it with them."

His heart thrummed so violently now that he could feel it shaking his ribcage. It was nonsense; the heart didn't move from its titled spot over the diaphragm, but it made all the sense in the world for him to feel as he did.

"*Prumblim,*" Thea nodded. "*Rasinu kalatin plomp.*"

"What?" Andre reached for Thea and lifted her chin with his thumb. She smirked, making his heart nearly burst out of his ribcage.

And when she blinked at him, her dark eyes saw straight into his soul. He tucked a few shimmering strands of her blonde curls behind her ear as if he had to bring order to the disarray her golden locks had brought into his life.

But the only way things would be in order was if he kissed her.

Right then.

"*Rasinu kalatin plomp?*" He rasped. "Is that in her language?"

"It means whatever you wish for it to mean in *Quinovinum.*" Now Thea tilted her head slightly and smiled, but her gaze fell from his eyes lower.

He hoped it was to his mouth as he closed the distance. "You have an affinity for languages, Princess."

His lips touched hers.

"I have an affinity for you," she said in his mouth just before he inhaled. "I've fallen in love with you." She opened her mouth to receive his and wrapped her arms around his neck, pulling him closer.

"Me too," he managed before there was no more time to speak.

Chapter Twenty-Nine

C LOVERDALE HOUSE WAS full of patients, and with the other doctors back, Andre finally had time to see the patient Thea had mentioned before, a woman reluctant to receive the discharge order required before her husband would come to pick her up. Odd, truly, because patients were usually eager to go home after extended recoveries.

The aroma of freshly brewed tea wove through the air, blending with the soft sounds of birds chirping in the garden. Andre ran a hand through his hair and shifted the leather medical bag. As he stepped further down the hall, he heard excited women's chatter, and when he recognized Thea's voice, he couldn't help but smile. Perhaps he could say hello to her before retreating into the exam room with the next patient. Much had remained unsaid between them, and he didn't know how to forge the future he so desperately wanted with her, but, at the same time, the most important words had been uttered. With those words, Andre had a newfound hope that life would turn out alright.

He followed her voice into the south-facing parlor room and noticed Thea sitting beside a woman with her back toward the door. Both had delicate porcelain teacups cradled carefully in their hands. A flicker of warmth washed over him as he caught Thea's optimistic words floating toward him.

"Once your leg heals, I shall take you for a stroll through the gardens," Thea said, her voice brimming with hope.

Andre felt the familiar pull of emotions as he turned his gaze to the patient's leg. She sat with a bandaged leg propped on a cushioned stool, a grateful smile lighting up her face. Sunlight caught her golden hair, framing her like an ethereal vision.

In that instant, Andre felt his heart tighten; it had been too long since he had seen her. The recognition struck him like a lightning bolt, illuminating a past he thought was forever lost.

His gaze remained locked on Anna for a moment longer, sensing her struggle to anchor herself amid the conflicting emotions. He instinctively glanced at Thea, catching her furrowing her brow in concern; she must have realized something was underway. Then, his eyes returned to Anna, and when they met, a jolt of recognition surged through him. It was as if the air crackled with unspoken words, heavy with the weight of their shared past. In that instant, everything shifted—time seemed to hold its breath—as they stood on the precipice of rekindling a bond tarnished by silence.

As he stood there, frozen in the moment, he first noticed how the sunlight glinted off her hair, reminiscent of his father's. It was a striking reflection of the von Dürer lineage; only the von Dürer side of the family sported such blonde locks. She looked so familiar yet different—a hauntingly older and sadder version of the sister he had cherished in his youth. It was as if the weight of the years had etched sorrow into her features, revealing the toll of sleepless nights and tears shed in sorrow.

Andre watched as Anna's chest rose, and she held her breath. A growing drumbeat from his heart echoed joy and apprehension when he realized she'd recognized him, too. The corners of her mouth twitched instantly; then she pursed her lips as if to say something. Instead, she inhaled deeply, and a warm and inviting smile appeared on her lips, yet it felt almost foreign to him. It was a smile that hinted at shared memories and the companionship that had anchored her through tough times. But as quickly as it emerged, it faded, replaced by a wave of uncertainty that washed over her.

"Anna," he whispered, almost inaudibly.

In her gaze, he saw echoes of their childhood—but the years of separation had weighed heavily upon them, infusing the air between them with unvoiced pain and an undeniable sense of loss. Andre felt a deep ache in his heart, recognizing the distance that had formed in the absence of their shared lives.

As Anna's smile slipped away, a painful twist of emotion knotted in his stomach. Memories of their last encounter flooded back. His mind raced, but time felt inexplicably slow. A flood of vivid and poignant childhood memories surged through him. But now, as he looked at her, she had transformed into a lady—a stranger yet undeniably his sister. The emotions churned within him, a storm of joy and disbelief.

Then, in a moment that felt like a scene from a dream, she dropped her teacup with a clang, the sound sharp against the silence that enveloped them. The hot liquid nearly spilled onto her lap, and without thinking, Andre instinctively reached out, catching the cup with the saucer just in time.

"Andre," she said, her voice a melody that stirred something deep within him, a connection that transcended time.

It was then that Thea broke the spell, her curiosity piqued. "You know each other?" she asked, her eyes darting between them.

His heart tightened. "I thought I'd lost you forever."

THEA SAT IN the corner of the drawing room, the light filtering through the lace curtains, casting delicate patterns on the polished wooden floor. Her mind buzzed with disbelief and bewilderment. With trembling hands and eyes wide with shock, she watched as Anna pushed herself up from the floral-patterned chair.

"Andre!" Anna's voice trembled, barely a whisper yet filled

with urgency and surprise. She moved towards him, her steps quick and unsteady, a mix of hope and disbelief in every stride.

Andre froze for a moment, his eyes locking onto Anna's, a myriad of emotions flitting across his face—astonishment, joy, a desperate yearning. He closed the distance between them in two swift strides, pulling her into a fierce embrace. Thea felt her heart skip, the intensity of the reunion almost palpable in the room's heavy air.

Was he Anna's lost flame?

But he wouldn't reunite with her, not in front of Thea. Not after they'd… and then realization dawned on her.

Anna clung to Andre, her fingers digging into his coat as if she feared he might vanish again. The room seemed to hold its breath, the only sound being the rustle of Anna's silk gown as it brushed against Andre's boots.

Thea watched, her brow furrowing slightly.

Yet here he was, holding Anna with a desperation that was raw and unrestrained, just as Stan had when the highwaymen had captured Thea.

"Oh, Thea, please pardon me," Anna wiped tears from her face. "I didn't expect ever to see him again."

Thea's confusion deepened. She had heard whispers of André's past, tales of loss and sorrow that had shaped the man she had known. But seeing him now, reunited with a sister presumed lost, she realized how little she truly understood.

"Do you remember the brother I mentioned to you?"

"You mentioned me?" Andre shot a look at Thea as if afraid a secret had been divulged.

It had.

"Yes," Thea stammered. "The Habsburg brother who was born too early?"

Andre swallowed hard and slumped his shoulders. "That's me. I'm the bastard."

Then his gaze lifted to Thea, but there was an ocean between them.

Andre—a Habsburg? The enormity of it pressed down on her, making the fragile hope that had budded between them feel like a foolish misstep. His lineage, so near to royalty, was a chasm she could not cross because she was promised to some other distant relation of his. Yet, no matter how her mind tried to armor itself with reason, her heart would not listen. It betrayed her every time, pulling her thoughts back to him with a yearning she couldn't quite voice.

It wasn't just the power of his parentage that weighed upon her; it was what it *meant*. If Andre weren't born too early, he'd be a Habsburg, and she could… but he wasn't, and that was almost worse than what she'd thought earlier, that he was just a commoner.

Her duty, her family's expectations—those unyielding forces that would make love a reckless impossibility—had he hidden who he was on purpose? Did he even see it? Understand it? She doubted it, not when he looked at her with such disarming sincerity or kissed her as though nothing else mattered. Her chest ached with the memory, fraught with longing and fear in equal measure. She wanted so much to believe and trust the sparks between them at that moment, but doubt coiled around her like an unforgiving chain. How could something so beautiful survive the cold, unspoken laws of society—laws that reminded her of exactly who she was and why he could never truly be hers?

Thea inhaled the soft scent of roses mingling with the faint bitterness of tea, a delicate tether to the moment as she took in the scene before her. She felt like an outsider, an intruder on something sacred, yet she couldn't stop looking away. The siblings' reunion was a quiet testament to the strength of love and family—a bond that endured time and loss, a bond that only deepened her own sense of isolation. How cruel it seemed that such love could flourish for them while hers felt doomed to wither before it even began. It had been one thing to love a doctor, a commoner who'd earned an honest living and much respect through skill.

It was another problem entirely to fall for a bastard Habsburg son while she was promised to a Habsburg prince. Scandals at London balls ruined lives. What she'd done could wage wars.

Andre finally released Anna, stepping back slightly but keeping her hands clasped in his. His usually controlled voice was thick with emotion. "I thought you were gone forever."

Anna smiled through her tears, her grip on Andre's hands unwavering. "And I believed you to be lost to me." Her words hung in the air, resonant with the weight of years spent apart.

Thea took a deep breath, feeling the sun's warmth on her skin as it peeked through the window. She realized that this moment, filled with unexpected joy and raw emotion, had changed everything. For Andre, for Anna, and perhaps even for her.

Aware that she was, for now, forgotten, Thea slipped out of the room and left the happy siblings to share their joy...without her.

Chapter Thirty

THEY TALKED FOR hours. Andre told Anna about his studies in Vienna, his apprenticeship in India, and how he started the practice at 87 Harley Street with his friends. In turn, Anna told him about her marriage, that her father had been appointed professor emeritus in Edinburgh and lived there with her mother. She even told him how she fell from the horse and broke her leg.

They'd exhausted every possible way to search for each other in secret, out of fear, yet Thea finally brought them together.

"Where is she?" Andre asked.

"She left us alone to speak, I suppose."

Or perhaps she left because she realized I could ruin her beyond ruination. The Habsburg bastard was even lower in rank than the orthopedist without any links to the aristocracy.

"I'm going home to plan the ball. There's still much to be done."

"Are you quite certain that you feel ready to return home?" Andre asked when his sister gripped his arm tightly in a shaky effort to rise from her chair. He handed her one of the crutches, leaning against the wall.

She winced. "This hurts my arms," she said, reluctantly taking the crutch.

"You're not ready to go home alone," Andre said.

"I won't be alone at home; we have a staff of fourteen people.

I'm never alone." She sighed as if it were a bad thing to have so much help. "There's always something to do, someone to receive or call on, and readying to leave or upon my return—but my husband put me here to isolate me."

"The life of a lady sounds like a chore to you."

Anna gave him the look she used to have when Mama sent them to the nursery if they ate pudding in the kitchen before dinner.

"I did everything I was supposed to," Anna said.

"And it doesn't make you happy." Andre didn't need to ask; it was plain to see.

"Nobody ever asked me what would make me happy, Andre. Everyone assumed that following the aristocratic path was right for me, and now"—she stroked her belly—"if I bear him a son, I will have accomplished everything I ought at two-and-twenty."

"And then?"

She raised her brows. "You're the first to ask."

"You seem to have an answer. Do you care to share it?"

She gave a half smile. He had her. "Well, I'll be a mother. And Mother said she'd come to help. But I don't intend to remain at Paul's disposal."

"Mother is coming to London? When?"

Andre's heart quickened.

"I don't know exactly. The last letter came from Father. She'd left Edinburgh and was going to Italy to visit Lorenzo. Papa won't join us till Christmas."

His parents were coming to London. He thought he should feel whole again, relieved they were alive and restored, but all he could think of was Thea. How would she react?

And where had she gone?

"I won't remain in London when the baby arrives."

"I beg your pardon? You're leaving London?" How could he already lose the family he'd barely reunited with?

"As part of my marriage settlement, Papa ensured I'd have a castle in my name."

"Where is it?"

"Not too far, only about a day's ride by carriage. You could probably ride there in half a day when you wish to visit. And you shall. It has eight bedrooms and more than enough room for all of us when Lorenzo comes for Christmas."

⋙❋⋘

"HAS SHE LEFT Cloverdale House?" Andre asked every servant who passed. He feared Thea had run away and could be in danger, so he searched for her everywhere.

When the scent of citrus and damp earth wrapped around Andre as he stepped into the orangery, he heard her—soft, muffled weeping.

His gaze caught her instantly. Thea. She was folded into herself on a stone bench beneath a potted myrtle tree, the fragile lace of her handkerchief pressed tight against her face. Her shoulders shook with the force of her sobs, and the sight twisted something deep in his chest. He'd seen despair before, countless faces contorted with pain, yet her tears struck him with unrelenting force.

Andre approached her cautiously, boots nearly soundless against the tiled floor. "Thea," he murmured, his tone low, meant only for her.

She stiffened, startled, and quickly pressed the back of her hand to her cheeks as if to erase the evidence of her distress.

"Oh," she whispered hoarsely, her voice breaking. "Andre... I didn't hear—"

"I'm sorry," he interrupted softly, easing down onto the bench beside her. He made no movement to touch her, giving her space, though every nerve in his body urged him closer.

Her lips parted, but no protest came. Instead, she lowered her gaze to the crumpled handkerchief she twisted between her fingers, as though even looking at him might undo her. They sat in breathless silence for a moment, broken only by the faint rustle of leaves and her uneven breaths.

"You don't have to hold this alone," he said finally, his voice gentle but firm. Her response was a sharp shake of the head, her knuckles white around the damasked fabric.

"You don't understand," she rasped. "What I've done…" She bit her lips to stop their trembling. "What I've set into motion. It isn't something you—or anyone—can fix."

"Tell me anyway," he urged, leaning forward, his elbows on his knees. "Test me."

She huffed a laugh, light and humorless, only for it to dissolve into another wave of tears. At last, as though some internal dam had collapsed, she began to speak, her words spilling out in fervent, broken bursts.

"I've ruined everything, Andre," she confessed, her voice shaking with anguish. "Refusing Prince Ralph wasn't just about myself. It was a blow—a public affront to the Habsburgs. The Transylvanian branches, they don't forgive. They conquer." She choked on air as her lashes fluttered, heavy with tears. "And I— I've given Baron von List exactly what he wanted. I've done it. I've played into his hand."

The silence was deafening after her words fell. Andre sat back, his mind unfurling the implications she hadn't said but that hung heavy between them. She was right—he understood just enough of alliances, power struggles, and ambition to know what she feared wasn't far-fetched. Thea wasn't caught in the web; she *was* the web. Every thread circled back to her, every knot tightening with her despair.

"This could mean war," she whispered, her voice raw. "A war I caused and that would implicate my brothers. All for… for…"

"For me?" he asked, though he had no need to. The answer hung between them like a fragile grape ripening too soon and rotting on the vine.

She raised her eyes then, amber and glassy, and met his gaze with searing honesty. "For someone I have no right to choose."

Her words cracked as they escaped her, raw and vulnerable.

Andre's chest burned with the need to speak but fear that anything he might say could make it worse. He reached for her hand instead, slid his palm over hers. Her skin was cold and unsteady—such a contradiction to the fire that burned within her.

"Thea," he said at last, his voice steady but low. "I know what it is to feel the consequences of my very existence. But this...? This war you fear? It is not your doing—at least, not yours alone."

"You don't understand!" she cried, her hands trembling under his. "I can't undo this, Andre. Don't you see? There's no going back."

"And who says going back is the solution?" His voice came suddenly, sharp and impassioned. "For years, I blamed myself for things that weren't my fault. Do you want to know what that granted me? Nothing." He paused, his hand tightening its hold on hers. "When I was eighteen, I fled—a decision that shaped my life. Napoleon's army..." His words faltered for a moment before he found strength again. "They would not have spared my family if they learned of me—a bastard. The timing of my birth stained us all."

She blinked at him, speechless for the first time since he entered.

"So I left," he continued, his words laden with memory. "I removed myself as if that would cleanse their name. I stopped using my full name. I clung to medicine like a drowning man to driftwood because in medicine, science mattered. Skill mattered. Not parentage—never blood." He leaned closer, his thumb brushing her knuckles. "It was society that cast the shadow, Thea. Not me. Not my family. Just misplaced judgment."

Her voice softened, tentative, as she asked, "You ran away to protect them?"

"I did," he admitted, the confession raw in his throat. "And while I ache for what I abandoned, I know it was my only choice. But now that Anna told me about her awful husband, I wonder if I should have stayed. And I'm not running away from you. Not now, not ever—for as long as you want me by your side."

"And yet I risk everything now," she said faintly. "My family's lives. My home…"

"No, you don't." His voice caused her gaze to snap to his. "If alliances crumble or conquest is plotted, that is far bigger than you, Thea. They might wield you as an excuse, but it's not your doing. And you have me now," he added, his voice softening. "You have my family at your back."

Tears shimmered in her eyes anew, though something unspoken passed between them—a flicker of hope in the midst of despair. Her free hand sought his, trembling and light. "I'm dragging you into this," she murmured. "Into me."

Andre shook his head at once, his thumb brushing the edge of her hand. "You're not dragging me anywhere. I *choose* this, Thea. I choose *you*. Whatever comes next—we'll face it together. Do you want that?"

For a long moment, her dark gaze searched his, words beyond her grasp. Then, as sunlight dappled the leaves around them, she gave the faintest of nods, her lips tilting into something fragile but real.

Andre allowed himself to forget, just for a moment, the weight of his past. Timing, his mother had once said, mattered little. And now, with Thea's hand in his, he dared to believe she'd been right all along.

Chapter Thirty-One

ANDRE LET THEA find her brother while he brought the discharge papers to Anna, who was standing with a crutch under her arm in the room where he'd found her.

Found her... Andre considered the words. He never expected to find his sister again.

"Anna, there you are!" A short, half-bald man arrived empty-handed but for a smug grin.

This was the husband who'd cheated on Anna and whom she'd caught with a mistress? *This?*

Andre balled his fists, but Anna squeezed his arm and put on a fake smile.

"Husband..." she said to the man, who was notably shorter than her, and twitched.

His eyes darted from her to Andre and back but when Anna narrowed her gaze, he jerked his head back as if he'd been stung.

"May I present to you Dr. Andre Fernando von Dürer?"

Etiquette required Andre to bow to her sister's husband, but he couldn't get himself to bow to the cheating, twitching figure before him. It was almost comical that he gave Andre a once-over and had to look up for it. A meager man like that should treat his sister like a queen, not discard her and break her heart. For a broken heart, one needs to fall in love first. Anna didn't seem to love this man beyond the excellent sentiment of tolerating his presence.

Paul reached out, and she jerked back.

Oh, she couldn't bear his touch.

Andre's insides churned at the sight of his sister's unhappy marriage. This was not what he'd wished for her. Love, passion, devotion, and a man with integrity were the least she deserved.

"So I heard," Paul started, showing his crooked teeth. "Your brother is a doctor."

He twitched again and tugged at the back seams of his breeches.

Anna pretended to be impervious to the jerking movements of her husband. Her smile faltered, replaced by a fleeting grimace, as she cast a sidelong glance, her expression carefully schooled to neutrality.

"*Was ist mit dem Hampelmann?*" What is it with the jumping jack? Andre whispered to Anna.

She burst into laughter.

Andre joined her.

It was just when they were like children, and Andre's heart swelled with love for his long-lost sister. Oh, how he'd missed his family.

"*Wahrscheinlich hat er sich wieder was eingefangen.*" He probably caught something again.

"What are you saying to him?" Paul demanded in a tone Andre didn't appreciate when his sister was addressed.

"Do you suffer from an itch?" Andre asked Paul.

The man narrowed his eyes, but Andre paid more attention to his sister's grimace. No woman should feel disgust for her husband. How could he help his sister out of this union?

"It's been going on for a while," Paul admitted. "Have you an ointment for it?"

Andre's eyes met Anna's, but she crinkled her lips and gave a faint shake of her head.

Good, at least you don't have it.

"I'd need to examine you before I can make a diagnosis."

At first, Paul stood stiffly in the room, but the silence, which couldn't have been more than a second, stretched into what felt like an awkward hour.

"May we leave you here for a moment?" Andre asked his sister.

"Certainly, I shall have another cup of tea." Anna's hand slid down Andre's arm, and she sank back into the armchair.

Less than fifteen minutes later, Andre considered the Hippocratic Oath he'd sworn in the exam room at Cloverdale House. "First, do no harm" was its essence. Yet, he wished for nothing more than to rip Paul's arms out for how he treated his little sister.

"You have a boil," Andre said as he dropped his probe into the metal bucket prepared for dirty instruments. The instruments would be carried outside in the bucket and rinsed with boiling water before being touched by hand.

Paul pulled his breeches back up and tied the laces.

He didn't seem rueful for having contracted a disease that was a testament to his indiscretions.

"Does your mistress have it, too?" Andre asked. His duty as a doctor was to stop any spread of infection and warn his patients—even if his instinct was to let this particular man suffer.

"How dare you imply infidelity? Why don't you ask whether your sister gave me this?" Paul fastened the last button and sucked his belly in like a rooster. "Perhaps she's the one—"

Andre rose from the chair, dashed around the desk, and towered over Paul, balling his fists so tightly that his palms hurt. "You listen to me very carefully—"

"My lord." Paul looked up at Andre with a vicious stare. "You're a mere physician. Address me with my title, bastard."

Andre was seething with rage.

"That is Dr. Andre Fernando von Dürer for you, Paul." Andre dragged the last word out as if it were an insult to the lord. "I would strike you that you'd spit your teeth further than you can see, milord, but I know that you feel it where I wouldn't even slap you. It'll always come back."

Paul's eyes grew wide. "You know—"

"I know because I studied medicine. I am a man of science. You pretend to be a man of honor, but you have nothing to show for it, not even your own wife's respect or affection."

Paul formed his lips as if to speak, but nothing came out.

He leaned in slightly, his voice lowering to a near growl. "You owe her an apology. Not for her sake, but for yours. Otherwise..." He allowed the unspoken threat to linger, not needing to finish it.

Andre straightened, smoothing his cuff with deliberate precision, his gaze slicing through the man like steel. His temper was banked—for now. "Consider this your only warning. Anna is under my protection. Do not forget it."

The man swallowed hard, his face pale and taut. He gave a jerky nod but did not speak further, his confidence thoroughly shaken by the weight of each of Andre's words.

Andre tilted his head, his lips curling into another chilling smile—one that didn't reach his eyes.

"Just give me the ointment. That's your job." Paul still had a self-indulgent smugness that provoked Andre even further.

"It's not."

"You're a mere doctor, a bastard. I'm a lord. Give me the ointment."

"Exactly, I am a doctor. I'm not an apothecary. And if you'd like me to ensure that my friend, the apothecary, gives you the right medicine, you'll have to ask for it as a patient."

"It's a disgrace. How dare you?"

"How. Dare. You. Cheating on my sister, sullying your line, and now you're threatening me when it is you in need of my medicine?"

"But I am—"

"Titled? You're *entitled*. But you have not earned my respect. Even though I may not have a title, I'm a hundred times a better man than you'll ever be. And I am a very, very, very dangerous man when my little sister is imperiled."

"I've done nothing to imperil her or the baby."

"And you will do nothing. Do you understand my words?"

Paul raised a brow.

"I will make myself very clear. You will uphold the clause and support her and the child, but you will never interfere with their lives. Should you as much as breathe in the direction of my sister's bed chambers, I will come to you at night. Not bound by the duties of my profession or any rules that keep me from inflicting upon you what I know you deserve."

"You have no right to stop me from visiting my wife."

"I do! As your doctor and hers, I'm bound to ensure that neither of you imperil your health. If you were to cross me or my pregnant sister, or the baby when he or she is born, there's no way to tell how far I will go to protect my sister. I lost her once and will not risk it again. I'm not ever going to turn away from my family again. You'll have to get past me—but you won't—do you understand?"

"But she's bearing my heir!"

"Yes, she might be. And she's bearing my niece or nephew. They are under my protection."

"And under my roof!"

"You can take the roof but not them. What will you do with a roof, hm?"

Paul didn't respond.

"Then our roles are defined. Are there any questions?"

"Your mother told me that she missed you." Paul tsked. "I didn't realize it was a hound she'd been looking for."

"Better a hound than a rat spreading disease wherever it goes. Now, get out."

"I'll take Anna with—"

"You'll not remove a patient from this rehabilitation center without the doctor's explicit permission. And that doctor is me."

With these words, Andre opened the door, and Paul huffed as he left.

Chapter Thirty-Two

THEA WAS SURE she'd heard Andre's voice but came to the sunlit parlor and found Anna shuffling impatiently in the armchair.

"Oh, Anna, good afternoon!" Thea said when she saw a knocked-over cup and a puddle of cold tea in the saucer and on the doily.

"I wish it were, Thea," Anna said, padding the mess with an already-soaked cotton napkin.

"I should ring for help—" Thea said, but Anna shook her head.

"Nobody can help me anymore." And suddenly, leaning back in the chair, Anna seemed to have forgotten the spilled tea. Her gaze was so calm and absent when Thea followed it out the window that a shiver traveled down her back. Something terrible was the matter, not merely the spilled tea.

"Anna, please tell me what preoccupies you so much." Thea sat in the chair across from Anna and reached for her friend's hand.

But Anna withdrew and folded both of her hands over her stomach.

"He's come to take me away," Anna spoke in the direction of the window as if a ghostly figure had her captivated somewhere in the distance. "And then he will come to me, and I will lose the baby." Anna stroked her stomach as if the tiny being inside of her needed her comfort, not vice versa. "I hoped my mother would be here when I left the rehabilitation center. I sent to her, but she's older now and cannot travel as fast as he did. And now he's going to."

Thea swallowed hard, afraid to imagine what Anna's husband would do to her.

A single tear ran down Anna's right cheek, and she let it roll off her face and fall on the hand covering her stomach. "I thought that it would take longer. Somehow, I was glad I only broke my leg and that the baby was well." She turned to Thea and blinked at her as if she'd seen her for the first time. "Do you know that Andre could hear the baby's heartbeat with his stethoscope?"

Thea's breath caught. "I didn't."

Anna beamed like the proud mother she'd be. "It's swift, much faster than our adult heartbeats. But he said that's normal for a tiny baby—" Suddenly, her breath hitched, and she nearly choked on tears, no doubt. "I don't want my baby to die, Thea." Anna broke into tears.

Thea was at sea—one filled with emotions she'd never known, yet they were coming all at once.

Thea stared down into her teacup, the remnants of the brew swirling like her thoughts. She felt a pang of guilt for Anna—yes, guilt had anchored itself firmly in her chest. But guilt wasn't all. There was something sharper, deeper.

Fear.

Anna's bravery inspired her, but it also terrified her. The woman was not much older than she, yet burdened with so much. And somehow, that realization shifted something inside Thea. She'd come to England to escape a loveless marriage, a trap. She'd started to look after Mary—to teach her Latin, arithmetic, and give her structure. But over the weeks, her purpose had grown. It wasn't just about Mary anymore. She wanted to protect, to nurture, to care for a child. To have a family.

Her breath hitched, her fingers tightening around the fragile porcelain cup. Since Andre… since she'd fallen in love with Andre, it was clear. Her heart was ready.

Lost in the swirl of her own emotions, the sound of a voice echoed through the hall, wrenching her from her thoughts.

"We have to carry our trunks here?"

Thea's stomach twisted violently as her pulse quickened. She knew that voice, though it took a full moment for her mind to align with recognition. Before she could breathe, Stan's response followed, clipped and petulant. "No, but they are here for patients, not you."

A dull rustling noise reverberated, unmistakably the sound of one brother giving another a shove—or maybe a punch. Thea's pulse drummed in her ears, drowning out everything but the implications. Her brothers. Here.

She rose so suddenly that her teacup rattled against the saucer, nearly toppling onto the carpet. Her hands trembled as she set it down without noticing Anna's gaze, sharp and concerned.

"Thea?" Anna's voice was soft but probing. "Is something wrong?"

Thea grasped at words, desperate to form a coherent thought amidst the rising panic. "Anna… I—" she faltered, then tried again. "I mean, there's someone—I should—"

"Who is it, dear?" Anna asked gently, already reaching for her crutch with slow, practiced movements.

Thea's chest constricted painfully. She couldn't evade this now. Anna, her dear friend, needed her. And yet, all Thea could think of was running—escaping far, far away before whatever storm lay waiting in the hall swept her up completely.

She swallowed hard, forcing herself to move, to stand beside Anna and offer her arm in assistance. She owed her that much. If anything, Anna's quiet strength anchored her in that moment.

And then, the voices grew nearer.

"Thea!"

Her head whipped toward the door. The voice was loud,

laden with authority, and it struck her like a whip. Not Stan. It was Alex. The weight of it slashed through her, both familiar and imposing.

Panic crawled up her throat, and her grip on Anna's arm tightened.

"Alex," Thea smiled through her teeth.

"Aren't you going to introduce me to your companion?" he asked, standing tall and eyeing Thea with the same demanding stare that his father had. Alex had always been the one to make his father proud.

Introductions were made, and Thea tried to excuse herself.

Anna tilted her head. "You're not pleased to see your brother." It wasn't a question.

Thea swallowed hard, unable to pull her gaze from her brother who was a foot taller than her.

"Pleased is not... exactly the word I'd use."

His coat was immaculately tailored, his boots gleaming with polish, his hat perched at the slightest rakish angle—not for charm, but for calculated effect. Even the air around him seemed sharp, as if he carried expectation on the soles of his boots.

And then came Stan. His disheveled dark hair popped out first as he plopped into the armchair and winced. The shoulder... He had dressed appropriately, of course, but there was none of Alex's ironclad perfection. There never was.

"I should go," Anna said as she stepped toward the door. Thea nodded. It was better that Andre's sister didn't see this.

"Sit," Alex said, waving to the settee once Anna had left the room.

It was just the three of them, and they switched to their native language, Romanian.

"Are you mad?" Alex asked Thea. "You ran away!"

Oh good, no time wasted on platitudes.

Thea bristled against his condescending tone. "It would have been madness to stay and wait for the Habsburgs."

"But that's exactly what you were supposed to do."

Stan cleared his throat. "That's not all."

Alex groaned. "How much do you need? I didn't bring that much with me."

"It's not money. It's a blessing she needs." Stan nudged in Thea's direction.

Oh no, he was forcing her to say it.

"I wish to dissolve the agreement with the Habsburgs entirely." Thea folded her hand on her lap.

Alex sucked his lips in. "Don't tell me—"

But he asked Stan and not her.

"Why would he know better than me? Why don't you ask me?" Thea put her arms on her hips and realized she sounded precisely like Mother.

"Because you're an innocent!" Stan shrugged as if she couldn't possibly know her own heart.

"No, I'm not!" And just as she spoke the words, Thea bit her tongue. Oh no, she shouldn't have implied…

"I beg your pardon?" Stan asked in German now, a language reserved for official meetings and correspondence. He was taking notes.

"I merely mean that I know my own heart." Yes, that sounded harmless enough.

"And does anyone else know it?" Stan asked.

"Yes," she said with a curt smile. Long sentences could get her into too much trouble.

Alex crossed his arms.

That was unlike him. In fact, he looked rather wild. Not in the wilderness sense, because he was clean-shaven and well-coiffed, as usual, but there was a fierceness to his gaze— impossible!

"You're in love!" Thea exclaimed.

Alex jerked his head back. "What?"

"With whom?" Stan now joined the commotion.

"How did she turn this around to me?" Alex's voice cracked when he switched back to Romanian and addressed Stan.

"That doesn't matter, just tell me!" Stan seemed not quite like himself. "You haven't been introduced to Lady Seraphina yet. So who?"

"Just someone I met in Cornwall," Alex spoke silently. Thea and Stan cast each other a look.

"Is it that serious?" Thea asked.

"No, it can't be." Alex swallowed visibly and inhaled deeply. "It must not be."

"And yet, it is too late, isn't it?" Thea asked, holding her hand up when Stan groaned and rose to pace the room. "You love her?"

Alex slumped and gave Thea a rueful look.

That's what it was. He'd blossomed somehow. The charade of the first to follow all the rules seemed to have cracked, and what it revealed was the faithful Alex, the one she hadn't seen since they'd been children.

"And now you must marry Lady Seraphina?" Stan tsked. "Nothing's lost. It's perfectly well for you to bring some experience into the marriage." Then Stan paused and gave Thea a severe look. "But not for you!"

Alex blinked a few times. "How do you know that I did—"

"I knew the moment I saw you, Alex." Stan gestured as if he were brushing Stan from head to toe with paste. "Your voice is deeper, your gaze steady, and your voice cracks when you're absent-minded. Whoever this girl is, she affected you deeply."

Alex leaned his upper body forward and buried his face in his hands. "I feel split in two when she's not with me."

Thea's hands flew to her mouth. "I cannot believe the hypocrisy!"

"I mean, I was fine. When Mama said I could meet Lady Seraphina while coming to England and escort Thea home, I didn't think much of it. Life was fine."

"Escort me home? When did I agree to come back?" Thea interrupted Alex, but he didn't seem to pay attention.

He looked up at Stan, who had assumed a wide stance next to

Alex's chair. "And now that I left her in Cornwall, I feel like I'm not me."

Stan narrowed his gaze and tilted his head to the side.

"I can't describe it; it's just that I'm not me without her."

"You feel like a husk of your life that only she can fill?" Thea asked knowing the feeling all too well.

"Yes," Alex said.

"And as soon as you don't feel her close to you, you already miss her?" Thea pressed on.

Alex nodded.

"Even if she's only in the next room?"

Alex nodded again.

"Colors, scents, and even the sounds in the world are better when she's near and fade to shades of fog when she's not?"

"Exactly." But when Alex spoke the words, his eyes locked with Thea.

"Oh no!" Stan joined Thea on the settee. "Do you feel like that about Andre?"

Thea saw her father's eyes in both brothers, but it wasn't him. The young men looking at her were the same who'd taught her how to climb the tree to get over the palace walls, the same who brought her honey cake and half-fermented wine after bedtime, the same who left their books out so she could learn about subjects that her tutors didn't deem fit for a girl.

"Yes, Andre means everything to me," she admitted.

And when she did, it was as if a boulder had rolled off her lungs because she could breathe easier.

"So when you said you're not that innocent, you meant—" Stan barely managed to speak it, he was the youngest of the brothers, but she was his little sister, after all.

"We didn't."

But I want to.

Stan cringed but remained silent.

Alex—and that was a genuine surprise—didn't jump out of his chair to scream about how she'd ruined her life. Instead, he melted into the cushions like he'd stolen something valuable.

"I did," Alex mumbled. "In Cornwall."

"It's not a problem for you, Alex." Stan rubbed his forehead and sank onto the settee, lifting a hand to rub Thea's back. "For a girl, it's rather a complication."

"I wanted to save myself for my bride, but that was before I knew—"

"Then you understand that I want to marry Andre." Thea decided that honesty in this situation may not be the best policy, but it was her only chance.

"You're betrothed to Prince Ralph." Alex and Stan said it at the same time and in the same tone.

"She can't break the engagement," Stan said.

"She can't marry him either. Not now," Alex added.

"What if we don't tell?" Stan pursed his lips.

"I don't wish to marry anyone besides Andre."

"Tell me more about him?" Alex asked Stan.

"He's a doctor. He is specialized as an orthopedist but when he touches people… for example, when he touched my ankle the day I was injured—" Thea replied before Stan could say a word.

"You were injured?" Alex cried out.

"It's why I called you. We're in grave danger." Stan rubbed his face with both hands.

"And Andre rescued me."

Her love.

Alex and Stan cast each other a look that said more than she could fathom, though seemed like *I-can't-believe-we-have-to-do-this-with-our-baby-sister.*

Silence followed.

Stan shifted in the seat, and the springs in the cushions creaked.

"I want only Andre," Thea's voice pierced the silence.

Except that it didn't pierce the silence.

Her brothers remained motionless.

"As soon as possible, of course," Thea added for good measure.

Stan blinked a few times, but it was Alex who spoke first. "That's the problem. It's not possible.

"Do I have to explain it to her? Are you jesting?" Alex turned to Stan. "What did you do while you've been here?"

"Quite a lot, thank you for asking. In all the *minutes* since you've arrived, you haven't even asked about any of the diplomatic accomplishments of my time in England—"

"Well, because you let our sister fall in love." Alex gestured grandly.

"What was am I supposed to do, catch her mid-fall and stop the landing?"

"Perhaps yes, if it was the doctor she landed on."

"Enough!" Thea rose and inhaled so that her chest swelled with the courage she didn't have. "I am indeed going to marry Andre. Yes, it is complicated because I must first breach the betrothal agreement with Ralph. But this is my life, and I will not be a bystander while you two think you have the authority to rule over me in Father's absence."

Both Stan and Alex stared at her, eyes wide and mouths agape.

"It won't work," Alex said.

"I will make it work!" Thea's voice betrayed the anger bubbling within her.

"That's not what I mean. It will work with him if you love him." Alex sighed. "I wish you nothing more than happiness."

"Me too," Stan added. "Frankly, I haven't said anything until now because I cannot blame you for not wanting to marry the Habsburg prince."

Thea couldn't believe the words that came out of her brothers.

"B-But you said—" she croaked. Oh no, Stan must have told Alex…

"It won't work in that Father will never agree to swap a Habsburg prince for a Habsburg bastard. It has to be a done deal."

Stan narrowed his eyes, and Alex shook his head, his lips flat in a line in resignation.

"But he doesn't know Andre the way you do," Thea plead to Stan.

"That's why." Stan raised his eyebrows. Then he shifted in the settee and scratched his chin. "I would prefer a man like Andre for my dear sister over the Habsburg prince a million times."

Alex raised his chin. "As your older brother, I must remind you that you have dynastic responsibilities, Thea. You're not anybody. You are a princess."

"And our little sister," Stan added, which earned him an approving nod from Alex.

"What about your dynastic obligations and the girl in Cornwall?" she asked.

Alex's mien fell. "I don't know what to do."

"Because it just happened, and the feelings are so grand that you cannot contain the joy in your heart?"

Alex furrowed his brows. Stan shifted again.

A pall of silence hung in the air, thick and oppressive, until he coughed, his voice breaking the stillness with an edge of uncertainty. "I—should we—perhaps this isn't the moment..." His words trailed off, his resolve fading under the weight of her unyielding silence.

"You have a responsibility to me, too," Thea mumbled. "I'm not a political bargaining chip. I was born to make political alliances but I want to do more. And if Stan can resolve the matter with Baron von List here, I would be sent to Prince Ralph in vain. You mustn't allow it."

"It would break your heart?" Alex asked. "That's what she said the last time I saw her."

"Yes, it would. Do you want that to happen, or will you represent our family and show that we are—"

"Wait, what did you say?" Alex asked.

"It's Father's letter. He said that we should represent him

while we are in England," Stan said.

Thea felt her eyes widen and her pulse rise. "Then do it!"

"He surely meant in diplomacy," Alex tried, but his tone betrayed that he'd lost this battle.

"He didn't limit the authority he granted you. And you're the oldest brother here. Oh, Alex!" Thea rose and darted to his side. She took his hand and gave him a squeeze. "Please don't turn Andre down when he asks for my hand!"

Alex looked at Stan, but Thea ignored their unspoken brotherly messages. "Please don't deny me the chance to a life filled with love."

Alex sighed and then turned to Stan. "And you say he is a good man?"

"Worthy to be one of us, brother," Stan said.

Thea's heart swelled with joy. "Then let me speak to him first."

Chapter Thirty-Three

DESPITE ALL HER best efforts, Thea could not find Andre anywhere at Cloverdale House. Was it possible that he had returned to Harley Street without telling her?

She convinced Stan to let her take the carriage there, searching for him and when she opened the door to the practice, there was a flurry of activity. Patients waited in the hall, some women chattered excitedly in the apothecary, which had a door ajar, and a man with a small parcel of ice came down the stairs, holding it to his cheek.

There was ice.

Andre couldn't be far if he was the one to chisel it off the block in the cellar.

"Princess?" a voice came from the side room. "Can I help you?" It was the nurse Mary had liked so much.

"Miss Wendy Folsham?"

The young woman nodded gently. "Is Prince Stan alright?"

"Oh yes. I'm looking for Andre."

A hollow ache joined the turmoil in her chest—an ache she despised for its weakness.

Wendy showed Thea the way to Andre's chambers upstairs. Thea knocked.

"I'm not home," came Andre's voice. He'd left without speaking to her.

The anger wanted to bloom, demanded it, but so too did hurt. There was no room in her heart for both, and yet both surged, unwilling to be silenced. She swallowed hard, forcing her chin up, though the trembling of her shoulders betrayed her.

"Me neither," she called back.

The door opened abruptly. "Thea! What are you doing here?

"I could ask you the same! Where have you been?"

His eyes narrowed, and Thea entered his small but neat room, shutting the door behind her. An overstuffed bookshelf leaned against the wall, with a desk, lamp, wash basin, and bed. But what Thea noticed was that the scent of Andre was amplified in this room. This was him, raw and unkempt in simple beige breeches and a white linen shirt.

"I've been looking for you at Cloverdale House, and you didn't return."

"I can't be with you, Thea. I'd drag you down." His voice sounded unconvinced and sad, as if he were forcing himself to speak to them.

"That's not true. Everything I know about tells me you would only lift me up."

He dropped his head and avoided her gaze.

Thea's heart leaped at the sight of this firm, tall, and ruggedly handsome man with the manners and breeding of a prince but the golden hands of the doctor. "You're too humble."

She crinkled her nose. "It doesn't suit you."

At that, he met her gaze. "Humility has nothing to do with insufficiency. I wish I were enough for you, but I can't ever be. And now that you know why, I can bear the loss. I knew I couldn't have you, but losing you hurts even more."

She knew what he meant, of course. Although he was born an illegitimate child, his parents married and gave birth to his siblings after that. By blood, he was a Habsburg. He could just never be legitimized.

"Let me ask you this. If I told you that my parents had me out of wedlock, would you feel differently about me?" Thea asked.

He swept toward her, put his arms on her shoulders, and let them rise slowly to her cheeks until he cupped her face and drew her closer. "Nothing in the world, especially no trifles like society's rules and technicalities, could ever affect how deeply and fiercely I love you, Thea."

"That's exactly how I feel."

He exhaled, and his hands melted off her. Then he took a step back. "Thea, this is different. You're a princess. A princess! I'm nothing."

Enough was enough.

"First of all, I may be a princess, but that doesn't mean that all the men in my life, my father, my brothers, and now you have the right to tell me what to think, do, and feel. I love you and don't need anybody's permission but yours to show it."

"Show it?"

She had his attention again.

Good!

"Second, I am supposed to become a Habsburg, and besides your sister Anna, you're the only one I've ever met—and I know most of them personally or by reputation—who has a beating human heart inside that rock-hard ribcage of yours."

"Ribs are bones; they're supposed to be hard."

"Well, the ribs, maybe, but everything about you is just so… so…" She sucked in the air between her lips and then bit her lower lip. "Hard."

"Hard? Yes, so hard, difficult, Thea." He took a step back and almost reached the door with his back. "But it shouldn't be so difficult."

"It's not difficult at all."

"Yes, it is! I can't stop thinking about it, and no matter how I look at it, there's no angle here that I can use to set things right."

"I'm not a dislocated shoulder, Andre; this is my life. And my heart."

"And I won't break it."

"Then you have no choice but to be with me."

He blew out the air. "Thea—"

"I mean it."

"It's too difficult." His protest sounded even less convincing now, yet he seemed to resist her with all his might.

"Then let me explain it for you." Thea spoke in her governess voice that she'd reserved for Mary, but apparently, the most accomplished orthopedist in London needed a lesson. "I love you."

He slumped.

"Wait!" She held out her index finger to enumerate the elements of this theory that would make her—make her heart—whole, she hoped. "You love me, don't you?"

His eyes found hers and glistened with something black as if there were a void only she could fill.

"That's what I hoped. Good. So it's a simple equation: a plus b makes—"

"Thea, we're not variables. There's no way to recalculate that I'm just not enough."

She narrowed her eyes. "You're just right for me. No other variable—person—that fits into the equation... heart... life, I mean... argh! Andre, why don't you understand that you are the only one right for me?"

He swallowed hard and looked rueful. His Adam's apple bobbed, but he didn't speak.

"The decision is mine. If everyone thinks I have such authority in diplomacy and importance for the kingdom, how is it that nobody thinks I can know my heart enough to decide—with all I am—that it beats for you?"

"Thea," he rasped, his voice dropping.

"Don't *Thea* me, Andre! This is between you and me, a man and a woman. If you want me, allow *me* to decide to give myself to you." Her index finger bore into his chest. "You don't need anybody else's permission."

Thea stood in the middle of Andre's bedchamber, her heart thudding so fiercely she could almost feel it in her throat, and then… she felt something change. Although the room was only dimly lit, the soft flicker of the gas light cast long shadows on the walls; it seemed as bright as if a new dawn had brought on another chapter in her life. The clip-clopping of hooves from the street outside served as a reminder of the world beyond these walls. But there, at 87 Harley Street, they were finally alone, and nothing else mattered.

Andre squared his shoulders as if he'd come to a new realization. He fumbled behind his back, and Thea noticed that he had turned the key in the door, the metallic click echoing in the stillness. He looked at Thea, his dark eyes searching hers for the implicit permission she had already granted with a nod. Her breath hitched as he stepped closer, deftly untying the band that held his white linen shirt together at the neck. The shirt fell open, revealing the expanse of his chest, and the distance between them evaporated.

"Then take what you want and claim me, Your Royal Highness."

She furrowed her brows.

"I mean it. You're the princess and my superior. Do with me whatever you wish, for I'm yours with heart and soul and for as long as I shall live. If it is truly your wish—"

"It is."

He exhaled, and his face brightened into a fleeting smile before his gaze locked on her lips.

"I only wish for you."

"I'm not much," he protested.

"You're everything for me. Forever."

He seemed unable to contradict her now, but when he pressed his lips against hers, Thea gasped, her mouth parting in surprise and desire. Andre deepened the kiss, his tongue exploring with such deliberate intensity that her knees nearly buckled. Each stroke of his tongue sent waves of pleasure coursing through her, making her insides clench and tremble.

Andre's hands roamed up her back, his touch firm and possessive. He pulled her closer, the heat of his body seeping into hers. His scent—clean linen mixed with a hint of sandalwood—invaded her senses, intoxicating her further. She threaded her fingers through his dark hair, feeling the silken strands slide between her fingers as she pulled him closer. She wanted him, not merely to claim him, but with a ferocity that she couldn't explain.

Yet, he seemed to know exactly how to proceed. Every touch and kiss of his was precisely what she hadn't known she needed, and only he could complete her.

His lips left hers, trailing a path of kisses down her jawline and to the sensitive skin of her neck. Thea's breath came in short, ragged gasps as he nipped and sucked, leaving a trail of heated sensations in his wake. She arched her neck, giving him better access, and he took full advantage, his mouth working magic on her skin.

Thea's hands moved to his chest, fingers splaying across the hard planes of muscle. She felt the rapid beat of his heart beneath her palm, mirroring her frantic pulse. She pushed the shirt off his shoulders, letting it fall to the floor. Her hands explored the contours of his back, feeling the strength and sinew under the smooth skin.

Andre lifted his head, his eyes locking onto hers with an intensity that made her shiver. "Thea," he murmured, his voice rough with desire. "Are you sure you choose me? Here and now and forever?"

She nodded, unable to form words, her body already answering for her. She wanted this—wanted him—with a desperation that bordered on madness if she were denied.

Andre's hands moved to the laces of her dress, his fingers working quickly to undo the intricate ties. Thea felt the fabric loosen and slip from her shoulders, pooling at her feet. She stood before him in her chemise, the thin fabric doing little to conceal her heaving chest and the stiff peaks of her nipples under her stays.

He gazed at her, his eyes darkening with hunger. "You're so

beautiful," he whispered, his voice laden with reverence and longing.

Thea felt a flush creep up her neck. His words and gaze made her feel both exposed and cherished. She reached for him and pulled him back to her. Their bodies pressed together, and the heat between them was almost unbearable.

Andre's hands slid beneath her chemise, skimming over the smooth skin of her back before cupping her buttocks. He lifted her effortlessly, carrying her to the examination table that doubled as a makeshift bed in his private moments of respite. He set her down gently, his hands never leaving her body.

Thea lay back, her hair fanning out around her like a halo. She watched as Andre shrugged off the rest of his clothes, the candlelight casting a golden glow on his bronzed skin. When he was finally as bare as she, he climbed onto the table, positioning himself above her.

Their eyes met, and a silent understanding passed between them. Andre kissed her again, his mouth claiming hers with a fierce tenderness that made her heartache. His hands caressed her skin, mapping every curve and dip, leaving no inch unexplored.

Thea's breath came in shallow, staccato bursts as his lips traveled lower, worshipping her body with a devotion that left her trembling. He suckled her breasts, his tongue flicking over the sensitive peaks until she moaned, arching into his touch.

His hand slid between her thighs, finding her slick and ready. He teased her, his fingers dancing over her most intimate place, coaxing her pleasure higher and higher. Thea writhed beneath him, her body tightening with anticipation and need.

"Please, Andre," she whispered, her voice barely more than a breath. "Show me how you feel."

HE OBLIGED, POSITIONING himself at her entrance.

"I don't know how not to hurt you," he said, frozen and looking down.

"I want to feel you all over," Thea said, surprised at the urgency in her voice. She knew she was out of control, but she was so full of anticipation that she was both giddy with joy and quivering with excitement. Andre was perfect in every way that mattered, as a human being with a big heart, and she had no reservations about giving herself.

But what she didn't anticipate was how much he could give her.

When he entered her, she felt a slight burn. He paused for an instant, but not too long. Then, with a slow, deliberate thrust, he entered her, filling her. Thea gasped, her hands clutching at his shoulders as he moved within her. He was large and complex. Somehow, she hadn't expected him to fit inside of her as he did, but she considered it for a moment, pressed her hips against his, and it felt right. Oh, so right! The sensation was overwhelming, a perfect blend of pleasure and pain, making her feel more alive than ever before.

The discomfort had subsided momentarily, and she felt their bodies meld into perfect harmony.

"Does it hurt?" Andre asked, concern etched on his face.

"You feel as good inside my body as in my heart," Thea rasped.

Andre held Thea's gaze, his words a tender caress. "Thea, you are the flame in my heart and the calm in my soul. With you, I've found the love I never knew I craved, but I do. You've become my light and the reason for every heartbeat."

She inhaled at his words, unsure how to answer. He slid even more profoundly with the motion, and she arched her head back.

She felt her cheeks tighten, her brow furrow because nothing was left to say—they could only show each other how deep their love ran.

Andre set a steady rhythm, each stroke eliciting cries of pleasure from Thea. She matched his movements, meeting him thrust for thrust, their bodies moving in perfect harmony. The world outside ceased to exist; there was only that moment, that connection, that shared ecstasy.

As the tension built, Andre's movements became more urgent, and his control slipped. Thea felt herself nearing the edge, the pressure mounting almost unbearable. They both shattered with a final, powerful thrust, the release crashing over them like a tidal wave.

Andre collapsed onto her, his breath hot against her neck. They lay there, tangled in each other, their hearts pounding in unison. Thea's body hummed with the aftershocks of their lovemaking, a contented smile playing on her lips.

At that moment, she knew she was irrevocably his and he, hers. There was no going back, no denying the truth of what they had become together.

Andre lifted his head, his eyes soft and filled with a tenderness that melted her heart. He brushed a strand of hair from her face, his thumb tracing the curve of her cheek. "Thea," he whispered, his voice a gentle caress. "I love you so very much."

Tears welled in her eyes, not from sorrow but from his words' overwhelming joy and certainty. She cupped his face, her thumb brushing over his lips. "I love you too, Andre," she replied, her voice steady and sure. And she'd hold on to him forever.

※

Chapter Thirty-Four

A few hours later, at Cloverdale House…

"GO ON," THEA whispered and nudged Andre toward the door of his treatment room.

"I don't even know your older brother," Andre protested.

"You know, they're four of them."

"You said two are here."

"Yes, so go and speak with them. They're expecting you."

That's what he feared. They'd expect him, the commoner who'd compromised their sister due to marry a Habsburg—one of his distant cousins no less—and now it was his judgment day.

"They'll kill me."

"No, they won't. And I'll stand right here."

She was going to eavesdrop; there was no doubt in his mind. But he had to hold his own and defend a position he'd put himself into, while in actuality, it was the brothers he could relate to.

After all, he'd love to give Paul, his younger sister's husband, what he deserved. Andre realized the situation was different. Paul had betrayed Anna. He would never do that to Thea.

"Alright, I'm going in." Andre squared his shoulders, and Thea grabbed his collar.

"Just one kiss for good luck," she said, pressing her lips against this.

Instantly, his body hardened, and his resolve solidified. He'd lay his life down for his princess, no questions asked. But he could use the good luck.

So, he kissed her back, pulled her closer, and deepened the kiss.

"Ahem!"

Stan cleared his throat.

Thea jumped away, pressing her hands over her mouth, but it was useless; her lips were swollen with desire. Andre would continue where they'd left off, but first, he needed her brother's blessing.

"Our brother is waiting," Stan said and inclined his head, signaling Andre to step in.

Wait, this was his treatment room, and yet another man stood in the center, just under the gas lamp.

"May I present Prince Alexander von Hohenzollern-Sigmaringen to you?" Stan started, and Andre put one hand behind his back and bowed. "This is Dr. Andre Fernando von Dürer."

"The professor's son from Florence?"

"Yes, Your Royal Highness." Andre couldn't decide whether to stand en garde or ramrod. He felt that flight was the better response than fighting with two men his size.

"And you studied in Vienna?" Prince Alex pressed on.

"I completed my studies at the faculty of medicine and then continued with an apprenticeship in Delhi."

"India?"

"Yes, Your Royal Highness."

Alex gave Stan a look, but Stan remained placid. He'd learned much in India. And yes, he wanted to teach their younger sister everything. Andre felt their pain, yet that was one aspect he couldn't get himself to regret. And he was sure Thea would not.

"My brother tells me that you compromised our sister," Alex said.

Well, Alex was undoubtedly the more direct one.

"I don't have much to offer besides my heart, but I would like to—"

Alex didn't let Andre finish. "Why is that, Dr. Fernando Von Dürer, that you have nothing to offer besides your heart? Aren't you a Habsburg?"

Of course, his accent was as flawless in pronouncing the Italian as well as the German parts of Andre's names.

Andre swallowed. He went right for the Achilles heel. "It's because I was born out of wedlock."

"Because your father is…"

"Dr. Johann von Dürer, of Vienna, and then of Florence. My mother is Sophie von Dürer, born de Lorraine."

Alex looked at Stan, who responded with a shrug. "You didn't know about this?"

Stan shook his head.

"Your mother's a Lorraine?" Alex asked.

"And a granddaughter of the Grimaldis?" Stan asked.

"On my mother's maternal side, yes."

"He's related to the Habsburgs and the Lorraines?" Stan said. "A relation of the House of Lorraine, the Grand Duchy of Tuscany."

"Thea told me your family was scattered throughout Europe, but you didn't say you're related to some of the most royal and noble houses in Europe!" Stan said.

"Except that none of them ever acknowledged you?" Alex added.

"My parents had arranged their wedding, but I was born early. Bein Catholic, there was no way…"

"It couldn't have been that early, and surely at least six months is enough time to plan a wedding to ensure that one's child is not a bastard," Alex said.

Andre bristled, fully knowing that Alex was right, but Thea was listening, and he wouldn't let the shame of a mishap in timing sully his person. It was enough that he couldn't redeem his line.

"My father was studying and deeply involved in the effort to advance medicine. He had my mother's support—"

"But she was with child."

"And she didn't have to doubt his love and devotion, so she didn't want to rush the wedding."

"Hmpf!" Alex went, but that earned him a gentle punch in the side from Stan.

"Very well, so you wish to marry soon?"

"Yes, Your Royal Highness."

"What if I say no?"

"I'm afraid you might try to defy the laws of nature."

"I hardly think unearthing gravitational forces—"

"But biology, perhaps," Andre said. "The body doesn't respond to exterior motives and works on its timeline, much like the heart finds its rightful place with the person we love."

"You mean she might be…?" Alex's eyes grew wide, and Stan combed both hands through his hair. "She just told us no… so this *just* happened?"

"If Father knew, he'd kill us for allowing this," Stan said.

"You let it happen. She was under your watch!" Alex called out.

"While you were doing the same thing at some beach… where were you? Cornwall?" Stan squared his shoulders.

"How dare you speak to your big brother in such a fashion?" Alex faced Stan with his chest stretched out like a peacock.

"Big? You think you're so grand, but I'm taller."

Alex slapped his hand flat on Stan's head. "There, flatten your curls, and you're just as tall as I am."

"Short."

"I'm not short, but you seem rather short-sighted."

Andre cleared his throat.

And then Thea stepped in. "You behave like two schoolboys while he's standing here waiting for your blessing and approval. I don't even know why I asked him for the formalities if this was what he'd be presented with."

Stan and Alex gave her rueful smiles, and Andre suppressed a chuckle. It appeared the little sister had the big brothers under control.

"You'll have to marry soon." Stan nodded and crossed his arms.

"Before Father and Mother arrive for Christmas."

"What did you say?" Thea blinked.

Were those tears welling in her eyes?

"Well, just in case. If you are…" Alex groaned and turned to Stan. "I can't say it. She'll always be the girl with the *Affenschaukeln*."

Pigtail loops, truly? Thea?

Andre couldn't imagine the slender princess with pigtails climbing trees outside Bran Castle, but perhaps that was the beauty of a future with her: she'd always surprise him.

Andre looked at her, and she beamed. "So, you say yes?" She clasped her hands over her heart and brought them to her cheeks. "Please say yes!"

Alex and Stan feigned severe looks, but Andre now knew that they'd accept him.

"First of all, you weren't truly asking us; you were telling," Alex said. "And second, Andre is a thousand times a better man than any of the Habsburgs we know—" Alex elbowed Stan lightly. "Present company excluded."

"I'm not truly a Habsburg," Andre smiled. In the Habsburg dynasty, the issue of legitimacy, especially concerning sons, was tied to the strict rules of succession and marriage.

"You have Habsburg blood; you're a Habsburg. And that's what I will tell Father," Stan said. "I can't remember the last time someone asked when I was born. The parents are the same; the rest is merely a detail on paper as far as I'm concerned."

Andre could not be legitimized because doing so would disrupt the established order of succession and potentially lead to disputes over claims to titles and lands. Still, it didn't matter if he didn't threaten to lay a claim—except on Thea.

Then she turned to Andre and squealed. "We have a wedding to plan."

➤➤➤✦◄◄◄

"YOU NEED A ball!" Anna declared when Andre and Thea told her their brothers had given their blessings. "And a dress."

"It's too soon for a wedding dress; we don't even have a license yet," Thea protested, giving Andre an insecure look over her shoulder. "We can't marry the Anglican way, we're Catholic. There's no special license for us."

"Not a dress for the ceremony, for the ball! You, Thea, will come stay with me and I will introduce you to society properly." Anna twisted on her crutches but then winced. "I don't think I shall dance until my leg is fully healed and the baby is born, but that doesn't mean I cannot throw the most lavish ball of the season."

And just like that, Andre's treatment room turned into a bridal-planning headquarters.

"I don't know anybody here; whom shall we invite?" Thea asked.

"Everyone! We have a few cousins in town this season, extended relatives, my husband's relations, some of whom are very well connected, and a few of my closest acquaintances. Give or take two or three hundred guests?"

Andre's eyes widened, but he seemed to know to remain silent at his desk.

"And the doctors and nurses?" Thea asked.

"Naturally. I know Andre's connections to the Earl and Countess of Langley, so they shall be on my list."

Anna was in a whirlwind of planning. She took the pencil from Andre's desk and sat across from him. "Paper!"

Andre handed her a blank sheet.

"Now, the decorations. What's your favorite color?"

"Purple."

"And flower?"

"Roses."

"There are no purple roses in England. How about pink?"

"It's not Mary's ball you are hosting, is it?" Thea asked, and both women laughed heartily.

Andre rose and seemed ready to leave them to plan the event of the season when Anna grabbed his arm. "Brother, you need evening attire."

I need reinforcememts to keep Thea and Mary safe among three hundred guests plus the staff. List won't remain far off.

"I have evening attire. My friends were just married, and I have—"

"No. You need light drab colored kerseymere breeches and blue tailcoats with large flat gilt buttons and with or without black-velvet collars; that's your choice. It's our Viennese tradition."

"Ehm..." Andre sent Thea a please-help-me look, but she merely giggled. "I don't like black collars. What's the matter with my cravat?" Not that he cared about the cravat considering Thea was going to be in a crowd with three hundred people and List would likely be there with who knew how many of his lackeys.

"Ah!" Anna rubbed her forehead. "He's like Father, always more focused on practical clothing than the looks."

"What's wrong with how I look?" Andre crossed his arms and tilted his head. Thea eyed him top to bottom and seemed to rather like how he looked. *She needs to stop looking at me like that...*

"Turn around," Anna said in a swirling motion. "There we have it, "She pointed at his bottom.

Thea tilted her head. She looked long and hard, but there wasn't anything amiss with the shapely and muscular bottom of her fiancé.

"It's lovely, sister, truly. In all these years that I've missed you, nobody has commented on the shape of my bottom quite as much as you. Especially in front of—"

"A princess?" Thea giggled.

Andre sighed.

"You are wearing clothes tailored for practicality, Andre. You look as if you were riding daily, taming wild horses, or cutting wood for the winter."

"What does that even mean?" Andre grimaced.

Thea shrugged but blushed rather pleasingly.

"Just go to the tailor and have him measure you. If our mother sees you like this... you look like a wild stallion with all this muscle."

Andre suppressed a grin and winked at Thea. She giggled again.

Thus, an hour later, Andre stepped into the tailor's shop, the smell of rich fabrics and freshly pressed linens enveloping him. The quiet shuffle of the older tailor, Mr. Hollingsworth, filled the small room as he approached with purpose, tape measure in hand.

"Ah, Dr. Fernando," Hollingsworth greeted, his voice warm and familiar. "A pleasure to see you. I've been hoping to repay you for your ingenious treatment of my hands."

"I'm glad to have been of help." Andre inclined his head.

"And you finally decided that I may repay you?" Mr. Hollingsworth rang a bell and Margaret from the store on Regent Street appeared. Oh how good of Mr. Hollingsworth to have hired her. She had the bandage on and walked with a crutch but sat down at a comfortable-looking chair, and had a sewing table near a brightly lit window.

"With evening wear." Andre smiled.

"For a wedding?"

"A Viennese ball. For an engagement."

"I see." The older man turned his head down.

Then he slumped some more.

"Are you making me ask, or may I congratulate you now?"

"You may," Andre smiled. "Thank you."

The tailor waved off the formalities, his eyes twinkling with gratitude and excitement. "You saved me from a fate worse than poorly sewn seams. Now, let's get you suited for the evening, shall we?"

Andre stood straight on a wooden stool a minute later, allowing the tailor to begin his work. The feel of the tape against his shoulders was familiar, and he welcomed the distraction. "I trust you'll work to make me look less like a man taming wild horses?" Andre teased lightly. "I come with specific criteria from my sister and fiancée." It was the first time he'd called Thea that and his chest filled with pride.

The older man chuckled. "If I had your build, Dr. Fernando, I wouldn't hide any of it. But I understand the request and shall oblige. Leave it to me; you'll be the best-dressed man at the ball. Indeed," Hollingsworth replied with a wink. "But I must admit, I have a selfish motive. Dressing you well reflects splendidly on me."

They laughed, the camaraderie easing the tension that had clung to Andre's thoughts since the afternoon's events. Here, he found peace among the bolts of fabric and the rhythmic snip of scissors. But he still wondered how he could best keep Thea safe among the bustling crowd at the ball.

Chapter Thirty-Five

THE NEXT DAY, Thea felt lighthearted and was glad to hold Andre.

"These madeleines are delicious," Thea said, clinging onto Andre's arm as they stepped back up the low stairs to the practice. "They're just the right amount of sweet," she said, when Andre handed her the little parcel with the extra pastries for Mary.

"You are just the right amount of sweet," he said with a glint in his eyes that made her heart skip.

Andre pushed the door open, and they stepped into the waiting room. Just when Thea wanted to set the parcel aside and take her gloves off, Nurse Wendy and Alfie, the apothecary, stepped out into the hall.

"Andre, there's someone waiting for you in your treatment room," Wendy said.

She was usually the one to assign patients, *but at this hour?*

"Aren't we supposed to get ready for the ball?" Thea asked when she saw the confusion on Andre's face.

"It's an emergency," Alfie said and gave Andre a meaningful nod.

Thea observed her with growing curiosity. Wendy was not a woman easily flustered; her urgency hinted at the severity of the situation. Before she had the chance to reflect further, the door opened, and Andre pushed his sleeves up just a touch, as though he'd already been hard at work. His gaze flickered from Wendy to the end of the hall.

Thea saw Andre's demeanor change, she recognized it now. When he was needed as a doctor, there was nothing that could hold him back. Thus, she followed him down the hall to his room, Nick, the oculist appeared from his room. And down the stairs came Felix, the dentist.

"Is he here?" Felix said, and then smiled when he spotted Andre.

How oddly the doctors were all behaving. How terrible could the emergency be that only Andre was able to take the patient on?

The smell of polished wood and faintly medicinal tinctures filled the air, mingling with the warmth of the early afternoon sun spilling through the tall windows. The hall buzzed with quiet activity—everyone strode purposefully through the hall, their boots echoing slightly on the wooden floors, while they followed Andre to his room.

"Wendy, you said there was a patient who needed me immediately?" Andre asked.

And then time stood still. The industrious hum turned to silence. Andre was frozen in the doorway of his room, and two women waited inside.

"I said it was an emergency," Alfie corrected him.

But Andre didn't seem to hear him anymore.

"Anna," he said simply, his tone steady. He slipped past Thea without sparing so much as a glance, his focus entirely on the woman who stood next to his sister.

"What's going on?" Thea asked, her voice cutting through the low murmur of the room. She glanced between Andre, Anna, and the woman she'd never seen before—her posture elegant but reserved, her hands clasped tightly together, the fingers almost bloodless with force. There was something unmistakably familiar about her features.

Thea's breath caught as realization dawned. She recognized

those same sharp cheekbones, that same determined set of the jaw. They belonged to Andre. This must be his mother. Anna turned to Thea, whose expression had shifted from curiosity to stunned awareness.

"She just arrived, and I brought her straight here to find you," Anna said with a smile, wiping tears from her face at the same time.

At the far end of the room, blocking the window as if she were an apparition illuminated from the back, the older woman lifted her hands to her mouth, then clasped her chest as she gasped. Andre's eyes were locked with the woman standing there but his gaze didn't falter, and Thea watched as the bustling practice around him seeming to fade as recognition settled over him. It was not joy that softened his jaw, but something closer to disbelief, threaded through with a restrained ache that spoke of years gone by.

Thea felt her chest grow heavy, though she wasn't sure why. She took a step back so as not to intrude but couldn't stop watching. It was a moment not meant for her, perhaps not meant for anyone, but it was impossible to ignore the way Andre froze in place, torn between moving forward and staying rooted. He blinked a few times when his eyes turned red rimmed. And then he stepped forward, calling out "Mama!" as he, the tall and strong man, fell into the embrace of the woman who'd outstretched her arms. It was not Thea's moment, but she knew instinctively that something important had shifted here at Harley Street, in that very moment a miracle had occurred in matters of the heart.

THE LAST HOUR unraveled like a dream Andre hadn't dared to entertain. His mother, here, standing before him, the years of separation dissolving in the hum of conversation and the surprised laughter of introductions. Anna, stalwart and composed, had stayed by his mother's side through it all. Meanwhile, the parade of his friends—Nick with his steady presence, Wendy's pragmatic efficiency, Alfie's wide-eyed wonder, and Felix's easy charm—had one by one made their bows, their genuine warmth smoothing what could have remained stilted and cautious.

Then Wendy had ushered in Pippa and Bea, followed shortly by Stan and Alex, each of them adding another layer of light-hearted acceptance, drawing his mother into their circle of aristocrats. His new family combined with his old. Andre still struggled to grasp his fortune. The somber weight he'd carried for years, the silence he'd told himself might stretch forever, was lifting. It wasn't just unexpected; it was unimaginable. And all this time, Thea remained by his side, and he felt his chest fill with the love surrounding him.

The moment didn't linger—the looming ball called them all away soon after. One by one, his friends departed to prepare, joking about last-minute wardrobe disasters and the inevitable rush. Even Anna offered a gentle farewell, leaving their mother only briefly to retrieve her things.

"*Andre, il mio caro ragazzo ormai cresciuto.*" Andre, my dear boy, all grown up. His mother's gentle voice roused him from his inner thoughts. Her gaze settled on him, misty and soft, as though she had spent the better part of the hour reflecting, herself. "To see you here, to see this life you've built... I wondered—" Her voice caught briefly, and she gathered herself. "I wondered, sometimes, if you'd forgotten how much you always meant to me. I see now you never forgot who you were."

Andre swallowed hard and worked to keep his voice steady, though his heart thudded in his chest. "Mama, I—"

She held up a hand, her lips curving faintly before turning her attention to Thea, who stood at his side. "And you," she continued, her voice warming, as though drawing Thea into the intimacy of years-long affection. "You see him, don't you? Not for his name, not for his position, but for who he is. I always knew... I always knew there would be someone who could love him for the man I raised him to be. But to meet you and see the happiness he wears so plainly now…" She paused with a teary smile. "There are no words for how proud I am. Of both of you."

Thea's hand tightened around Andre's. He glanced at her, noticing the glimmer pooling in her eyes, though she blinked quickly to keep it from spilling over. Pride stirred in his chest, but it was accompanied by something deeper, something closer to gratitude. He nodded once to his mother, not trusting himself to speak right away, and settled his free hand over the one Thea clasped in his.

The flickering warmth of the gas lights in his treatment room offset the empty quiet that filled the space without the others. His mother stepped closer, soft fabric brushing against the polished wood floor as she extended a palm, revealing a small velvet box. She opened it with the care of someone unveiling a treasure.

Inside sat a ring that caught the hearth's glow and magnified it—an imposing ruby circled by sapphires and a halo of diamonds, all set meticulously in gold.

"This," his mother began, her voice imbued with a reverence that made even Thea fall utterly still, "belonged to my grandmother. It is part of the Grimaldi jewels, passed down only when the heart finds its home." She exhaled softly and looked at Andre, her eyes piercing as though they shared a secret no one else could understand. "It belongs to you now, if you'll take it, my son."

Andre, for once at a loss, closed the box and met his mother's gaze. Her slight nod encouraged him, steadied him. Then, before hesitation could creep in, he turned to Thea. She stared up at him, her lips parting in a soft gasp as her gaze darted between his face and the closed box still in his hand. He dropped to one knee, lifting her hand into his, and opened the box once again.

When he slipped the ring onto her finger, tears glistened across her cheeks, though she smiled through them, luminous as dawn. Andre looked at her, his free hand framing hers around the ring.

"Thea," he said, his voice steady now as warmth swelled

within him. "No wealth, no treasure could surpass you. You are my greatest riches, and I will protect you always."

Thea's lips trembled as her smile widened. "Andre," she murmured, her voice barely above breath, "you've already given me everything my heart desired."

The weight of the moment wrapped around them as his mother pressed a hand to her chest, emotion evident in her shining eyes. Andre's resolve deepened, his heart declaring what words could only begin to say. This was more than a reunion. It was a new beginning.

Chapter Thirty-Six

T HIS WAS THE end.

That night at Anna's townhouse, where the ball was about to begin, Thea had a foreboding sensation.

Andre could feel the danger vibrating in the air. Although he'd agreed with Alex and Stan that they wouldn't leave Baron von List out of sight, the moment the Prussian stepped into the ballroom, Andre's heart fell to his knees. He'd also seen it in the eyes of Nick, Alfie, and Felix, when their eyes met Andre's—List entered as if he'd been invited.

Stan came to Andre's side just as he did the night Thea had been abducted.

"I can't fight with my injury," Stan said, "but if he as much as tries to come close to my sister again, I'll find a way to—"

"It won't come to that," Alfie said when he came between them. This time, Bea wasn't with him, rather she stood next to Thea. And with them were Nick and his wife Pippa. As the daughters of an earl and a duke, they were following the princess everywhere that evening.

"The ladies will not be leaving her alone, and we won't let List out of sight."

In the far end of the room, however, Andre spotted Alex. He spoke agitatedly with another man who looked royal, dressed in an impeccable uniform.

"I'm going to see what the matter is," Stan announced and walked away.

Laughter and music intertwined with the clinking of crystal glasses, as the crowd ebbed and flowed in a seamless, elegant chaos. Yet, amid the splendor, Andre's eyes never strayed far from Thea. The air felt just like that night at Alfie's wedding, his chest tightening with an unrelenting unease—the kind that turned even the most gilded gathering into a place fraught with shadows only he could see. But Thea smiled graciously, holding court in the ballroom. She belonged there like the chandeliers, she was the sparkling light of the ball.

And then Andre's breath hitched. That night that seemed like so long ago, it was Mary who'd been caught, too.

At first, he walked. Yet, his heartbeat quickened and by the time he reached the stairs, he took two at a time. He rushed upstairs and saw a door open. He followed it and saw little Mary wrapped in what seemed like a tablecloth with a doily over her head. Alone.

Phew! Relief washed over him when she smiled at him.

Her room was a full nursery stuffed with toys, a rocking horse, and lovingly decorated with frilly curtains. In the back of his mind, he wondered why his sister had a nursery if she was only pregnant now, but sadness washed over him, and he realized it hadn't been a room as much as an unfulfilled dream.

"Shouldn't you be asleep?" Andre asked.

"I'm trying to dance to the music, but I don't know how," she said, tugging at the sash at her waist.

Andre remembered his sister, Anna, when she was a little girl. She also put doilies over her head and wore shawls, pretending to be a princess dancing at the balls in Vienna.

The music swelled, and he counted. "One, two, three. One, two, three."

Mary eyed him with an innocent vulnerability that shattered his resolve to only pay her a short visit and return downstairs.

So he reached out, took a long and deep bow, and offered his hand. "May I have this dance, Miss Mary?"

She beamed at him and hopped onto his feet just as before; the doily fell off her head, and she hugged his stomach. "Thank you, Andre."

"It is my honor and greatest pleasure, Miss Mary." He spoke with all the pomp he could muster.

And so they went through the room, the dolls sitting on the bed being the onlookers, and the milk and biscuits on the side table taking the place of a buffet with punch.

But when the music died downstairs, Andre heard the metal clinking on the glass.

An announcement.

Whatever it was, he felt he didn't belong and wished to reach for Thea, pull her out and into his arms. But he couldn't love his princess and remove her from this world he'd only known from the margins. For as long as Andre could remember, he'd been with the Habsburgs, just not one of them.

"You ought to go to her," Mary said. "I saw the bouquet of roses."

"My sister prepared them," Andre muttered. "Now, I'm here to dance with you."

"But isn't Thea waiting downstairs for you?"

Andre dropped his shoulders, and Mary stepped off his feet. "She's in love with you. I know it, she told me."

She told me, too.

"Don't you wish to marry her? Shouldn't you announce your engagement downstairs?"

"I do, very much, but it's not that simple." How could he ever explain the hierarchy of aristocracy to the child without a title? And how could he tell her that he was a bastard himself? Otherwise, he'd be the Habsburg offering for Thea's hand now. She was holding court among the cream of the crop of the ton, while he just couldn't get past the fact that he was the bastard who wanted to marry her more than he wanted to breathe the air that kept him alive. Just for a little while longer, he wanted to allow her to shine and remain shielded from the scandal their union would surely cause.

Andre tried to hear what was going on in the ballroom downstairs. He went closer to the open doors to the balcony of Mary's chamber, and there was barely a sound emanating from the ball.

"What do you think is going on downstairs?" Mary asked.

"I don't know. All I can hear are the crickets chirping."

"Crickets? The little beetles?"

Crickets were not beetles, but considering Mary's grimace, Andre thought it better not to tell her about the distinctions of insects. He remembered Anna's dislike of the smaller crawling creatures, while he and his brother liked to see them hop in Tuscany and follow them around the cypress trees. Anna preferred kittens and puppies.

"I don't hear any crickets. Beetles don't make sounds," Mary said matter-of-factly.

"Then what do you think this sound is?"

It was loud and clear.

"Stars."

"What?" Andre squatted so he could face Mary.

"The sounds at night. Like this—" She cupped her ear to show she was listening to the chirping outside. "This is the sound the stars make when they sparkle."

"That's so sweet," Andre said. His chest tightened. A sense of romanticism in Mary's worldview gave him hope. It was children like her that made the world a better place.

"You have to go and tell Thea that you love her," Mary said.

"She knows."

"But she's alone at a ball, and you are here with me. You have to claim your princess, or else someone else will."

And then there was a thud and a scream.

Andre's arms grew cold, and his legs heavy.

Thea cried out nearby.

A FEW MINUTES earlier, downstairs at the ball…

Thea felt as though this was the ball she'd missed the night she refused Prince Ralph. Well, truth be told, she hadn't made it to the ball that night, and this was different. Tonight, she knew she'd find Andre and nestle into his embrace… but where was Andre?

Thea scanned the room and saw Stan approaching Alex who seemed consumed in an argument with another man.

Oh no! White breeches, a black coat with golden buttons…

Thea excused herself from Pippa and Bea and felt all the eyes on her as she walked toward her brothers.

Red cuffs and golden lapels.

Thea's pulse quickened and she wasn't sure how her feet carried her there, but she wasn't going to run away this time.

And when she came to her brothers' side, they stilled.

Before her, the man bowed, and Anna appeared with a bouquet of red roses.

The Viennese tradition was the crowning event of the evening. The prince would offer a bouquet of roses—and if she accepted them, they'd be effectively betrothed.

Never!

The man in the Viennese uniform was Prince Ralph, Thea knew it the moment she saw Anna's look. He turned to receive the flowers from the hostess of the ball, but Anna stepped back, clutching the roses in her arms.

"What is the meaning of this?" Prince Ralph asked.

The music stopped.

As did Thea's heart.

"As I tried to explain, she doesn't wish to marry you." Stan squared his shoulders.

"And we represent our father while on diplomatic mission in England, thus, as we explained, we'd like to dissolve the betrothal agreement," Alex said.

"No."

Thea narrowed her eyes. That was all he had to say, no?

"Is something the matter?" A tall blond man stepped through the crows with a smug grin that seemed as unsettling as a Venetian theatrical mask.

"Baron von List," Stan nodded politely, shooting Alex and Thea warning looks, "this is a private matter."

"Apparently not, or else you wouldn't make such a spectacle of yourselves," the Prussian said with a slightly open vowel sound that betrayed his accent.

Prince Ralph turned to Anna. "Can we speak in private somewhere?"

Anna pointed at a door off the side wall. "In the library over there, Your Royal Highness."

Where's Andre? Thea's heart thrummed as she led the way as etiquette required, followed by her brothers and Prince Ralph. Everyone watched her, the runaway princess's fall from grace. The scandal would fuel enough shame from England to Transylvania, there was no doubt. But that didn't matter.

As long as they don't wage war over me…

Chapter Thirty-Seven

"THIS IS GOING to cost you," Prince Ralph said when he slammed the door to the library shut. Thea cringed but Stan and Alex remained steadfast.

"As I said, our gold mines are being plundered," Alex said. "We don't have the funds to pay you off."

"Then I want her. I am entitled to her!" Ralph pointed at Thea as if she were a statue in the room.

"I never agreed to marry you," she said as calmly as she could.

Ralph grimaced. "Why would anyone even ask?"

At that, Stan and Alex quirked their brows.

"Perhaps we can find a more diplomatic solution to unite our families' interests?" Alex said.

"What else is there besides strategic marriages? We've been planning on this for as long as... I mean... even before I went on the grand tour of Europe, I knew the Hohenzollern-Sigmaringen princess would be at the ready for me."

Thea bristled against that.

"First of all, Prince Ralph, I'm right here and shall be addressed with respect."

Ralph sputtered something in German that Thea rather wished she hadn't understood. But she saw her brothers' faces and Stan balled his fists.

"The princess is addressing you, and you will listen," Alex commanded. He was the older brother and raised his chin just like Father did when he accepted no rebuttal.

"What do you have to say, Princess," Ralph muttered and gave her a once-over that made her feel instantly dirty. If she couldn't even bear for him to look at her, she couldn't ever bear his touch.

"Instead of using me as a bargaining chip, why don't you consider a charter to prevent the exploitation of Transylvanian gold from its mines?"

Ralph waved her off as if she were an annoying fly.

"Hear her out, she's a political mastermind." Stan smiled in her direction and Thea's chest warmed when she looked at her brothers' supportive expressions.

"There's nobody to give enough signatures to such a charter, even if I considered it." Ralph shrugged.

"There's an English earl, the Earl of Langley. A French marquis, a German count, two Transylvanian royals, and a de Lorraine from Italy in the ballroom. Shall I request their presence for an international convention—"

"You can't be serious," Ralph shouted, combing both hands through his thinning hair.

"She is. They are some of our closest friends and will gladly sign a document that stifles your hold on our sister, and plays into Baron von List's enrichment schemes," Stan said, now stepping close to Ralph. He was half a foot taller, and it pleased Thea immensely that Ralph had to look up at him.

"Call them in," Stan said, and Alex left the room.

"Let me see it." Ralph waved at Thea. "Do you have the charter here?"

"It's upstairs," she said. "I can bring it here."

Stan crossed his arms and nodded in Thea's direction.

Thea's slippers barely made a sound against the carpeted steps as she hurried up the staircase, her heart racing in time with each step. The walls seemed to press in on her, the scent of old wood mingling with the faint smokiness of candles burning downstairs. She burst into her room and closed the door behind her, her breath shallow. On the small writing desk by the window, the charter lay folded and unassuming, yet it held everything. Her fingers trembled as she reached for it, the weight of its words mounting in her mind. Was it as complete as it needed to be? Could it guarantee the freedom she had fought for—the freedom she needed to forge a life with Andre? She unfolded the paper carefully and began scanning the lines, her determination flaring once more. It had to be enough. It just had to.

"Don't!" a voice echoed through the hall. Thea froze at the sound of a muffled shout wafting through the upper halls, followed by the sharp crack of something breaking—porcelain, perhaps? Her breath caught as silence fell once again, tense and suffocating. No audible footsteps followed, but then her door flew open with a force that rattled the hinges. Prince Ralph stood in the doorway, his shadow dark and foreboding against the light from the hall. Alone.

"You can't be here," Thea said sharply, her voice low but dripping with fury. "Get out!"

Ralph's lips curled into a mocking smirk as he stepped inside, shutting the door behind him with a deliberate click.

"Wouldn't you want that, Princess?" he drawled, his tone oozing with malice. "Or should I better stay and make sure we are found in a *compromising* position? Then you'll have to marry me, charter or not."

Her blood turned to ice as his hand moved to the key, turning it with a mocking slowness. The lock clicked once, twice, and she flinched. Swiftly closing the distance between them, he gripped her arms before she could shove past him. She thrashed, refusing to make it easy for him, but Ralph was fiercer. His hand came over her mouth, silencing her protests, while the other tore the charter from her trembling fingers.

"No!" her scream was swallowed by his palm as she watched

him fling the papers onto the bed.

Thea's breathing quickened. Cold sweat drenched her neck as her eyes darted to Ralph's menacing body—far too close. His grip tightened, and he shoved her against the wall with a thud that knocked the air from her lungs.

Panic churned in Thea's chest. She needed to escape. Now. Her body tensed, her mind racing for any opportunity. With every ounce of strength, she drove her knee upward. Ralph's strangled growl of pain broke through the roar of her racing pulse as he staggered back, releasing her momentarily.

"You'll set me on fire in bed, whether we're married or not," Ralph spoke onto his hand as if he tried to spit the words in her face.

But Thea didn't listen.

She moved swiftly past him and to the connecting door to Mary's room, gasping for air, but then the doorframe filled with another figure.

⊱⊰

ANDRE'S GRIP WAS iron as he slammed Ralph against the heavy oak door, the force rattling the wall. The venom in his voice dripped with barely contained fury as he growled, "How dare you lay a hand on my fiancée?"

Ralph smirked faintly, the smugness of a man who had pushed too far, even in the face of being caught. His lack of fear only fanned the fire in Andre's chest, his hands tightening at the man's collar. "You'll regret this, bastard!" Ralph began, but Andre wasn't there for threats.

"I don't care what you call me, but the bastard here is you!"

Before Ralph could answer, the thunder of hurried footsteps filled the hallway. Stan appeared first, breathing heavily, his arm cradled protectively to his chest. Alex followed right behind, with Nick, Alfie, and Felix surging into the corridor like a calculated wave of reinforcements. "Where's Princess Thea?" they called in unison.

"He knew," Stan called out, his voice strained but steady as he shot Ralph a murderous glare. "He knew exactly where I was injured. Twisted my arm just the right way—he wanted to make sure I was out of the picture completely."

This was premeditated.

Andre's head pivoted sharply toward Stan, and suddenly, a sickening sense of clarity slammed into him. The missing piece of this sprawling and vile puzzle fell into its rightful place.

"Ralph…" Andre said through gritted teeth, his voice low yet deadly. "It wasn't just List, was it? You've been working with him. All this time."

"He's been sabotaging our gold mines to force me to marry him!" Thea called.

Ralph's silence spoke louder than any denial could have. The faint sneer pulling at his lips stung like salt on an open wound, confirming Andre's worst suspicions.

Stan took a slow step forward, pain evident in the way he moved, but determined, nonetheless. "You're a coward," he stated coldly, his words each like a dagger being driven home. "Using List to cover your tracks. Sending his lackeys to do your dirty work."

"You're not a man deserving of your title," Andre barked, his rage barely tamed as he finally released Ralph, shoving him toward Alex and Alfie, who were ready to hold him down. The prince stumbled, but his expression's momentary flare of indignation was quickly suppressed when Alex reached for him, his grip unrelenting.

"You won't get away with this!" Ralph hissed through clenched teeth as Alex twisted his arm behind his back with little effort.

"Keep him out of my sight," Thea called bitterly, apparently unable to stomach another moment of the man's presence.

"You'll pay for this!" Ralph spat toward Stan and Alex, but

neither responded. They were already hauling him down the hallway, with Nick, Alfie, and Felix ensuring no escape would be possible.

Andre watched the group for a long moment, the weight of adrenaline still coursing through his veins—and yet, the moment his eyes settled on Thea, his world grew still.

From behind, he heard the quick sweep of skirts against the floor. "What's all this commotion?" a familiar voice exclaimed, pulling him temporarily from his focus. Andre looked toward the staircase, where Anna appeared, her face flushed with worry. His mother trailed her, her sharp gaze scanning the chaotic aftermath. Her expression was just as it had been all those years ago in Florence.

This time, I didn't run, Mama.

But all the noise, the shifting shadows, and the looming judgment melted into the background for Andre. He stepped closer to Thea, his voice soft now as he spoke just for her. "Are you all right?"

The world could burn. Ralph could scream. But in that moment, all Andre could see—truly see—was his princess.

Chapter Thirty-Eight

THEA STOOD ON the side of the ballroom with only her brothers. This was their life, danger and attention colliding in the least fortunate moments. She smoothed the soft folds of her gown, the shock of the attack still present in her mind. The ball had to go on though, lest she cause a scandal and attract undue attention. If Prince Ralph had colluded with Baron von List, then danger could still be lurking everywhere.

But for now, as discretely as possible despite the crowd of onlookers, Thea looked at her Andre speaking to Anna and their mother out of earshot. Her protector. Her love.

Despite the chaos that had unraveled earlier, there was a quiet hush within her now, a newfound peace that settled into all the cracked corners of her heart. She looked up, seeing Stan beside her, his arm still wrapped in a hastily knotted sling, his steady presence a reassuring anchor.

"I'm glad we're here," she said, her voice soft but sure.

Stan gave a small, crooked smile, his hand brushing a stray tear from her cheek. "We will always be your home, Thea. No matter where you run, you'll always have us." Alex nodded his assent.

She felt her lips tremble as warmth spread through her chest. She hadn't realized how much she needed this—how much she needed *them*. Despite the pain from the past and the storm of betrayal she had weathered, here they were. Stan, Alex, and even Alfie, Nick, and Felix who had come to rescue her. They had come for her, believed in her, defended her when it mattered most. And Andre, he had her heart.

Alex stepped forward, his usual mischievous expression replaced by something softer. "Everything's fixed for now," he began, though his tone betrayed the challenge ahead. "Ralph and List won't crawl out of this unscathed, not with what we've uncovered."

"Don't tell me they are still here." Thea put her hand on her forehead.

"Saving face among the ton," Stan said with palpable disgust. "But under guard."

Thea glanced toward Stan, recalling his earlier vow. "I trust you'll do what needs to be done," she said, her voice steadier now than it had been in days.

"We will," he said simply, the weight behind his words leaving no room for doubt.

Anna's rustling skirts gently broke through the serious air, her hands clasped as she stepped forward. "But none of that is for tonight," she announced with purpose, her eyes gleaming with excitement. "Tonight is for your celebration, Princess. Don't let them steal your moment."

Thea blinked, startled out of her thoughts as Anna gestured toward the doors that led back to the ballroom. Faint strains of music drifted through, light and lilting, a stark contrast to the chaos that had shaken the house to its core earlier.

"It's time for the bride's dance," Anna stated firmly, a playful smirk tugging at her lips.

Thea opened her mouth in protest before pausing, catching sight of Andre outside the doorway. He stood just at the edge, his dark hair catching the glow of the gilded lights beyond. His eyes met hers, warm, steady, unyieldingly full of love.

Her heart curled softly, the memories of this long, torturous road fading against the promise of him. He crossed the threshold easily, his movements graceful and composed as he extended a hand toward her.

"Thea," he murmured, her name a secret on his lips. He didn't need to say more.

She stared at him for a moment and then placed her hand in his. His fingers curled around hers, the heat of his touch grounding her in a way nothing else could. She looked up into his face—intelligent and kind, strong yet gentle—and her pulse quickened, not with panic as it once had but with a giddy, fluttering joy.

"I'll warn you now," she whispered, her lips curving into a small smile as he guided her toward the ballroom, "I've never been much good at waltzing."

Andre chuckled, his deep laugh vibrating in his chest as he pulled her close. "If I have you close to me, nothing else matters, my princess."

The ballroom welcomed them with open arms, a sea of dazzling lights and soft colors. Their audience paused in anticipation, every gaze trained on the princess and prince who had fought harder than anyone could imagine arriving there.

Thea took a breath, letting it unfurl the lingering tension in her chest as Andre held her hand tightly. The music swelled, spiraling upward like the hope brimming in her heart. Her past had scorched and blinded her, but it hadn't broken her. She lifted her chin, meeting Andre's mother's proud smile and Anna's encouraging nod. Stan's watchful gaze added strength, while Alex winked cheekily, earning a rare laugh from her.

This was her moment to step onto the parquet.

She moved with Andre, their movements far from perfect yet full of an ease that only came from love. Her world had been remade—not only because of him but because of herself and the people around her.

The glow of the chandeliers blurred into stars above as they danced, and Thea allowed herself to close her eyes, feeling the rhythm of possibility unfolding beneath her feet. One, two, three. One, two, three. Tonight was theirs, but it was also the beginning of something greater. Beyond the music, the evening, and even the warmth of Andre's grasp, she could sense that freedom she had once only dreamed of was now a freedom earned and cherished, burning with a soft, reassuring glow in her soul.

Thea opened her eyes and met Andre's gaze once again, the noise of the ballroom fading into nothing. He smiled down at her, his promise wordless yet unmistakable.

Thea felt truly, wonderfully, free for the first time in what felt like forever.

Chapter Thirty-Nine

"WHERE ARE WE going?" Thea asked.

"We must face our fears, Miss Thea," Mary said as she put her small hand into Thea's.

Thea furrowed her brows. This was what she'd told Mary the night the highwaymen took them. And then the prince.

Mary led her through the corridor and into one of the bedrooms of Anna's house.

"Whose room is this?" Thea asked, surveying the large bed chamber with a door connecting to another. It seemed like a room big enough for the masters of this grand house, but it looked as though it were made up for guests. The covers on the sizeable four-post bed were turned down; a fire crackled in the elegant hearth, with a brass clock and small dancing balls that caught the light from the crystal chandelier over her head.

"This way." Mary led Thea to the white-framed double glass doors and onto a balcony.

The cool night air should have made breathing easy for Thea, but the sight before her cut her breath off. Andre was in all his evening finery: a small table set for two, a candelabra, chilled wine, and napkins folded as tiny hats on the fine china. Even though it was dark, the polished silver and the candles added a sparkle to the balcony scene, but nothing compared to the mesmerizing smile Andre cast her.

"Good evening, Princess Thea," he said as he bowed and reached for her hand. She complied, and he placed a tender and lingering kiss on her knuckles that sent a jolt through her body.

And he didn't let go of her hand.

"What are we doing on the balcony in the middle of the night?" Thea asked, unable to fathom the romantic scene that unfolded before her.

"Don't worry if a branch out there frightens you; we'll track it down and prove that it's nothing more than twigs and leaves," Mary said with a wink.

Then Andre nodded at her, and she pivoted like when she'd received praise.

Once Mary had left and closed the double-glazed doors, Thea stepped closer to Andre, still holding her hand.

She shivered.

"Are you cold, my love?" he rasped.

Thea shook her head. It wasn't the crisp night air that made her shiver but the realization that she'd found the place where she belonged—or with whom. As long as she was with Andre, it mattered little where she was.

"I ordered a little dinner for us," Andre said when he reached around Thea, and she stepped slightly out of his embrace. Not too far, for he felt so wonderfully strong, solid, and warm that she'd gladly remain there forever.

"There's something you once said you'd missed."

Thea couldn't think of what she'd said when her stomach lurched as she held Andre's gaze. His deep-brown eyes sparkled like their own universes, and the reflections from the room behind her, the lights from the chandelier and the crystal chandeliers sparkling in his eyes, were just too beautiful for her to form coherent thoughts.

Thea sank onto one of the two chairs and looked at the lovingly arranged plate.

"Where did you get this from?"

Andre took the seat across from her.

"Anna's cook is from Brașov." He reached for the spoon to his right but then waited.

His elevated upbringing truly shone through, especially when his manners were as impeccable as his looks. He wasn't the doctor in charge of dinner but the gentleman treating her like a princess. And even though Thea had run away from this life, she was glad for the pieces Andre brought back to her. She had a different perspective on her life with him by her side—especially in her heart.

"Thank you for this," Thea said, loading her spoon with the soft yellow corn and then a generous dollop of cream.

"This isn't the same cheese," she observed, patting her mouth with a napkin.

"I know. The closest to the creamy cheeses we are used to is Devonshire Cream. It's not too bad once you get used to it." Andre joined her and ate the food that had been a pillar of comfort from her childhood.

"It's different but better with you." Thea cast him a smile and he froze.

"That's what I wanted to ask you again, alone." He used his napkin, placed it on the table, and then rose. But before Thea could join him, he knelt beside her.

"If I didn't compromise you, and Alex hadn't come… would you still wish to remain in London?"

What a silly series of hypothetical scenarios!

"Why?"

"Because I don't want to force you into a life you do not want." He swallowed, his Adam's apple bobbing visibly as he looked up at her.

Thea reached for his hand. "Where does this come from? I thought the engagement was—"

Andre shook his head. "The engagement is chiseled in stone, Thea. I will never leave your side unless you want me to."

"Never!" Thea cupped his face with both of her hands. "Don't ever say such a thing."

"If you would like to wait to see if you are with child, I won't pressure you."

"Andre!"

"Please hear me out. In a few weeks, you'd know. And if you want to erase all of this, I will not stand in your way." His voice sounded unsteady, but his gaze was firm.

It was too dark to tell if his eyes had gotten redder, but more tears seemed to be welling up, sparkling even more in the dim light on the balcony.

"Is this because of something Alex said?"

"Yes."

Thea inhaled. Sometimes, she wished she could still pull her brother's hair, as she had done when she was three years old, and make him scream.

"Not like that," Andre said. "He said that he'd speak to your father on my behalf because he and Stan gave their blessings in his stead."

"So?"

"So, if you'd rather forget about the Habsburg bastard from Florence sullying your line, I just wanted to ask you again if you'd like me to step away."

"And go where?"

"Out of your life."

"Like you did with your family?"

He nodded.

"No! Don't you see they've been searching for you all these years? And I want you in my life! If a baby is inside me, it should only ever be yours."

"But everyone knows I'm a bastard now, and you're this precious, beautiful, intelligent, and oh… Thea, my princess!" He mumbled the last words because she'd pulled his face closer and pressed her lips onto his.

"I only fear one thing," she said to his mouth.

"What?"

"That a few weeks is too long a wait."

He jerked his head back and gave her a shocked look.

"If there might be a baby, why not make it a certainty."

⫸⫷

ANDRE'S BODY WAS instantly hard, but it was his heart that remained soft.

"Not like this," he said, placing a chaste kiss on Thea's lips. "Not a bastard."

She blinked as though she'd understood.

"When?" Her question was but a whisper.

"Thea, you deserve the wedding of a princess, not a small ceremony."

Andre looked at Thea, his chest tightening at the sight of her. The delicate flush on her cheeks, the way her lips parted as though she had words she wasn't quite ready to say—it was all too much and yet exactly what he needed. He reached for her hand and intertwined his fingers with hers, the simple touch grounding him, bringing a calm he hadn't felt in years.

"Thea," he murmured, his voice soft but weighted with a thousand unspoken promises. She met his gaze, and the world seemed to fall away. No grand ballroom, no watchful eyes, only her—the woman who had unraveled every broken part of him and pieced him back together.

Her brow furrowed slightly, a question lingering in her eyes, a quiet vulnerability she rarely allowed anyone to see. He responded the only way he could, his hands lifting to gently cradle her face as though she held the very essence of his being. "You make me whole," he whispered, his voice steady and honest. "I didn't think I'd find my family again. Or myself. But then you came into my life, and everything shifted."

Thea blinked, her expression softening into something un-readable yet breathtakingly beautiful. He leaned in then, brushing his lips against hers in a kiss that was tender, heartfelt, but filled

307

with all the love that had swelled and swelled until it could no longer remain contained. It wasn't a kiss to stake a claim or make a vow. It was a kiss meant to say *thank you.*

Thank you for saving me, for showing me what life could truly be.

When they broke apart, Thea rested her forehead against his, her breath mingling with his. For a moment, neither of them spoke, as though even the air around them was holding its breath, unwilling to shatter the perfection of this tiny, infinite universe they had created between them.

"You've given me everything I didn't know I needed," Andre said finally, his voice almost trembling under the weight of his emotions. His heart was full, so full he wondered how it could possibly contain it all. "Because of you, I found not just my family, but myself. And I swear I'll spend the rest of my life doing everything I can to give that back to you."

Her lips curved into a smile that sent warmth coursing through him, thawing even the deepest, coldest corners of his once-lonely heart. "Andre," she whispered softly, her hand brushing his cheek. No other words followed, but she didn't need them. Everything they had been through, every unspoken truth, was in her eyes.

Andre kissed her hand then, reverently as though she were sacred, and drew her closer. The music swelled downstairs, but nothing could muffle the joy in their hearts as they moved through the dance, their own rhythm took over, unhurried and timeless. For the first time in his life, Andre wasn't looking ahead or behind. He was there, present, with her.

Thea's head rested lightly on his chest, and Andre closed his eyes, feeling her heartbeat against his. It was steady, sure—just like his love for her. For the first time, he didn't feel the ache of something missing. His family was there with him. Thea was there, with him.

And for the first time, he felt whole.

Epilogue

Dearest Miss Thea,

I trust this letter finds you in excellent health and spirits. My husband and I wish to extend our deepest gratitude for your kindness and good care of our dear Mary during our prolonged absence. It is a great comfort to know that she is under your watchful and affectionate eye, thriving as she does in such a warm and nurturing care. Your attentiveness brings us both great peace of mind, as no other arrangement could have been more suitable or delightful for our Mary.

It is with much joy and anticipation that we give our consent for Mary to attend your forthcoming nuptials. The thought of her partaking in such a splendid event, in the company of so much happiness, has brought a smile to our faces. She wrote to us in a letter, full of anticipation of your wedding with an enthusiasm that is simply heartwarming, and we are certain it will be a most memorable and joyous occasion.

My husband and I grieve only that we cannot be present to witness what I am assured will be an affair of unmatched elegance and beauty. May the day bring you nothing but bliss and herald the beginning of a matrimonial union as harmonious and fulfilling as ours, dear Thea.

Believe me to be,

Yours most sincerely,
Mrs. Adelaide White

Thea folded the letter with care, her heart swelling with affection at Mrs. White's kind words. She rose and stepped out of the sitting room at Cloverdale House, the sound of distant voices guiding her steps down the long, quiet corridor but Cloverdale was never short of distractions, especially when Mary was around.

She found the girl in Andre's treatment room, sitting perched on a high stool. A piece of parchment rested on her lap, and she was diligently sketching with a pencil. Beside her stood Andre gesturing to the skeleton hanging against the wall—a rather macabre but educational addition to the room. He must have brought it from the practice on Harley Street so Mary could study it again.

"And this," Andre was saying as he pointed to a broad, curved bone, "is the largest bone in the human body. The hip bone, or as we say in Latin, the *os coxae.*"

"Sounds like it's an oxen!" Mary looked up with bright eyes, her pencil pausing mid-stroke. Catching sight of Thea, she beamed with pride. "Oh, Thea! We are studying anatomy!"

"Is that so?" Thea replied, stepping into the room fully. Her eyes met Andre's briefly, and she felt herself flush at the warm spark in his gaze, one that seemed to glow only for her. The smallest of smiles tugged at the corner of his mouth, and she found herself momentarily breathless.

"I had a short break between patients," Andre explained, his tone light but his eyes lingering on hers, "and our apprentice nurse here had a few queries. I thought answering them would be a productive use of our time."

Thea approached with a soft laugh, holding out the letter. "Speaking of productive use of time, Mary, I've just received word from your mother. She has given you permission to attend our wedding."

Mary's pencil clattered to the floor as she clasped her hands together, her face lighting up with joy. "Oh, Thea! Truly? I can come?"

"Truly," Thea said warmly.

With a delighted squeal, Mary hopped off the stool, leaving her sketch behind as she darted past Thea. "I must tell everyone! Everyone must know!" she called out as she disappeared down the hall, her voice fading into the hum of the busy house.

Andre chuckled softly, stepping closer to Thea. "She's certainly not lacking in enthusiasm."

"She never is," Thea agreed, but her words faltered as Andre took another step toward her. His gaze now held a simmering intensity, and her heart gave a small, traitorous leap.

"You know," he said quietly, his voice rich and low, "nobody is more excited for this wedding than I am."

Before she could summon a reply—or even banter some light tease in return—Andre leaned in, capturing her lips in a kiss that banished all coherent thought. It was not the gentle, tentative sort of kiss one might expect in a quiet corner of Cloverdale House, but rather the kind that left her utterly breathless, dizzy, and wholly undone.

When at last they parted, his forehead rested against hers, and the unspoken promise of all that lay ahead filled the small space between them.

"My Princess Thea," he murmured, her name on his lips an unspoken vow.

She smiled softly, her body humming with warmth as she glanced at the open doorway. Somewhere down the hall, Mary was no doubt regaling the staff with her news. And right here, in this quiet moment, with Andre at her side, Thea felt the future spread before her, bright and limitless.

This was happiness.

This was love.

And the rest of her life began now.

The series continues with Prince Stan's story in *The Sound of Seduction*, book 4 in the *Miracles on Harley Street* series. Find out how Nurse Wendy conquers his heart when she returns alongside the Doctors on Harley Street. Find out more at www.SaraAdrien.com.

Author's Note

Neem and the medicinal plants at Cloverdale House:

You may have noticed, dear Reader, that the characters in this series all benefit from the orangery at Cloverdale House—not only because it functions as a secluded indoor paradise for secret trysts, but also because it binds the characters in many ways. One of the plants that received special attention in this book was neem. Let me tell you what made it special:

The inclusion of neem, a highly regarded medicinal plant from the Indian subcontinent, in this Regency romance reflects the growing influence of global trade and intercultural exchange during the early 19th century. Known in its native land as *Azadirachta indica*, the neem tree has been a staple of traditional Indian medicine, or Ayurveda, for centuries. Its remarkable properties for cleansing the blood, supporting the skin, and detoxifying the body were invaluable in treating ailments ranging from fevers to infections.

By the early 1800s, neem became a subject of fascination within England's expanding botanical and scientific circles. Of course, Alfie (the hero from book 2, *The Scent of Intuition*), the apothecary at 87 Harley Street, would have known about it and shared his knowledge with the others. However, since Andre, the hero in this book, was in India with Alfie before they came to London and cofounded the practice, it is likely that Andre could hold down the fort at Cloverdale House and dispense the best medicines he had at hand for his patients.

Its exotic origins no doubt added to its allure among the upper echelons of society, particularly those with an interest in the fashionable pursuit of botany. Thus, it is likely that Pippa (the heroine from book 1, *A Sight to Behold*) would have embraced neem as one of the plants in the orangery at Cloverdale House.

For this story, neem represents not only the practicalities of early 19th-century medicine but also the romantic and cultural intrigue of a world growing rapidly interconnected. Its inclusion highlights the dynamic interplay of tradition, science, and discovery that shaped Regency-era approaches to health and healing.

Cloverdale House:

In crafting the world of my novel, I embraced the delightful freedom of artistic license to breathe life into Cloverdale House, an estate of unmatched splendor and imagination. While Cloverdale House is a creation of fiction, it is richly inspired by the historical grandeur of Carlton House. This esteemed mansion, nestled in Westminster, served as the opulent town residence of King Paul IV during his regency and time as prince regent. Its distinguished location faced the south side of Pall Mall, with its enchanting gardens flowing seamlessly into St James's Park, embodying the elegance of its era.

Carlton House's architectural journey began with its reconstruction in 1709 for Henry Boyle, later Lord Carleton, who eventually passed it to his nephew, Lord Burlington. The estate's narrative continued as it was sold in 1732 to Frederick, Prince of Wales, whose vision, alongside the renowned William Kent, reshaped the gardens into a masterpiece. With the expansion efforts of Frederick's widow, Princess Augusta, the house became a quintessential emblem of royal luxury.

Yet, in the tapestry of my imagination, had such a majestic house not been enlarged and entwined with royal legacy, it might have found itself in the hands of a character like Pippa, an heiress of charm and fortune. If Pippa had indeed owned such a grand house, the doctors on Harley Street would have surely dubbed it a palace. Coming from their modestly furnished rooms on the top two floors above their practice, they would see a rehabilitation center as a chance of a lifetime.

This imagination springs from my own experience of awe when visiting the large medical complex in Houston, Texas, where entire blocks are devoted to clinics and hospitals. With such a grand vision in mind, how could I not bestow such a wealth of resources, space, and beautiful clinical settings to my beloved doctors from this series? I hope you enjoyed their stories and embraced the deviations from fact, finding joy in the blend of history and fantasy.

Andre's Backstory:

For Dr. Andre Fernando's backstory, I aimed to blend fictional elements with true historical context to create a vivid and plausible narrative. The following historical details serve as the backdrop for Andre's family's dramatic story.

Timing of the Massacre in Florence:

Napoleon's invasion and subsequent control over parts of Italy, including Florence, brought about significant turmoil and conflict. In April 1797, during Napoleon's Italian campaign, the region experienced severe unrest marked by battles, raids, and social upheaval. This period of conflict saw many noble families, especially those with ties to enemy states like the Habsburgs, face persecution and displacement. The chaos and violence of this era provide a credible setting for Andre's harrowing escape from his home in Florence.

University Semester Start in Vienna:

In the early 19th century, universities in Europe, including the University of Vienna, adhered to an academic calendar with two primary semesters:

Winter Semester: Typically began in October and lasted until February.

Summer Semester: Usually started in April and continued until July.

Given this structure, it is plausible that Andre would have enrolled at the University of Vienna for the start of the summer semester in April 1817. This timing aligns with his urgent departure from Florence and highlights the immediacy with which he had to adapt to his new life focused on education and survival.

By grounding Andre's story in these historical facts, I hope to enhance the authenticity of his journey, making his struggles and triumphs all the more compelling. Through Andre's eyes, we witness not only the personal cost of war but also the relentless drive for self-reliance and excellence that defines his path to becoming a distinguished orthopedist at 87 Harley Street.

Princess Thea's Backstory:

As you turn the final pages of *A Touch of Charm*, I would like to take a moment to reflect on the historical backdrop and the delightful blend of fact and fiction that shaped Princess Thea's journey. This tale weaves together the early 19th-century Transylvania, the intricate dance of European politics, and the timeless quest for love and autonomy even though the timeline is fictional.

In the period when *A Touch of Charm* is set, Transylvania was a captivating and ethnically diverse region. Nestled within the Carpathian Mountains, it was part of the Habsburg monarchy's extensive realm. The early 1800s marked a time of intricate social and political landscapes, where Romanians, Hungarians, Saxons, and other ethnicities coexisted, each contributing to the area's distinctive cultural mosaic.

Governance in Transylvania was under the influence of the Habsburgs, who appointed regional delegates to administer their policies. Although devoid of independent royal families, the area was dotted with influential noble houses that played crucial roles in local governance and society.

In crafting the world of *A Touch of Charm*, I introduced the fictional von Hohenzollern-Sigmaringen family who actually came later in history to influence the region, residing in the storied Bran Castle. While Bran Castle is a historical fortress renowned for its dramatic architecture and later associations with the Dracula legend, its portrayal as the home of this noble family is a flight of creative fancy because that is where I imagine such a splendid family to exist.

In my narrative, Princess Thea, Prince Stan, and Prince Alex's father is Prince Ferdinand von Hohenzollern-Sigmaringen who serves as a delegate of the Austrian Emperor. This fictional role underscores the historical significance of Habsburg influence while adding layers of intrigue and political maneuvering to the plot. His distant kinship with the actual Hohenzollern-Sigmaringen line, notable figures in subsequent Romanian history, further enriches the story, offering a plausible yet imaginative connection to European aristocracy.

Ferdinand's lineage traces back to the illustrious Hohenzollern-Sigmaringen family, a branch of the storied Hohenzollern dynasty, known for its significant role in shaping the history of Germany and Romania. This hereditary link, though distant, grants Ferdinand a veneer of imperial legitimacy and a claim to nobility that few can dispute. The Hohenzollern-Sigmaringen family would later rise to prominence in Romanian history, most notably with Prince Carol I, who would become the first King of Romania, solidifying the family's legacy within European aristocracy.

However, in the intricate web of 19th-century European politics, Ferdinand's role is not merely ceremonial. He acts as a linchpin in the delicate balance of power, where diplomacy and strategic marriages are tools of statecraft as potent as armies, which is why Thea's marriage to a Habsburg was so important. His presence in Transylvania is a testament to the Habsburgs' desire to maintain authority over their territories through trusted and influential figures and Andre was instrumental in that.

As a sidenote, Bran Castle's historical allure and strategic location make it an ideal setting for Princess Thea's childhood. Historically, the castle served as a fortress and later as a royal residence, so I borrowed it a bit earlier for my stories. There will be more about Bran Castle in Prince Stan's story, *The Sound of Seduction*, in the next book of this series.

As you know, at the heart of this Regency romance is Princess Thea, a character embodying the era's tension between familial duty and personal ambition. Her fictional engagement to a Habsburg prince underscores the strategic nature of noble marriages, often orchestrated to forge alliances and secure power.

Her longing fueled Thea's daring escape to London for freedom and genuine affection, mirroring the burgeoning spirit of Romanticism in the early 19th century. London, with its vibrant social scene and cultural shifts, becomes the perfect stage for Thea's adventure (and those of her brothers, Stan and Alex, too!). Her arrival in England, with the allure of her noble lineage and exotic Transylvanian roots, captures the imagination, setting the scene for her quest to define love on her own terms.

In weaving *A Touch of Charm*, my aim was to blend entertainment with historical depth. While the von Hohenzollern-Sigmaringen family and Princess Thea are products of fiction, their story is anchored in the historical context of the time. This fusion of fact and fiction allows for a captivating exploration of identity, freedom, and love's complexities.

Thank you for joining me on this adventure. May you find joy and inspiration in Thea's pursuit of her heart's desires, and may her story resonate with your own dreams of love and freedom, which you'll find again in Prince Stan's story that follows next in *The Sound of Intuition*.

About the Author

Bestselling author Sara Adrien writes hot and heart-melting Regency romance with a Jewish twist. As a law professor-turned-author, she writes about clandestine identities, whims of fate, and sizzling seduction. If you like unique and intelligent characters, deliciously sexy scenes, and the nostalgia of afternoon tea, then you'll adore Sara Adrien's tender tear-jerkers.

For more information and exclusive sneak peeks, audiobooks, new releases, and more, sign up for Sara Adrien's newsletter at www.SaraAdrien.com.

Catch up with Sara Adrien here:
linktr.ee/jewishregencyromance
saraadrien.com
instagram.com/jewishregencyromance
facebook.com/AuthorSaraAdrien
bookbub.com/authors/sara-adrien
goodreads.com/author/show/22249825.Sara_Adrien
youtube.com/channel/UCK9OLp1wN6IaGkXe7OugfHg

ALSO BY SARA ADRIEN

Books with the doctors on Harley Street:

A Sight to Behold
(Nick and Pippa's story)

A Touch of Charm
(Andre's story)

The Sound of Seduction
(Wendy's story)

A Touch of Gold
(Felix's story)

Bring Me A Winter Miracle
(holiday special)

Lyon's Den books with Doctors on Harley Street by Sara Adrien:

Don't Wake A Sleeping Lyon
The Lyon's First Choice
The Lyon's Golden Touch
The Lyon's Legacy
and many more!

Find out more at www.SaraAdrien.com